FALKIRK COMMUNITY TRUST

30124 02691163 8

CANCELLED

SPECIAL MESSAGE TO READERS

THE ULVERSCROFT FOUNDATION
(registered UK charity number 264873)
was established in 1972 to provide funds for
research, diagnosis and treatment of eye diseases.
Examples of major projects funded by
the Ulverscroft Foundation are:-

- The Children's Eye Unit at Moorfields Eye Hospital, London
- The Ulverscroft Children's Eye Unit at Great Ormond Street Hospital for Sick Children
- Funding research into eye diseases and treatment at the Department of Ophthalmology, University of Leicester
- The Ulverscroft Vision Research Group, Institute of Child Health
- Twin operating theatres at the Western Ophthalmic Hospital, London
- The Chair of Ophthalmology at the Royal Australian College of Ophthalmologists

You can help further the work of the Foundation
by making a donation or leaving a legacy.
Every contribution is gratefully received. If you
would like to help support the Foundation or
require further information, please contact:

THE ULVERSCROFT FOUNDATION
The Green, Bradgate Road, Anstey
Leicester LE7 7FU, England
Tel: (0116) 236 4325

website: www.ulverscroft-foundation.org.uk

FOR THE LOVE OF LIVERPOOL

Leaving a rewarding job in London, Kate Owen has uprooted her life and given away her daughter to keep them both safe. Damaged from a traumatic event that broke her family apart, she attempts to find peace in Liverpool. There she meets the seemingly eligible Alex Price, who offers her a glimpse of a happy future. But there are those in London who can never forget what she did, and believe she holds the key to the unfinished business she left behind in the capital. Growing closer to Alex, Kate realises he is also hurting from painful memories. Will they ever find happiness together in Liverpool?

RUTH HAMILTON

FOR THE LOVE OF LIVERPOOL

Complete and Unabridged

MAGNA
Leicester

First published in Great Britain in 2018 by
Macmillan
an imprint of Pan Macmillan
London

First Ulverscroft Edition
published 2020
by arrangement with
Pan Macmillan
London

A catalogue record for this book is available
from the British Library.

ISBN 978–0–7505–4775–8

Published by
Ulverscroft Limited
Anstey, Leicestershire

Set by Words & Graphics Ltd.
Anstey, Leicestershire
Printed and bound in Great Britain by
T. J. International Ltd., Padstow, Cornwall

This book is printed on acid-free paper

1

'So what the hell happened to you? Did you drive through a hedge backwards in a tractor?' Tim Dyson threw up his hands in a gesture of mock despair. Although tempted to manufacture a chuckle, he managed to contain his false mirth. 'You come here to see me twice a month, give or take, face set in stone, no feelings on show — God forbid you should turn to worry or laughter or a bit of grief. And once, just once, you arrive flustered and two minutes plus some seconds late. Beads of sweat on your brow, too. And it's all about a woman? A bloody woman and a stranger to boot?'

Alex Price, hands still dug deep in pockets, shrugged. 'She wasn't wearing boots. Her shoe broke. Those skyscraper heels should come with a government health warning.' *Don't look at me like that, as if you expect me to be normal. I don't do the emotion thing. Shit, I need to get out of here. There — that's a feeling, isn't it? Impatience?*

'For your benefit or for hers? The health warning, I mean.'

Alex continued to gaze out of the window at Rodney Street, the place where some ills might be cured and the bank accounts of many customers became noticeably diminished. It had to be one of the costliest streets in Liverpool. 'She was . . . different,' he admitted finally.

'Different from the not-quite-Stepford Wives

1

you employ at your head office?' Tim kept his tone light. 'Do you clone them like Dolly the sheep? Tell me, do your female employees work on batteries or do they need winding up each morning? Come on, Alex — react, for heaven's sake.' Tim studied his old mate, the slope of his shoulders, the hands hidden deep in his pockets.

Sometimes, riling and tormenting his friend from childhood actually provoked a reaction, but this evening Alex remained quiet while Tim rattled on. 'The Price girls aren't ugly, but they're not pretty, and none will see thirty-five again.' He waited for a moment before asking, 'Do they make you feel safe?' But Alex was still refusing to rise to the bait.

Ah. The man swung round. 'You're the one winding me up, Tim. Well, you're trying to.' Alex paused. 'I should have gone for actual therapy to someone I don't know, but old school tie and all that, misplaced loyalties, and — '

'And I'm familiar with what happened to you.' Tim rose to his feet and walked round the desk, placing himself within reach of his complex, damaged friend. 'I was there, remember? Look, I'm happy to be your dustpan and brush, but you have to let the crumbs hit ground level before I can sweep up. How did you feel? You must feel something, sometimes. I repeat — how did you feel, you aggravating bastard?'

'What? When?'

Sighing, the psychologist shook his head. 'When you saved that woman from having a nasty accident, possibly a broken ankle — how did you feel?'

2

After a contemplative pause, Alex answered. 'Shaken. And . . . odd. I felt odd.' *She looked through me, as if those bright eyes scorched all the way to my spine, but I'm not going to say that, because you'd have a field and flag day with it. Should I go for counselling rather than rehash the same old arguments with my best friend? I suppose the result would be the same, because I built this cage myself.*

Here came progress, Tim decided. Odd was an emotion, wasn't it? 'Right. Good odd, or bad odd?'

'I don't know.' *Well, that's true enough, I suppose.*

Tim returned to his chair. Getting Alex to express feelings was like pulling a tiger's teeth without anaesthetic. 'Not that I've any experience with tiger dentistry,' he muttered.

'What? Are you considering becoming an animal behaviourist? Because I'm not sharing a sofa with an orangutan.'

'Alex, you're driving me crazy. I'll be the one wearing a back-to-front coat in a padded cell.' Tim closed his laptop. 'A short time ago, you helped a woman who had broken a shoe as she stepped out of a cab. That affected you.'

'Did it?'

'And when you arrived here a few minutes late — and you don't do late — you were preoccupied. In fact, you looked like a man about to face a firing squad.'

'Did I?'

'Yes. Was she pretty?'

'Possibly.'

3

'Eyes?'

'Two. Yes, she had two. Two is clearly her favourite number, because she had two legs, two arms and two — '

'Colour of the eyes?'

'Blue.'

'Hair?'

'A lot of it. Medium blonde, I think would fit. Dark for a blonde, too light for brown. She was sad. Not just about the shoe, but about life. Downturned mouth. Or perhaps the shoes were Louboutins — a lot to lose. Are you satisfied with my description?'

'Ah. Are you after my job?'

Alex shook his head. 'I haven't time for your job. Too busy cloning sheep and Stepford Wives.' At last, he sat on the couch. 'The dreams are back.'

'Nightmares?'

'Sometimes. Occasionally, it's all been a mistake and we're together, the whole family, including an improved Susan, having a meal or running around on a beach somewhere. She's your next client, by the way.'

'Who is?'

'The broken-heel woman. She's sitting in your waiting room, barefoot and carrying one shoe.'

Tim Dyson raised the lid of his sleeping laptop and clicked the screen on. 'Ah, yes. But you're here to tell me about you. Go back to the dreams, because it's vital that you talk about the ones that stick in your mind.' He should have read the new woman's notes earlier on, but he'd had a difficult day.

4

Alex had had enough of talking about his dreams — a little went a long way. Unable to sit on the couch a moment longer he jumped to his feet, donated the extra time to Cinderella, ordered his friend to keep the woman here, and made for the door.

'Cinderella?' Tim asked, a glimmer of mischief in his eyes. He could use those free minutes to scan the neglected notes.

Alex stopped and turned. 'That story was about shoes, right?'

The therapist stayed where he was; once Alex Price made a decision, there was no holding him. 'You're going for shoes, aren't you, Prince Charming?'

'See you in a fortnight. I'm off to find glass slippers. I wonder if she has ugly sisters?'

★ ★ ★

Alone, Tim Dyson looked at the notes about Miss One Shoe. She seemed to have some baggage, although certainly not enough to fill the hold of a jumbo jet, and her early history was not as dramatic as Alex's. He read on. Oh, but it became dramatic, heavily so. Two injured people, then. 'And there's chemistry,' he said to himself. 'Alex felt odd. Strange, since he's felt nothing since the 1990s. Or he pretends he's felt nothing. This has the potential to become one big bloody mess.'

He continued to stare at Miss One Shoe's notes, but his mind refused to focus, too full of thoughts of his close friend. Alex Price was a talented man. Locals had been heard to describe him as a bloke with so many fingers in so many pies that they didn't know whether to offer him gravy or custard. The reason why he hired the Stepfords was simple — attractive women affected him, just as they affected all healthy young men. Price females needed to be plain.

'Bugger this — concentrate!' he ordered himself. His next patient, Katherine Owen, had OCD, PTSD, abandonment issues (weren't they a Yankee invention?), anxiety, depression and now a broken shoe. Panic attacks were frequent and free-floating, usually with no immediately visible trigger. And the police had . . . 'Oh, my God.' No way. No way should Alex Price take an interest in Miss Owen. A bell rang deep inside Tim's brain. It had been in all the dailies, had merited bold headlines. Details? He would find them.

But he couldn't put a stop to a relationship that hadn't started. He was a qualified physician, so his mouth was glued shut by the Hippocratic Oath. Yet he had also become a psychologist because listening was often better and more effective than writing prescriptions. Bugger. Oh, well; it was time to face the music.

He pressed the buzzer and she floated in. She wasn't exactly barefoot; she wore stockings or tights, and the surviving shoe dangled from her left hand.

'Good evening, Miss Owen.'

She waved the bereaved footwear. 'Sorry about the disarray, but I lost a heel. This shoe is now a very sad object, as its identical twin is deceased.

6

Requiescat,' she whispered, placing the item on the floor.

'Sorry to hear that,' Tim said, a friendly smile visiting his face. She was feisty for a depressive. He paused. 'Do you feel like talking?' After Alex, someone willing to communicate might make a healthy change.

The woman fixed him with eyes of a startling shade of blue; this one wasn't merely pretty — she was a bloody stunner. English rose complexion, full lips, good figure. 'You have my history?' she asked.

'Yes.' Again, he waited; again, he wished he'd done a better job with her notes. He amended his statement. 'The more salient points, anyway.'

She raised her beautifully shaped eyebrows. 'If you've read the best bits, then you know I'm a mess.'

Tim shook his head. 'I know no such thing, Miss Owen. You're a client. I have a tendency not to attach labels to people who've travelled a hard road. Are you taking medication?'

She nodded once. 'Anti-depressants, Diazepam and Armagnac.'

'Not all at once, surely?'

'Panic attacks equal one and a half Diazepam and a slug of brandy. If it works, don't knock it.'

Tim grinned at her. He'd met this type before, of course. She was confrontational, challenging and well educated. Miss Owen aimed barbs at herself in order to deflect attention from her pain; she didn't want pity, hated empathy, was almost totally guarded. Tall and elegant, she surely accepted and embraced her beauty — or did she? If not, she would hardly be the first occupant of this room to underestimate his or her own physical attractiveness. Alex Price was similar. Tim was realistic — he knew that he himself was more than just average-looking, and some had even called him handsome, but Alex and this woman were in a different league. 'Promise me that you won't ever use all three at the same time.'

'No, I'm not suicidal. The don't-jump-off-the-bridge pills I take at night. I've been prescribed those since long before the . . . incident. I was diagnosed several years ago. Well, misdiagnosed might be nearer the mark. I am not bipolar, not psychotic. My illness was created by . . . circumstance.'

He watched as a pale pink blush travelled across her cheekbones. The woman didn't know him from Adam, and it was her first appointment. This was getting-to-know-you time, and she might not like him as a therapist, so he took the usual mental step back. 'No need to talk about the details just yet,' he advised her, 'but I'd like to know something about you.'

She inhaled deeply, exhaled through her mouth. 'I was born in London, raised in London, attended Imperial College, London, worked in London. I had to leave after the event. So I've given up my name, my home and my job.'

'Your daughter?' he asked, his tone gentle. He watched the pain in her eyes, the way her shoulders suddenly dropped slightly.

'Is abroad with my parents. I'm hoping she'll

be bilingual in a few years.'

Tim nodded encouragingly. 'So your mum and dad are giving her a sense of continuity?'

'Yes. And in case you're wondering, the answer is no, I didn't find it easy to let her go. Fortunately, my parents have been taking Amelia abroad since she was very young — just for holidays, of course.' The woman straightened her spine. 'My daughter was and is my world, doctor — '

'Tim. Call me Tim.'

'Right, Tim. I'm Kate and I had to disappear. People will be searching for a brunette with a four-year-old daughter.' She almost smiled at his shocked expression. 'Yes, it's a good wig, one of several in the same shade. I have two more styled in up-dos. Real hair. I sometimes wonder whether some poor nuns have contributed their crowning glory to help me find safety. The point is, I had to keep my little girl protected and her mother alive, since grandparents do not last forever. They're a very close couple. If one died, the other wouldn't cope with life, let alone with a small child. Suicide is not an option for me.'

'I understand.'

She closed her eyes for a moment. When she opened them, they blazed with a mixture of grief and anger. 'Sleep eludes me,' she stated baldly. 'And I'm living proof that sleeping pills are not the best idea. Their efficacy fades, and eventually I had to take them with alcohol. A dessertspoonful of brandy for a panic attack is one thing, but a large glass of red wine with pills at bedtime is a slippery slope, and I have too much to do.'

He nodded. At least this one was talking.

'I was a set designer for London theatres.'

'Yes?'

'I loved my job. My qualification is in chemistry, but I've always been what my father calls arty-farty, so I followed my heart, not my extremely boring honours degree.'

'Not easy,' Tim said.

'It is if you know the right people, some of whom managed to be the wrong people. Anyway, that was then and this is now. I've bought a crumbling mess in Blundellsands and I shall renovate and style it, sell it, then start again with another piece of dilapidation. It's just a bigger stage on different levels, and I know I can do it. Apart from a few tradesmen coming and going, I'll be alone. No one here knows me, and that makes me feel safer.'

'And hopefully, not buried under crumbling brickwork,' Tim chuckled.

She laughed. 'God, I never thought of that.'

He had to ask. 'Do you have what is semantically termed a significant other? Someone you left behind, perhaps?'

Her reply was immediate. 'Amelia is my only significant other. Without her to live for, I'd probably have been dredged out of sediment in the Thames some time ago.'

'Witness Protection?'

'The police know where I am, yes.'

'Bodyguard?'

'Two failed police dogs. They respond if I tell them to kill. They also accept those I nominate as friends, so they're not dangerous unless they need to be.'

'Joke?'

'No. I trusted humanity for a while, but . . . well, the way things were, I knew plenty of bodyguards. They existed on the rim of criminality, and although I'm not saying that all security people are open to bribery, my own experiences have made me wary. I trust my dogs. They have worried to death many a second-hand mannequin no longer fit for shop windows. As long as I don't shout the k-word in a certain tone of voice, they're tranquil and quite good fun. I love them, they love me; it's a simple enough equation.'

The conversation died a natural death. Kate made a second appointment before picking up her shoe and leaving for the waiting room, where she found herself in the company of Alex Price and three rectangular boxes on the floor in front of him. 'Ah,' was all she managed.

He fared slightly better. 'Choose shoes,' he mumbled.

'Poetic.' She waited while he removed lids. 'No stilettos,' was her next statement. 'I suppose you're trying to help me avoid another accident. Thank you.'

He handed her the broken shoe she'd left behind in the street. 'This may be repairable. I got your size from it, so it was useful after all. The shop had closed, but he opened up for me.'

'You're an influential man, then?'

'According to legend, yes. I own the block of shops, and he gave me these. Apparently, they're very last year.'

She bent to study the footwear.

11

Alex, determinedly unimpressed, shifted his gaze from a pair of legs that seemed to go on until a week on Tuesday. She was beautiful and was, therefore, an item to be avoided.

'I like them all,' she said. 'Tell me where the shop is, and I'll pop in and pay what I owe.'

'No need. They were taking up space and gathering dust. Keep them.'

'Are you sure?'

'Yes.'

'Is the shoe shop man sure?'

'Yes.'

They bent simultaneously to pick up a box, and their fingers collided for a fraction of a second. Each backed away quickly from the pulse that passed between them, shorter than a heartbeat, sharper than a honed knife.

Kate straightened and looked into dark chocolate brown eyes. She thought she glimpsed a cocktail of fear, confusion and hurt. Then the eyes cleared, and she saw nothing at all. How did he manage that, and why did he do it? The man wasn't merely handsome; he was beautiful, with a square jaw, untamed hair, a straight nose and a damned good body. But she got the distinct impression he didn't like himself. Could she help him, and could he help her?

Alex lowered himself into a chair, his gaze magnetically locked with hers. This was great, just great — wasn't it? He'd run business meetings full of sharks and wild cats almost biting each other; he'd bidden high and partly blind on the stock exchange, and he'd been ruthless when buying companies, smashing them up, selling off pieces and people . . . and here she was. Such bright, clear eyes she had. They were eating into him with questions to which there were probably no answers, and he noticed in her face — just for a moment — something that was no stranger to desire. Had he met his Waterloo? Because there was no denying that she was very lovely.

'Thank you,' she said again, her voice shaky.

He managed to look away, but continued to feel the burn of her eyes. Burn? Blue was a cold colour . . . 'Would you like me to drive you home?' Where had that come from? His mouth seemed to be working of its own accord; no connection whatsoever to his brain.

'I have my phone, so I'll call a cab.'

The inner door opened and Tim Dyson strolled out. Prince Charming and his Cinderella were still here. 'No glass slippers, Alex?' he joked before turning to Kate. 'I suspected that your hero might have gone to fetch shoes, and I was right. If you've no car, I'm sure he'll drive you home with those three boxes and your other bag.'

'No need,' Kate began, but Tim hadn't finished.

'You'd better hurry, you two, because Mrs Melia will be here shortly with the Mad Moppers. You mustn't come between Mrs Melia and her disinfectant. She can be very fierce.'

'And so can I,' Kate promised.

Tim chuckled as he descended the stairs. Perhaps the two sorely mismatched people in the waiting room might even be good for each other.

Explosions sometimes cleared the air, and there was definitely an attraction between them. Predictably, Alex's body language had been reminiscent of a tranquillized sloth, but Kate had appeared . . . hungry? Was that the right word? Bugger psychology, anyway; this was poker night.

★ ★ ★

I am driving the Merc, but something is driving me, and I'm moving too fast. Must get a grip, because I don't want to drown. Dad taught me to swim when I was about four, but he didn't live long enough to advise me with regard to avoiding certain women. Yes, I'm afraid of them and yes, I know why. So does Tim.

'Turn left before that level crossing,' Kate Owen says as we pass the entrance to the West Lancashire Golf Club. She's in the passenger seat with a large handbag on her knee and two shoeboxes in the footwell. The third ended up in a rubbish bin once she'd decided which pair to wear. Her broken stiletto and its intact partner are in the capacious bag that bears an insignia suspiciously like the Gucci logo.

Merrilocks Road, the sign says. 'Strange name,' I remark.

'I think it's pretty,' she replies. She's probably one of those females who own an answer for everything. A slender finger points right. 'That's my house.'

There are two pairs of old, drunken gates, one at each end of a semicircular driveway. I park near the front door of a three-storey house, once

14

grand but now sad and dilapidated.

'Come in and look at the 'before' picture, Alex. I shall be turning it into apartments.'

I shouldn't go in. I know full bloody well that I should drive off back to Strawberry Mead, my safe place, the house I've had designed to please me and me alone. Well, me and the memory of Lennon, a hero of mine. She's lovely. I like her. She makes me laugh, so I should get the hell out of here pronto. Very few people cause me to grin, but she's one of those very few.

She offers what she must believe is a sweetener to get me inside the house. 'Come and meet Castor and Pollux. They're guard dogs, but they won't hurt you. Don't be intimidated by their size.'

I hesitate, though I'm used to dogs. 'Why? Are they unusually big?'

'Yes, but you're more likely to have your ankle bitten by a terrier. I'm not a fan of small dogs.'

Dogs are my weakness; I am currently the property of two Labradors and two huskies, all rescued. Now I'm out of the Merc while she opens her front door, and I'm faced by two of the hugest Alsatians I ever saw. They are gorgeous. When they notice me, they grind to a halt, sit, and stare at their owner, clearly awaiting commands.

'Friend,' she tells them.

They start doing what might be called a happy dance, though they wouldn't get far on Strictly. Also, rather too large for such frivolous behaviour, they might cause a shift in tectonic plates or movement in the house's foundations.

My hands are licked until they are almost dripping wet. Next, I am led on a tour of the neglected and very large property. It seems to go on forever; she says she'll be turning it into three luxury apartments. Then she comes to life, telling me about her job as a theatre set designer.

'Lucky, no licky,' she commands, and I laugh. She explains that shouting the dog's name on Crosby beach is not a good idea. 'He got reduced to Lucky. Pollux sounds like male reproductive equipment. Mind, they still show me up by peeing all over Gormley's statues.'

Why do I ache? This isn't the first beautiful woman I've encountered. My mother was stunning. There's something else, isn't there? This evening, in the presence of a female stranger, I almost feel the water closing over my head, and I've forgotten how to swim and when to breathe. I feel. She makes me feel. And I don't like it. It's unsafe.

She breaks my train of thought. 'And this is my safe place, humble but my own.' She's chosen to live in three of eighteen rooms.

Her area, her curl-up-and-be-myself spot, is vast and on the ground floor. She's gone minimalist when it comes to decor, and I guess she's one of those rare people who could stick a second class stamp in a huge, gilded frame, call it art, and get away with it. The bed's a king size — is she expecting company? Her gaze accompanies mine. 'I tend to sleep diagonally,' she explains. Yes, she's very tall.

The dogs' beds are on the floor near the sofa. 'My bathroom's through that door, kitchen

16

through the other.' There's the sleeping area with drawers and wardrobes, then a living area with a dining set in light oak, a very plain L-shaped sofa with scatter cushions, and a flat screen TV over a magnificent fireplace. In a recess next to the chimney breast sits a desk with a computer and a tidy pile of papers. Everything is super-organized, super-clean.

Like a third guard dog. I follow her into the kitchen. It's pristine, with everything in its proper place, no clutter, no sign of human life. It looks as if it's never been used.

She reads my thoughts. 'I have OCD,' she explains. 'I'm told it happens when fight-or-flight doesn't work, when life gets too complicated to control. We freeze. A thaw sets in, and we sometimes get OCD. That's when this starts, the need to be in charge of small things, like salt, pepper, sugar, coffee and tea.' She sighs. 'I do hope I'll grow out of it.'

'May I sit?'

'Sorry — of course.'

I place myself at the kitchen table.

'Coffee? Tea?' she asks.

'No, thanks. I can't stay long. Mrs Boswell will be champing at the bit. She's my housekeeper, and her hours are variable, but she likes to go to the pub on a Friday night. She and her husband have an annexe attached to my house, though they'll be dog-sitting.'

'You have dogs? Wonderful.'

'No, no — dogs have me. Churchill and Mac are black Labradors, Laurel and Hardy blue-eyed huskies. The Labs are placid, but the others cling to their wolf ancestors — just a wee bit on the wild side.'

'You're not married?'

'No. You?'

She lowers her eyelids for a second. 'He died.'

'I'm sorry.'

Those bluest of blue eyes fix on me again. 'I'm not.'

I'm lost for words. She isn't. She's rattling on again about her work, about being an assistant something or other on The Mousetrap — isn't that the one that's been running forever? I suppose they'll have to keep renewing bits and pieces on the stage. The Donmar Warehouse is mentioned, as is the Adelphi — even the Palladium. The subject has changed completely since the mention of her dead husband. Why is she in Liverpool?

'Why are you in Liverpool?' she asks. Does this woman have satnav attached to my brain?

'I like Liverpool, always have. I've been here since I was at uni.'

'And Tim?'

'The same. He studied medicine.'

'What about you?'

God, she's nosy. 'English literature. I dropped out.'

'Why?'

Bloody hell. 'I inherited a sum of money from my paternal grandparents, went into property, bought some shops and houses, opened various sorts of clubs in the city. Tim stayed, too.'

She sits opposite me. 'You're both from further inland,' she says.

'Yes, cotton and coal country. Bolton. He's a year or two older than I am.' And he was there for me all those years ago, has been with me ever since. I have many acquaintances, dozens of business connections but few friends. I trust my dogs, my housekeeper, her husband and Tim. Beyond them, I'm not sure I trust many people, especially those of the female persuasion.

'Do you have friends?'

Here we go again. She's invading my very personal space. 'Just a few. My business is time-consuming.'

'So how do you relax?'

Is this the bloody Spanish Inquisition? Speak up for yourself, Alex. 'Why do I feel as if I'm being interviewed for a job?' I ask her.

Kate frowns. 'Sorry. I don't get out much these days, so you're probably my first real victim. My car's having surgery, and I've been shut in for days.'

I give her a small, apologetic smile. 'I don't get out much, either. I do play squash very badly in one of the clubs I own. I walk my dogs. Sometimes, I do a round of the clubs, like a spot check — I even serve behind a bar from time to time. You?'

She shrugs. 'I've been here for just a few weeks. I've spoken to shopkeepers, three plumbers, the mechanic who's mending my car, a couple of electricians, Tim and you. Blundellsands keeps itself to itself, I think. That suits me, because I do the same.'

I wait before speaking. 'I hope you don't mind my asking, but are you in hiding?'

19

'Aren't we all? We wouldn't need counselling otherwise. Yes, I'm keeping a low profile. But you might be able to cheer me up.'

I'm panicking. The way she's looking at me, as if I'm some kind of saviour, a lifeline. I could get lost in those eyes. Kate Owen is special. For me, she's dangerous. The idea of what some call true love scares the hell out of me. True love means giving someone the ability to hurt you. I can't go there; will not go there.

She's grinning mischievously.

'How do I cheer you up?' I ask finally.

'A dog picnic,' she replies. 'If teddy bears can have a picnic in the woods, Castor and Lucky, Laurel and Hardy, Churchill and Mac can enjoy a party on Crosby beach. Sunday morning, eleven o'clock. Bring treats, poo bags and leads.'

She remembers the names of my dogs. And I know I'm already dangerously close to losing myself in her, though I mustn't let it show.

'Do I get an answer?' she's asking now. 'Because you're hardly the most communicative of people.'

I tell her I'm thinking through my weekend schedule. And the snare tightens when she asks for my mobile number. She taps it into her Samsung, and mine rings. 'Right,' she says, 'done and dusted — we each have the other's number.'

Oh well, that's me sorted out for the rest of my flaming life. This isn't about Sunday and six dogs on a beach; it's about forever. She thinks I haven't noticed her eyes wandering over me, but I've had my rogue female alert system fine-tuned for years. I'm not bragging when I describe myself as handsome — it's a clinical fact. Yes, I am responding at animal level, but that's something I can cope with. What bothers me is that I don't know how to deal with feelings, since I built a wall round me years ago.

Why her, why now? Why not one of what Tim calls my Stepfords, or the manager at Charm, a barmaid at Cheers, one of the many members at Check Mate, my club for singles? There are women a-plenty at Chillex, my newly acquired health centre, but nobody stands out as The One. And after spending a couple of hours in the company of Kate Owen . . . Oh, bugger it. I'd better go and face Mrs Boswell's music.

★　★　★

The Boswells were Alex's two Bees — Brenda and Brian. Brian looked after the grounds and did minor repairs and decorating in the house, but the place was 100 per cent Brenda's. It mattered not that an architect had designed it, that craftsmen had built it, that Alex had paid for it; this was her baby. She employed a couple of 'scrubbers' during the week, tough and brawny women who attacked floors and windows, but Brenda was definitely ringmaster. No one touched 'her' silver, 'her' china, 'her' kitchen cabinets. Alex sometimes wondered whether he'd be missed if he disappeared.

He'd been missed tonight. The diminutive figure of Mrs Bee was standing in the entrance hall with her arms folded across her second best coat, and a foot tapping on the parquet. She didn't tap frequently, using the habit only when extremely agitated. 'You're late,' she accused.

'Yes, I am.'

She inhaled deeply. 'You smell of perfume, expensive perfume. I think it's that Channel Five.'

'Really?'

'Really.' The foot continued to tap.

He hung his coat in the cloaks cupboard. She was dying to ask, but he played along for a while. 'We ran late at the office, then I went to see Tim. He was in let's-make-Alex-laugh mode. He failed.'

Brenda straightened in a vain attempt to look taller.

'Are the dogs all right?' Alex asked.

'Fine. They're in the paddock with Brian. Has Tim Dyson joined Champs aux Fraises?' Her French accent left a lot to be desired.

Champs aux Fraises was Alex's gay club in Liverpool. 'No,' he replied. 'Try the English version, Brenda. Champs aux Fraises means Strawberry Fields. And very few men wear women's perfumes, though some of the lesbians might.'

Brenda shook her head. He had to have been close to a woman tonight. She spent her days vacillating between worrying about his remaining single and wondering whether a wife might get rid of housekeeper and handyman. But now wasn't the occasion for imagining; this was bull-by-the-horns time. 'Who is she?'

He chuckled. 'Kate Owen. She broke her shoe, and I drove her home. She lives in Blundell-sands.'

But Brenda Boswell hadn't been on the planet for over sixty years without learning about undercurrents, tensions in the air, and expressions on the face and in the voice of a man she'd worked for for over five of those years. 'You like her,' she stated.

'And?'

She was flustered. 'I'm just saying.' She cleared her throat. 'Are you seeing her again?'

'Yes. You'll be late for the pub. Brian will have been replaced on the darts team, and your friends will have started the dominoes marathon. Think of all the gossip you'll be missing.'

'When?'

'Now — this very minute. You are late.'

'I know we're late. We're late because you're late.'

'Sorry.'

Her mouth tightened. She knew he was playing her like an old fiddle, and she knew that he knew that she knew. 'I didn't mean *that* when. I meant when will you be seeing — '

'Brenda, leave me alone, love.'

She didn't move, though Alex did. Within seconds, he was on the floor under four dogs, each animal vying for attention. Brian stood over the tangle of limbs and tails. 'We'll be off, then,' he called.

Alex waited until he heard the front door close. 'Peace, perfect peace,' he murmured while extricating himself from four wet tongues, four happy tails and sixteen feet. They sniffed. Chanel No. 5 didn't bother them, though they needed to assimilate the aroma of Kate's dogs.

He knew how to distract them. 'Food,' he yelled, and four dogs disappeared through the kitchen and into the utility room. He followed. Unless he was away on business, the dogs were his. He fed them, walked them and, when he could catch them before they fled, he showered them. The canny creatures knew when their master planned to attack with water, so containing them on shower days was not easy.

The Labradors, furry vacuum cleaners, inhaled their dinner, while their lupine companions ate more delicately. Alex let Churchill and Mac into the dog run outside before sitting on a stool to watch the beautiful huskies. Labradors were very attached to humans, but the winning over of Laurel and Hardy, whose mother had died, had been hard work. Alex had been their new mother; he was the one who'd taken over a month off work to get them feeding from bottles. They were beautiful dogs, with thick coats and blue eyes. She had blue eyes . . .

As a picture of Kate Owen filled his imagination, his mobile phone belted out the tune from *Match of the Day*. It was her. 'Hello,' he said.

'Thank you for helping me.'

'Think nothing of it.' He could sense her smile.

'Just returning the favour, making sure you got home safely.' She laughed.

'I did.'

'What are you doing?'

'Feeding the hungry. Churchill and Mac have finished. Laurel and Hardy have better manners.'

There was a pause of several seconds. 'Will you come on Sunday, Alex?'

'Yes. Have you checked the tides?'

She had. Of course she had. 'Let's go to the part near the lifeguard station,' she suggested.

'OK, boss.'

She laughed again. 'See you Sunday.'

'Yes, see you then.'

The connection died. Alex turned to Laurel. 'And here's another fine mess you're getting me into.' He let the huskies out into the run for ten minutes. Experiencing a strange mixture of trepidation and excitement, he found his supper and went to seek his DVD of *Turner & Hooch;* it was Churchill's favourite. It would soon be Sunday.

2

It was a warm day for mid-April. A couple of light showers had washed the world clean just after dawn, and the air was freshened by a light breeze. As the sun neared its zenith, rays played on the water like excited children, while shadows of statues depicting Gormley's *Another Place* began to shrink on the sands of Crosby.

Alex Price sat on the erosion steps, two Labradors to his left, two huskies to his right. As keeper of several dogs, he had to make sure they knew the rules, the first of which was *Thou shalt not bother strangers*, while the second, *Sit still until I tell you to move*, had all members of the tribe quivering expectantly. Well, Alex wasn't exactly quivering, though his heart and mind were both busy.

She was here. He knew that, because several males stopped on the sand and stared over his head through the rails that separated the steps from a tarmac-covered parking and walking area. And he was feeling again, because he didn't like other people looking at her. She wasn't his; she was just a woman who'd broken a shoe and asked a lot of questions. Was this jealousy? Whatever its name, it was new and confusing, and he hoped it would disappear soon.

Kate Owen, in skin-tight jeans twinned with a sweater in a lighter blue, was coming down the slope with her magnificent Alsatian guards. Her hair was up, serving to emphasize her jawline and a long, slender neck. Men continued to stare, but she had eyes only for him. 'Hello,' she yelled. 'Glad you made it.'

Alex held up leads, treats and a bundle of bags for dog waste. 'I'm armed,' he warned.

Kate released her dogs. They turned right and made for the river.

'Go,' Alex ordered, and his four dogs ran in pursuit of Kate's two. He stood up, but Kate was having none of it. She sat and pulled his hand until he joined her. 'They'll be fine, Alex. My dogs know the scent of yours from Friday, from your clothes, and you took the smell of Castor and Lucky home to your lot.'

'Pollux,' he said, retrieving his tingling hand.

'Same to you. May I press you to a chicken salad sandwich?'

The dogs came and went, came and went, keen to have treats of chicken and dog biscuits. Their significant humans talked of matters mundane — the cost of a new clutch for her car, the weather, the Viking settlements of Great Crosby, Little Crosby, Thornton and Blundell-sands.

She swallowed. 'Over there, I saw thousands of bricks worn down by the tides. Why? They run parallel with the golf course.'

'Houses fell into the river.'

'No!'

He grinned, unable to look at her, yet not wanting to take his eyes off her. 'That's why these steps were built. The river is a hungry animal, very invasive. At one time, there was a theory that Blundellsands would be under water in a hundred years. This is called the erosion with good reason. We're literally holding back the tide.'

'Oh dear.' She paused. 'Alex?'

He still couldn't look at her directly.

'Are you afraid of me?'

He was. 'Not at all,' he lied.

'Back in a moment. I'm going dolloping.' She grabbed a pile of dog bags and ran off to clean up after their canine charges. Ah, so 'dolloping' was her word for scooping up dog muck. The unsavoury task seemed not to faze her in the least — she even chatted to other walkers while she cleaned patches of the beach and shoved her finds into a Tesco carrier bag before tying it. It seemed as if the whole world followed in her footsteps, though few females took part in what looked rather like a casual bridal procession, except for the absence of flowers.

On her return, she placed her burden in a larger bin liner, whipped a packet of Simple wipes from her bag, scrubbed her hands, returned to her bag and smeared both hands with antiseptic from a plastic bottle.

'Are you sure that you picked up after just our dogs and not a whole zoo?' he asked.

With no hesitation, she put him in his place. 'Dog faeces can blind a child. I didn't stop to measure the items to assess which breed they came from. Now' — she smiled broadly — 'tell me about your clubs. They will be my next adventure.'

Alex shrugged. Her next adventure? Oh, hell

on toast. 'I have five.'

'Exciting.'

'And they all begin with C-h.'

'Why?'

'Why not? They are Charm, Cheers, Checkmate, Chillex and Champs aux Fraises. That last one means Strawberry Fields.'

'I know. I have A-level French.'

Of course she did. She was probably proficient in many disciplines. 'A woman of many talents, then.'

'Charm?' she prompted.

'It's a dance club with a good sprung floor, ballroom lessons two nights a week, salsa night, jive night. It's busy. Patrons tend to be on the mature side, though salsa and jive both attract some younger people. Charm's doing well. They have tea dances in the afternoons for retired people. Most clubs are for younger folk, so I plugged a gap in the market.'

'Your face lit up just now,' she observed. 'That means you enjoy your clubs. What about Cheers, then?'

Alex grinned. 'I share ownership with an American who has a passion for Liverpool, for Texas and for the TV show. He puts a joke across the counter with most drinks, runs quiz nights, and hires very pretty Scouse girls. Calls himself Bobby Ray Carson, though his Southern accent is dodgy — he's from New York. Cheers has regulars, just like the TV show. It also attracts alcoholics and binge drinkers, so security is tight.'

Simultaneously, they realized that they were being stared at by six very bedraggled animals.

'Oh, God,' Kate exclaimed. 'They look like filthy strays.'

'It's not God, it's the river,' Alex replied. 'It's a sight cleaner than it used to be, but it still serves up some crap.'

She jumped to her feet. 'Let's walk them round to my place. I have a doggy wet room just inside the back door.'

'I came in the dog van, Kate. It will take six in the back, so I'll drive you home, and you can take Castor and Pollux inside while I get my four back to my house.'

'Nonsense. I'll clean all the dogs. Oh, and I made scouse for later, thought it might help you feel at home. I got the recipe from a Liverpool group on Facebook. Very helpful people, these Scousers.'

Alex nodded, acknowledging the truth of that. 'All right, it's a deal. I have to warn you, though, my lot have an allergy to legal water. I can take them into a dry field and they'll find one small puddle and cover themselves in mud, and then refuse to be washed by me. They love only naturally occurring waters.' It was becoming clear that she would go to any lengths to keep him by her side. She had planned all this in the full knowledge that the animals would get filthy. He had been selected, so he owned no choice in the matter, because she'd stolen his free will. So who was he to disagree? 'As long as you're OK with that, it sounds like a good plan.'

He spent the first half hour in her house lighting a fire in the living-sleeping-eating-study room and spreading old towels on the rug.

Finally she entered with six drip-dry dogs and more towels. The scent of washed fur filled the air; both were used to the smell of wet dogs.

'They were very well-behaved,' she said. 'There's not a lot of choice, because there are side jets as well as the overhead ones.' She threw a towel at him. 'Here. Catch a dog and dry it.' She began to rub Churchill's fur. Looking up from her task, she asked, 'What?' He was staring hard at her. 'What, Alex?'

'Did you go into the shower with them?'

Kate glanced down at her fluffy white bathrobe. 'Just for a while, yes.'

'But — '

'But what? I cleaned them two at a time.'

'I may hire you as a dog-washer.' His tone was dry.

'What's wrong?' she asked.

Alex inhaled deeply. She had short, loosely curled brunette hair. 'Did you dye and cut your hair while you were cleaning dogs?' She blushed, and he felt guilty. *Feeling again. Her embarrassment is affecting me, and I know now that this woman is a part of my danger zone, the place I try not to visit.*

A hand flew to her head. 'Oh, hell,' she snapped.

Nothing further was said until the animals lay in a slightly tangled row in front of the log fire. Kate walked to the door. 'I'll be five minutes at the most,' she promised.

It was a long five minutes. She was in disguise, on the run from something or other, or from someone. Was Kate Owen a criminal? Surely not. But she'd left London and a job she had clearly

31

loved, had turned her back on friends and on a way of life offered only by the greatest city in the country. What was going on?

She returned sporting a dress and the dark blonde/ light brown wig, the loose one she'd worn on Friday. 'Sorry,' was the single word she offered.

'Why?' he asked. She had looked even prettier as a gamine brunette.

'I can't talk about it, Alex.'

'May I ask whether Kate Owen is your true name?'

'No.'

He allowed a few beats of time to pass. 'No, I mustn't ask, or no it isn't your real name?'

'It isn't my name. I am Katherine, but not Owen.'

He stood up.

'Please stay,' she begged. 'I've made too much of that Liverpool stew, and dogs can't digest potatoes.'

'I have to change the cover on the floor of the van. It will need washing. I always carry a spare.' It was there in her eyes, the need, the desire, the hunger. 'I can't do this . . . stuff, Kate. Like you, I have issues, things, events in my life I can't talk about. We're damaged people.'

'So? Everybody suffers damage of one sort or another — that's life.'

'But I don't want to talk about my history, and you clearly don't want to talk about yours. So what do you need from me, Kate? Straight answer.'

She studied him. He was a sight for anyone's eyes, sore or not. And there was something else, something they had shared from the moment he'd picked her up after the shoe had broken. 'I like you a lot,' she murmured truthfully. Her tone grew more challenging. 'And I think you like me, too. You're fighting it, but you do like me.'

A heavy silence followed.

'Why can't we be reborn?' Kate persisted. 'It's just a case of discarding the past and living in the moment. A person's history is old clothing, isn't it?'

At last, he spoke. 'If we were able to do that, you wouldn't be in therapy, and Tim would be short of money.'

Kate could find no direct answer to his statement. 'You're my only friend in Liverpool. I'm a refugee from London, and I seek asylum.'

They both burst out laughing. 'We'll end up in one,' Alex managed.

'We could share a cell,' she suggested.

'Kate — stop it. I can't share, I can't . . . commit.'

'Phobic?' she asked.

'Yes. It's a nurture rather than nature thing, or so I'm told on good authority. I can't be half a couple. It's also part of the stuff we don't talk about. I'll go and change the cover in the back of my van.' He left her in the company of six drying dogs.

I am going to sit right here till he comes back. He can take his dogs and leave, because I have a plan. I've always had a plan; I'm here in Liverpool because I had a plan. OK, it was a bit drastic, but it saved me and my darling Amelia.

Now, I'm moving too fast, plotting too quickly and too soon. I've frightened him off. Yet I know he's a good man.

He cares for me — I'm not blind and not stupid. It crackles between us like static electricity, has done right from the start. Alex is the sort of man I need; he's a dog-lover, a mover and shaker — he lights up the room and makes me smile. Feelings like this don't travel in one direction only. I catch him looking at me, see him grinning to himself, head bent to one side because I've said something slightly outrageous. Ah, here he comes.

'Right, all done. Come along, boys.'

The 'boys' obeyed him immediately.

'Goodbye, Kate,' he said. 'Phone me if you need anything.'

She exhaled loudly. 'Go, then.' She tried to keep the petulance out of her tone, keen not to sound like the spoilt child she had been. 'And I plan not to need anything from you, thanks.' Now that had sounded petulant. Until her unfortunate marriage, she'd always had her own way with parents who still doted on their only child and her daughter. It was about time to grow up.

He shrugged, took his dogs and left.

★   ★   ★

Kate dragged one of her 'killer' dresses from a wardrobe. It was silver, corseted, and needed no bra. After choosing shoes and a clutch bag, she went into her own shower and thought through

34

her plan. Oh, she would show him. She might not see him tonight, but she would make sure as hell that he would hear about her very, very soon. 'Keep a low profile,' the police had said, but she had no intention of planting herself permanently in the silent Viking village known as Blundellsands. She was smartly bewigged, made up like a film star and dressed like a rather naughty princess. 'Watch this space, Alex Price,' she muttered. Then she sat and waited for time to pass.

★ ★ ★

Although somewhat overdressed for Cheers, Kate was a woman who could carry herself no matter what the situation. With a wrap of silver-grey lace, she managed to conceal much of her upper body, so the sweetheart, corseted dress was immediately less revealing.

Cheers was impressive. A squarish bar imitated the layout of the TV show. Alongside Bobby Ray Carson, three pretty girls served drinks. Kate, very much aware of the crowd's quietening mood, moved towards the co-owner of the club. She introduced herself. 'I'm Kate Owen, a friend of your partner's.' Alex had never mentioned that his partner was black — and very handsome. These days, many people tended to be colour blind when it came to shades of skin, which was more than acceptable in Kate's book.

Bobby Ray shook her proffered hand. 'Welcome, Kate. Did security stamp your hand?'

'Yes.'

'Marked for life,' he jested. 'Name your favourite poison, and your first drink's free.'

She ordered a diet lemonade spritzer and perched on a bar stool. On the opposite side of the large room, a juke-box played while a few couples jumped about to the music. Kate became aware of two or three people moving behind her. She sipped at her drink while males close by argued. When security removed them to a different area, her wig never turned a hair. 'Another, please,' she asked when her glass was empty. They had all probably wanted to dance with her, but she wanted just one man, and he wasn't here. Yet. Ah well, she could wait. At last, she was learning patience. Wasn't she?

Bobby Ray handed over her second drink. 'You're causing quite a stir,' he said quietly. She glanced round the room. A few men in a huddle kept turning to look at her. 'Am I in trouble?' she asked innocently. She was good at innocence; she'd practised it for years when confronted by her parents. 'It's a pity Alex isn't here,' she told him. 'If he were here, I think your security guards would be redundant. He seems to be a very determined man.'

Bobby Ray had been a bartender in New York, Boston and Chicago, and had become astute when it came to judging character. It was time for a break, anyway, so he nipped out for a cigarette, picking up his phone before leaving. She was a predator, and Bobby needed to talk to Alex about his huntress.

Kate smiled to herself. The American would have a conversation with his partner, thereby providing what her evening lacked. Alex would come, wouldn't he? She needed to talk to him, to convince him that they might just move on together as a couple.

When the man in charge returned, he placed his phone under the bar and plugged in its charger. She awarded him the best smile in her collection, since he seemed to be fitting in very well with her latest plan. He gave her a brief nod before moving to the opposite side of the bar.

The night passed in a blur while she danced with at least a dozen men; Alex was not one of that number. At just before one in the morning, Bobby Ray cut in to dance with her. 'You're going home,' he whispered into her ear. 'And I mean right now.'

'I'm not drunk — '

'I know.'

'I've had three spritzers all night.'

'I know that, too. I'm leaving the bar to one security and three young women. These are my instructions from Alex, my partner and friend. I'm doing as he advised.'

Kate stopped dancing, standing with closed fists on her hips. 'You'll have to carry me, then.'

'No problem.' He walked to the bar and picked up Kate's clutch bag from its place of safekeeping. Handing the item to its owner, he asked, 'Are you going to leave under your own steam?'

Either way, this was a fight she couldn't win. She was going to walk, or she would be lifted like a child. She walked.

When they reached Bobby Ray's car, Kate

clouted the six feet and four inches of solid man with her silver clutch. 'Do not make the mistake of ordering me about — ever. Now, go away and let me be while I phone for a taxi.'

'No.'

'Then I'm going back into the club — just as far as the entrance — and I'll phone from there.'

A voice came from behind them.

'Get in my fucking car, Kate. Thanks, Bob.'

She spun round and found herself face to face with Alex. 'Get in the back seat. Now.' His expression was grim. 'Don't mess about with my clubs, with me, or even with my dogs. Any more of your nonsense, and I'll slap a restraining order on you before you can say knife. This smells suspiciously like harassment, and you will stop.' He nodded at his partner. 'Go inside, Bob. I'll take this one home.'

'This one' was ushered into the rear of Alex's Merc. She was shaking; he wouldn't even allow her up front next to the driver's seat. What had she done wrong? Her spine tingled. It had started with . . . she didn't want to think his name. It had started with a man she'd grown to hate and, having dealt with him, she had taken charge of everything and everyone. 'I don't know how to stop.'

'What did you say?'

'Did I just speak out loud?'

'You did.'

Kate sighed. 'I don't know how to stop being in charge; everything in rows, like soldiers. And I saw you, wanted you, planned how to get you.' She waited in vain for a response, as Alex seemed buried beneath his vow of silence. 'It's a huge part of what's wrong with me,' she added. 'I had to do something really big a few months ago. I gave away my daughter just to make her safe. You'll have heard of the Kray twins, I presume. They're still around, people like those two. And if you step, however accidentally, into their world, you are doomed. What you see now, the harassment, the needy woman, was created by other people. I shifted Amelia — my daughter — and I was placed in a safe house until the court case was over, then I bought wigs and fled north. I'm a pest, but I'm most definitely not a monster.'

He pulled up outside her front door and turned off lights and engine. 'Thank you for talking,' he said. 'May I come in?'

'Of course.'

The fire had died, though the dogs remained in situ, two tails banging on the rug in lazy greeting. After stroking the good boys' heads, Alex and Kate sat on the sofa, leaving space between them.

'Close your eyes,' he said.

'Why?'

'Just do it and shut up, will you?'

She obeyed.

'I was eleven years of age, Kate, but even now, it's printed on the insides of my eyelids. Not all the time, of course. I have dreams, and they sometimes come when I'm awake, too. Imagine feeling unable to close your eyes.'

'I can't,' she whispered.

'Exactly. I'm letting you in as far as I can,

because you did me the great honour of opening up as much as you dared. The picture I carry is violent. I am just an onlooker, and I can't look away. My problem with women stems from that horrible vision. Like you, I lost someone who was dear to me but, unlike Amelia, my loved one can't ever come back. I . . . I also think my love was undeserved.'

'Dead?' Kate whispered, opening her eyes.

'Yes. You have a fear of abandonment. I'm almost the exact opposite, since I dread becoming attached. We're both crackers, aren't we?'

'Probably. Sorry about tonight, Alex. I was a very spoilt only child, and there's been no discernible improvement. If I stamped my little foot, my parents caved. I still have a tendency to stamp.' She waited a few seconds before continuing, 'What do you do about sex? Feel free not to reply, of course.'

'Friends with benefits,' was his immediate answer. 'It works for me and for them.'

'And are you happy with things as they are?' She opened her eyes.

'No, I'm not happy, Kate. I don't actually look for happiness; my preferred destination would be contentment. I'd like the ordinary life, two children, some dogs, family holidays in Spain or Italy.'

'And you can't have any of that.' This was not a question.

'Not yet,' was his reply. 'I move forward an inch at a time with Tim's help. He's a good man, and he was a great kid. At the age of thirteen, he saw what I saw and dragged me out of there, out of the place I can still see. And although he takes the pee out of me, he's my main support.'

'Such sad creatures we are,' she breathed.

He turned and looked at her. 'You are now another problem for me. Tim taunts me relentlessly about my Stepford Wives, plain women I employ in the central office. He accuses me of cloning them. The truth is that I am not attracted to any of them, so I'm safe.' He pondered for a moment. 'The answer to the question in those wonderful eyes is yes, I am attracted to you, but I'm not ready. And I believe that you, too, exist in a state of unreadiness.'

Kate chewed her lip thoughtfully. 'You're probably right. So where do we go from here?'

Alex raised his shoulders. 'I carry on with my job, you do yours. If there's a film we want to see, or a concert we want to attend, we go. And we continue to see Tim regularly. He should be told that we are friends. Not yet an item, but keeping company from time to time. I'll come here for an evening meal on Friday, and you will come to my place the following Friday. We'll spread the load.'

'You're going to trust my cooking, Alex?'

'I could ask you the same, because Mrs Bee won't be preparing food on a Friday. She goes out and leaves me with the microwave. Look, we're equally crazy, equally alone, and we probably deserve one another. Let's live a little and hope not to suffer from food poisoning.'

'OK.'

'And I can't wait to watch you in that kitchen,' he said. 'I've never studied an OCD sufferer cooking a meal. Should be fun.'

'Do not mock the afflicted.'

'Do not deprive me of my hobby,' was his swift response. 'That would be cruel beyond measure.'

'Alex?'

'What?'

'Do you have siblings?'

The smile was replaced by a thoughtful expression. 'An older brother. He's in Australia. And a younger sister. She's in a home for disabled people. I was raised by my paternal grandparents from the age of almost twelve, and Stephen, my brother, was taken in by a wealthy aunt and uncle in Sydney. Susan is in Fleetwood; she was born handicapped.'

Kate swallowed. 'I'm so, so sorry.'

'The poor girl doesn't know anything different, so she's happy enough. She speaks her own language and has a beautiful dolls' house — yes, she's a young adult, but she still needs her playthings. Paints, crayons and chalks all make her happy, like a child on her birthday. She has dozens of soft toys, and she recognizes me. My name is Ta-da, which is probably her version of teddy, because every time I visit I take her a teddy bear. Her favourite is a tiny one in a container slightly bigger than a matchbox. He has a sheet and a pillow, and she keeps the lid open so she can see him. He's her baby, the only one she'll ever have.'

I will not cry; I won't make him any more miserable than he already is. Such sadness, such grief. Apart from Tim, I'm probably the only person he's confided in. There's more to it, just

42

as there's more to my story, so I won't push him, because I understand only too well what he's enduring. I tell him life's tough, and he just nods and says he'd better go.

And he's gone. No hug, no kiss, no fuss. But at least he admitted that it's there, the attraction between us. I suspect that a hug or a kiss would have led somewhere, and neither of us is fit to travel. He uses women, just as I have used men to relieve tension or take my mind off something. Alex and I are bonding, so neither a quick roll in the hay nor a romp round a bedroom offers an answer. This selfish woman is going to learn to be extremely patient.

Castor and Pollux move to their beds, and I start to shed the glad rags, silver dress, silver shoes, silver jewellery. Tonight worked. Daddy's little rich girl got what she needed, which was more than a dance in Alex's arms. Instead, we both gave each other a little piece of ourselves. He's worth waiting for, and so am I.

★   ★   ★

In a bruised, battered and abandoned high-rise building in London's East End that reeked of urine and rat droppings, four men sat on plastic chairs round a plastic table. Like an army with no leader, they were confused and angry, at a loose end while they awaited instruction from captive superiors in three separate prisons. One boss was contained in Wandsworth, another in Durham, and a third in Walton, Liverpool. The fourth, Gentleman Jim Latimer, known to his friends as Jimmy, was dead, his ashes supposedly scattered on the Thames and on his parents' grave in Chelsea.

'I think we should bugger off and forget it,' Weasel said. 'I mean, they kept our names out of the hat, they've gone down for the big job, we don't know where the rest of the stash is, so what's going to be in it for us? We may not be top of the tree, but we have to live, innit? We got to start thinking about ourselves and what we want.'

Mad Max jumped to his feet, knocking over his chair. Max had two modes — silent or seething. 'Listen, you rat-faced skinny bastard, Jimmy died. They're not all inside, are they? Only three are in jail, because the fourth is dead. He was the star, he done all the planning. We have to get the one who shot him, right?'

The other two agreed with Mad Max. Anyone with a desire to remain alive tended to agree with the big man. Even Weasel, number four and least important, was nodding vigorously.

'They'll send word to us; they'll find a way,' Max said fiercely. 'If they want us to get her, we will. No matter how long it takes, we'll find the bitch. She's easy to recognize, and the kid will be with her.'

Trev shrugged. 'I don't know about that. Seems her mum and dad have done a disappearing act. My auntie that cleans in the same Kensington block as they live in says she heard they'd gone to France. And when they go away, see, they often take the kid with them. Wouldn't surprise me if Mrs Katherine Latimer handed her over to them and took off on her own.' He scratched his head. 'I just can't work out how we can get to the bottom of any of it. It's like a jigsaw with half the pieces gone walkabout.'

The third man shrugged. The pecking order among the bottom four was Max, Trev, him, then Weasel. They were couriers for much of the time, carrying drugs or money or both to constantly changing locations. The third man's nickname was Brains, as he could get into and out of anywhere, including most safes, though aside from that gift he was a slow thinker. 'It's worth millions,' he mused, almost as if talking to himself. 'We done a good job, all of us — even Weasel. I wonder if Jimmy's wife took off with the rest of the loot? The papers say there's still a load missing.' He shook his head. 'She could have took it, Max.'

'Nah.' The big man scowled. 'She's straight — that's why she shot him. Anyway, things out of private bank security boxes aren't easy to offload, and some are good for blackmail. She wouldn't know where to start, and neither would we.'

Trev agreed. 'Yeah, she's no crim, and she didn't shoot him for the stash. He kicked the kid.' He shrugged. 'So she blew his head off. I'm not saying what she done was right, but the kid was in hospital with broken bones. That's why she was found not guilty. But she put Jimmy's other mates inside, didn't she? And we don't know where nothing is.'

'We're lucky she didn't know any of us, or

45

we'd be locked up too,' Mad Max growled. 'Funny how I'm the one that gets called Mad just because I'm big. Gentleman Jim was the real nutter, beating his wife up and nearly killing the little 'un. Still, respect and all that — he paid a big price.'

'We just got to wait, then,' Brains said. 'But while we wait, can we get pie and mash? Me stomach thinks me throat's been cut.' They hastened towards a door that hung crookedly from one hinge. It was time to get out of this stinking hole and go to hunt for supper. Who knew, with appetites satisfied, they might just conjure up a plan. But come what may, Katherine Latimer must be found.

★ ★ ★

Another man, in circumstances far removed from the decay of a high rise waiting to be demolished, was thinking about Kate. He occupied a mews that clung to the fringes of Chelsea's better side, and he, too, was determined to find the runaway, because he loved her. 'Why didn't she tell me she was going?' he whispered.

Dr Giles Girling, known to his friends, patients and colleagues as Dr Gee-Gee, paced about the small room. He'd been on duty when Amelia Latimer had been brought in by her beautiful mother, who had screamed like a banshee until an orderly had turned up with a trolley and two nurses. The little girl had appeared dead, but she'd eventually been saved, thanks to God and a very good surgeon.

Giles had assisted Mr Moores in theatre, where a piece of the little girl's skull had been removed to allow for swelling. A punctured lung had been remedied, a broken ankle set, and after many weeks in hospital the child had been well on the way to a full recovery. Miraculously, there had been no obvious brain damage.

He remembered coming out of theatre and standing by the surgeon while everything was explained to Katherine Latimer, whose face had been whiter than her daughter's. After Mr Moores had left the waiting room, Giles had listened to Kate's confession. She had shot the man who'd injured her child. Yes, he'd owned guns, and she'd used the one kept in a drawer with napkins, coasters, playing cards and bullets. 'My husband,' she had concluded. 'Now, take me to my daughter, please, then telephone the police.' So he took her, left her, and followed her instructions.

He stood by the window, eyes closed as he replayed the terrible scene. Officers from the Met had arrived. Kate had simply sat in the corridor and spoken in a monotone reminiscent of a robot. This was a woman in deep shock. She had been looking through a pane of glass at her child.

'He did that,' she had said, waving her arm towards her little girl, so frail, head bandaged. 'Something major went down yesterday evening. I can always tell when it's a big job, because he hits the vodka like a ton of bricks. His eyes were wild. Aside from that, he's meticulous, very much the city gent, sets off every morning in his pinstripe suit, carrying the compulsory umbrella and document case. I thought I'd married a stockbroker; I was wrong. He was very, very far removed from the stock exchange.' At last, she had referred to her husband in the past tense.

'He took two bags up to the guest room last night. Amelia was already in bed, and I was watching a *Blackadder* repeat. He was upstairs for quite some time before coming down to get another slug of vodka. Now, this is the really out of character part. He must have left one of the bags open, and the door to the guest room ajar too. He went back upstairs, and started shouting at Amelia. She screamed for me, and I knew he was in danger mode. Not that he ever hurt her before — I was the one who kept falling downstairs, so to speak — but she was still screaming, so I grabbed the gun and ran up. As I crossed the landing I could hear him kicking her little body against the wall. She must have helped herself to pearls — there were pearls scattered all over the carpet after I shot him. If he'd closed the door like he always did before, this wouldn't have happened.'

'Are you sure there were just two bags, Mrs Latimer? It was a very big job. Safety deposit boxes have been emptied — many of them.'

'I only noticed two, but I was in a hurry. There may be others further inside the room — I don't know.' She turned to Giles. 'Please let me go back in now,' she said.

Now Giles sat on a small window seat and allowed his thoughts to wander through nearly two months of almost daily contact. She told

48

him about her life as spouse to a gangster. 'He was a good-looking man, always perfectly turned out. Said his money was tied up in stocks, so he moved into my house after the wedding. Amelia was only a few weeks old the first time he came home covered in blood and said he'd been mugged. I was suspicious, but unsure of what the hell he'd been up to. And I wasn't allowed to ask questions, of course.

'The next morning, I heard that a young policeman had been found dead in Maida Vale. It was much later on that I realized Jimmy might have played a part in that murder. When I questioned him, he broke my arm. Every time I came to A and E, he was with me. He promised that if I ever spoke up, he would kill me — that was the only one of his many promises that I actually believed. The police know everything now. We will go through the motions of a court case, but I probably won't serve time, because I've helped by giving the police the names of three of his cronies. They're in custody.'

Giles hadn't expected her to leave London. One friendly sergeant told him eventually that her identity had been changed and that she had moved far away. And that was that. He couldn't cheat and call in hospital or family doctors' details, because Katherine Latimer no longer existed on anyone's books or computer screens. Had she changed the child's surname? Or were the grandparents looking after Amelia?

He had reached an impasse. Kate had worked in London theatres, so where might she go to find similar work?

He poured himself a double Armagnac. After twelve years in the making, it slid down like honey with a bit of heat in the tail. 'I told you I'd fallen for you, Kate, but you said you weren't fit for marriage.' Was she fit for it now? Oh, if only he could find out . . .

3

Although I'm not exactly one of the party people, I do like to choose where I spend my free time, and a busy Merseyside A & E would not be my destination of choice, especially on a Saturday night. In the short hallway, we encounter a collection of drunks and their various contributions to the scene: tuneless singing, vomit, urine, and a stench for which I can discover few words. Just think pigpen and have done with it.

My father drank. He didn't indulge every day, but he'd go out on a binge, come home during the night and all hell would ensue. I keep a fairly good cellar and enjoy my wines, but I feel sorry for these guys in the hallway. They aren't people any longer; even animals don't lie in their own effluent.

Of course, Powder Puff Pete has to have his say, so I drag him by the good arm into the unit before he starts World War Three among the inebriated and liver-damaged. God knows there's enough trouble on this globe without him throwing his five quids' worth into the mix. He's going to be difficult. I can tell he's going to be difficult because he won't sit down; says he's still recovering from being in my car.

'Listen, boss,' he announces as we enter the main area, 'you want to try wearing this corset. Even with a couple of ribs removed, it kills me when I sit. I blame Jane Fonda; she kicked off with the lose-some-ribs idea.'

Across the packed room, voices recede until silence reigns. Now, I've had some awkward moments in my life, but this should rank somewhere high on that lengthy list. Not that I keep a written account, but Pete and I must present as a very strange couple. I, Alex Price, am a reasonably normal-looking bloke, but Pete? Where to begin?

He's extraordinarily tall and lathered in makeup. The wig is yellow blonde and piled up enough to give him an extra five inches in height. A pink dress covered in sparkles dominates the picture until you see the shoes — hot pink, peep-toed and peppered with sequins. Size twelves. His nickname — Powder Puff Pete — was bestowed on him by other performers at *Champs aux Fraises*, as he owns a dark and rampant beard that seems to grow in minutes. This nuisance he paints with some strange liquid probably manufactured by Dulux; on top of that, he applies a prodigious amount of powder using something on the lines of a Brillo pad. This is his powder puff, and no one must touch it.

He suddenly realizes that he has a captive audience. In spite of a possibly broken arm, he delivers 'Tragedy' in a falsetto that would challenge Barry Gibb of the Bee Gees, followed by 'Tiptoe through the Tulips'. The ensuing round of applause is not appreciated by staff, and Pete gets processed immediately. Shunted off, probably to X-ray, he leaves me to answer a barrage of questions about my companion. Yes, he's a man, yes, he can sing in a normal voice too, and no, he doesn't make his own frocks. He's here because he slipped in onion gravy and might have broken his arm.

Things settle, and I have a read of my Liverpool Echo. I'm looking at an article about Liverpool One, the relatively new and vibrant shopping centre in the city, when my second tormentor arrives. I lift the newspaper in an attempt to conceal myself, but she homes in. Monica. Monica Hargreaves is Powder Puff Pete's wife and nemesis. In her wake drift four children. There's Our Kylie, Our Britney, Our Chelsea and, on reins, Our Troy, youngest and sole male offspring. At fourteen, Kylie has decided to dye her hair orange and purple. With a bit of green, which may be accidental.

The entourage stops. Monica confronts me. 'Where the blood and guts is he, and what the f — what the hell has he done this time?' She is wearing her don't-you-dare-mess-with-me face. I wouldn't dream of messing with her; I'd have a better chance of survival in a vat filled with rattlesnakes.

I explain that he slipped in some spilt onion gravy and fell on his arm against a porcelain sink. 'He's getting X-rayed, I think.'

'What the Holy Mary was he doing in the cookhouse again?'

I shrug. 'He was teaching them how to pipe duchesse potatoes.'

'So it's banquet Saturday, is it?'

'Yes.'

'He's a singer, not a bleeding piper. Britney, wipe Troy's nose.'

Britney does as she's told. Most people do as they're told where Monica's concerned. 'He's called himself a chef ever since he served slops in the army, daft bugger. Burnt sausages with cold beans and he thinks he's Janie Oliver.'

'Jamie Oliver,' I say. 'He's a man.'

'Is he?' She lowers her tone. 'Tell me Pete changed out of his frock and scraped all the muck off his gob, please.'

I shake my head. Having witnessed Monica in full flood on a couple of occasions, I nurse no wish to annoy her. She's tiny, unpredictable, quick to laughter and quicker to anger. 'He's got three gigs in Canal Street next week,' she snaps. 'I can't see him belting out 'I Will Survive' with a pot on his arm.' She pauses. 'I could sue you for loss of earnings.'

I must be firm before she loses her rag and fetches a lawyer. 'You can try, but it's in his contract and plastered all over the kitchen door, authorized personnel only. He might be daft, Monica, but he's not blind. And I'm not hiring an extra guard just to keep your man out of the kitchen. By the way, your little boy's eating crisps off the floor.'

I think about Kate and the supper we had last night at my house. It was my first attempt at lasagne, and we really enjoyed the fish, chips and mushy peas we had to buy instead. I decided in the queue that I must acquire a cookery book.

After eating, we wandered into the zone of ancient Greece, its writers and philosophers. We talked about Plato, Aristotle and Socrates before moving on to the Shakespeare game, disagreeing about everything. Kate lights up when arguing. In the end, we agreed to differ and drank mugs of hot chocolate with marshmallows on top. It was disgusting — we managed to agree on that score, and she promised to lend me some recipe books. Lasagne, here I come. She says she'll give me marks out of ten. I can't wait.

Monica has found someone else to mither, but I seem to have inherited Our Kylie. She's at that difficult age, I deduce, all wide eyes and coloured hair. 'Kylie?' I keep my voice low.

She bats purple eyelashes. 'What?'

Deep breath, Alex. 'You don't need to do all that with your hair. You look great without it.' She's gone bright red, a shade that clashes loudly with the orange streaks on top of her head. It's one of those moments when you wish you could snap your teeth together and bite words back. Being cruel to be kind can be horrible. It is horrible.

The woman-child runs away, probably in search of a loo. Right. I am out of here. After giving Monica thirty quid — they may need more than one taxi — I leave her to it. But I don't go home. No, I need to talk to someone, and the someone I need to talk to is Tim or Kate. Tim will be out doing whatever single, lovelorn medics do on a Saturday night, but Cinderella is a night owl. If she's asleep or reading in bed, I'll know, because the light will be dim and in one area only of the big room.

She's awake. The place is lit like Blackpool illuminations, light streaming through temporary and unlined cream curtains. I guess she's *probably still doing her drawings and looking at swatches, and I find myself grinning. Kate is fierce. I should drive away and go home. My feet and hands don't agree, because I'm braking and pulling into the kerb.*

'Just a friend,' I say aloud as I park on the street. 'She's my friend.' Who am I kidding?

★ ★ ★

Alex could 'feel' her eye staring at him through the peephole in the front door. The dogs weren't growling; they would probably have recognized his scent even if he'd arrived in a lead-lined container. He should have texted her, at least, because this was rather late for a passing caller to visit.

She opened the door. 'Hello, stranger. So long since last we met.'

'Twenty-four whole hours,' he managed. No wig this time, just wilful curls in a wonderful, dark mahogany shade. He wanted to reopen the Shakespeare fight with a quote from *Romeo and Juliet*, but he didn't dare. '*From rest and sleep, which but thy pictures be —* '

Kate cut him off in the doorway. ''Death, be not proud' by John Donne. Gotcha. See? How brilliant am I?'

'This isn't fair,' he told her. 'I'm the English literature student.'

'Who never finished the course.'

'But you're a chemistry graduate.'

She winked at him. 'There's plenty of chemistry in poetry. Come in.'

He did so and the dogs made the sudden, compulsory fuss of him.

'Sit down,' she said.

He wasn't sure how to start. 'I needed to talk to someone.'

'And I'm someone?'

'Of course you are. Aside from Tim Dyson, you're the only person who knows anything about my past.'

'Ditto,' she whispered. He was grateful that she hadn't objected to his turning up unannounced like this.

'I've been at Champs aux Fraises,' he began. 'It's popular on banquet night, which happens on the third Saturday of each month. Food *and* entertainment, meaning that the acts on stage need to be good so that people will care enough to stop talking and clattering cutlery. That's why I booked Powder Puff Pete. He was his usual self, up to the eyebrow pencil in mischief.'

She grinned. 'So he's one of your gay cabaret acts?'

'Gay? Pete Hargreaves? He's got four kids and a little wife whose tongue's sharp enough to slice carrots without a knife. Pete dresses to sing, and he takes the job seriously, so he's in demand — sometimes goes to London. Even had surgery to give himself a waist. He works hard and earns well. He ended up in A and E, and I was his unfortunate driver and companion. Somebody at Champs must have phoned Monica, and she joined me at the hospital while Pete was being treated. She gave me the rounds of the kitchen — that's Liverpoolese for being told off. She's a little tigress, and I was in deep trouble.'

'Oh no. You've been thoroughly Monica-ed.'

'Oh yes.' *She's laughing at me again, and I love it.*

'Poor you,' she said. 'We think life's hard, then a Monica makes it worse.'

He turned serious. 'I like to be there on banquet nights. Of course, the place is packed to bursting with heteros, because Champs is the best club in the north.' *I'm bragging; almost preening, as if I'm cock of the henhouse. Pull yourself together, Price.* 'So I was available to drive Pete to the hospital after his fateful encounter with spilt onion gravy.' *Well, it is the best club in the north.*

Kate interrupted his thoughts. 'Do they fall in love with you, the gay men? Do they send you billets-doux and flowers?'

'It has been known. And I'm one of the few males who can say he's been stalked for weeks by a lesbian. She was probably having a month off to see if my grass was greener. The men have given up on me.'

'What a shame, Alex. So cruelly abandoned through no fault of your own.'

'Indeed. My heart is broken.'

'So what happened tonight? Turf wars? A demo against gays?'

He told her everything, from duchesse potatoes through the drunks, the singing, Monica and the off-spring, all the way to Kylie with the inappropriate hair.

Kate, never adept at concealing her emotions, finished up on the floor with two Alsatians and cheeks wet from tears born of laughter. 'Troy?' she managed, almost spluttering with glee.

'Yes, Troy. I gave him a wooden horse for his second birthday, but I suspect that the reference remains unnoticed to this day by his parents. He loves his rocking horse — '

'The siege of Troy,' she shouted. 'Stop it, Alex. Did you give Kylie a boomerang? Because that's what the word *kylie* means.'

'No.'

'Or Chelsea a season ticket for the Blues?'

'Stop it. I'm a Liverpool supporter.'

'What about Britney? Singing lessons? Gym membership?'

He, too, was done for. Both ended up shrieking with laughter. 'Stop it. You're killing me,' he gasped.

Kate stopped giggling immediately. 'That's almost exactly what happened to me. Not physically, but my character came close to death while my husband was still alive. He hurt me badly several times, but I never pressed charges because I existed in fear of him and his gangster friends. I loved my daughter and my work. Beyond those two, I had nothing. That bastard sucked the soul out of me.'

Alex waited. 'And after his death?' he asked eventually.

'Amelia and I escaped when she'd recovered and I'd put his most dangerous colleagues in jail. My daughter was in hospital for weeks.'

He pondered for a few moments. 'He hurt her?'

She nodded. 'The three who ran the show

with him are locked up. I never knew the names of the other members of the gang, but they're in London. I think they deal drugs and run errands — they're lower down the food chain. But they're out there, Alex, and those in jail can get messages to them.'

He frowned. 'Are any of the gang in Walton?'

'Yes. Eric Mansell, my husband's right-hand man. He started off in Manchester, but got moved here after a few weeks. The thing is, I'd made my plans to come to Liverpool before that happened, and I decided I would stick with them. A person can't run forever.'

He might have missed her. The realization hit him in the chest like a kick from a heavyweight wrestler in steel-toecapped boots. She was the one, and he wasn't ready. Would he ever be ready? Was he good enough for her?

'What are you thinking?'

Here she came again with that private hotline ringing loudly in his ears. 'That we might never have met,' he answered truthfully.

'So you like me?'

A beat passed between them. 'Of course I do. You're confrontational, annoying, funny, controlling, ferocious, ambitious and beautiful.' He grinned while a blush spread across her cheekbones.

The smile she donated in return was unsteady, almost embarrassed. 'And I like you because you're decent, smart, handsome, hardworking, kind — and you love your dogs.'

Alex ran a hand over his hair. 'Right, that's the mutual admiration society up and running. Go easy on me, Kate. When it comes to emotional involvement, I should wear L-plates. I'm a virgin.'

She gave him another shaky smile. 'Stay with me tonight, Alex.' She touched his arm, and he managed not to shiver when goose bumps arrived.

'I can't,' he replied quickly. 'The Bees will be in bed, so I can't ask them to look after the dogs.'

'Bees?'

'Yes. I keep two kinds of bees. The humans are Brenda and Brian Boswell, and the honey bees are housed in a special environment. Hives in what looks like a giant greenhouse in which ideal conditions are maintained. They don't know they aren't outside, because they have their own hives for the queen and drones, while the workers bring home the lavender. I make mead from their honey, add a bit of strawberry flavour and give it away in the clubs. Honey nights are well attended.'

'Strawberry mead?'

He smiled. 'That's the name of my house. The whole thing's a tribute to John Lennon.'

'Strawberry Fields?'

'Yes. I nearly bankrupted myself to buy the land. It's near enough to the orphanage site, and it cost a bomb. I had the rare privilege of meeting Yoko when she came over for what would have been John's seventieth birthday. I suspect that she had something to do with my plans' being accepted.'

'Really?'

'Oh yes. She was wife and lover, but she's a

supremely wise woman and she was all he needed. The females in his life had disappeared; Julia the mother died, while Julia the sister, adopted when young, was God alone knew where. Yoko was one of the few people who could manage Lennon simply by being at his side. Best friend and confidante — the whole package contained within one tiny female. She had the ability to deal with near-genius.'

Kate changed the subject. 'Can't I be just for sex? I won't mind.'

'I would mind. And I'm sure you would. No, you're not fit for purpose.'

She slapped his knee. 'Not good enough for you? Try me and see.'

'Too good, Kate. There's other stuff running along at the side of physical need here, and you know it. Like John Lennon, I lost my mother, and my sister isn't really there. People like me get confused.'

'So you're an orphan?'

'Yes. My dad died first, then my mother killed herself when I was still relatively young. As she gradually lost her senses, my paternal grand-parents took over and I lived with them all the time, stopped going home at weekends.'

Kate stared at him. 'You blame yourself for her suicide?'

'She'd lost everything, right down to the family cat. When I stopped visiting, she didn't leave the house, didn't have baths, didn't clean up after herself — she was living in squalor. Grandma and Grandpa got someone to shop, cook and clean, but that didn't save her.'

He paused, then exhaled as if relieved. 'Tim's tried to get through to me for years, but you're the one who managed it. He predicted this, you see. 'Someone will come along and drag the rug from under your feet,' he often said. But it wasn't my feet, was it? It was yours.'

'Yes — the stiletto. Those shoes cost a fortune. But you're worth it.'

'Am I?' he asked, his tone dry.

'You know you are, and I don't mean money or shoes or anything tangible. Alex, I just have this strange feeling that we were made for each other.'

He cupped her face in his hands, and her skin felt so soft and smooth. 'Kate, you will have to bear with me. I'm a mess.'

'I told Tim *I* was a mess, and he says not to be judgemental about people who've been through bad stuff. Your bad stuff started much earlier than my terrible time, so yes, recovery might take longer for you. Is it OK if I wait to see what happens?'

'Yes. And I'll do my best to hurry up.'

'For me?'

'For us.' Then he kissed her. Oh yes, this definitely went way beyond the merely physical . . .

* * *

Tim was in. 'What do you want, Pricey? It's gone midnight.'

'Nothing. I kissed her.' He felt like a Catholic teenager at confession.

'And? Have you had a tetanus injection?'

'Behave yourself. It was like arriving home. She's wonderful, affectionate, a nuisance — '

'Slow down, Alex. And don't shout into the phone — I'm not deaf yet.'

'I'd like to see you as soon as possible.'

After a short pause, Alex's best friend and unofficial counsellor spoke. 'Come round to my house tomorrow afternoon,' he suggested. 'I'll throw in a sandwich and a cuppa.'

'Thanks. See you about three.'

'I look forward to it.' Tim ended the call. Oh, what a perfect end to a wonderful day. Not! Alex Price had fallen for an exquisite woman who'd shot her husband dead. 'This is crazy.' He paced about. 'She mustn't have told him what happened to her. I'd bet my last quid that he hasn't told her much about his past, either. And I can't say a bloody word,' he muttered while pouring himself a generous measure of Scotch. He took a mouthful, shuddering as the heat of it hit his throat. What a bloody fiasco.

'I shouldn't drink so bloody fast,' he told himself aloud before emptying the contents of the glass down his throat. This was a dilemma. As an eleven-year-old boy, Alex had watched a scene that could easily have come from a horror movie, though it had been all too real. For weeks after the event, the lad had been traumatized to the point where his speech had been affected, he'd refused food, and his grades in school had taken a serious nosedive.

Alex's paternal grandparents, who had been awarded custody, had sent him to a facility in the south where he was treated before returning to live with them in Bolton, visiting his mother only at weekends. These visits had been made with reluctance on the boy's part, since Mildred Price was sitting on the hem of insanity, and in view of her deterioration the grandparents had put a stop to any overnight contact. 'And the guilt has lived on in Alex,' Tim muttered.

Mr and Mrs Price continued to allow brief visits as long as he was accompanied by one or both of them, but the lad was never again to sleep in his parents' house. When the place became filthy, Grandpa and Grandma brought in outside help and stayed away from the Blackburn Road semi, feeling there was no more they could do for their daughter-in-law.

Tim stared at the chimney breast. Love at first sight? Oh, he knew how that felt, didn't he? Julia. On the first day at Liverpool's School of Medicine he had tumbled, becoming increasingly besotted with Julia Kavanagh, an American student who had returned to Vermont when her course ended. She loved him. She loved England. But her father was dying, and she needed to go home.

'Bugger it,' Tim shouted, resisting a strong urge to smash his whisky glass into the fireplace. Three or four times a year, he crossed the Atlantic to see her.

'Bugger it,' he repeated. Having nursed her father as he travelled a long path through stage four, Julia now awaited the death of a beloved mother, another victim of the big C. She had promised to return to Liverpool after it happened. She would need to refresh her qualifications, as the only medicine she had practised after qualifying had been nursing at home, but she was a good, solid student, and she would make it as a paediatrician. Yes, love at first sight existed.

'Alex, what the hell can I do for you?' Tim asked the room. Throughout his time as a therapist on Rodney Street, he had noticed that damaged people seemed to be automatically attracted to each other. An illustration of that particular fact was now happening in glorious Technicolor. Alex had suffered an arrest in emotional development at a very vulnerable age, while Kate needed someone on whom she might depend, someone worthy of her trust and love.

It was in all those newspaper cuttings Tim had in his desk. Kate Owen, really Katherine Latimer, had shot her husband in the face while holding the weapon very close to him. The bullet had later been dug out of a wall after blood and brain had been shifted about a bit . . . Tim didn't blame her in the least, after all she'd been through.

'She did right,' he told himself. 'That child almost died, and all female animals will go to extreme measures to protect their young. There's stuff still missing from that bank raid, too, and the three prisoners might send people to seek her out. Would Alex cope? Would she? God help them — and me, too.'

He went to put the kettle on. Where booze was concerned, enough was enough.

★ ★ ★

Everyone on nodding terms with Gentleman Jim's lower order of four knew that Brains was, when it came to driving, something akin to the *Titanic* approaching its iceberg. Brains called it 'living on the edge', though passengers of his were more inclined towards 'Nearer my God to Thee'.

He and Weasel died instantly on the M25 when lane-hopping at rush hour. For most of the time, the word 'rush' was not applicable to that particular route, but Brains was in a hurry, and disaster ensued when he twisted and turned his way between queues of traffic, lost control and smashed through a barrier into the path of a lorry travelling in the opposite direction. The motorway ground to a halt for several very long hours, during which time tempers and radiators became overheated and many phoned home to be told that supper had been eaten, burnt, or fed to the family dog.

'Just us now,' Trev said as they drank pints in the Bow Bells.

Sombre for once, Max grunted. 'Even Weasel had his good points. Remember how when us four kept watch he could smell a cop before it walked round the corner?'

'Yeah, he was good with the pigs, I admit. Always called them Officer and pretended he was lost or confused. Mind, he was the only one of us who had no record, and that made him useful.' Trev paused. 'I'll have to work on my auntie, see if she can find out where Jimmy's

67

wife's mum and dad have gone. If they have the kid with them, we follow. The kid is the weakest link; if we snatch her, that'll smoke Katherine out of her hiding place. I'm not talking ransom money; we just have to find out where Jimmy hid the rest of the stuff.'

They carried on drinking as a tribute to their lost pals. It was a hard life, but they must not weaken, even if, later on, it would be pie and mash for just two this time.

* * *

Tim Dyson opened his front door. Alex's facial expression was that of a naughty three-year-old who'd stolen all the biscuits. 'Welcome, stranger. Step into my parlour, said the spider to the fly . . . because I'm going to do a 'me too' on you.'

'A what?'

'A 'me too'. It's like when you have a headache, there's always somebody who says those words, and that person's headache is much worse than your trifling pain. You have indigestion? Me too. That's how it goes.'

'Don't joke, Tim — I'm a desperate man. Spent most of last night in A and E with Pete, Monica and the tribe. Pete was in pink, while Monica was in a state worthy of treatment in the psychiatric department. She was one hundred per cent dislocated in the temper zone.'

'Then you went to see Kate.'

'Right.'

'And you kissed her.'

'Yes.'

68

Tim poured the coffee, and each man sat in an arm-chair. 'Right, brother — here comes the 'me too'. You ready?'

Alex shrugged. 'I don't know what the hell you're going on about, but get a shift on with it, because my lavender's growing and the bees are noticing already.'

'Deep joy. Do you still talk to insects?'

'Yup. I should see a therapist.'

'Ha-bleeding-ha. Anyway, here it comes. You fell in love at first sight — me too, which is terrible English. Julia. We shared a man the day we met. He was dead at the time, and we had to locate, identify and display various body parts. We were together for over four years, as well you know. I fell. You seem to have tumbled now. So that's how I know, and I'm well placed to tell you, that love's a crazy business — it's an accident. Companies should allow us to insure against it. You're happy and miserable simulta-neously. You hand yourself over to somebody else, and that somebody can make or break you. When in love, you're no longer in charge. It's very frightening.'

'Me too,' Alex said, a grin on his face. 'I'm scared.'

Tim shook his head. 'I almost did it, came very close to giving up my family, my friends, the city I love in the country I love. I was going to join her in Vermont, but she stopped me. She probably didn't want me to regret such a huge move, and she'll return to Liverpool after her mother's death, because she likes Liverpool and loves me. It's been hell, Alex. I've done my best to carry on as normal and even you might not have noticed, but seeing her just three or four times a year is not enough. Finding trust takes time, and trust is necessary before the fear goes.'

'But I'm not in the same position, Tim. Kate's going nowhere.'

'You're in danger.'

'How?'

The therapist shrugged. 'Is your heart lost irretrievably? Is hers? Are the risks equal? Have you told her what happened the day you came home for your rugby kit, the day I accompanied you after visiting the dentist all those years ago? Have you painted that vivid picture for her?'

'No. She knows I suffered a trauma, but not all the details.'

Tim paused for several seconds. 'And has Kate told you any of her history?'

'Some. Her husband beat her up, attacked their daughter. He died. She's afraid of his associates, so she came north and sent Amelia away with her parents.'

Tim chewed his lip for a moment. 'Your Stepford Wives — the plain ones — I understand. I even understand your distaste for and your fear of beautiful women. Now you fall for a stunning show-stopper. How will you stop fearing and start trusting?'

'I have no idea.'

'Men will lust after her, just as women keep their eyes on you.'

'She's different. I'm different.'

'We're all different, Alex. In some basic respects we're similar, but mankind is a mixture

70

of all sorts of things, good, bad and indifferent, especially when it comes to the way we think, the way we act or react. Now, I can't tell you what I know about Kate, and I won't tell her about your blackest day and the lasting effect it's had. But I will allow myself to warn both of you to be careful. Until you are damned sure that you each know the history of the other, take things as slowly as you can manage. Danger lies in ignorance.'

Alex shifted in his seat. 'Has she done something wrong?'

'No comment. Save to say that in my book, the answer would be an emphatic no.'

'And yours is the only book that matters, isn't it?'

'Definitely not.'

Alex studied the floor for some moments. 'Kate is so straight, she's almost ferocious. She says what she sees, and to hell with it. If you don't like her expressed opinion, that doesn't matter. But if she perceives a wrong, she'll do her damnedest to right it.' He raised his eyes. 'Ah, you're wearing the poker face, your Friday night expression. From this rigmarole of yours, I am now almost convinced that she killed her husband.'

The ensuing silence was weighted by unspoken words. Alex fractured it. 'And her husband deserved it?'

'No comment.'

'No comment. No bleeding comment? Will she kill me? Because the way things are going at the moment, she won't need to — you're doing it.'

'Don't panic, Alex.'

'Don't panic? I don't need permission from you to feel nervous.'

Tim leant forward. 'By having you in my house, by allowing you to crawl towards a conclusion, I am already in trouble. She's my patient — you know what level of confidentiality that entails. All I'm saying is that she needs to come clean with you, and vice versa.'

Without offering another word, Alex Price jumped to his feet, banged his way out of the house and drove off. To describe his mood as dark would be an understatement; he was livid. Like many adopted Scousers, he copied the indigenous habit and made for the river. In her depths, whether calm or boiling, many found solace without knowing why.

★   ★   ★

I'm in my parked car with the erosion steps beneath me, and I'm staring down at the stretch of sand on which our six dogs ran together. I am crazily, stupidly in love. She held my hand, and I can still feel the tingle that ran up my arm. I saw her with her guard dropped, no wig to conceal her identity. Nothing fazes her; she copes with burnt lasagne, fish and chips, dog muck, me. I need her, God help me. She's colour in a monochrome world.

Tim Dyson's car slides into the space beside me. Buggeration. I need 'me time' in order to recover from the 'me too' experience. He eases his way into my passenger seat; I should have used central locking.

'Are you suicidal, Alex?'

'No.'

'Then I suggest a refresher course in driving. You went through a stop sign and two red lights.'

'Mea maxima culpa.'

'I forgive you. Not that I'm pretending to be God, of course.'

I look him up and down. 'You're not handsome enough to be God.' He didn't deny my conclusion earlier, so I can now assume that Kate did kill her husband, and I feel like . . . I feel like running.

'What are you going to do?' he asks.

'I've got to get away.' I refuse to meet his eyes. The combination of suddenly finding I'm finally in love and that the woman in question has killed — even if for good reason — is more than I can take. 'I'll probably hand over to my second in command and lose myself for a few weeks or months.'

'Will you tell her you're going?'

I shrug. 'I have to think about that.'

'You'll break her heart, Alex. She may present as strong, but she's still papering over the cracks.'

'Aren't we all? You've been papering over the Atlantic Ocean for years, and I'm sure it hurts. I'll tell her I'm going away to think about business, perhaps sell Chillex to that American chain.'

'Right,' he says, though his voice isn't steady.

I sure as hell am not going to tell anyone

about my destination. Not Kate or Tim or anyone at work.

'Will you keep in touch?' he asks me next.

'No. I'm going away to find what's left of me. And don't tell anyone to look for me in any of my regular holiday haunts like Wales or Cornwall, because I won't be there.'

He's gone, thank goodness. And he hasn't turned into the road that leads to Kate's house, so I'm safe for now. But I have no time to linger.

I drive homeward to speak to Brenda and Brian. I'd trust them with my life.

4

Still angry and confused, on his way back home Alex found himself wrestling many mixed emotions. He'd forgotten what that was like and how exhausting it could be. And there was packing to be done. So this was feeling, and feeling was painful.

While folding clothes in his room, he stopped for a breather; he could not leave the country without at least seeing her again.

Brenda Boswell knocked before poking her head round the door. 'I would have packed for you,' she grumbled. 'I know what I'm doing when I pack.'

'I need to be messing about with something while I think.'

She nodded sagely. 'You've been like a cat on hot bricks since you met that nice young woman. Has she given you the push, then? Is that why you're scarpering off abroad without any real warning?'

'Er . . . no. Well, partly, I suppose. I need some distance from work, from her — '

'And from me and my Brian?'

'Never. Aside from my dogs and my honey bees, you're the only living creatures I trust completely.' He sighed heavily. 'She's pushy, Brenda. She needs a permanent fixture in her life . . . a husband. I'm not ready, and although I've told her that neither is she, her hormones are fighting an unfair war. I need to escape from the firing line.'

The housekeeper smiled. 'Put your foot down, son.'

'She'd stamp on it.'

Brenda laughed. She had a big laugh, one that sounded as if it couldn't possibly have emerged from so tiny a body. The trouble was that she often cried after laughing. 'I like the cut of her jib,' she said. 'See, sit down with me a minute.' She perched on the edge of his bed and took his hand as he joined her. 'You mean a lot to me and my Brian — you know you do.'

Alex managed not to roll his eyes. Brenda's emotional moments were usually accompanied by a tale she had told so many times that its socks were full of holes and the shoes needed soling and heeling. Shoes. He mustn't think about shoes. Kate had at least a hundred pairs. She should be called Imelda.

'We never had kids of our own.'

She was off. It was a sad tale, though it had become somewhat threadbare with the passing of time. Oh, God, she had the handkerchief out already. Poor Brenda.

'I know you didn't have children,' he said softly. 'And I'm sorry.'

'He was perfect,' she whispered. 'Just like a little doll after they'd cleaned him up a bit. Tiny, he was, and his lips were a bit blue. He never breathed.'

Alex patted her hand. 'Sad, love.'

'Years passed and we struggled on, even after all my operations what made me barren. Brian

76

said he didn't mind, but we both minded. Then you came along, like, and gave us that little shop to run while this house got built. Nice, comfortable flat with the shop, too. And now we're here, the three of us — '

'And the dogs.'

'Yes. And you're like a son to us.'

'Don't upset yourself, please. I think you've done a very good job of bringing me up. I can use cutlery and wipe my nose all by myself.'

She dabbed at her eyes.

'I've made my decision, but I must go and speak to her first.'

She squeezed his hand. Again, he noticed the strength she owned in those little digits. 'Where you come from, in Woollyback land, they'd say you've been and gone and done it, eh? You love that young woman.'

He ran the free hand through his mop of hair. 'I don't know what state I'm in, Other Mother,' he muttered, knowing how she loved it when he used that term. 'According to Tim, I have to get past the fear to find the trust. According to myself, I need to run and think for a few weeks. So much for getting past the fear. But I have to tell Kate . . . yet I don't know if I can face her.'

She stood up. 'Look, son. Look at me. I want you to go now and get over to that house of hers. Remember telling me and Brian how you shut down when you were a first-year at Bolton School? Well, we can't be having a repeat performance. Open up to her.'

'She'll kill me,' he replied with a wry smile. 'She has what one might call a volatile temper.'

77

The rest of Kate's secrets would remain with him; it was not his story to tell. 'I suppose I'd better go and get the deed done,' he said.

'That's my boy. Face the music as soon as you can, because that's better than hanging about. I'll be here when you get back, son.'

He kissed her furrowed brow. 'I'm going to have a word or three with my river first. If anybody phones, I've gone out and you don't know where I am. I've switched off my work mobile, but you can reach me on the private one. If it's work, they'll phone the land line.'

'Good luck, Alex. I'll pray to St Jude — he's for hopeless cases.'

'You are joking?'

'Would I do that? Go and have words with the Mersey and with Kate.'

He squeezed her hand.

'Course I'm joking.'

He managed a grin. 'I love you, Other Mother. See you later.'

Brenda stayed where she was for a few minutes. 'You've never fooled me for a minute,' she told her adopted son when the front door closed behind him. 'All that rubbish about not having feelings — well, I've watched you, and listened to you. You might act the cold fish in business, but I know you're a good man. Look after him, St Jude. He's the daft so-and-so on his way to the river. And make Kate hang on to her temper. Amen. Now, where did I put my beeswax polish?' She bustled about and got on with her day.

★ ★ ★

I hope nobody who knows me passes by.

What's just happened to me is common or garden in these parts, because people seem to know when you're the right type for the job. I was in the right place at the right time. Or the wrong time, depending on your point of view. And I don't look like an axe murderer, which fact probably helped in my promotion to childminder. I hadn't intended to stop here for long, but somehow this place always gets to me. And of course I'm dreading telling Kate about my plans. So now I've got a good reason for hanging around a little longer.

A beautiful blonde from Southport has left me with a Libby. Libby is three going on forty, and she's dressed up like a princess from that *Frozen* film. When she clicks a button, the edges of her cloak light up with those new LED fairy lights that don't get warm. She fascinates me. She has a Granny Linda who lives down the road, and she's here for a birthday party.

'But you've a beach in Southport,' I remind her.

She gives me a look that makes me feel like something that fell out of a Christmas cracker a couple of years ago. 'There's no water,' she says as if talking to a brain-damaged person. 'It's Lucy's birthday, and Lucy likes water.' She points to the river. 'That is water.'

She's right — it's definitely water. This is one gorgeous child, strawberry blonde hair, peaches and cream skin, bright blue eyes.

79

The beautiful mother is dragging two little girls away from the river's edge. It's clear that Lucy's affection for water is shared by her friend, because both children look dampish. They arrive. 'Sorry,' the mother says.

I tell her it's fine, but I have to go now because I'm meeting someone.

Unfortunately, Libby has taken a liking to me. 'Don't go,' she begs. 'Sandcastles. We have flags.'

Well, what can I do? Seduced by the promise of flags and banana yogurt, I descend the steps and am handed another job on a plate — well, in a bucket — and I am now chief architect of this newly established company. Unlike Southport sand, this stuff is actually wet, so I don't need to work hard at shaping a palace fit for Princess Libby.

'Sand lets water soak in cos it's all parcel cells,' Libby informs me.

'Is it?' I ask.

'She means particles. Daddy told her about particles,' says the mother, busily drying off the two intrepid would-be swimmers who had attempted to conquer the Mersey, the Irish Sea and, no doubt, the Atlantic.

Although I have to get to Kate, first I talk to Libby's mother. She says her job is parenthood, and she earns a living by twisting arms to collect money for charity, so I give her a card. 'Ah, you're Alex Price, then?' There's a gleam in her eye, and I know she'll be hitting the Price charity department with a big stick.

'Yes, I am. Libby, I must go now. If Mummy

lets me know you're coming again, I'll bring my dogs to meet you.'

It's the innocence in the eyes, isn't it? So pure, so clever, so endearing, this little girl. And I suddenly know I want children of my own, and that their mother must be Kate Owen. Well, it seems I'm taking great strides in the emotional department . . . What was it Tim said? 'One day, someone will come along and drag the rug from under your feet.' The someone has finally arrived. Kate.

★ ★ ★

Kate Owen's temper was straining on its leash. 'How did you find me?' she roared for the third time. 'And don't say you used medical records, because I've changed my name as well as my appearance. All that aside, I haven't yet registered with a local doctor. So out with it, Giles.'

He took a backward step. 'I'm sorry.'

'You will be. I can make sure you lose your job.'

The young doctor hung his head. 'You must have realized how I felt about you. I loved you then, and I love you now. There are no pills to cure this.'

Kate shook her head in dismay. 'You were my anchor, or my spine, or my rock — whatever. I talked to no one else apart from the police. It was the end of my bad life as long as my baby survived; then, when I knew she was going to make it, my good life began. You were part of

81

that, and I'm grateful. You helped me out of hell and into the light, but I don't love you. Giles, you were a good friend — no more than that. And I'm . . . well, with someone else now.'

The front doorbell sounded. To Kate's astonishment it was Alex. His arrival was a miracle, but she had no time to explain why. 'Thank goodness. Come in, and go along with what I say. I'm in a bit of a pickle,' she whispered. She led him into her Jill-of-all-trades living space. 'Alex Price, this is Dr Giles Girling, paediatrician. He assisted the surgeon throughout Amelia's operations when we were still in London.'

Each man awarded the other a perfunctory nod, but neither said a word.

'Alex is my fiancé,' she went on. 'We plan to have an autumn or winter wedding, don't we, sweetheart? I want crunchy leaves or snow under my feet.'

'Sweetheart' nodded. Life today had been somewhat odd thus far.

'Giles may be a consultant in the not too distant future.'

'Well done,' was Sweetheart's reply.

'Your shoes are sandy, darling.'

He glanced down at his feet. 'I've been on the beach with some children.'

'Lovely.' She stared hard at Giles. 'If I wish, I can make sure you're awarded no consultancy. Your career lies in my hands, so don't forget that. For the fourth and final time, how did you discover my location? Answer me.'

It was the doctor's turn to look at his feet. 'I bought it.'

'From a Met officer?'

'I think he might have been a policeman, yes.'

Kate exploded. 'I shall inform the inspector in charge of my case, and that sergeant of his will be discarded immediately. But he will still know my address, so I now have to sell up, and I might well lose money because of you. It means another change of name, too. You have gone too far, and you know it.'

'I'm sorry,' Giles mumbled. 'I didn't think.'

'Well I hope you manage to think in theatre when next removing the top of an infant's skull.' She was now in thunder mode. 'I shall never, ever forgive you for this. Even if I decide to keep your name out of things at this juncture, I shall continue to hold the power to drop you in it at some future date. There's also a chance that the policeman might mention your name. Get out, and don't come back. I mean it, Giles — go!'

'You heard the lady,' Alex growled, pleased to see her in a very unladylike morph.

Giles Girling slunk out of the house. The two remaining occupants were quiet for several minutes before Kate moved to pick up her phone. After pressing just one button, she spoke. Her hand was not quite steady. 'Inspector Allen? Yes, yes, it's Kate. Quite well, thank you. Yourself? Oh good.'

Alex came to stand beside her, placing an arm round her slender waist.

'How many people have my details? Ah, just as I thought — you and your bagman. Well, I've been found.' She paused while receiving a lengthy answer. 'Then it must be DS Makin. The guy said he'd paid for the information. What? He thought it could have been a policeman, but who knows? What if it was a journalist? You do realize Jim's right-hand men may well be searching for me from jail? Yes, I'll change the SIM card and send my new number by courier. Right. I'll await your call.'

She broke the connection and sat on the sofa, all fire draining from her. 'Put the kettle on, Alex,' she begged. 'It might not have been the sergeant, just someone good at breaking private passwords on computers. I hope the inspector realizes that.'

'What are you going to do?' he asked.

'I shall sit here and wait for you to bring me a cup of tea. Sorry. I'm being obtuse again. The inspector will sort everything out, and I'll take it from there.'

He remained where he was, as if riveted to the spot. 'Will you leave Liverpool?'

She awarded him a cheeky wink. 'No. I'm changing my name to Price.'

Alex went off to make tea as commanded for the queen of Merrilocks Road. Their little girl would have dark hair and blue or brown eyes. She would also have an excellent mother, though her potential father's hands shook as he waited for the kettle to boil. Plain biscuits. Kate didn't take sugar, but she needed some carbohydrate after the shock she'd just endured. She was changing her name to Price? Was this fear or excitement? He had absolutely no bloody idea.

'I wish you'd come earlier,' she said as he placed the tray on a small coffee table. 'Though I

84

wasn't expecting you at all, so I must be grateful for small mercies.'

He handed her a cup of tea with two rich tea fingers in the saucer. It occurred to him that he needed not only to confess his own escape plans; it was also necessary to tell her that he knew details of her history. 'There you go. Semi-sweet biscuits will settle your stomach.' He had learnt that line from Other Mother.

He sat on the sofa, deliberately leaving room between them. He didn't relish the idea of being on the receiving end of her wrath. After waiting while she dunked her biscuits, he cleared his throat. 'I did some thinking. This has all been so fast . . . I thought it would be better if I gave us some space. Well, that is to say, gave me some space.'

'Oh?'

He inhaled deeply, remembering times when he'd been sent to sit outside the head teacher's office after breaking the rules. 'I've just packed my cases for an extended stay abroad. I've . . . I've got to go and see some Americans about a partnership deal for Chillex.'

Kate's jaw closed with a snap that was almost audible. 'Don't leave me,' she begged. 'I need you here now that Giles has ruined my new identity. I have no way of knowing if I'm safe or not. The only good thing is that at least Amelia is fine. Even the police don't know her where-abouts.'

This was far removed from the reaction he'd expected. Phew. He'd got away with it. He softened his tone. 'All right, the Americans can wait. This is far more important than that. I won't leave you, now that I know what's happened. That copper might sell your address a dozen times over, especially if he gets the push for unacceptable behaviour.'

'Yes, that's only too possible. So I can't stay here in my bolthole any longer. So where do I go?'

'With two lion-sized dogs? Where are they, by the way?'

'In the back garden — it's secure.'

He smiled broadly, because she'd forgiven him without saying so.

'You're coming with me. We'll get contractors round here to finish off this place to your specifications, and I'll hire a personal bodyguard for you.'

Kate remained silent for a few seconds. 'No,' she whispered eventually.

'Why?'

'Because I'm ninety per cent sure that my husband collected his gang members from the ranks of security people. That's why I have Castor and Pollux. Dogs can't be bribed with money, and you'll notice that I've recently blanked off the letterbox in my front door here. Dogs like food, and baddies poison it. A human bodyguard is the last thing I need.'

Alex nodded. 'I never thought of that.'

'You haven't lived my life. You should try my shoes for size some time — though possibly not the stilettos. It was a shitty marriage built on lies — his lies. He was a man with no conscience, and no empathy whatsoever.'

'A sociopath, then.' It was not a question.

'Very much so. He almost killed our daughter.'

Alex realized that he was holding his breath. Would she? Wouldn't she?

Kate grabbed a cushion and clutched it to her chest. 'There were guns hidden all over the house. The revolver in the sideboard was always loaded, so I took that one. Amelia was unconscious after bouncing off the wall — a proper wall, not the plasterboard partitions they have in modern houses. Real bricks.'

'I have a modern house with real bricks throughout.'

She glanced at him. 'You would.' After a short pause, she continued. 'I made sure he saw his own death. He was coming towards me when I pulled the trigger. I blew his face off.'

'I know.' Alex's voice was almost as soft as a whisper.

She turned and stared at him. 'Who told you?'

He had prepared and honed the answer to what he hoped was perfection. He needed to protect Tim, the lad who had saved him, the man who had helped him for years. 'After you told me you were glad he'd died, I suspected that you might have killed him. Reams of microfiche later, I found you in the library. Amelia was with you in the photograph, but her face was blanked out.'

'So was Jim's,' she said. 'He haunts me sometimes.'

Alex blinked dampness from his eyes. 'I'll look after you.'

'I don't want you to feel you have to.'

He jumped to his feet. 'Pack your stuff now.

Don't give yourself time to think — I'll think for you. I'll have Brian bring the dog van round. We have your car and mine, so we'll get the dogs in the van with some of your things, and our boots and rear seats will carry a fair amount. We can manage the move as long as we stay calm.'

'But — '

'But what?'

'What are the arrangements? Do we share a room?'

'No. You'll be in the roof with the bats and the pigeons.'

'Another of your pathetic jokes, Alex Price?'

He nodded, chuckling. 'There's a small suite of rooms up there. Bedroom, bathroom, sitting room and kitchen.' He grinned broadly. 'The dogs can go up with you, or stay down in the mud room with mine. I find that dogs tend to make their own arrangements, so we'll let them choose.'

For a moment she wavered and then made her decision. 'OK, boss, let's do it.'

They filled all her suitcases before resorting to black binbags. She found a teddy with one eye and alopecia. 'This is William,' she announced.

'Shakespeare?'

'Wordsworth. For a Lakeland poet, he did a good job on Westminster Bridge.'

'You miss London?' he asked.

She walked towards him, raised a hand and touched his face. 'Not as badly as I'd miss you. And I like Liverpool, because it's a more manageable size. From the erosion, I can see New Brighton, the Wirral and Wales. And the sunsets are fabulous.'

'You won't see any of those places from my house.'

'I'll see you.' Her hand moved over his newly sprouted facial hair. 'All that testosterone,' she mumbled. 'I'm sure we could find a use for it.'

He was a hopeless case, and he knew it, knew he'd been hers from the moment that heel had snapped. 'Slowly, Kate.'

'I don't do slowly.'

'I noticed.'

'When I go on a reading spree, I get through three books in two days.'

'I need to take things at my pace, Kate. We have to wing it until I'm ready to tell you what happened to me when I was eleven years old. I'll know when it's time to let you walk through my deepest, darkest secret.'

'Did you kill anyone?'

'No.'

She took both his hands in hers. 'Was it horrendous? Do you still dream about it?'

'Yes.'

'That's a problem we share. In my nightmare, I shoot him, but he remains intact and grabs me. All I can think about is my daughter, but he has me trapped, so I can do nothing for her.'

'While I see a room — a whole house — filling with blood. I'm a good swimmer, but blood's thicker than water. Tim drags me out of the red stuff.'

'Oh, Alex.' She placed her arms on his shoulders, clasping hands behind his neck.

'We're a mess,' he whispered.

Well, I'm installed. Alex is downstairs talking to the two Bees.

This is where Alex's brother stays when he comes from Australia for a visit. Stephen is his name, I believe. It is quite large and airy, with several Velux windows allowing light into kitchen and bathroom, while both bedroom and living room have large dormers perched on the roof of the house. I'm home. I'm home with Alex. Sometimes a bad thing happens — poor, love-struck Dr Giles was a bad thing — yet turns in a matter of minutes into something excellent. Alex wants to take care of me.

I've been through testing by the two Bees. Brian wanted to know whether I needed any decorating, while Brenda was all a-fluster about my cleaning. She wasn't pleased when I said I'd be doing my own housework, but I told her it's just the way I am, and nothing personal. In truth, it's my OCD making me worry about her altering my pattern, but I don't know her well enough to admit that.

Alex has asked me to dress in a smart suit, because he's taking me to Chester — rather exciting, as there are Roman ruins there. He's acting somewhat strangely, and I can't work out whether he's excited or scared. Oh well, I had better just go along with him, because the dogs are settled with Alex's four, and all are out in the back 'helping' Brian with the compost heap. Poor Brian. Enduring help from six dogs must be a chore.

I'm wearing fine mohair in charcoal with a cerise blouse and gloves, black shoes and bag. He's waiting for me in the hall, and he tells me I look lovely. So does he, but I just smile. He has to know how women covet him.

Chester is special. It's walled apart from one small section, and it's next to the River Dee. There are The Rows, which have tiers of shops stacked one on top of another, and although much of the city was renovated in the nineteenth century, the work remained faithful to the Jacobean period, right up to the crazy, twisted chimneys.

Alex tells me that there are three levels in most rows, and that the lowest lies below pavement and road, where there are still Roman remains. I'm awestruck. The legions were here in this beautiful place, and evidence endures of central heating systems and crude bathroom arrangements. I feel right in Chester, as right as I do in Liverpool, and no longer miss the London Eye, Tower Bridge and the Thames. Some Londoners to this day view the north as flat cap, whippet and ferret territory, but how wrong can they be?

My companion is nervous, and it's nothing to do with the way women size him up as we walk along the row towards the church of St Peter. Alex stops outside a jeweller's. He tells me that this is our pretend wedding day and only the two Bees will know the truth. What? I blink in confusion. Has he gone mad?

'If the world believes we're married, you will automatically be far, far safer. It's well known how far I go to look after my employees, so my wife will be even better protected. It's the best way I can think of to minimize the danger you're in.'

I'm still gobsmacked.

And we are still standing outside the jeweller's. Walking behind me with his hands on my shoulders, Alex guides me inside.

The man asks if he can help us.

I try to smile, but I feel beyond help.

Alex asks for wedding and engagement rings before turning to me. 'Gold or white metal, my love?'

'White,' is my answer once my tongue unties itself.

'White,' Alex repeats as if the shop owner hasn't heard me. 'One for Kate, and a match for me. Platinum.'

We acquire matching wedding rings, and Alex says he will bring them back for engraving at some later date. He also insists on buying me an engagement ring to convince everyone still further. A diamond on a plain platinum band works perfectly.

I need something like sugar, or perhaps a gin and tonic. I'll probably wake up shortly from this very vivid dream.

The man boxes and wraps the jewellery, and takes Alex's Amex. I go outside and lean against the window, arms folded across my chest. I'm sulking. Why am I sulking? I am displeased because he just told me what was going to happen. There was no discussion, no consultation, no chance for me to agree or disagree. Jim was like that. But no, no, Alex is nothing like Jim.

He joins me and asks me what my problem is. So I tell him, holding nothing back. Nobody organizes me. I've waded through enough dung already, and I absolutely refuse to be managed without prior consultation. He says he told me what was happening, and I accuse him of telling the Bees first. Then he apologizes and begs me to stop shouting in the street. So I stop. He's doing it to protect me, the best way he knows. It's hard to stay mad at him, anyway, because something of the boy still remains in him, probably because he suffered that emotional arrest at a very young age. I shudder as I remember him telling me about swimming through blood. What did he see? Will his nightmares ever end?

'So our marriage is just pretend?' I ask.

'For now, yes. We need to sift through our options for the future, sort out Amelia and your parents, decide where everyone will live, and how we might manage to escape your past.' He pauses. 'And mine.'

In tea rooms at ground level, we are presented with high tea as ordered by Mr Price. We have an ornate silver teapot with a matching, lidded jug containing hot water to weaken our brew should we so wish, sugar and milk in smaller silver pots, and a three-tier cake stand with enough confectionery on its levels to drive a whole classroom full of children crazy.

Sandwiches are without crusts and placed beautifully on oblong platters in white ceramic. Between these regimented lines of triangular delights sit tiny fronds of parsley and little radishes carved into flowers. I wonder what all this is about, but the man I love is busy peeling back top layers of bread in order to assess the contents. Again, I see the child in him.

'Be Mother,' he suggests, wiping his hands on a napkin before digging them into pockets. I pour the tea, and I suddenly know what's happening, though I'm not going to spoil things for him. A few expletives later, he appears to have found what he has sought. 'Three bloody boxes, and it has to be the last one,' he grumbles quietly.

Despite the fact that the place is nearly full, he stands and moves to the side before kneeling next to me. 'Kate whatever your name is today, will you marry me in the not too distant future? Like next year?'

I have never cried in public since childhood, but I'm weepy now. People are standing and applauding, while our waitress takes photographs with Alex's phone. And, as the tears wash my face, all I can think is that he loves me. He wants to keep me safe, and soon enough we will be properly married.

He tells me not to cry.

He stands and returns to his seat after taking a bow to his audience. Conversation hums once more, and he asks me to give him my thoughts, so I tell him I want more children. And he smiles as he relates his tale of Libby-on-the-beach. This man, this beautiful boy in the body of an adult, this chief executive of a thriving business, will make an excellent father and stepfather. It's time to go home.

They returned to Strawberry Mead at about six o'clock and walked straight into trouble. Bobby Ray Carson was striding about in Mrs Bee's kitchen, while two policemen, their warrant cards on display, sat drinking tea at a small breakfast table. 'What's going on?' Alex asked.

Bobby Ray answered. 'I've closed Cheers, and colleagues of these gentlemen are with your two girlfriends at Chillex and Checkmate.'

Alex's mouth twitched. 'Not in front of my wife, Bob.'

'Sorry.' Bobby Ray gave them a look of surprise but then grinned. 'Congratulations.'

'Girlfriends?' Kate raised her left hand to display wedding and engagement rings.

'Tell you later,' Alex promised before returning to the business in hand. 'Is it drugs?' he asked.

The men at the table nodded. 'Nothing obvious at the gay club, and Charm seems clear. Steroids among other nasties at Chillex, all kinds of stuff at Cheers. London boys, we believe.'

Kate clutched at Alex's hand. 'Do you have any names?' she asked.

'No, but they were noticed outside Chillex and inside Cheers. Mr Carson had his usual eagle eye on the club, and when he saw business taking place he phoned us. We know you keep a tight and tidy fleet of ships, so we moved fast, but not fast enough. People who bought the drugs are enjoying the happy ambience at various stations, and they all said the men had London accents.'

Alex spoke to Bobby Ray. 'You got the buyers' names?'

'Yes.'

'Stick them on the banned list. I want all five clubs taken apart by the police if they have time. Yes, all five. We shall reopen when we're judged clean.'

The officers stood up. 'If everybody cooperated like you, Mr Price, the world would be a cleaner and safer place.'

Alex shook their hands. 'I've heard of too many deaths from drugs, gentlemen. As long as I have a say in such matters, the clubs will be clean. Mr Carson here agrees with me — he owns half of Cheers.'

Bobby Ray nodded his agreement. 'So we whiten all windows and show a closed for refurb sign, yes?'

'Yes. I'll send painters in. Good luck to you, gentlemen, and bad luck to dealers.' The police left, and Bobby Ray followed within minutes.

To distract her man, Kate placed herself in front of him. 'Girlfriends? Tell me,' she insisted.

He took a handkerchief from his pocket and waved the white flag. 'Well, there's Amber Simpson, manager of Chillex. If she stood sideways behind a lamp post, you wouldn't see much of her. She needs a few good meals, so perhaps she was thinking of eating me.'

'Pretty?'

He shrugged. 'Peroxide blonde, muscular and ambitious. Not my type at all. She probably sees me as a man with just about enough money to get her to where she thinks she wants to be.'

'And number two?'

'Marty — really Martina Nelson. She manages the singles club, and she does it very well. Checkmate has its own specific problems, because singletons who are not singletons are often pursued by spouses. There are some spectacular fights, so Marty depends heavily on security, though I've heard some customers complaining that Marty's armlocks are extremely painful.'

'Is she pretty?'

'Compared to whom?'

'Compared to me, of course.'

He touched her face. 'You aren't merely pretty — you're perfectly beautiful.'

'Good answer. In fact, the only acceptable one.'

His thumb travelled gently across her cheekbone. 'Just give me time, Kate. I must go out now. Fortunately, my clubs are fairly close to each other behind Hope Street, but I may be gone for a few hours.'

'See you later.'

'That you will. Bye for now.' And he left.

5

Kate woke suddenly in the dark, wondering where on earth she was. After blinking stupidly for a moment or two, she remembered: she was pretend-married and properly engaged to a beautiful, difficult and stubborn man. And she loved him.

Yes, she was at Alex's house. She pulled at the duvet, realizing as she did so that someone was sitting at the bottom of her bed. 'Alex?' she asked, turning to switch on a lamp, blinking against its glow.

'Were you expecting someone else?'

'There's a sizeable list, but you're at the top, I promise.'

He shifted to the side of the divan, so that he could hold her hand. 'No joking. First, your dogs are settled with mine. But we have serious business, so I hope you're fully awake. There are drug hits all over Liverpool, stuff ranging from so-called legal highs all the way to some supposedly Chinese stuff that is unevenly cut, so when it's too pure it might kill.'

'God.'

'Not God — it's more likely to be the work of the lower, hotter section of the afterlife. But . . . ' He paused for several seconds. 'I know London's a big city, but the two guys selling the drugs just happen to have East End accents. Might those voices possibly belong to what you described as gang members lower down the food chain, the men with no names? It may sound far-fetched, but what do you think?'

'Jim's pond life?'

'Your dear departed's runners, yes. They'd do the work too menial for him and his sidekicks. I suppose they kept watch when a big job went on, protected people who wouldn't have needed protection had it not been for Jim — and yes, there would be drugs. But . . . Kate, stay strong.'

'What? Why?'

'The house you were renovating on Merrilocks Road has been ransacked. Yes, hang on to my hand. I went up there to check when I left the clubs, just in case. Couldn't go inside, because it's a crime scene — fingerprints and so forth.'

Kate let go of his hand and sat bolt upright. 'If they are Jim's men, they'll leave no evidence. He'll have trained them to be meticulous. But they were lucky, because my dogs would have ripped their throats out.' She drew up her knees and rested her chin on the raised duvet. 'Your fingerprints will be in there.'

He lifted his hands, displaying grey fingertips. 'See? I'm being eliminated. It's a dirty business.'

'Oh, Alex, fingerprinted because of me. What have I pulled you into? You have your business to run, your life to live, and I come along — '

'You will be my business; you will be my life. When I'm ready and you're ready — when we know the time is right and Amelia can come home, there'll be big changes. We can live anywhere in the world — '

'Eric Mansell,' she cried. 'The one in Walton Jail, Jim's right-hand man. What if he knows I'm

99

here? He might have got the lower orders to come up from London to find me. Drugs were always the basis of the business, their fuel, their bread-and-butter money. I used to thank God that I had my own salary and the house my parents bought for me, because I didn't want anything to do with heroin, cocaine or whatever . . . ' Her voice died of exhaustion, while the grip on his hand was renewed.

'You may be on the right track, but it could be the other way round, Kate. The London guys might have bought your address from the same source as Dr Girling. The man in Walton may have nothing to do with what's happening. But Merrilocks Road was targeted — that was personal. What do they want from you?'

She bit her lip. 'I killed their boss and put three criminals in jail.'

'And they want to kill you?'

'Not necessarily. They'll want to know where the rest of the stuff is from the Hatton Garden job, and they probably think I can tell them. And maybe I could, though I only just thought of it myself. Jim's dad died a couple of weeks before Jim's . . . death. If the police dug up the grave site . . . It would be typical of Jim — he hated his dad, who was a decent man. Yes, his father is probably buried under a dozen safety deposit boxes. I must speak to Inspector Allen.'

'Go to sleep now, princess.'

Unexpectedly, she laughed. 'I'm no princess.' Again, she became serious. 'It's amazing how one forgets things after a trauma — and how precisely they can come back to you in certain circumstances. Of course, I carry a clear picture of Jim's face just before I shot him, but today, after Giles had gone, I suddenly remembered how very dirty it was.

'Jim was meticulous when it came to personal hygiene. Two showers a day, two shirts, two of everything. Yet he was hitting the vodka that night, and while he was pouring it I noticed rims of black stuff under his fingernails too. He was filthy, Alex. He looked like he'd done a shift in a coal mine. Gentleman Jim didn't do filthy. He was OK with theft, murder, wife-beating . . . he was fine with protection rackets, drugs and fraud. But untidiness and dirt? Never, not even when gardening.

'I don't want to make Inspector Allen follow a red herring, but this particular fish is worth bait on a line. I do realize that the dirt might well have come from the tunnel they made in order to gain access to the safety deposit boxes, but I also believe Jim was capable of dishonouring his father in the worst way. He hadn't even bothered to attend the funeral. Mr Latimer was a train driver, an honest working man with . . . ' she paused through several beats of time, 'with an allotment where he grew prize-winning flowers and vegetables. He specialized in chrysanthemums. Dull but serviceable blooms, didn't someone say?'

She sighed. 'It won't be the allotment, because there's always a lengthy queue for those, and Mr Latimer ceased to be a tenant when he died. So it's the grave — it has to be.'

'It could be the tunnel,' Alex reminded her.

'I'm almost sure it was black soil, so the grave's worth checking.' She shuddered. 'Imagine being among the dead in almost total darkness, digging and . . . ugh.' She shivered again. 'But I have this feeling, and the inspector said I must tell him every lead I can think of, even if it seems silly. Is it silly?'

'No. Go to sleep. Perhaps I should have left all this until daylight, though I knew you might tell me off for not waking you.'

Kate scarcely heard him. 'Jim knew where the grave was, because he took flowers for his mother several times a year; he adored his old girl, as he called her. Yes, it makes sense. The grave was recently disturbed for his father's burial, so no one would notice any change.' At last, she gave her attention to Alex. 'If you're not happy to sleep with me, go away.'

'I'd be more than happy, but remember, I have never been in this situation before. Sex was just exercise with no real affection in the mix. With you, it would be different — and my hands are covered in fingerprint stuff. Mrs Bee bought lovely new bedding recently, and she'd kill us if we messed it up. Believe me, Kate, you don't want to upset my housekeeper.'

'I don't care,' was her answer.

Alex laughed.

'And we don't need sex; we need sleep,' was her next contribution.

'And dirty Mrs Bee's covers? Have you seen her in high dudgeon? She makes the incredible hulk look like a children's entertainer.'

'She's tiny, Alex.'

He shook his head. 'In her mind, she's *Tyrannosaurus regina* crossed with a medieval witch. Even Mr Bee keeps his head down when she's on one.'

Kate tossed back the duvet; she was wearing very little. 'Come on, we'll just sleep. On my life, I promise not to interfere with your person, and your moral virginity will remain intact.'

'You think I'm a dumbo, don't you?'

'I would never be engaged to a dumbo. I've nothing against elephants — in fact, I contribute to the protection of African wildlife. Take your outer clothes off and get in this bed. The child in you still needs a mum. Sleep with me, and I'll protect you from your nightmares.'

'Is that an order, ma'am?'

'Yes.'

He gave up the fight, undressed, and joined her.

★　★　★

Kate woke wrapped in his arms with warm brown eyes looking at her.

'Any dreams?' he asked.

'Can't remember. You?'

'Ditto. This is the first time I've spent most of a night with a woman.'

'And we were very, very good.' She giggled. 'Sleep without sex. Quite an achievement in my book.'

They stayed together for a few minutes before he jumped out of bed wearing only a big smile and boxer shorts.

Kate drank in her first real sight of him, carefully noting his assets. 'Pecs good. Six-pack not horribly pronounced. Abs great. Love handles, none. Handsome, tick.'

He felt the heat in his face; yes, she embarrassed him, but Alex wanted children with backbone and brain, and this woman had both.

'Payback time,' he announced. 'Beautiful, definitely. Natural hair, soft and shiny. Good body . . . ' He made a ticking motion over his palm.

'Except for the scars.' Her voice was low. 'I have a metal plate in my right leg, so doctors have given me a chance of arthritis as I age.'

Alex swallowed a lump of sadness that had settled in his throat. 'I wish I'd killed him with my own hands. But now you are definitely, absolutely mine. Tell me — is Amelia like you? Her personality, I mean.'

'Yes, she's a handful. That's why he almost kicked the life out of her, I suppose. She's a very girly girl — beads, sequins, separate dressing-up wardrobe full of princessy stuff. She took pearls out of his stash, you know, and her intention would have been to keep them.'

'So he half killed a child?'

She nodded. 'His own child.'

Again, he swallowed. 'She sounds like the little girl I met on the beach yesterday. An answer for everything, she had. Her two friends were trying to drown themselves in the river, while little madam was bribing me with paper flags for sandcastles, and banana yogurt for pudding.'

'Did they drown?'

'No. Princess Libby's mother saved them while I sat and learnt how clever small female children can be. I imagine your Amelia as being in the same bracket as Libby.'

'She has French lessons with my parents twice a week. She'll be able to argue back in two languages soon.'

Alex jumped to his feet. 'I'll throw something on and exercise the dogs. There's a new phone charging in your living room, so use that. Remember? You told the inspector you would change your SIM card. Get him up to scratch. Tell him you're in my care, that we're going to be married when everything's sorted out, and that we're truly engaged. He needs to know what happened here last night.' He blew her a kiss and left. After a few seconds, his head returned. 'The pretend marriage — he needs to know that.'

Kate pulled a pillow over her face. Like an ostrich with its head in the sand, she could see nothing for a few moments, and that was fine by her. The project in Blundellsands had been taken away from her, some dangerous people were looking for her, but that was all peripheral. Alex loved her. Alex was her core; he was all she truly needed.

★   ★   ★

I feel there's a disease that's spreading to embrace England and, perhaps, France. Inspector Allen has found and given me the names of two men who were Jim's runners. There's a Max Alton, usually known as Mad Max, and a Trevor

Jones who's normally Trev. There used to be two more, but there was an accident on the M25 and they died.

The inspector has been in touch with Liverpool's Chief Constable. Max and Trev were seen near Euston station, and possibly caught the train to Lime Street from there. It all dovetails together quite sweetly except for one problem. The bastards (Inspector Allen's word for them) have done a disappearing act. So they are the ones who invaded my space and ruined my project. Even though he no longer walks the earth, Gentleman Jim continues to spoil lives and destroy any hope nursed by those among us who want to move on and forget our nightmare pasts.

I told the inspector I had changed address and that my house had been ransacked. 'There wasn't much to ransack — I lived in one room,' I said. 'And I'm pretend-married to Alex Price. Look him up — he got a warning for knocking the Master of Foxhounds off his horse in the nineties. Probably Holcombe Hunt.'

Of course, he wanted the pretend-married bit explained, so I told him Alex has superb security people and we'll be truly married when everything calms down and Amelia comes home. He tutted and laughed, telling me that if he lives to be a hundred he'll never work me out. I said snap, because I don't always know who and what I am, either.

He now has my theory about the Latimer grave, so that will be investigated almost immediately. Once the missing boxes are found,

Max and Trev will have no further use for me, but I won't feel completely safe until they're locked up. Oh, how I hope I'm right about the grave.

I shower, make sure I'm wearing the wedding band as well as the engagement ring, slip into a blue dress and flat navy shoes. With the shoulder-length blonde wig covering my own hair, I descend two flights and meet Mrs Bee in the downstairs hall. 'Good girl,' she whispers. 'I see you've got the wedding ring on. He's in the sitting room with Bob, that good-looking black man from Cheers. I get the feeling there's more trouble, something to do with one of the clubs.'

She seems flustered when I give her a hug and a quick kiss on her forehead. Brenda is so small, I could probably tuck her head under my chin. I leave her and go in search of my man.

When I enter the sitting room I find he and Bobby Ray are clinging to each other, and Alex is actually sobbing.

My fiancé, my husband, my beloved, is in tears, and the mother in me rushes to comfort him. 'What happened?' I ask Bobby Ray. 'He was fine upstairs a few minutes ago. Alex?'

Being unable to speak, he gives me no answer.

'Bobby Ray? What's going on?'

Clearly choked himself, the man dries his dark eyes. 'We couldn't open the broom cupboard in the back of the club.' Bob inhales a shuddering breath. 'There was a dead boy behind the door, needle still in his arm. There were no tracks or old injection marks, so he's been killed by his first hit. He looks about sixteen or seventeen and there was no club stamp on his hand. Alex can't cope with shit like this. Excuse me.' Desperate for air, he makes for the door, leaving his partner in my useless hands.

'I'm here, my love, I'm here,' I say.

'Somebody killed that boy. Oh, Kate, he was a novice. Whoever gave him the drugs buggered off and left him to die behind that door. His arm had a band on to tighten it and make the veins swell. Someone did this in my club, then escaped through a window.'

'Your and Bobby Ray's club,' I remind him.

'It's not his fault.' Alex dries his eyes.

'It's not yours, either. You were with me — '

'Not all the time. I was back and forth to the clubs, up at your house, and back here only from three in the morning,' he says, his tone steadying. 'I'm going now with Bob to talk to the police. There's a meeting this afternoon at my office. I'll send a car for you.'

'Why?'

'Because you're part of my life,' he says simply.

I hand him back to Bobby Ray when he returns. One way or another, I have to get to the bottom of Alex's historic problem. He's my man. I must mend my man.

★   ★   ★

To begin with, it was sheer bloody murder. They had to drive on the right side, which was the wrong side, their passports were forgeries, and they had no French beyond *Voulez-vous coucher*

108

avec moi ce soir?, which was of little use when they were hungry and searching for food. Of course, Trev had forgotten to bring the French phrase book he'd pinched from W H Smith.

Max, who had hired the Renault via forged documents, took about an hour adjusting to the rules of the road, and they ended up in Saint-Malo, which was nowhere near the Haute-Loire area for which they were supposedly heading. In fact, they were still near the English Channel. Driving wasn't too bad once he got used to it; the driver still sat in the middle of the road, and he became better with practice. Right was now the easier turn, but that was all.

He found a parking spot. 'See them walls?' he asked.

Trev sighed. 'Course I do.'

'In 1963, I read about this place in the papers. I was a kid, but I knew what they were on about. The Great Train Robbery had just happened, and somebody said they thought they'd seen one of the robbers here. These walls were crawling with Frog cops all shouting and blowing whistles. It's part of our history,' he said proudly. 'They done a job that was dangerous and daring. Several months ago, we watched Hatton Garden while Jim and the others done a job worth millions.' He closed his eyes. France and action were exercising a beneficial effect on Max's temper.

'Are you gonna drive with your eyes shut?'

'No. Just thinking about Ronnie Biggs. He was the one that got away.'

'To Hot Lo-higher?'

109

'No. South America. And the river's Lo-ire, no aitch in it.'

'I hope there's fish in it. I'm bloody starving.'

'We won't get there today, you tinhead. We need a *carte*.'

'We've got a car.'

'*Carte* means map. Wait here. I'm going in that shop over there to see what they've got for us to eat.'

'Don't get none of that quiche crap. Cold egg and bacon pie makes me want to chuck.'

Max opened his door. 'This is a small car, so no chucking up in it. I should have come on my own.' He marched off to the nearby bakery.

Trev was fed up. Max was right — this country was a damned sight bigger than mainland Britain. He wanted to go home. He could have been running drugs for Fat Arthur, having a pint down the Beggar, game of arrows, pie and mash.

He watched as Max came out of the food shop and went into another place. God, he was buying a tent. How long would they be staying in a country with folk Trev couldn't stand? Even their bloody president had hidden in England during the war. They were all white flags and unused guns, the French. And they talked daft. And his stomach was rumbling. And Max was back, throwing things in the car.

'What the hell's that bloody lot?' Trev wanted to know.

'Tent and fixings. Matches, kettle, tins of food, tin plates, tin cups and sleeping bags. Oh, and a couple of pans, coffee, tea, sugar and dried milk.'

Once Max was back in the driving seat, they sat in a silence that was punctuated only by the clacking of Max's ill-fitting dentures. Trev didn't even stop to think about what he was eating — food was fuel, and fuel was what he needed.

'It's a long river,' Max said when he'd finished eating.

'I'd worked that out,' Trev snapped. 'It was my old auntie that got the address, remember? She copied it off that letter she found where she cleans. Thank God Katherine Latimer's mother writes to her neighbours. I'm not as daft as you try to make out.'

Max grinned. 'Did you enjoy your French smelly-feet cheese?'

'Is that what I've ate? Yeah, it was OK.' He picked his teeth with a fingernail.

Max opened the map. 'We're here,' he explained, 'and they're all the way over there, something like Martin Fleurs, it's called. The man in the camping shop had a bit of English, and he showed me the place on the map. He says if we get lost, follow the river.'

Trev took a loud swig of pop. 'And we can't just pounce when we get there. We've got to stop and watch the house, the comings and goings.' He paused. 'Speaking of movements, what about when we need a toilet?'

'You're getting on my tits now, Trev. I have a tin opener for when we're shoving the food down our throats, and a spade for when it comes out. Dig a hole, soft arse. Yes, I've got baby wipes and loo roll. If I'd left it to you, we'd have arrived here with sod all.'

111

'Sorry, Max. I know I can be a muppet sometimes.'

Max grinned. 'You're good in other ways, mate. When it comes to shifting drugs, you're ace.'

'Thanks. Right, where are we going now?'

'Paris.'

'Is that near the river?'

'A different river. It's spelt S-e-i-n-e, but you say sane.'

'Why?'

'Because it's French.'

'No, I mean why are we going to Paris?'

Max shook his head slowly. 'It's like London. When people visit England, they don't give London a miss, do they? We've come all this way, so why not?'

Trev couldn't think of a why not, so he sat back and fastened his seat belt. Paris? It would be packed solid with French folk all dressed up as if they'd come straight off the gangplank, or whatever they called the thing models walked and posed on. 'There's no ballroom under the tower like what they have at Blackpool.'

'What?'

'Well, it's just stuck in the middle of the road, innit? No candy floss and ice cream, no arcades. And it looks rusty.'

Max rolled his eyes heavenward. It was going to be a series of long, long days with Trev moaning his way through every single second. 'Listen to me. If I'd wanted a foghorn complaining down my ear'ole, I'd have brought the missus instead. So shut up and put up.' He

112

pondered. 'When did you go to Blackpool?'

'When I was ten.'

'Right. And now, we're going to Paris.' Max turned on the engine and pulled away. Whether he liked it or not, Trev was going to see the capital of France. It was what normal people did, wasn't it?

★ ★ ★

Dressed once more in the elegant charcoal suit, except now teamed with emerald green blouse and gloves, Kate alighted from the chauffeur-driven car. Alex was waiting for her, and he took her hand as she stepped on the pavement outside Price Partners.

She whispered in his ear, 'I can't marry you for real, darling. I'll be Katie Price if I do. I wouldn't make a very good Jordan.'

'Then you'll be Katherine or Kat.'

'Whatever you choose.' Although she was trying to keep the atmosphere light, she knew that he was still in a bad place. Goose bumps travelled up her arms, and a slight headache threatened to strengthen its grip if she didn't stop worrying about Alex worrying Tim. She needed to get hold of Tim, who knew the past and helped Alex through his nightmares.

'Are you all right?' he asked.

'Are *you* all right?' was her reply.

He stopped in the empty foyer. 'He was celebrating his sixteenth, Kate. His mother thought he'd gone round to a friend's house, but . . . '

113

'No one will blame you.'

He inhaled sharply. 'I blame me.'

'Why?'

'My club, my staff, my security guards.'

She pulled at his hand and led him to a leather sofa; the foyer probably doubled as waiting area. They sat. 'Alex, at any given time, we can manage to be in one place, and in that place only. Bobby Ray owns half the club — does he blame himself?'

'I'm not sure. He's upset.'

'Where's this meeting?'

'Upstairs. The conference room is not huge, so it's packed. Everyone is here — well, everyone connected to the clubs. First, I shall introduce you as my wife. That's for your own safety. Then I have to cut them all to the quick, because I'll get to the bottom of this lad's death if it's the last meaningful thing I do. Don't be afraid of me when I'm in CEO mode.'

'I won't.' Kate smiled as relief coursed through her veins. Apart from the ill-conceived guilt, he was speaking rationally. 'I love you, beautiful boy,' she whispered.

He smiled and led her upstairs. This was it, he realized; this was the day on which Kate would meet both sides of him. He would be showing the power he had assumed as a businessman, the role he had been forced to play on the road to success; she already knew the damaged child who hid under the cloak of managing director. Today, she might accept the part she would have to play as partner of a crazy man. Or, God forbid, she might abandon him. He'd been right

114

— love was painful. He was held in her capable hands, and she had the ability to make or break him. Like . . . like when there'd been all that blood. He mustn't think about that wretched, heartbreaking time. He took a deep breath before leading her into the centre of his working universe.

Alex liked to keep things simple, Kate decided after they had walked to the front of the gathering. There were few pictures on the walls, and furniture was sturdy, modern and plain. She stood next to him when the silence instigated by their arrival was broken. A low buzz rippled through the room as Alex took her hand. 'This is Katherine Price, my wife,' he announced.

Applause followed his brief statement and he asked her to be seated. 'Stay with us,' he told her quietly. 'This won't be pretty, but it must be done. You need to know the business.'

Kate wondered why, but said nothing.

While Alex remained standing, she sat by him at the end of a large table, hands clasped on its surface. People she presumed to be managers and staff from the clubs were clustered round the table, while large men, who had to be security, lined the walls. Some occupants of the room smiled at her, although she noticed two or three females staring at her with daggers in their eyes. *Bring it on*, she said inwardly.

Glancing sideways, she watched her man as he drew himself up like a warrior preparing for battle. He seemed taller, broader and older, yet she knew in her heart of hearts that he was still suffering.

115

'A boy died,' he stated baldly, 'and we are all to blame. The body was hidden away in a cupboard, in Cheers. There were all manner of drugs there too. The police also discovered something labelled imaginatively as natural steroidal pills in Chillex.' He banged a closed fist on the table, causing everyone in the room to jump.

'All our businesses will remain closed to the public until I know who bought and distributed these poisons. Who is responsible for the boy's death? Who gave him that needle before escaping through the window? Who allowed people into Cheers without stamps on hands? You know the score — all of you. Goodness knows we've been through it often enough. Security, you must give me the names of any colleagues who broke this most important of rules.'

He moved his head and stared into the eyes of every security guard. 'The alternative will be the dismissal of all minders at all five locations. There are many jobless people out there who will step up to the mark. Any reprisals arising from those dismissals would be dealt with quickly and legally — that's a promise. Once reopened, the clubs will be guarded round the clock.' He glanced at Kate. 'My wife will help with ongoing refurbishment; she is a designer and therefore is perfectly suited to the role of artistic director.'

Kate looked at him. Here was another fine mess he was dragging her into, though she had to admit that Alex's clubs would benefit from her theatrical flair and experience. Yes, this would be better than mending a house.

Alex continued. 'You must all take a card from the table near the door. On each card is a phone number dedicated to the subject of this meeting. Put that number in your mobiles and destroy the card. I know that grassing up a workmate seems harsh, but this is about a dead teenager whose family is reeling in shock. He died on his sixteenth birthday. Phone me. Tell me who allowed this to happen, and your name will be kept out of the mix unless the police force my hand. Think about the boy. As I said, if I get no response, the security teams at all five nightclubs will be replaced.

'I repeat — any information passed to me will be treated as anonymous unless the boys in blue kick up an unmanageable fuss. Go home and think about this.' He dropped into his chair. 'If it's not one thing, it's your mother,' he said without thinking, as his members of staff began to file out of the room, many of them looking dazed.

Kate froze. Could she? Should she? She must. While people continued to pick up cards and leave, she said it softly. 'Is your mother part of all those swimming-through-blood scenes you dream about?'

He nodded just once. 'Not yet, Kate. I can't even think the words yet. For months, I blanked it. My mother was insane, and I thought I was following the same route, as if I'd inherited it from her. All this . . . ' he waved a hand across the room, 'all this is just salad dressing. I buried myself in literature, then in commerce. Outwardly, I'm successful, but . . . ' He ran out of steam.

117

Kate smiled at him. 'The success doesn't bother me — but what does upset me is my need to help you.'

'Why?'

'Because I don't know how or where to start.'

With the room empty, he found the courage to slide his arm across her shoulders. 'Begin with this,' he said. 'I have already started to learn something. A man can know so much about himself that he thinks it's enough, the whole package, the full deal. It's no such thing. Only when a woman — *the* woman — fills in the gaps does he realize who and what he is.'

'I don't always know who or what I am, Alex.'

'Even Tim, the expert, could not have managed in two years what you've achieved in weeks. Your courage, your defiance, your affection and humour have seeped into my brickwork and formed a bond ten times stronger than any mortar. This dead boy in Cheers has rattled the slates on my roof. The shock was a force ten gale, Kate. Stay with me. I need you.'

'And I need you,' she whispered. 'It works both ways.'

'Do you find it scary?' he asked.

'Of course. It's always a matter of chance, luck and management — I loved Jim until I learnt he was a criminal. Once he realized that I knew what he was, the beatings started. But this is different, as if I've always known you.'

Alex managed a cheeky grin. 'Remembering from the future. How very poetic.'

'Marriage is not poetic; it's like a small business,' she said. 'It needs to be kept in good order. Yes, there's love in the mix, but there has to be sense, too. Good sense and good times are the glue.' She stared at him to make sure he understood what she meant. 'Let's go home,' she suggested.

They went home.

★　★　★

When the remote controlled gates opened, Alex and Kate noticed Mrs Bee in the front doorway, arms folded tightly across her chest, face like thunder, a foot tapping on the step. 'Oh, God,' Alex breathed, 'she's on one.'

Kate studied the housekeeper as they neared the door. 'Home is where the heart is — that's the theory,' she commented. 'But we get a gargoyle in a temper. Great. I'll deal with her while you put the car away.'

'Are you sure?'

'I'm always sure; get used to it.'

As soon as the car stopped, Kate jumped out. 'Hello, Brenda. You look as if you swallowed a wasp. What's going on?'

Mrs Bee huffed. 'My husband is down below in his underpants in the swimming pool.'

Kate shrugged. 'We all need a hobby, and swimming's good exercise.'

A second huff fought its way through Brenda's tightly clenched teeth. 'He's not swimming.'

'I'm sorry. He isn't drowning, is he?'

'No. Well, I hope not, because he needs to trim his topiary and it's my sister's birthday down the Legion tonight. We've bought her a spa weekend down Chester way and a nice lace tablecloth.'

Kate fought to swallow an explosion of laughter. Scousers were brilliant. They answered all questions except for the important one, placing special emphasis on enquiries that remained unasked. 'What's going on, Brenda?'

'Dogs. Dogs is what's going on.'

'Oh, I see.' She didn't, but knew there was more to come.

'Probably my fault, Kate. I must have left the door open a bit.'

'Which door?'

'The door to the stairs going down to the gym and the pool. I've been doing a bit of cleaning down there, and I mustn't have shut it proper, like. Then we noticed. We'd gone from six dogs to no dogs, and we were up and down this house like shoplifters fleeing out of Asda. Six dogs is a lot of dogs to lose.'

'Yes, it would be.'

Brenda relaxed slightly. 'You tell him, love.'

'Brian?'

'No, he's not fit to be seen. Tell Alex.'

'Tell him what?'

'That there's six big dogs in his pool, his filters will be clogged with hair, and my Brian's trying to catch the buggers. Every time he gets one out, it jumps back in again. It's his death of cold he'll be catching, my Brian, never mind dogs.'

Brenda retreated while Kate made her way to the garages. By the time she reached her beloved, tears were coursing down her face.

'What happened?' he asked, concern in his tone.

After several moments, she gained enough composure to tell him, though further gales of laughter impeded proceedings. When in possession of the tale, Alex found himself reduced to a quivering mass of near-hysteria. 'Jeez,' he managed. 'I can't wait to see Brian in his knickers.'

'Stop it,' she begged. 'Think about your filters all clogged up with hair.'

'I'll do my best. I'd better go down there now.'

Abandoned, Kate sat in the Mercedes and chuckled. Life with Alex was full of surprises — and glee. 'He'll tell me soon,' she whispered to herself when the giggling ceased. 'He'll let me in, allow me to know who he is.'

Mrs Bee tapped on the window. She pointed to a workbench. 'Cup of tea and a bit of ginger cake, love. Thanks for telling him.'

Kate climbed out of the car. 'The dogs?' she asked.

'One word from Alex and they were all out of the water. He found Brian a robe, and they're both drying dogs in the utility. Alex says you've to come in soon and get one of the hairdryers out. Them hounds is saturdated.'

'Saturated?'

'Yes. Wet through.'

Kate feasted on Mrs Bee's very special ginger cake and a cup of hot tea. In this house with six dogs, a difficult housekeeper and a man who suffered flashbacks, she was happier than she'd ever been since her own childhood. Ah, here he came.

'Get inside, and make with the hairdryer. Tour

of the clubs tomorrow, see what you think.'

'Finish your cake,' Mrs Bee told Kate, and then looked Alex up and down. 'I've got my eye on you, Alex Price.'

'I know, Other Mother. Go away while I pinch half of that cake.'

Kate grinned. Yes, she was finally at home.

6

Kate's special phone is ringing, and she's outside playing with six dogs and one tennis ball. I can see twenty-six legs, six tails and one human head in the mix. Where's the ball? It's probably buried somewhere underneath that confused bundle of life. For the first time in my life, I'm with a beautiful, strong woman, and am unafraid.

Thinking about that, I remember just one more beautiful woman, but I will not swim through blood today. The phone's still ringing. Through her Zedge app, Kate has chosen the theme from The Good, the Bad and the Ugly — a very apt app, considering the reason for this phone's existence.

Knowing that Scotland Yard is trying to contact her, I answer. 'This is Kate's phone; Alex Price speaking.'

'My surname's Allen,' says the inspector, 'and I must speak to Kate and only to Kate.'

I tell him I understand and explain that I will need to go and rescue her, as she's a bit tied up just now. 'I'll get her straight away,' I promise.

A shrill whistle from me brings the dogs to heel — well, most come to heel. Castor and Pollux remain with their mistress, because they are her guards. She stands. No wig. Those dark, shining curls cling to her head, and she's dressed in torn jeans and one of my T-shirts, which looks like a two-man tent on her. Yet the woman takes my breath away . . .

'What?' she shouts, fists resting on hips buried beneath my filthy T-shirt.

'Your phone — the Scotland Yard one.'

I stay outside with my dogs; I know the call will be about her father-in-law's grave and that she was very fond of the old man. Old man? He was in his sixties when he died, and I'd bet my boots that Latimer the elder was thoroughly ashamed of Latimer the younger.

Here she comes, tears streaming down her face leaving in their wake two narrow routes of cleanliness. 'I was right,' she sobs.

Of course she was right. 'Have a shower,' I advise, 'and we'll go to Crosby beach with the dogs. We can talk while sitting on the erosion steps.'

She nods, but the tears continue to course down that wonderful, dirty face. 'How could he do that to his father, Alex?'

I tell her that Jim probably wasn't an out-and-out sociopath, because he'd loved his mother. 'How could he hurt his daughter?' I ask. 'He was a criminal. They're usually made rather than born, sweetheart. Yes, he could have curbed his temper, but no doubt it became harder to control as he grew older. He fell in with a bad crowd when young, I expect. Don't cry. Let's go and wear out the animals. By the way, you look like an over-grown four-year-old, black as a chimney that wants a sweep. I think we need the power hose.'

'I need only you,' she whispers, hiccuping against more sobs. Even when she cries, she's beautiful.

'Do the police have everything now?'

She nods. 'Even the pearls. The owner is donating them to Amelia. I'll get them restrung when she's old enough to appreciate such a valuable piece.'

'Good. Now, go and clean up the act. We'll have a look at the clubs later. Between us, the inspector, the dogs and I will keep you safe. Have the police picked up those two loose ends?'

'No, not yet.'

'Are they searching for them?'

She nods her head. 'But they're lying low; there's no sign of them. Anyway, Scotland Yard will tell the press that the missing safety deposit boxes have been found, so I should be safer now.'

I ask if Amelia might come home, but Kate's not ready for that. Only when the loose ends are in jail will she consider bringing home her daughter and her parents. 'In case the loose ends don't believe press statements. They may continue to suspect that I have some of the haul, though they'll know I'm not a thief. I wasn't involved in any of Jim's schemes. Let's wait a while.' She leaves me and goes to shower. My arms are empty and my heart is sore. I hate seeing her suffering. To distract myself, I make a promised phone call.

★   ★   ★

There was a skittish breeze whistling its way across the beach in Liverpool North, acting as if it attempted to compete with crying gulls.

125

Starlings, too, were in the mix; they had learnt that better spring weather brought picnics, a hot dog van and the ice cream man.

Kate and Alex kept the dogs beside them on the steps; there were two children on the sands near the lifeguard station. Laurel and Hardy, who appreciated a little wildness in the weather, were anxious to be up and away, but Alex held them back until he heard the voice. It was Libby, the little princess in charge of paper flags and banana yogurt, and an older boy who seemed to be looking after her. Two mothers stood at the water's edge and watched a tanker drifting its lazy way into the Port of Liverpool.

'It's the man,' Libby screamed, 'and he brought his dogs. He promised he would.' She pulled the boy with her. 'This is my cousin Matthew,' she announced. 'I told him about you and how you build the best sandcastles. Auntie Sue is with Mummy near the water. You phoned Mummy.'

The children sat with Kate and Alex while the dogs were released. 'I hope they don't knock over those two mothers,' Alex whispered to Kate. 'They might sue for damages.'

'Thank you for bringing me here,' she replied. 'This place seems to clear my head. So this is the young lady you told me about? Pleased to meet you, Libby — and you, Matthew.' She turned to her adult companion. 'Right, Alex. Go and make sandcastles and I'll be the judge of your efforts.'

He laughed. 'Aren't you always?'

'It's my job,' was her answer to that.

On this occasion, however, Alex's skills were

not required. 'I'm doing Libby's castle,' Matthew insisted. 'I am her cousin.'

Alex, redundant, returned to Kate on the erosion barrier, watching while Matthew entertained his younger cousin. The boy was thorough. Using a small ruler and string, he made a drawbridge over the moat, created slits through which arrows might be fired in the event of intrusion, and finished with an item that was almost as tall as he was. All the time, he talked Libby through what he was doing.

'A born teacher,' Kate said to her companion.

He agreed. 'He's a nurturer. Here come the mothers.'

Southport Mother spoke to Alex. 'Thank you for phoning to say you would bring your dogs. Libby loves animals. We have a cat, but no dog just yet.'

Matthew's mother was from the Wirral. She, too, was a dog person, though she seemed taken aback by the pack of six. 'We have two, and I sometimes think that's one too many.' She was a pleasant woman, open-faced and natural.

He introduced them to Kate before leaving the three women and making his way back to the children. Matthew had just turned eleven, and he jerked a thumb in Libby's direction. 'She's only three, but she's quite clever for a girl. Except she still says she wants to be a princess when she grows up.'

Matthew's favourite subjects were dinosaurs, Romans and Vikings, but not necessarily in that order. He liked boats, Tenerife, caravans, Kentucky Fried Chicken, history and maths.

'She likes clothes with glitter on,' he complained. 'When I get home, I'm sometimes covered in it. My mum says Libby moults glitter and our dogs moult hair — she doesn't know which is worst.'

Kate watched the man she seemed to love more with each passing day. He was a natural, and Amelia would probably take to him. He picked up Libby and ran along with Matthew in pursuit of six fast dogs. Libby squealed, as did Matthew when soggy animals made contact with him. Alex was probably going to want more children, and that thought sat well with Kate. Amelia was lonely, and the solution to that was currently running himself daft round Gormley's statues with two children and six hounds.

When mothers and children had left, the couple watched the dogs until they slowed down and returned to the steps. 'Not too wet this time,' Kate remarked. She studied her man's face. 'Do you want children?' she asked after a few moments.

'Not yet,' was his reply. 'We'll have to settle Amelia first. We need to give her time to adjust.'

'Ah, the man has wisdom, so not just a pretty face. That was the right answer, Mr Price.'

He grinned. 'And I want you to be mother to my kids, too.'

'How many?'

He placed a possessive hand on her denim-clad knee. 'We'll see how we go, yes? If you have a hard time, it'll be just one. But if you give birth as easily as Birds Eye pop peas from the pod, we might have several.'

'Several? What about my figure?'

The grin broadened. 'Worry not; I'll keep an eye on that.' She wasn't wearing her wig, and that pleased him, though he failed to understand why. 'You look beautiful with real hair.'

Kate covered his hand with hers. 'And I grew it all by myself.'

★   ★   ★

Max loved Paris. In truth, he had enjoyed every bit of France he'd seen so far. The language barrier scarcely bothered him, since many people understood and even spoke some English, and sign language filled in the gaps. Villages were quiet and beautiful, while Paris was amazing. Trev hated it. He had no time for cathedrals, museums or walking. He was East End of London right through to the bone, and he wanted to go home, to escape all the 'bleeding foreigners.'

'Me legs ache.' Trev stopped for a third time and rubbed the backs of his knees. 'Can't we just go? It's only two hundred miles from Paris, and — '

'Yes, I know. Once you'd learnt to hold the map the right way up, things got a whole lot better. Are you coming or what? It's late.'

'I have to go with you; this is a foreign country, and I'd get lost on me own. Anyway, we've seen everything except for that red windmill place full of naked girls. Now, if we were going there, I'd — '

'You ain't half getting on my tits, Trev — '

'Well, it's been bloody boring, walk, walk, look

129

at this, look at that.'

They perched on some steps leading up to a closed bank. 'You showed me up in that museum,' Max grumbled. 'Top of your voice, asking who broke the arms off the Venus, and you bet he'd lost his job. Them Americans was crying with laughter. As for what you call the Moaning Lisa . . . Gawd.'

'Well, she was ugly. No eyebrows and skin like wet tripe. Where's the smile everybody talks about, eh? If I woke up with a face like that on the next pillow, I'd be out of there quicker than a ferret down a rabbit hole. She was worse-looking than Fat Arthur, and he's got a physog like a smacked arse.'

Max, who considered himself educated after gaining three GCSEs, shook his head. Some people had no sense of art or history, no soul, no hunger for information. He pointed down the wide avenue. 'This is the Champs Elysées.'

'I know. Four quid for a thimble-size cup of coffee. Daylight robbery.'

'Never mind that. Down the bottom there's the Arch of Triumph built for that short-arse pillock called Napoleon. He was celebrating his victories over the wotsnames — aristocrats or summink. Well, he crowed too soon, because Russia done for his army good and proper and he got exiled. Underneath that arch is the tomb of the unknown soldier. Unless you want to join him underground, stop bloody going on about you don't like this, you're not eating horse, and why did we have to go in the room where Marie Antoinette spent her last night before they cut her head off. It's history, so it's important.'

Trev answered back again. 'I never bothered with history. They were all dead, so I didn't see the point.'

The bigger man owned a retort, of course. 'A nation with no history is like a man with no memory.'

'History is rubbish and me legs is sore.'

'I feel sorry for you, because you've no brain and no imagination. And forget the Moulin Rouge — no chance.'

'Why's that?'

'Because I said so. We've a child to kidnap, in case you've forgotten.'

Trev decided to stop complaining, because it wasn't getting him anywhere. Max was a big reader, while Trev had a bit of trouble with the written word, though he enjoyed his children's *Beano* comics. He was good at flogging drugs, but he'd no bits of paper saying he'd passed exams. Max had English, Art and Maths, and he made damned sure everybody knew it. 'And it was small,' he muttered to himself.

'What?'

'That painting of that ugly woman.'

'You're right there, Trev. Worth millions and no bigger than our kitchen calendar. Right. Latin quarter and the Sacré Coeur, and we're done.'

'What's Latin, then?'

'Where all the artists and writers live.'

'Well, let's hope they can do better pictures than him what done the Moaning Lisa.'

Max unfolded his large frame and stood up. There was no future in talking sense to the senseless. 'Stay here, then. I'll pick you up on the way back to that grotty hotel.'

'What?'

'You heard — wait here while I go and do the Latin quarter.'

Although Trev didn't share Max's affection for wandering about, he didn't relish the idea of being abandoned on alien soil. 'I'll come,' he muttered. 'But can't you walk a bit slower?'

★   ★   ★

Mrs Bee was having a Holy Day. Once a month, she shut herself in a small room on the ground floor. It reminded her of a coffin, as it had no windows, though air was allowed to circulate via a system installed by Alex's builders, and coffins probably didn't have that particular facility. Oh yes, this was Alex Price's sacred place. And he was in the process of bidding for a lock of a man's hair to go in it, which fact made Brenda's skin crawl, because it seemed almost cannibalistic. A dead man's hair?

She didn't give much more than a hoot about John Lennon. He'd been one of the Beatles — so what? Years back, she'd had cockroaches, which were a bit like beetles, but she never bragged about it. Grumbling quietly, she began the ritual according to St Alex, who was as daft as three brushes plus a couple of wet mops where this particular Beatle was concerned. 'Stick an a where there should be an e, do a bit of yeah, yeah, yeah-ing, then bugger off to America abandoning a wife and a son here. So soft Alex goes and buys all this rubbish, leaving me — leaving Liverpool — to clear your mess.'

There were songs he'd been writing, drawings he'd done at school, Mathew Street paintings of him, vinyl records, CDs, films, letters, carvings, a banjo he'd used, a jacket, a shirt, a cap. She spoke to a drawing of Lennon's face made from the titles of his songs — even the glasses were outlined in words. 'Sorry you got killed, though. You didn't deserve that, lad. Forty years old. No sense to what happened.'

She dusted a framed drawing, a caricature of Ringo. Poor Ringo was 90 per cent nose; John Lennon knew how to exaggerate a person's least prepossessing assets. A framed YOU ARE HERE sign was displayed over the door, so she poked a long-handled feather duster on that. She would clean the glass next month. Lennon and Yoko used YOU ARE HERE wherever they went. 'You were a character — I'll give you that much. Losing your mam, then your mate with a brain tumour, wasn't easy, was it? God keep you. I'll try to imagine all the people living life in peace. Ta-ra till next month.' Heaving a sigh of relief, she left the claustrophobic space.

Over coffee at the kitchen table, she considered, not for the first time, Alex's fixation with John Lennon. Both had endured loss and disturbance in childhood; both had suffered bereavement and the vagaries of adults who had moved them from one place to another. Alex had lost his parents, his brother and to all intents and purposes his poor sister. John had lost his mother and his nomadic father, and had failed to find his sister, who had been adopted in Liverpool and had lived most of her life just seven miles from the city centre. 'Twin souls,' she whispered to herself. 'Alex and John, John and Alex. What a bloody shame.'

She was dipping a fourth rich tea finger in her coffee when all hell broke loose. The front doorbell sounded repeatedly, while the knocker crashed in time with the bell. Where was Brian? Oh yes, he'd gone to buy paint and wallpaper for the Boswells' living room in the annexe. Should she open the door?

In the hall, she stopped, as did bell and door knocker.

'Alex?' a man's voice yelled. 'Alex, let us in, for God's sake.'

She opened the door. 'Yes?' Outside, the tallest man she'd ever seen stood with a girl in her early teens, an interesting specimen with multi-coloured hair and a small suitcase. 'Who are you?' Brenda asked. 'Alex has gone up the coast with Kate and the dogs.'

'I'm Pete. This is Kylie, my daughter. We went to the office, but he wasn't there. The clubs are shut, and the staff can manage the rest of his properties while he has a bit of a honeymoon, I suppose.' He glanced at his companion. 'My daughter's an asylum seeker.'

'Where from?'

'Bootle.'

Brenda folded her arms across a flat chest. 'Does the government have an agreement with Bootle?'

'When will Alex be back? I'm Pete Hargreaves

— some call me Powder Puff Pete. I work at Champs sometimes.'

Brenda blinked rapidly. 'But you have a daughter?'

He sighed. 'I'm just a bloke who can sing falsetto and wear frocks. I'm a professional. Married, four kids and a fierce wife who's hunting for this one. Kylie's just fourteen, pregnant, and her mam wants to kill her.'

Brenda widened the door. 'Come in. You can wait with me in the kitchen.' She led the way, asking Rainbow Head if she was hungry.

Pete answered for his eldest. 'She's still throwing everything up till the afternoons. Give her a bit of water in case she's dehydrating.'

Brenda brought the water. So far, Kylie hadn't uttered a single syllable. 'Who's the daddy, love?' Brenda asked.

'She won't say.'

'She will if you'll stop answering for her.'

Pete glared at the older female. 'With a mam like Monica, my kids have to be very careful what they say. She's bloody dynamite with a very short fuse, is Monica. Ask Alex — he's seen her when she's been on one. It's like Chernobyl — God love them poor souls — but in a Bootle semi. I swear she's radioactive. She's decided our Kylie has to have an abortion, so my daughter's in need of somewhere to stay and some counselling while she makes up her own mind.'

Brenda was wondering whether Kylie came fully furnished in the brain department when the teenager finally opened her mouth to speak. 'We only done it once. I told him I was sixteen, see. I

135

thought you couldn't have a baby if you only done it once.'

'You lied about your age, then.' The housekeeper wasn't criticizing, and her tone was calm. 'You're not the first, and you won't be the last.' She turned to Pete. 'Me and my Brian have a spare bedroom in the annexe. We'll look after her, love, I promise.'

Pete blinked. 'You'd do that?'

'Course we would. Alex is much the same, as you probably know already. I'll ask him to sort out doctor visits and counselling.'

At last, a little colour arrived in the pregnant girl's cheeks. It clashed with her hair, but it showed that she was bucking up a bit. 'Thank you,' she said.

'No need to be frightened here, lovely. Nobody's going to make you do anything you don't want to do.'

Pete glanced at his watch. 'I'll have to go and tell Monica I've put our Kylie out of reach.' Just as he finished speaking, a car arrived.

'Stop there,' Brenda ordered. 'I'll make sure it's him and not your missus on the warpath.' She sniffed. 'Mind, I'm probably fit for her.'

At last, Kylie smiled. 'You're about the same size as me mam.'

Brenda tapped the side of her nose. 'Poison comes in small bottles, sweetheart.' She left the room.

Alone with his daughter, Pete held her close. He loved his kids no matter what, and he kissed the top of her very undecided hair. 'Don't let anybody drag you down whatever reason they think they have, queen. You fell pregnant while loads of others were lucky or clever, and they got away with it. Now, make sure you decide what you want, yeah?'

'Yes, Dad.'

'I'll help you. Alex will help you, I know he will.' He pulled away from her. 'Why are you blushing?'

'He's important.' It wasn't Alex's position in society that bothered her; it was his comments in the hospital and how embarrassed she'd felt.

Alex and Kate arrived, with Brenda bringing up the rear.

'Hello, Kylie.' Kate shook the girl's hand. 'You can stay here with us or with Mr and Mrs Bee. Your mother's just upset; I'm sure she'll calm down in time.'

'She will if I get rid of it,' was Kylie's stark reply. She sniffed and continued, 'See, this is a human being inside me, so it would feel like murder.'

'Catholic?' Kate asked Pete.

'Yes,' was his reply. 'But not so as you'd notice where my wife's concerned. She's all about what the neighbours will say and can she get her nets whiter than theirs. When it comes to gardening, she doesn't mow the grass, she bloody manicures it. Tulips have soft stems and heavy heads, so she ties them to knitting needles or bits of cane. Drives me daft, she does.'

Alex placed an arm round Kylie's shoulders. 'You'll be fine, love. As long as you like dogs. We have six of them.'

The girl grinned from ear to ear. 'Yes, please,'

137

she managed. 'And can I have something to eat? I'm starving now.'

⋆ ⋆ ⋆

Kylie's dad has gone, thank goodness. I don't like the thought of an annoying female mosquito arriving to buzz around my man. Those bugs carry all kinds of illnesses in their bites; anyway, I've never liked short people — except Mrs Bee. Most of them compensate for lack of stature by making sure they're heard — I remember my Latin teacher. She was tiny, all mouth and anger, so I swapped her for Greek. Greek was male, tall, dark and handsome.

I take Kylie upstairs. She tells me she's grown about six inches since her tenth birthday and that she's glad she's not going to be a short-arse like her mam. After bemoaning the lack of breasts, she lets me start her makeover. My blouses look deliberately loose but OK on her, though I'll need to work on skirts, jeans and shorts. Her hair is no problem to me because I have the shoulder-length blonde wig. Alex loves my real hair, so I've stopped covering it since the rest of the loot was recovered from my pa-in-law's grave.

After covering the poor girl's ruined head with a cap, I put the wig on her, and she bursts into tears. 'I look like a model,' she sobs.

She's right. Kylie has her father's good looks, just softer, more feminine.

'You're a beautiful young woman,' I tell her, 'and the person who made you pregnant could

go to jail, because technically you're still a child.'

Her truth pours like magma from a volcano, heated by fear of her mother, the dread of abortion, and concern for the foreign sailor responsible for her condition. 'We done it stood up,' she wails. 'He said stood up meant there'd be no baby.'

'Where is he now?'

She shrugs. 'His ship sailed weeks ago.'

I pull her close and hug her while she weeps. Her ship has sailed in many ways; she has a harsh mother, a dad who dresses up and earns his money by pretending to be a woman, and a criminal whose name sounds like Leaf as father to her unborn child. She tells me of the cruelty of classmates who insist that Pete is gay and her mother is a witch. 'Mam's not a witch; she's just house-proud. She always has a duster in one hand and a paintbrush in the other. And my dad isn't gay at all — he's a professional entertainer. In a good week, he comes home with a grand or more.' She sniffs. 'My mam says I have to kill the baby.'

There's more to it than that, but I can't tell her just now about HIV, chlamydia and all the other diseases that might befall a girl whose virginity has been stolen by a globe-trotter. I'm so angry, so bloody furious, that I feel like punching somebody. I tell her I think her father's wonderful, but I haven't met her mother, so I'm in no position to judge.

'Mam's clever,' she tells me while drying her eyes. 'Dad says if she'd been educated, she'd be dangerous, but we've had one Maggie Thatcher and we don't need another.'

Well, I have to agree with that. 'Now, don't lock yourself in the house. We all need fresh air, and no one will recognize you once I've organized your clothing. Alex won't let anything happen to you.'

She nods. 'My dad thinks the world of him. I'm glad he chose you, though. There's women at the clubs who fall over one another to get near him. He's kind as well as handsome.'

'Yes, he is.' Wondering who those women are, I lead Kylie downstairs to show her off, but Alex is in that huge greenhouse with his honey bees.

'He's not got them daft clothes on what they wear,' Kylie remarks.

'He doesn't need cover, because they don't sting him,' I tell her.

'Would they sting me and you?'

'Probably. As you've noticed, Alex is special. Ah, look, Kylie, the dogs are in the run.'

She laughs. 'God, they're big.'

I tell her we like big dogs, because once settled they're gentler than smaller breeds.

We watch while he carefully picks bees off his clothing and exits the massive glass building, an edifice that is his contribution towards saving the human race. I smile as I remember one tile in his kitchen that states WITHOUT HONEY-BEES, MANKIND IS BUGGERED.

'Whoa,' he shouts as he comes in, 'who is this beautiful young lady?'

Kylie giggles. 'It's me — Kylie.'

'Well,' he says, rubbing his hands together,

140

'this calls for a visit to Tweeners. Get in the car, you two.'

Kylie remains planted near the window.

'Come on,' Alex urges.

She shakes her head. 'It's in Bootle.'

He tells her he knows where it is, because he owns the shop's lease.

'Me mam's looking for me,' she whines.

'Kylie, your mother's looking for a girl who's been dipping her head in gloss paint — '

'It's not gloss — it's proper hair colour,' she answers quickly.

'And you're a beautiful blonde now, so get in the car.'

She follows me out while Alex goes up to change in case he's covered in bee shit. 'Is he always like this?' she asks.

I sit with her in the rear seat. 'I'm afraid so,' I tell her with mock seriousness. 'When it comes to men, I usually get rid of mine when they start thinking for themselves, but I'm afraid this one's a keeper.'

For a reason neither of us understands, we explode with laughter.

Alex returns to find a pair of hysterical females in the back of his car. 'What's so hilarious?' he asks, but we are laughing too much to speak.

Wisely, my darling does not pursue the matter. He sticks the car in Drive and pulls away towards the main gates. Adjusting the rear-view mirror, he sends me a wink. He's pleased with me because I've helped Kylie, and I'm ridiculously pleased because he's pleased. In some ways, I haven't matured since being in Greek class with that *gorgeous specimen whose name I can't recall. Not that it matters, because we called him Zorba anyway . . .*

★ ★ ★

As the Mercedes turned out of the unadopted lane on which Alex Price had been allowed to build his house, a short woman hid behind a hedge. His wife was beautiful. 'But so am I — and why is the wife in the back of the car?' Ah, there was somebody with her, a young girl with blonde hair . . .

'Where did I go wrong?' Chillex ran like a well-oiled machine because of her, Amber Simpson . . . and the wife's hair was now dark, so what the hell was going on? Had Katherine Price been wearing wigs after chemo? Was she playing the sympathy card in order to entrap him? And who the hell had planted so-called steroids in the club? Might it have been Martina Nelson, manager of Checkmate? She came to keep fit and chill out in the sofa area, hanging round for hours in case Alex put in an appearance.

Amber looked down at patches of damp on her clothing. The club was shut, but she wasn't going to allow the situation to outdo her, because maintaining her level of fitness was vital. The fat girl from schooldays was now a perfect specimen: toned muscle, long blonde hair with highlights lifting the colour, good skin and amazing legs. She had run all the way from town just to catch a glimpse of him, though she told

142

herself that she was simply exercising.

The car disappeared. She knew she should admit defeat gracefully because he was married, but what was marriage these days? It was a piece of paper signed by two people, and it could be torn in half by a divorce court. 'He still wouldn't look at me.' Somewhere inside herself, she was still the fat girl who went home from school alone every afternoon. Once she reached the safety of her bedroom, she found her friends — crisps, Mars bars and fizzy pop.

Amber Simpson could never return to those secret feasts. While focused on Alex, she'd had a reason to keep herself on track . . . On track? She remembered coming off the rails when she'd reached sixteen, hiding food, pushing it round her plate, going dizzy on the stairs; living on water, the odd bit of salad and daily laxatives.

She turned to jog back to town. Mum had found her passed out on the floor of her bedroom. They'd sent her to a place hundreds of miles from home — just outside Brighton. In that food prison, she'd been taught how to eat, how to mix with her peers, how to stay slim without anorexia. And she'd never looked back. After becoming a personal trainer, she'd found the confidence to apply for a job at Chillex and had won her place.

When the manager resigned to take a position on ocean-going liners, Amber had accepted his post. Alex had smiled at her during the interview. He'd asked her what was the most important part of the job, and she'd given the right answer. 'People,' she'd replied. 'They need to be at ease with the staff and with themselves. Many who come in have body issues, some real, some imagined. They must be helped to feel safe.' Oh yes, she had known what Chillex was all about, hadn't she?

And now he was married to a southerner who spoke with a gobful of plums, all correct and beautifully dressed. No interview for her, of course. Oh no, she'd been elected Director of Design or something like that. It was nepotism, nothing more, nothing less. Chillex was perfect; Chillex didn't need a bloody Londoner to improve it.

She jogged down Wood Street and cut through to Back Bold Street. Chillex remained closed, though the police had finished searching it. The 'steroids', once analysed, had turned out to be concentrated vitamin capsules, not a trace of steroid in the mix. Amber grinned; it had been a win for her when she'd heard the news. However, she remained suspended on full pay, because Lord and Master Alex Price had decreed that no club would open until he knew the truth about the dead boy in Cheers.

'So much for Bobby Ray and his wealth of experience,' she mumbled.

It was time to go home. Home was a bedsit above a newsagent in Litherland. Amber was saving up to buy a car, so she paid low rent. She hated sharing bathroom and kitchen, so she usually ate and showered at the club, but those facilities were off limit just now.

Her mobile rang as she entered her much-hated home. It was Bobby Ray Carson. 'Amber?'

'That's me.'

'We open again on Friday.'

She absorbed the news. 'What about Alex's wife? Isn't she going to improve us all?' She waited. 'Bobby? You still there?'

'Let it go, Amber,' he said quietly. 'And tell Martina Nelson to do the same.'

She kept her breathing as even as possible. 'What are you talking about?'

'The way you and Marty look at Alex. I don't think he's noticed, but — '

'I can't speak for Martina, but I'm getting engaged soon. Yes, I like Alex, because he's the first fair boss I've ever had, but that's all. I admire him.'

'Good. Keep it like that. I've had to interview a couple of new security blokes for Cheers. The old ones' mates grassed. They bought stuff from a couple of London blokes, but all they know is that one was named Max, because when the other one called him that they had a bit of a scuffle.'

'Bloody hell, Bob. You know we had no steroids at Chillex — they were just vitamins?'

'Yes, Alex said.'

'So no alterations for the time being?'

'I doubt it. Mrs Price did sets for London theatres, so I guess her ideas will be radical and dramatic — not the sort of thing that can be done overnight. Mine's the Cheers set, just like on the TV, so I don't expect too many alterations, and yours should be pretty safe. Chillex is what the name says it is, a place to exercise and chill out. I suppose we must wait until she has spoken. Now, there's a meeting Thursday afternoon for managers and security. Three o'clock. Be there.'

'See you then, Bobby.' She switched off the phone.

The Chinese takeaway two doors down had started cooking, so she closed her window. What with that stench, late night revellers, stray cockroaches looking for a number 47 with fried rice, and the odd rat in the back yard, this dump was more than she could bear.

She would have to go for a used car and a decent flat, or she might well be back on the Mars bars . . .

★ ★ ★

The hospital was on Eaton Road, West Derby, Liverpool. He'd been in the city since last night, but the love of his life no longer lived in that huge house on Merrilocks Road, Blundellsands. Why had he come north? The reasonable answer was that he might do better here than at Great Ormond Street, where the queue for a consultancy would probably fill the empty seats in the House of Lords, thereby making the place look occupied by more than just comatose peers of the realm.

But was that his real reason? He was becoming a stalker. He'd never pursued a woman before, but Kate was . . . different. She was so alive. When Amelia had started to improve, her mother had become more beautiful, talkative, funny. Was she really with that other man?

146

Whatever, he was here now and here he must remain. The interview had been gruelling, but he'd beaten all other applicants, and Alder Hey Children's Hospital would look good on his CV, especially if he made consultant in the not too distant future. He had a flat nearby, a map of Liverpool and, on his laptop, details about Alex Price and his clubs.

He would find Kate. He had to, because life without her was dull and grey.

7

Tim Dyson hadn't seen either Alex or Kate for some time. A romantic soul when all was said and done, he was cautiously thrilled to have been the accidental reason why his long-term friend had finally had the rug pulled from beneath very stubborn feet. He knew that Alex Price was head over heels for the first time in his life, that he was engaged to Kate Owen, and that they were living together as man and wife, so that Alex could keep her safe. But when it came to details, Tim was stymied, because he couldn't be in two places at once.

The long expected problem at the other side of the Atlantic had finally arrived, and Tim needed to go to his beloved Julia in Vermont. Her mother was comatose, on a painkiller forty times stronger than mere morphine, and, as the only child, Julia was sitting with her last remaining relative. She had no sister, no brother, no aunts or uncles, no cousins. Friends and neighbours dropped by from time to time, but Mrs Kavanagh was taking an unconscionable time a-dying. God bless the poor woman, because she had battled her hardest until the crab inside her had won the war.

Tim's bags were packed, ticket and passport stowed in a bum bag, and his flight would leave at dawn in two days. When it came to Alex, the child he had saved all those years ago, he

148

couldn't just leave without speaking to him. Alex had not phoned; nor had Kate. So the mountain had to visit Muhammad.

He phoned. 'Alex?'

'That's me. Sorry, Tim, but we've been a bit busy.'

'Yes. I read about the drugs and the closing of your clubs. So sorry.'

'Not your fault. My so-called security team bought the stuff from a couple of Londoners. A boy died in Cheers, so I shut down until I found out why. I'll never know who injected him with the heroin, but I sacked the men who bought and sold the stuff. It was the lad's first time. He was sixteen, Tim.'

'That's shitty. Look, I'm off to the States soon and I'd like to come and see you before I leave. Julia's mother's definitely on the way out, so I'm needed.'

Alex pondered for a moment. 'Oh, I'm so sorry. Give Julia my regards. Yes, she needs you. As for your proposed visit, we have a big meeting on Thursday and open again on Friday, and — '

'And I hope to be in Vermont before then. May I come tonight?'

'Of course. We'll feed you. I'll inform Mrs Bee, and she'll furnish us with something edible.'

It was Tim's turn to stall.

'You still there?' Alex asked.

'Yup. I wanted to ask you something.'

'OK.'

After another short pause, Tim continued. 'Are you ready, Alex?'

'For what? Am I ready for what?'

'To get past the river of blood. If you're preparing for marriage . . . Look, I don't know how long I'll be gone. There could be an autopsy — though I seriously doubt that — when the poor old girl finally shuffles off, then the funeral, packing Julia's personal stuff, finding a realtor to sell the house. Complicated stuff.'

'I know, Tim. But I'm not ready.'

'Nightmares?'

'No. Kate's guarding and protecting me. But flashbacks still happen when I'm awake and tired. I've been worse, and Julia comes first.'

Tim doodled on a pad next to his blotter. 'You're sharing a bed every night, then?'

'Yes.'

'Sex?'

'One male, one female.'

Tim laughed, though the sound he made wasn't happy. 'I don't mean gender, you idiot.'

Alex blew a raspberry into the phone. 'Sorry, Tim. She makes me so glad to be alive. Even little outings with the dogs become adventurous. We want children. We're having fun; we're getting there. She's everything I knew I didn't want, but I love her. Kate is amazing.'

'She needs the details, though. If you get seriously depressed, how will she understand? You'll probably know whether or when you need chemical help, but she should be put in the picture. I'll be there tonight. With a bit of luck, you may not even remember what you've said.'

'How come? What do you mean?'

Tim cleared his throat. 'I want to bring a hypnotist with me. I'll be sitting beside you while

150

you go under, and we'll record what you say if you don't want Kate to be in the room. I'll probably be abroad for several weeks, and I want you to have the ability to inform her fully now you're engaged. I've been with you since that terrible day, and I'm not buggering off now to leave you floundering. This way, you'll have all you need in a recording. I advise you to listen to it with her; you can help each other get through it.'

Alex felt panic closing in like fingers round his throat. 'I'm not sure I want to be hypnotised. And no, I wouldn't want Kate in the room during the process.'

Tim tutted. 'Alex, you're going to marry the girl. You know her history, so don't you think she should be allowed the details of yours? She won't abandon you, I promise. She's just as daft about you as you are about her. Truth's important. I won't be here to help you for a while. Is it OK if I bring the man with me? If you don't want her to sit through the session, we'll do the recording. If you decide against it absolutely, I'll send him away. But you'll still have to pay him, because I've made the booking.'

Alex growled. 'It's always the money, isn't it?'

'He's the best,' Tim snapped. 'Nothing but the best for you. What happened to you all those years ago left Freddy Krueger at the bus stop in the rain. Come on, Alex, I've a lot on my mind.'

'I know. Please, please tell Julia I'm sorry. Yes, you must get to Vermont and stop thinking about me. I'm in a bit of a panic, but I'll man up by tonight and I'll send Kate and Kylie upstairs.'

151

'Who the hell's Kylie?' Tim asked.

'She's an asylum seeker from Bootle. She's into multi-coloured hair, she's fourteen, pregnant and on the run from a very fierce mother.'

In spite of everything, Tim laughed. 'How do you manage to pick up so many problems on your way through life?'

'It's a gift. Remember the broken shoe? That got me a wife, and Kylie can be bridesmaid if we don't wait too long. I don't want her going into labour halfway up the aisle.' He waited for a few seconds, wishing not to seem flippant. 'Tim, I wish you and Julia all the best. Phone me when . . . phone me.'

'I will. And now you've agreed to be hypnotised, forget about me and my companion being fed tonight. We can buy chips on our way home.'

'OK.'

Alex turned off his phone. Hypnotism. What next? A witch doctor from some jungle, herbal remedies, hanging upside down in one of those inversion frames, yoga? Or might he be awarded a padded cell and a straitjacket?

The girls wanted to begin their fashion show. Tweeners, a shop that catered for the young on the cusp between childhood and maturity, had been a great success for Kylie. She had more clothes than she'd ever owned, and she positively twinkled with happiness. Poor kid. Not all mothers were fit for the job, as he knew only too well. The same applied to fathers, too.

Kate and Kylie entered the sitting room with Kylie glowing in the blonde wig, jeans and a new

T-shirt. She paraded up and down like Kate Moss wearing something designed by Versace.

He had to stop them. 'Kylie, you look fantastic, but I need to talk to Kate. Can we finish the fashion show tomorrow? Something important has come up, and I must deal with it right away.'

She scuttled off, leaving Alex with a dart in his chest. 'Oh, God, that girl is fragile — I'm so sorry.'

Kate smiled at him. 'She has a strong character underneath the damage. So what's happening?'

He had to tell her the truth.

'Out with it, Alex.'

He asked her to speak to Brenda and Brian. 'Eat in the annexe with them. They can use our food if they haven't enough.'

Our food? She smiled again, because everything was now ours rather than his. From the first evening, after the shoe disaster, he had been hers.

'Kate?'

'What?

'Are you listening to me?'

'What did you say?'

He shook his head. 'Nothing.'

'That's OK, then. I'm good at listening to nothing.'

Always, always, the last word. 'I love you,' he whispered.

'Good. That makes me feel less guilty about having relieved you of your emotional virginity.'

'Kate!'

'What?'

'Shut the eff up, will you? Close the mouth

and pin back the lugholes. Immediately, if not sooner.'

She made a zipping motion across her lips before curling a hand round each ear.

'Tim's coming soon, and he's bringing someone with him. A hypnotist. The man is going to put me under — ha-bloody-ha, let's see if he manages — and it's for you.'

She blinked several times.

'A river of blood.' His tone was calm, yet his fists were closed tightly. 'You need to know all of it. Whatever I say will be taken down and used in evidence against me. The interview will be recorded, and my home is going to be like a bloody police station.'

She crossed the small space between them and placed her hands on his cheeks. 'Will that really be easier than telling me?'

Alex had no idea, and he said so.

'Promise me one thing,' she begged.

'I'll try.'

'We listen to that recording together. I don't want you to be alone when you play it — and no cheating. I've already lived with a cheat.'

'I promise. If the man succeeds in mesmerizing me, that is.'

'Just don't fight it. Relax for once in your life.'

'Tim did suggest an alternative, though I refused it.'

'Oh?'

He nodded just once. 'You could be there while I'm under the influence, but I'd rather do the recording alone and listen to it with you some other time.' He paused and stared thoughtfully into her eyes. 'I can begin now, just to let you know the start of it. Katherine, my mother killed my father. I saw the murder; Tim witnessed the aftermath and dragged me out of the house. It's the pictures in my head that stop me going any further, because I lost my way afterwards.'

She clung to him like an oversized kitten, claws digging through his shirt sleeves, then she broke away, her face revealing her shock and sympathy. 'I'll take Kylie next door. I shall bring us both back when it's all over.'

She left him in a hurry, and he knew she was fighting back tears. So he had to go through with hypnosis. Panic paid another brief visit when he closed his eyes and saw red. It was a beautiful colour, popular on Valentine's Day, the colour of love, hearts and roses, red ribbons on a box, red dripping from a tablecloth. No. He had no intention of going chemical again: take two at bedtime, breathe your way through the flash-back, it's only adrenalin, proof that you're alive . . .

Brenda bustled in. 'What's going on? Kate looks upset, Kylie wants her hair bleached all one colour, and one of your dogs has took off with my Brian's work boot, right foot.'

'Feed them.'

'The dogs?'

'No, Kylie and Kate. I'm having a meeting here tonight, so I'll warm some soup and make myself a sandwich.'

'But I've made you some — '

'Brenda?'

155

'What?'
'Go away.'
She went away.

* * *

*This is seriously weird. I can see him, but I can
also see through him, as if I'm some sort of time
traveller with special vision. It's all coming out of
me, the words, the descriptions, a younger Tim
trying to drag me while my feet are riveted to the
floor. The curtains are green with white flowers;
my mother was a very floral person. The cat,
Toodles, is a ginger tom with attitude and a blue
collar — I hear it jingling when he moves. That's
to warn the birds, of course.*

*There's a lot of red, but I just see it and say it,
no fear, no emotion of any kind. No panic. I
think I'm talking about Stephen and Susan and
Mum's hat and coat, and none of it makes full
sense, like an incomplete sentence, or a clause
without a proper conclusion. In the room in my
house, I see only the hypnotist and those strange
green eyes with streaks of yellow like the points
on a star near the pupils. A thought butts in;
only 2 per cent of the world's population has
green eyes.*

*The hypnotist knows I'm wandering off and
he gets me back, using a strange humming
sound. I think he asks a question, and I answer
it. I talk about the front garden, standing there
with Tim, bending down, hands on knees as if
I've run all the way down to Bolton town hall
and back again. Mum walks past me. She's*

156

going up the road in her best hat and coat, and this is not a Sunday. She wears her best only when visiting my paternal grandparents or going to church.

I turn and see red running over the doorstep, drip, drip, drip, and I am not frightened. It approaches me, but I know it's not real. It was real in the mind of the child who came home for his rugby kit, but Green-with-yellow-centres-eyes is talking or humming and I know now what wasn't real and what was. I suppose I've always known what was real, but the child inside me didn't.

There's a snap, and I'm back, blinking like someone who has slept too long. I have one thing only to say. 'Thank you.'

He smiles at me, and those feline eyes of his twinkle. 'Excellent, Mr Price. I have left my card on your hall table, though I suspect that you won't be needing me again any time soon. You are a very good and responsive subject.'

They must have come here in separate cars, because Tim returns after seeing the man out. I've forgotten his name.

'Bernard Humphries,' Tim tells me. 'How do you feel?'

'Good. I feel great.'

He sits and tells me that he's wanted me to see Bernie for some time, but he'd hesitated because of my prejudice against music hall acts.

I feel clean.

But now Tim clings to me, and it's my turn to be strong. I feel his fear, because, just now, I'm not locked in by a river of blood. It's all been

157

about me, me, me, a selfish little boy with a mad mother and a dead father. We're both weeping. Tim Dyson has a phobia about flying, but he loves his Julia and will sedate himself while crossing the Atlantic. When he gets there, he'll have to deal with a death, a heartbroken woman, a house and all Julia's chattels. 'Look after her, Tim. And tell her I'm thinking about both of you.'

'I will, I most certainly will.'

God, I hope this new me will last. If it doesn't, I have the man's card. Stop thinking about your bloody self, Price. Think about this friend and all he must face when he lands in America.

Tim leaves. I watch him driving away. This time, he'll be gone for more than the usual fortnight, because grim reality has finally surfaced and must be dealt with. I blink to clear water from my eyes. The man has been my rock, the one I've clung to since I was eleven years old. In a class above mine at school, he was bullied about being gay because of our friendship, and he took it all on the chin. If he could just conquer his flying phobia, he'd be sorted.

I should have listened to Tim years ago. He's right — I'm too stubborn for my own good. Even admitting that my best friend is right doesn't sit well with me. Still thinking about yourself, Alex Price? Consider Kate and this recording. After all she's been through, she needs no further shocks at present. And we must listen to it together, just as I promised. Will she notice I'm different? Will this improvement last, or is it temporary? It's not just about me!

I close the door and walk through the house to join the dogs. Dogs need conversation. They sit in a line and wait to hear their names. Only the one I call is allowed to run for the ball. They shiver with anticipation. For Castor and Pollux, this is a new game, but they're learning fast. Big dogs are so much easier to train.

Kate arrives with Kylie behind her. 'How about we pick up where we left off on the fashion parade,' I suggest.

Kylie's face lights up, and her smile threatens to cleave her face in two. She clearly needs to be the centre of someone's universe, and I wonder whether she might keep the baby for the love she will automatically receive from a newborn. I suppose we all go through life plugging holes in the dam, looking for love, affection, success. Perhaps Monica shouldn't have had children, but who am I to judge?

Kate turns to follow Kylie towards the house, and I glance at my watch. Good God, I must have been under the influence of Bernard for almost an hour, yet it felt like minutes. I look round. 'You OK?' she mouths.

I give her the thumbs up sign and follow the girls into the house with six large animals behind me. Perhaps dogs enjoy fashion shows? We'll soon have the answer to that one.

★ ★ ★

Monica Hargreaves had a cob on. Cobs happen only to Liverpool people, and Monica was 100 per cent cobby. At three in the morning, she was painting the kitchen ceiling after spending several hours grouting the tiled areas.

She was a meticulous woman. Her house was perfect. The master bedroom had an en suite, Kylie had abandoned a bedroom worthy of a princess, while the other two girls shared a very pretty boudoir. Troy had his own little play-and-sleep room, and Monica kept the whole place pristine. She worked hard at keeping up standards, and she wasn't appreciated.

Pete hadn't come home. Soft lad had taken Kylie and most of Kylie's stuff while Monica had been at Aldi buying meat. Britney and Chelsea reckoned they knew nothing, while Troy was still at the spitting-out-dummies age, so he was completely useless. 'Where's he taken her?' she asked the wall. 'Timbuktu?'

She climbed down the ladder and sat on a marble worktop. Marble looked great, but it was cold to the backside. Pete could be double-bluffing; he might have lodged Kylie close by, then stayed out as if he'd been to London and back.

She surveyed all she had achieved in this kitchen. Lights on kickboards, an Amtico floor, top of the range fixtures and fittings, an extension for family meals — nothing but the best, and now she had to move. 'We have to go,' she said aloud, 'because she'll be back with her baby, and the neighbours will have a right laugh, seeing as they're so jealous of me.'

'They're not jealous.'

She looked over her shoulder and saw Pete

160

standing in the doorway leading to the hall. 'Course they are,' she snapped.

'They think you're ridiculous, and so do I.'

The unexpected comment derailed her for a few moments. 'Where've you been?' she managed finally.

'I've been settling my eldest daughter in a place where she'll be cared for. She will receive the counselling she needs, any treatment she requires, and the respect she deserves.' Kylie's distress had been the last straw for Pete. She'd made a mistake by taking from a boy what she interpreted as love.

'Where did you leave her?' Monica shouted.

'Away from you. Then I had an appointment with a solicitor, then I went for a drink or three with him. I'm divorcing you for unreasonable behaviour and a total lack of love for our kids. If you fight my decision, I'll go to the newspapers with witnesses. Don't forget, I'm quite a star turn in this neck of the woods. I want custodial care of all four of them, because I wouldn't leave a tortoise in your selfish hands.'

Monica closed her mouth so quickly that she tasted blood on her tongue, and it hurt. This event served only to increase her anger, and she glared at him. Divorce? Never in this world — not on her watch.

Pete's verbal assault continued. 'When did you last read our Troy a story, eh? Who taught the girls to read while you were up to your eyes in paint and soapy water? All you care about is walls and floors and furniture.'

She returned fire. 'And when you have to go to

work? When you go away to London — what then? They're all well fed and decently dressed, so what's your problem?'

'I'll get a nanny. This house will be sold, half equity each.'

'I'm their mother,' Monica screamed.

'Lower your voice, or all the neighbours will hear what you really are, a bloody witch of a woman who'll walk over her kids to get what she wants. Our Troy needs new shoes and clothes, but no, you had to get the kitchen tarted up. Our girls were short of clothes, too, but they had to wait while you found table and chairs fancy enough for your family dining area. As a mother, you're a joke.'

'And, as a father in a frock, you're the creature that causes them to get bullied at school.'

'And, as a father in a frock, I earn a good sum, sometimes after working all day as a master plasterer. You don't know you're born, lady. Happy enough to take Powder Puff Pete's thousands to do up every room here, eh? Happy enough for me to plaster walls and ceilings in your mansion after a hard day working for a housing association? Well, your free ride's over. Get a flat, get a job, and you can see the children any time you like.'

Her temper was near boiling point, so she tried to cool it down towards a simmer. How was she going to win this one? The joint account. How much was in it? She could take the kids abroad and give them a decent holiday, Spain or Majorca, somewhere with sand and sea and nice hotels.

'I'll be sleeping in Kylie's room,' he said.

'You can't; our Britney's in it. She's fed up of sharing with Chelsea, so she's glad our Kylie's gone.'

So the mother's coldness had been passed to Britney. 'The sofa will do,' he replied. He just left her there, sitting by herself on a cold surface.

Monica quickly riffled through her options. She was minus one daughter, perhaps minus a four-bedroom house and the other three children and, for the first time in her married life, she was not getting her own way. Oh yes, she was going to be minus one husband, too. The neighbours would love that. Doing a disappearing act with four — no, three — children wasn't going to be easy. She needed a night-time flight out of John Lennon, to hell with Manchester. She must think.

Jumping down to floor level, she checked the clock. It was a quarter to four, and the kids would be awake at seven. 'It'll take some planning, but I'll cope,' she whispered. 'Just like I always have.'

★ ★ ★

The Thursday meeting of managers was a tough one. Kate mostly kept her eyes on Alex, occasionally looking about and inspecting women who looked at her man as if he were a mixed grill served up after a Friday night on the booze. Bobby Ray Carson, like Alex, looked angry, because it had been his club that the dead boy was found in. She decided that she liked

163

Bobby Ray, because he cared about Alex.

The rest were a mixed bunch. There was Amber Simpson from Chillex, the keep fit and chill out business. She scarcely took her eyes off Alex. Lily and Ian Mellor, who ran Charm, were middle-aged and earnest, keen to get back to having tea dances and giving lessons in the dying art of ballroom; they were OK. But Martina Nelson, manager at Checkmate, the singles meeting place, was another Amber — hungry and possibly desperate. Kate wondered about the singles; surely Marty could find someone among her clients?

Champs aux Fraises, Alex's newest baby, was run by two gay people, Nick Armstrong and Sandra Horrocks. Kate presumed Alex would be safe in their company. But Amber and Marty were in red hot love with him. Or red hot lust, perhaps.

Alex was speaking and she observed how he really was something, especially when angry. His voice was quiet, dangerously so.

'Any more incidents involving drugs, and you're all fired. Each manager will now be responsible for their security teams. If necessary, get a security body to watch your security body. The name of the company might need changing from Price Partners to Price Solo, and you'll all have to forget the annual bonuses, because I can dissolve the partnership as fast as this.' He banged on the table.

'The term partners means we're all in this mess together, which is why you get a cut of the profits.' He smiled at the couple in charge of

Charm. 'There are people here simply because they work for Price Partners, and they are not involved with current difficulties, yet they need to be watchful. Now, go home, because I'm tired of all this, bored with it. We reopen tomorrow.'

He sat, and Kate moved closer. 'You're so sexy when you're angry.'

'Am I?' The tone was dry.

'Yes, definitely.'

Alex grinned. 'Let's go home and explore that possibility.'

Her peripheral vision caught Amber and Martina hovering in the doorway. The urge to kiss Alex was strong, though she managed to overpower it. Why put on a demonstration for the girls? But she didn't need to put on a show, because he pounced first. She was so proud of him. Let them see, let them know that they had no chance, because he was hers.

When she and Alex surfaced from the embrace, Amber and Marty had disappeared.

'One nil,' Kate murmured.

'What?'

'Nothing. I was just being silly. Take me home, angry boy.'

★   ★   ★

They were walking down Dale Street towards a decent coffee house when Kate spotted him, the doctor who had helped save Amelia's life before pursuing her all the way from London to the house on Merrilocks Road. 'Alex,' she whispered.

'What?'

'Don't look now, but bandit at two o'clock on the other side of the street.'

Alex bent to fasten a shoelace, peering across the road to where Dr Giles Girling was standing while speaking into his mobile phone. 'Has he seen us?' he asked. 'And what is he still doing in Liverpool? Didn't you tell me he had something lined up at Great Ormond Street?'

She shrugged. 'That's what he said when Amelia was in hospital. I wonder if he's stalking me?'

'Don't joke, Kate. Stalking can get very nasty.'

He stood up and guided her into the Coffee Pot, where he ordered a latte for Kate and a black as hell espresso for himself. Kate studied him; his mood had darkened like his coffee. 'You said you were no longer drinking espresso because it puts you in overdrive and makes you snappy,' she reminded him.

'He's after you,' he stated.

'And?'

He stared at the door. 'Oh, hell, here he comes. Keep that wedding ring on.'

Kate placed her left hand on the table so that the platinum band and the engagement ring were on display for all to see.

Dr Giles walked straight to the counter and ordered his drink, casting not so much as a glance in the couple's direction. Nothing in his body language appeared awkward, so it was possible that he hadn't noticed them. Alex, who suddenly felt the need to take charge of the situation, called him over. 'Dr Girling, please join us.'

The handsome young man stopped in his tracks. 'Just a moment,' he replied, rooting in a pocket to find the price of his coffee.

'I love you, Alex Price,' Kate whispered. 'Don't you dare forget that, ever.'

'If I do forget?' he asked softly.

'You'll be dead, and I'll be in jail.' She returned his broad grin.

Giles joined them with his cappuccino. 'Full fat milk,' he said. 'Physician heal thyself?'

Kate's smile moved to encompass the newcomer. 'So what brings you back to these parts?' she asked.

He placed the tall cup on their table. 'I'm at Alder Hey doing the research I've been longing to have time for.' He sat next to Alex.

Kate noticed that the paediatrician did a double take on seeing her hand. Now he thought they were married.

'I'm interested in childhood cancers,' he said seriously. 'Too many die before reaching adulthood or even their teenage years. So I attend sessions at the Liverpool School of Medicine twice a week. London's OK, and Great Ormond Street would have been special, obviously, but Alder Hey was too good to miss, especially with the research offer contained in the job description.'

Alex didn't trust him. 'So you're no longer chasing my wife?'

Kate noted that the tone of his voice was deliberately light.

Giles shook his head. 'I've met a very pleasant nurse. Early days, but, you know?' He shrugged. 'Life's rather busy for personal encounters.'

Kate continued to watch him carefully. 'But unlike me, you are London to the bone. I thought I would never leave London, but Liverpool is great and I met my man.'

The medic took a sip of coffee. 'I've kept my house, and yes, I might return in time. Are you keeping your house?'

'Not sure. We could make good rent money, though I'm more likely to sell.'

Giles whistled. 'Well, that might put a couple of million in your bank account.'

Her eyes narrowed. 'Indeed,' she replied coldly. 'Alex and I are considering our options. My parents have a mansion flat, so they won't need their old home back.'

Alex could feel the tension. This poor man was suffering because of Kate. Perhaps he laboured under the mistaken concept that Kate owed him love due to the part he'd played in Amelia's treatment and eventual recovery.

A panic threatened, but Alex stamped it out. The doctor had too much to lose by stalking Kate and making a nuisance of himself. He might well be struck off if he didn't leave her alone. 'We must go, darling,' he said.

She held out a hand to shake the intruder's. 'Goodbye, Giles,' she said.

'You're no longer in Blundellsands?' he asked.

'No. I live with my husband, and he's getting the Merrilocks house finished in accordance with my plans.'

Alex said a short goodbye before following Kate to the door.

Outside, she awarded Alex a cheeky grin.

'Now you know how I feel.'

'What?'

'Jealous.'

'Why?'

'Those two women — Amber and Martina. They want to eat you alive, probably with gravy and roast potatoes.'

'Don't forget the vegetables. They need a balanced diet.'

She punched him none too gently on his upper arm.

'I shall join the battered husbands' society,' he grumbled. 'Anyway, I made sure they saw me kissing you.'

'So you kissed me for their benefit only?'

He chuckled. 'Well, I did enjoy the side effects. Kissing you is fast becoming another hobby of mine.'

'But you couldn't follow through in a meeting room.'

'No. So let's go, eh?'

He was impossible, and that fact was a huge slice of her reason for loving him. Her lover was never boring; he was a treasure and she would treat him as such.

★ ★ ★

Max Alton was in love with France; the more he saw of the Loire valley, the better he felt. He should have been born there; it felt like home.

As he and his reluctant companion made their way along the meandering queen of French rivers, Max was, according to Trev, losing his grip. 'You've lost your grip. We were supposed to be going to that one village where that kid and her grandparents are meant to be, St Martin's Flowers or whatever, and we've been back and forth like a pair of cockroaches in a kitchen.'

'Shut up.'

'Well, how many more bleeding chateaux? Where's the chateau with the gateau and the fallen Madonna with the big boobies?'

'It wasn't real, tinhead. It was just a sitcom on TV.'

'None of this is bloody real, either. If I get dragged into another church, I'll vomit.'

'Well, maybe you're related to Satan. Sit down a minute.' They sat on a low wall and watched the river bubbling gently over rocks. 'Take a gander at that clean water. When did you see the Thames that colour?'

Trev felt embarrassed on behalf of the only English river he knew. 'That's because the Thames is a working river. There's pretty and there's useful; give me useful any day of the week. And there's all kinds in that forest where our tent is, noises in the night, trees and bushes rustling, foxes howling — '

'Barking. They bark — I read it somewhere a while back. There's urban foxes on the streets of London now.'

'And if you see one vineyard, you've seen 'em all. We have to get back with the kid. We need to shove notes into that house we trashed, the one Jim's old lady was doing up.'

Max sighed. 'No, we don't. We've got new names — it says so on our passports. I'm

170

Michael Shipton and you're Thomas Saunders, and we don't need to go back.'

Trev's jaw dropped. 'What? Not go back to London? Staying here, living here?'

Max nodded. 'Yes, and going straight, going kosher. Look at it. Ever been to Ireland, the southern part?'

'No.'

'I thought not.' Max looked round at the land. The people who worked it were not like Parisians. They were laid back, come day, go day and God bless Sunday. The lowing of beasts with full udders was not allowed to interrupt a leisurely game of boules; fishermen with a promise on the end of a line finished the slow reeling in before returning to work. 'This place reminds me of what my mum used to say about Ireland. Good soil to work with, and pleasant folk who like a laugh and a pint or two. We've been living the wrong life, Trev.' The only differences between here and Ireland were the language and the weather.

'I'm going home,' Trev insisted.

Max shrugged. 'Please yourself.'

'I can't go on me own.'

'And I'm not risking a dud passport again. You can do as you like. I'll get you to Paris and the train to Dieppe, then you catch the Newhaven ferry. Somebody will be driving to London, so hitch a ride. You make your choice and get on with it, Trev. I'm staying in France.'

'And if I get caught?'

'You keep your gob shut about me, or I'll get your knees broke. But there'll be no kidnap,

171

because . . . ' Max opened his bag, 'I went to Saint-Martin-aux-Fleurs — that's what the village is called in French — and look what I found in their bin.' He spread open a copy of *The Times* and handed it over. 'You can get English newspapers, but you have to order them, and they come a day or two late. They found the rest of Gentleman Jim's stash. It says so here.'

'When did you go?'

'Last night. I knew you'd no idea that we were near the place, so I spiked your drink and went on a mooch.'

Although Trev wasn't the best reader on the planet, he wasn't as daft as he was treated. 'It's a scam,' he declared. 'They're trying to winkle us out of the woodwork. I've not got me glasses — they must be in the car, and I'm not walking that far. What's it say?'

'It says they found four boxes at an undisclosed location, rumoured by nearby residents to be a graveyard. Looks like the reason Jim went for the kid was because she pinched some pearls from the stuff he took home. The woman who owned the pearls says the kid can have them after what her dad did to her. They had to take the top of her skull off. I reckon she's been through enough without being snatched by us.'

Trev sighed. 'It's a load of cobblers, all of it. I don't believe a word of it. It's been put there for a reason, just mark my words. And we had a plan.'

'So we make a new one. Stop here, improve our French, work in a vineyard. It's a fresh start.'

'What about me mum?'

172

'She'll manage. She's a tough old bird.'

'And the wife and kids?'

Max glanced skywards. 'You can't stand Yvonne, and the kids get you down. Stay and get yourself a nice piece of French skirt.'

Trev stood up.

'Where are you going?' Max asked.

'Back to the tent. I need to think.'

'Sure you can find your way?'

'Oh, shut up.' Trev stormed off in a thunderous mood with a headache to match. He didn't want to live in France; it was full of French people. There were plenty of jokes about the French, and he even remembered one. For sale, one French machine gun. Never used, and dropped only once. White flag included.

Max stayed where he was, bare arms and legs soaking up the warm sunshine. Even now, in the month of May, this was blissful weather. But something was bothering him, buzzing round like the damned mosquitoes that forced him and Trev to sleep under nets. Trev was angry, and it wouldn't surprise Max if the fool attempted the kidnap himself. Shit.

He stood up and looked round the area described by many as the heart of France. The word beautiful was not enough. The way people lived here now, in the twenty-first century, could be traced back to medieval and earlier times. There had been fierce battles in the area, yet peace ruled now. To keep this, to hold on to his dream, Max would go to any lengths. First, he had to warn the kid's grandparents. It would mean another midnight walk and a letter written

173

with his left hand, but he would do it.

If Trev got out of order . . . well, he would be dealt with. Who would miss Trev, anyway?

8

Amber Simpson had to get out of the stifling, ugly flat she had occupied for what felt like a lifetime. She would never again eat anything Chinese, because the stench from the restaurant was beginning to choke her. There was probably nothing wrong with whatever was served in the Golden Willow, but it had infiltrated its way into her nostrils for too long, and she was at the end of her tether. Sometimes, she wondered whether she stank of the stuff, or whether she only imagined that it had made its way into her clothing.

The annual bonuses would be through soon enough; she knew Alex Price well enough to understand that he had no intention of denying his colleagues their share, and Chillex was exceeding all expectations. She had some money saved, and although interest rates were poor she had managed not to touch her deposit account. The car was off the list for now, because she was going for a flat of her own, a mortgage rather than a rented place. Alex might help; she knew he'd made sure that the old dears who managed Charm had got somewhere decent to live when they'd moved here from Warrington.

In her hands, she held details of a two-bedroom apartment on Mossley Hill Drive. It overlooked Sefton Park, had high ceilings and some of the original stained glass windows. It was pristine, newly refitted and a definite contrast to her current scruffy abode. Two large bedrooms, massive living area, decent kitchen, new bathroom — oh, it called out to her. At under £200,000, it was a snip. She had a deposit, would ask for advice from Alex, and mortgage rates were currently favourable.

Closing her eyes, she pictured the scene from earlier that day when she had followed an agent through the flat. If the man hadn't suffered from verbal diarrhoea she could have been in her element, but she hadn't been able to tune out his monotone as he'd indicated original ceiling roses, architraves, deep skirting boards and sash windows. She'd heard, though she hadn't listened. Men who were not Alex Price held no interest for her anyway, and she preferred the company of women for the most part. Well, most women. She didn't like Katherine Price, and Martina from Checkmate was a bit of a bore, too. Marty had no chance where Alex was concerned . . .

Did anyone have a chance with him? After all, he was married, and he was decent. His wife wasn't decent. She'd inveigled her husband into giving her a directorship, a post that had never been advertised, although the Price company always advertised internally as well as through the media.

Amber looked at her furniture. The bed was all right, and the main bedroom at the Mossley Hill Drive flat had furniture built in — wardrobes, dressing table and drawers. The second bedroom would be her office and keep fit room, but that vast living area required furniture. She needed couches, armchairs, bookcases, pictures for the walls, a statement clock, rugs for the oak floor, a TV, dining furniture. Charity shops. The hospice place took in loads of furniture, and she could clean it, perk it up with cushions and throws. Her eyes lit upon the coffee table. Right. Fine sandpaper, a dab of paint, rough it up so that it would look deliberately distressed. Oh, yes. It was all doable.

Then she would throw a housewarming party, show everyone that fabulous Victorian fireplace. Mr and Mrs Price were going to have pride of place at the top of the list. She would need a designer dress, so the charity shops of Liverpool North and South would require visits. In fur-coats-and-no-knickers territories, otherwise known as debtors' retreats, she would find something startling yet smart. Let him see what he was missing by fastening himself to a Londoner with a plum in her gob and a tendency to look down on other women at the table. Director of Design? Mrs Price couldn't direct traffic.

'I can still save,' she told herself. 'Eat at work, shower at work, and I won't need to heat the apartment except in the evenings and on my days off in the dark weeks of winter.'

She put her plans onto the laptop. First, see Alex to get advice about mortgages. Get the mortgage after making an offer a bit lower than the asking price. If that worked, the furniture problem would be solved in part. If necessary, pay the full price for the flat and buy second-hand items. There was a site on the internet, a place where one could buy curtains that had hung in stately homes: velvets, silks and the like. It might well be beyond her means, but trying never did harm.

Amber was a girl with a plan. She'd had a plan many years ago, and it had led to anorexia, bulimia and time in an institution where she had applied herself to the business of staying alive. She knew the absolute value of every food type. A certain amount of the right sort of fat helped maintain the skin; protein was vital, as were carbohydrates as long as they weren't always refined sugars; Tuesday was a small cake day, while Saturday was celebrated with a Milky Way. Amber ate fruit and vegetables every day, and her body was honed to perfection. Girls with plans had a better chance of success . . .

She smiled. If anything unfortunate were to befall Mrs Price, Amber Simpson would be there to comfort the widower.

★　★　★

Pete took some leave from the plastering job and turned down most offers of evening work in clubs. He drove Britney and Chelsea to school before spending the day with Troy, taking him to parks, teaching him the rudiments of swimming in the shallow pool at the baths, fastening him in the car seat while they went to pick up his sisters in the afternoon, reading to him at bedtime. He left Monica to her scrubbing and bleaching, since those activities kept her quiet.

Troy. Why had he allowed his idiot wife to

choose their names? There was a big-mouthed woman on TV who stated that you could judge others' level of education by the names they gave to their children. Mind, looking at the names with which she'd saddled her own three, Big Mouth should really swill her own back yard before jumping on the mess of others. He grinned. The nasty bag made money out of hating people. Monica was a dedicated hater, too, only she didn't get paid for it.

But why had he let that crazy woman get away with Kylie, Britney, Chelsea and Troy? They each had a decent middle name — Anne, Jane, Marie and Peter — but he had been allowed no say in their first names. 'I've been weak,' he said as he walked into Alex's house one early evening.

Alex and Kate shared a frown. 'Weak? How?' Alex asked.

Kate tutted. 'I'd have sacked Monica years ago,' she said. 'Give her the P45, Pete.'

'I let her choose the kids' names. I turned away when she started making the house into a showpiece — the area doesn't merit spending so much on a semi. I've given in to her just for a peaceful life, an easy way out. And with working all day and some evenings, I escaped quite often. Now, I see to the kids during the day, then I come here and make my Kylie-Anne's evening meal, then go back and sleep on the sofa and try to stay unconscious by blocking out the voice that's screamed at me down the years. She's bringing a counter-suit because I dress for performances. I don't know why she's bothering, because as my lawyer says, 'If one partner says he

or she can't hear music, then the dance is over.''
He scratched his head. 'Sorry. I'll go up and see
my eldest. She's taken a sudden fancy for eggs.'

Upstairs in the loft apartment, Pete found his
daughter in a pensive mood. She was staring at
herself in an over-mantel mirror when he
arrived. 'What's up, doc?' he asked.

'I'll get fat and ugly,' she replied softly.

'You'll swell up a bit, but you'll never be ugly,
love.'

'I don't know what to do, Dad.'

He stood behind her, his large hands cupping
her shoulders. 'Whatever you decide, I'll back
you up.'

'Even abortion?'

'Yes. See? I didn't even hesitate. You're
fourteen, a whole adult lifetime in front of you. A
child will slow you down and force you to take a
longer road to wherever you want to be. So you
can get rid of the problem, keep the baby, or give
birth and hand her or him over to some poor
couple who can't have kids. You could do a lot of
good that way.'

She placed a hand on her belly. 'It's growing.
Every day, it splits into more cells. Forty weeks
they take.'

'Yes, they grow quickly. Wait till they need
shoes; then you'll know exactly how fast they
grow. The size changes before the leather's worn
out. But never mind about all that now, love,
because we've a few weeks before you need to
make your decision.'

She pushed out a heavy sigh. 'I'm happier
here, Dad. Can we have omelettes? There's a bit

180

of that nice ham left.'

'Of course we can. I bought salad this afternoon.'

After the meal, Kylie washed up while Pete watched the news. As darkness descended from the heavens, they were both nodding towards slumber when his mobile rang. Fishing it out of a pocket, he yawned before answering. Almost immediately, he was on his feet and yelling, 'You've done what?'

He listened for a while, shouting 'Hello?' loudly when the caller ended the conversation. Frustrated, he pressed a button to reconnect, but the phone he tried to reach had gone dead. 'Oh, Kylie-Anne,' he said, his voice almost cracking with emotion.

She jumped up from the chair in which she'd been dozing. 'What, Dad?'

'She's gone.'

'Who's gone?'

'Your mother. She's getting on a plane with Britney and Chelsea, but she's left Troy at home. That little lad's on his own, two years old and his mum buggers off and abandons him. Go down and find Alex, tell him what's going on. I'll get our little lad.' He grabbed his keys and fled, almost tumbling down the stairs in his haste. Red hot anger raged until the pit of his stomach felt as if it had been burnt by a white-hot poker. Bloody, bloody Monica.

In the car, with his body drowning in adrenalin, he had some difficulty with steering and with control of the clutch pedal. 'Don't crash,' he ordered himself. God, he was livid.

That bitch was taking Britney-Jane and Chelsea-Marie to . . . who knew where? She'd left the baby because she couldn't manage him — Troy-Peter was only a boy, and didn't matter. Last and least important was the fact that she had emptied their joint account. 'Good job I stashed some, then.'

As he turned right off Queens Drive towards Bootle, his mind wandered about of its own accord to when he'd first met Monica. She'd been funny, sharp, quick-witted and good company. She'd sung a lot, laughed a lot, made love a lot. She'd given up singing for painting walls, dropped laughing for buying furniture, and when it came to the other business, there'd been nothing since Troy.

Living without physical contact with her had presented no problem. A careful man, he had a mistress who was the very soul of discretion, and he must talk to her later; she had to know that he would be occupied for the immediate future, at least.

Pulling onto the driveway of his house, he got out of the car and listened keenly; the baby wasn't crying. He had to do this right. Police? What did a man do in a situation like this? Then he remembered Molly Partington, a social worker who lived at number 62. She would know, wouldn't she?

She did. Molly rang her boss's private number before informing the police that a child well below the age of twelve years had been abandoned by his mother. 'His dad's going into the house now, and I shall go with him. The mother's gone abroad with two of her three daughters.' She paused. 'I'm a neighbour and a social worker, yes.'

A man interrupted her. 'Kylie is staying with me and my wife.'

The social worker turned and recognized Alex immediately. 'Mr Price — the one who owns clubs in town — is looking after the oldest girl. What? No, it's not an emergency, because Mrs Hargreaves left only about two hours ago, and there's no sound of distress. Yes, I'll stay on the phone while we go in.'

'John Lennon, then,' Alex said to Pete, who nodded in agreement.

'I've tried calling her back, but there's nothing. She must have changed the card in the phone. You followed me,' he said, his tone betraying relief. He scratched his head before thanking his temporary landlord. Some people were so good.

They crept into the house like three burglars looking for loot.

Pete entered the fourth and smallest bedroom alone. Little Troy lay curled in the foetal position, one arm thrown over a stuffed toy, dummy held in his hand. Soft breathing said the child was in a deep sleep.

'He's OK,' the relieved father whispered to Alex and Molly.

The neighbour relayed the message via her phone to the police. When she had finished, she informed Pete that a police car was on its way. 'No blues and twos,' she informed the two men, 'but they have to come out when there's a child involved.'

Alex was the first to notice that Pete was weeping. 'He's fine, Pete.'

'I've got to take responsibility for some of this, you see. If I'd cared enough for my kids, I should have locked her in the garden shed. This is about Kylie. Monica can't face the idea of our daughter arriving home with a baby. She's as shallow as they come, self, self, self.'

Alex placed a hand on the man's arm. 'I know all about selfishness.'

'She won't come back,' Pete wept. 'And the girls will miss their friends, they won't get an education — '

'I'll get them home, I promise.'

'How?'

'No idea yet. Interpol, private detective, whatever it takes.'

'We don't know where they've gone.'

Alex smiled. 'That's the easy part. The police will find out which plane they're on and where it's going to land. Go downstairs and look for travel brochures. An organized woman like Monica will have marked her destination. It will be an apartment, self-catering, outside some main resort.'

'Why?'

'Because she's methodical. Britney and Chelsea will talk, so Monica will need to keep them away from the crowds for a while. Go on. Find brochures. Look in the kitchen as well as the sitting room.'

Pete sniffed. 'She's methodical enough not to have left any evidence for us to find.'

'Go. You'll feel better if you're doing something.'

When Pete had left the landing area, Alex asked Molly to stay near the child. He then descended the stairs and waited at the open front door for the police. They knew him well. Not only had he closed his clubs to give them a free hand after drugs had been found, but each year at Christmas he donated to police widows and their dependants.

A car drew up and two detectives alighted. 'Mr Price,' the driver said by way of greeting.

Alex waded in straight away. 'The oldest daughter is staying at my house. The father has taken time off his plastering work to help look after her and the others. Monica, Britney and Chelsea Hargreaves are on a plane, probably from John Lennon. I want you to find out the flight and its destination. Monica, the mother, abandoned a two-year-old boy in this house. He's fine; a neighbour's with him. Pete will look after them all. It's a good job Pete had no booking tonight.'

'I see. Powder Puff Pete? I've seen him; he's brilliant.'

Alex motored on. 'The oldest teenager is pregnant and was ordered by Monica to have an abortion or piss off. Kylie chose the latter option. I want the police at the plane's destination to arrest Monica and fly them all home.' He looked at his watch. 'Is that doable?'

'Let me try.' The detective returned to the car in order to talk to base while his companion entered the house to check on the abandoned boy.

Pete, having failed to find travel magazines, returned to Troy's bedroom and lifted his son, wrapping him in a blue blanket. 'Hiya, kid,' he said. 'Let's go and see Kylie, eh?'

The child yawned, offered his father a beaming smile and said, 'Ky-we.'

'Yes. Another ride in the car.'

'Wide in ca-a-ar,' announced Troy to the assembly on the landing.

'Not much wrong with him,' commented the CID officer, grinning at the little boy.

Pete stopped. 'There might have been. She knows I work in clubs some nights, and I don't take my phone on stage. This little beggar could have been alone in his room right through till morning, and he has big back teeth coming through. I tell you now, I want my wife arrested and brought home to be charged with neglect of a baby.' He paused. 'And for removing my two daughters from this country without my permission.' He walked downstairs.

Outside, the second detective spoke to Alex. 'The Deputy Chief Constable's taken an interest. It's Barcelona, and they touch down at about half past one in the morning our time. She'll be detained, and there'll be an interpreter.'

'The girls will be looked after?' Alex asked.

'Of course.'

Pete was fastening Troy in his seat when Alex arrived at the car. 'The Deputy Chief Con's called in a few favours. Hopefully, your missus and the girls won't leave Barcelona airport. You'll have Britney and Chelsea back tomorrow or soon after — with a bit of luck and a following wind.' He paused as he processed an idea. 'Leave Troy with Kylie. I know he's not a newborn, but it might give her some idea of what she's letting herself in for.'

'Good thinking, Batman.'

From his own vehicle, Alex phoned Kate, but he didn't get the chance to speak. 'Is the little boy all right?' she cried.

'He's fine. Pete's bringing him to Kylie now. I'll see you soon.'

'Good. Mrs Bee's banging about in the kitchen. She says you're re-creating Strawberry Field orphanage, and that Monica should get life in prison.'

'That sounds pretty normal, then.'

'Yes. She's her usual fierce self.'

'As are you, Kate.' He paused, aware of the importance of what he was about to say. 'Your strength's what made me agree to be hypnotised. After what I've witnessed tonight, I feel ready.'

'For what?'

He swallowed. 'The recording. The real wedding. Children.'

'Then get back here, sexy. I'll be putty in your hands.'

He laughed. 'That would be a first, my love.'

⋆ ⋆ ⋆

Church bells rang. So it must be . . . was it Dimanche? Wasn't that French for Sunday? Even Trev had picked up an odd word here and there — and where was he? Ah, yes. The *boulangerie* opened for an hour or so even on Sundays, because people wanted their croissants fresh from the oven. Trev would buy the chocolate ones, his favourites. They sold butter and jam,

187

too, and Max hoped that his daft companion would remember to hand in the short shopping list. Max had copied the items he wanted in French from a phrase book he'd bought in the camping shop.

He turned over in his sleeping bag. He had plenty to think about. Trev wanted to go home, so Max would need to take him as far as Paris, stick him on a train and write down the word *Newhaven* so that somebody could point the fool in the direction of the right ferry in Dieppe. His stomach rumbled — where was the daft sod? 'At this rate, I'll die of starvation and he'll have all four croissants to himself.'

He found some soap and a towel that had dried while hanging from a tree. According to what he'd read, this had been a great forest, but locals had used huge amounts of timber while building houses hundreds of years ago. Pity. The trees were stunning. He walked to the river, jumped in, and waited for his breath to return. The water was very cold and so clean that he could see fish darting about to escape his sudden invasion of their domain.

After washing his hair, he dipped his head in the river and for a split second he saw . . . He straightened, shaking his head not only to rid it of water, but also to wipe out what he'd seen — what he thought he'd seen. A body? Had he just washed himself in water that contained decaying human remains? Fish shit was one thing, but . . .

Max Alton scrambled up the bank and dried himself while sitting on a tree stump. He peered over the river's edge, but all he could see was a shape. It could be . . . a pale stone on the river bed? Part of a tree? A very large dead fish? No, they never got to that size, surely? There were no sharks in the Loire . . . Oh, God, he and Trev had to pitch their tent elsewhere in case . . . in case it was a human corpse.

He had to warn Trev. But as the day went on, Trev failed to appear. Max went from irritated to concerned to outright panicked. There was nobody he could trust to share his worries with. The truth was nagging at him but he didn't want to believe it. It was too sudden, too final.

By nightfall, however, he had to accept that the river Loire was the temporary resting place of his mate Trev, now officially Thomas Saunders. Tomorrow, he must bury his colleague somewhere in these woods. Afterwards, he would destroy their camp as best he could and double back to another part of the valley. Empty of food and devoid of all thoughts except for the memory of poor Trev, he had a bad night.

★ ★ ★

He looks so tired.

We lie feet to feet on his large, L-shaped sofa while he tells me about the evening's events. I say that Monica sounds as if she ought to be housed in some place for the terminally bewildered, but Alex tells me it's probably like my OCD, but a bit worse. His opinion — never humble, not where my lover is concerned — is that Monica has probably had post-partum

189

depression since the delivery of Kylie, and too many pregnancies and births have tipped her into a kind of psychosis.

I accuse him of pretending to be Tim, and he just laughs and says the painting and decorating kept Monica's mind occupied, because subconsciously she didn't like the young creatures who had made her ill.

'Does she know she's ill, Dr Price?' I ask.

'Probably not.'

He falls asleep, so I get down on my hands and knees and crawl to him. He looks so young while sleeping, though the beard is erupting and giving him that dark and interesting appearance. Alex is gorgeous. Without the boardroom frown and the business suit, he's sweet. I'd better not tell him that, because sweet would sound too feminine. But yes, he's pretty.

One luscious brown eye opens. He tells me he's not asleep, then proves it by assaulting me. Kylie and Pete had better stay where they are, up in the gods with little Troy. This man, my man, is an excellent kisser. I must sneak up on Mr Alex Price more often . . .

★   ★   ★

Pete's phone rang at about two o'clock in the morning. It was Monica, and she was hysterical.

'Where are you?' he shouted. 'And are the girls all right? What the hell were you thinking of, playing a trick like that?' He knew she wasn't listening. She was too busy being upset because she'd been rumbled.

190

'Bloody Barcelona,' she wept. 'How could you do this to me?'

'How could you take Britney and Chelsea out of the country without letting me know? How could you leave a teething child on his own in the house? I could have been working for all you knew.'

'You've not worked for days — '

'That doesn't mean anything. And if my phone had been playing up? If I'd lost it?'

'I'd have found a way of getting in touch.'

'How? Pigeon post, smoke signals, telegram? Listen, you. The girls need to go to school. You've no right to interrupt their education — you'd get fined for that alone. Haven't we enough on with our Kylie taking time to make her mind up? Fortunately, I've phoned the head teacher and explained about Kylie's condition. Yes, I told him the whole truth.'

She inhaled deeply. 'The shame of it,' she managed.

'And Molly, the social worker from number sixty-two, got her boss and the police on the job for our Troy. He's with our Kylie, and I'm with both of them. Oh yes. Everybody will know how insane you are.'

Silence reigned. Barcelona suffered a sudden and deathly hush. Pete could almost hear the gears in Monica's head turning, engaging, changing up as she worried about the neighbours talking about her. 'Pig,' she managed eventually.

He imitated a boar by snorting twice.

'I want my stuff, but I'm not going back to that house.'

'Fine by me. Now, get my girls home.' He ended the call with a flourish.

'Dad?'

Pete turned to see his lovely Kylie-Anne standing in the doorway. She looked like a frightened little kid, and she had another child inside her, God bless them both. 'What, love?'

'Can I still stop here?'

'Of course you can. Alex will find somewhere for your mum, and I'll get help in the house. You take your time, queen.'

'I can think better here. And I don't mind having our Troy if you'll bring his clothes and toys.'

'I will.'

She settled on the sofa, knees drawn up, her outline reminiscent of Troy's just before he was lifted from his cot bed. Pete waited before easing his daughter's legs into a more comfortable position. He brought a duvet, covered her, then returned to the business of making himself into a barrier to prevent Troy from falling out of bed.

So, this was his life now; he had become a full-time parent.

Did he mind? Oh, he would find a way to cope. For a few moments, he even felt sorry for Monica. When a dad abandoned his family, the mother was expected to manage just because of her gender; but when a woman left home, she was painted blacker than hell in the minds of all who knew her. She would need somewhere to live, some sort of counselling. Alex would know; Alex Price was everyone's fall-back go-to man.

There was something different about France when it came to beginnings and endings. It wasn't as noticeable as it had been on the southern costas in Spain, where dawn was sudden and day turned to night with scarcely a hint of dusk, as if God had been doing paperwork instead of attending to heavenly and earthly bodies and the alignment of stars with planets.

Max remembered those far off lazy days in the sun with Mabel and the kids. The children had buried him in sand; now, he had to inter poor Trev, whose blood he had found on a rock. The lad had probably slipped, cracked his head and fallen unconscious into the river. Trev's clothes and towel were behind a few shrubs and bushes, his shoes were hidden under them, a clean sock shoved under the tongue and laces of each piece of footwear. There was something almost unbearably sad in Trev's careful little arrangements made while he prepared to clean himself before going up to the *boulangerie*.

In a jacket pocket, Max found the shopping list — *quatre croissants, beurre, confiture fraises* — all from a phrase book. Oh, God. All Trev had wanted was to get back home, and he wouldn't be going anywhere now, would he? To approach police would be folly, so Max was up before light warmed the earth, digging with what Trev had termed the shit-shifting shovel, lifting the clods of soft, fertile earth and laying them in a mound beside the grave. Now, he had to face the worst.

He stripped to his boxers, entered the water and heaved at the literally dead weight of a man who had accompanied him through life for twenty years. 'I all but brought you up, lad. I thought I'd see my own end long before yours. Come on, now. We have to get you out of this bloody water.'

Laid out on the bank, Trev looked so thin and shrivelled. He wasn't bloated by being in the river, and rigor had long passed, so the body was malleable. 'I'm sorry, Trev, sorry for how I treated you, how I spoke to you just because you can't bloody read.' Max sniffed. 'Couldn't read,' he amended.

For a reason he failed to understand, Max dressed the remains. No way could he pile soil on the frail, blue-white corpse. This was his mate, almost a son or a younger brother, so he was owed some dignity in his final resting place. It wasn't an easy job; the encasing of an oversized doll in trousers, shirt and pullover took some doing, but Max persevered. The flesh was so cold, as if it had been covered with ice at Billingsgate market.

After lowering the body into its grave, the older man stood. He was breathless, so he waited for his pulse to slow and for his lungs to remember what their function was before he covered Trev in the soil of a country for which he'd held no affection. 'If I do go home and come back, Trev, I'll fetch some British soil from Tower Hamlets Cemetery Park.'

He couldn't mark the grave with a cross, so he shifted two flattish stones to the site. Before leaving, he would take a photograph of the grave so that he would always have proof that Trev had lived. He stood staring at the ground that concealed the remains of one of London's best drug runners.

Sunday school. What was that song? Max was no singer, so he spoke the words. 'The Lord's my shepherd, I shall not want. He maketh me to lie down in green pastures . . . ' Defeated and utterly miserable, he allowed the tears to flow. He managed a few more words in a low and broken whisper. 'If there is a soul, fly free now. Fly home, Trev.'

★   ★   ★

I wake, and she's standing there in a crisp blue blouse and some jeans so tight that she may have painted them on. She has that expression on her face, the half smile, raised left eyebrow, mischief in the eyes. Is she going to jump on the bed, drag me out, pull my hair? I grin at her and cover the more delicate parts of my anatomy with her pillow. Her pillow on my bed — our bed. When she sleeps with me, I don't get haunted by a river of blood . . .

She grins and asks if I'm afraid of her; I reply in the negative, and she throws herself across the bed, pinning me in my place. 'I'm going with Pete to pick up Troy's stuff,' she tells me.

When I ask why, I am ordered to mind my own business, and she isn't going to get away with that. 'Then I'll come, too.'

'No need. Aren't you doing audits and

accounts and stuff today?'

'Later. This morning, I'm in a meeting with Amber Simpson.'

Kate frowns. 'One of your predators? She's the one from Chillex. When she stares at you, that one looks as if she wants a knife and fork, gravy, Yorkshire pudding and a — '

'No. She's careful with her diet. I'd be too much protein, even for her. Anyway, I'll postpone, because I'd rather be with you. Amber and Marty make my flesh crawl. Desperation doesn't suit a woman. Of course, being a man of good character, I've never been tempted by either of them.'

I gaze at her. The real hair is growing, and she blows a shiny dark ringlet away from her eyes. 'You are all my tomorrows,' I tell her, but in spite of my feeble attempt at romantic courtship the eyebrow stays raised. She's up to something. Kate has several 'tells', and she seems blissfully unaware of the fact that her body betrays her intentions. 'What?' she asks.

'When you're losing an argument, you cross your legs and swing a foot.'

'I never lose an argument.'

'Then stop lying across me, sit on the chair and we'll argue about whether you ever lose an argument.'

'No.'

See? I told you she's argumentative. 'I need to get out of bed.'

'OK.' She jumps up. 'I've held you back for long enough, and Pete will be in the car and ready to go.'

She moves towards the door and I throw the pillow at her.

'Bull's eye,' she calls. 'I'll get you later.'

The wonderful thing is that I know she will get me later; after her time spent living in fear, she has burst out of the chrysalis and is now newborn and colourful.

★ ★ ★

Leaving Troy with Kylie, Pete drove to Bootle with Kate in the passenger seat. He was grateful to her and Alex, and he said so.

'Well, there'll soon be another little girl running round at Strawberry Mead,' she told him. 'I shall bring my daughter back from France after the summer's over.'

'You've just the one?'

'So far. Today, I'd like to look at Monica's work.'

'Help yourself.' He shook his head. 'If she'd minded her children half as well as she looked after the house, we might not have reached this shitty situation.'

Kate knew a good man when she saw one, and Pete Hargreaves filled the bill perfectly. He was hardworking, morally sound, and he adored his children. 'So you taught them all to read?'

'I did. Got some books from the Picton so that I could learn how to teach — it's not rocket science. The doorway to arithmetic isn't numbers; it's sorting colours and shapes. They learn a lot from dominoes and snap games, too. Once we reached numbers, they counted

197

anything they could lay their hands or eyes on. I've got four clever kids whose mother spends her time up a ladder and her money on furniture, fixtures and wallpaper. The feature wall in the main bedroom cost four hundred quid a roll. She's a dedicated spender.'

He pulled into the driveway and turned off the engine.

'So you're going for a divorce?' Kate asked.

'You can bet your life I am.'

'And the children?'

He shrugged. 'Not easy. Too many dads divorce their children along with the wife. They start off filled with good intentions, then they miss a week, leave it a month, and end up seeing their kids a couple of times a year. But I'm not that sort of father, so I'm hanging on to my kids.' Again, he raised his shoulders. 'I've had a word with Lois.' He paused. 'Now I believe you're supposed to ask who Lois is.'

Kate grinned. 'OK, I'll play the game. Who is Lois?'

'My lover. There's been nothing between me and Monica since Troy was born. A man has needs.'

'So does a woman,' was her swift response.

Pete grinned. 'I wonder how I knew you were going to say that? Don't start being predictable. Alex loves your unpredictability.'

Kate dug her companion none too gently in the ribs. 'I know what my man likes, thank you muchly. Have you noticed I'm learning to talk Scouse?'

'A bit. But muchly is a Lancashire word.'

'I stand corrected.'

'All right, Mrs Clever Clogs. Come and have a look at my wife's palace.' He went off to collect clothes and toys for his little boy, and she followed him in, wandering around the place on her own, taking her time.

Kate was in the middle of scrutinizing the main bedroom when a pair of hands encircled her waist.

Alex noticed that she didn't flinch; she knew the feel of him, the scent of his body wash, the tempo of his breathing. 'What are you plotting?' he asked.

'Monica,' was her reply. 'Her taste and mine differ, but everything in Merrilocks is laid out for her in the plans. She can live there and make sure the tradesfolk are giving us our money's worth. Monica can be foreman. As long as she's not in jail, that is.'

'She won't go to jail.' Alex scratched his head. 'Are you sure you want her? She frightens me to death at times; she's like one of those small terriers created to nip the heels of cattle all the way to the milking shed.'

'Heelers. Manchester heelers.'

'We had cows round Bolton on the moors.'

Kate nodded pensively just as Pete joined them.

'Did I hear you mention the name of my dear departed?'

'Yes,' they replied simultaneously. 'Kate's giving her a job,' Alex went on. 'She'll be up in Blundellsands frightening plumbers and electricians to death. I'll light a candle for them in church. They're going to need divine intervention.'

'As long as she's not in jail, I'll offer her the job,' Kate announced.

Pete thought about that. 'If you need a plasterer, don't ask me. I won't be available.' He walked to the bedroom door and stopped. 'Who'll wash up? It was either me or the girls here. She never did that sort of job.'

'There's a dishwasher,' Kate told him. 'Ask your wife to contact me on my mobile when she gets back from Spain. She'll be of use to me, and she'll be out of your hair. You have my number. I'll arrange to meet her at the house on Merrilocks Road. If she's in prison, I'll interview her there.'

Alex threw up his hands in despair.

'Bloody women,' Pete muttered.

★ ★ ★

It wasn't far from Saint-Martin-aux-Fleurs to Saint-Martin-de-Fugères, but it felt like ten kilometres on a bike, though the French catered very well for walkers and bikers. There was a track running parallel with the main road, and it had been well laid out for travellers on foot or on pushbikes. England threw the odd narrow lane alongside dual carriageways, but the French did these things so much better.

Max had to return the borrowed bike, pick up the rental car and drive back to Fleurs. Trev's bicycle would be taken apart later, packed in the car with the rest of the camping gear and returned to the hire place in one piece some time later today. That was the theory, anyway. The striking of camp had been done at six in the morning; Max had demolished Trev's last place of abode. Everything was hidden as well as possible, and that included Trev's body.

He missed Trev, missed the complaining, the moaning, the help with day-to-day life in a part of the forest that was visited by very few people. In truth, they hadn't seen a soul since pitching, which was just as well. From time to time, Max stopped and rested, sweat pouring from his brow; France was certainly a few degrees warmer than London. It was May, and temperatures were on the up. Trev, on the other hand, was down.

Max, too, was down. Last night's dream continued to haunt him, and he still saw the dripping wet Trev standing there, asking even now to be taken home. Like most Londoners, the dead man would have chosen to be buried under English rather than French soil. 'Leave me alone, Trev,' he whispered. 'I did the best I could.'

He reached Fugères, and handed in his bike. The area was so seasoned in the art of dealing with visitors that most understood and spoke some English.

Sitting in the hire car, Max pinned his eyes to the police station. 'It's too late,' he whispered. 'And all my papers are false. I'm a crim. I can't prove I didn't murder him. They'd get my real name, and . . . ' There was more to it than that, wasn't there? Deportation. Standing in the dock

201

at the Bailey, twelve people deciding, one judge sentencing . . . Oh, hell, what if Trev's family came looking for him? 'And I've a history with police and courts.'

He drove away. He had things to do.

* * *

The child watched the big man as his car pulled onto the road. Very early this morning, she'd seen him pull a large dolly out of the river, dress it and put it in a hole. Then he'd filled the hole in. That was no way to treat a doll, even if it was big enough to wear frocks in a shop window. She'd run straight back to Grandmère and Grandpère's house for breakfast, because she wasn't allowed to stray. And now she couldn't tell, mustn't tell, because this was the second time she'd come to the woods today, and the woods were on the list of places she was forbidden to visit. But she was so worried about the big dolly.

9

To the great surprise and delight of both parties, Kate and Monica got on like the proverbial house on fire. After the first few minutes of slight awkwardness, they were seated near a coffee table in the multi-functional living area of Kate's house with cups of tea and bourbon biscuits.

'Is it OK if I dip?' Monica asked.

'Dunking is compulsory in any property of mine,' was the serious reply. 'My mother told me it was ill-mannered, so I have perfected the skill over many years.' She waited for a moment. 'So, you didn't get locked up, then?'

Her visitor blushed. 'No. Pete stuck up for me, said I needed to see a doctor. They brought one in, like, and I told him how I get through the days. So I have to go and see somebody at the hospital. What's OCD?'

Kate laughed, then coughed through a mouthful of tea, making an unsightly mess of her blouse. This broke any residual tension.

Once recovered, Kate rose to her feet. 'Follow me,' she said. In the kitchen, she threw open every cupboard door. 'That's OCD, though it's been slightly disordered by workmen. They must be stopped.'

Monica was still mopping tears of laughter from her cheeks. 'My kitchen's like that,' she announced. She sat at the table while Kate righted the sins of tradesmen.

'Can you read scale plans, Monica? I have everything worked out to the last centimetre. I paid a man to draw them up.'

'Can I read plans? I designed and fitted our kitchen myself, apart from heavy worktops, gas and electric. There's not much I can't do when it comes to fixtures, fittings and decorating.'

'Ah, but you'll be the supervisor. You'll live here and keep the men on their toes. I'll show you colour charts and fabrics et cetera later. There'll be a living wage, and you can have a break from recent . . . difficulties. Look. What you did was wrong and rather stupid, but you didn't kill anybody. Don't blush.'

'I love Pete, but I don't know how to show it. I get wound up.'

'And the children?' Kate's tone was gentle.

The shorter woman stared down at the table. 'My mam died when I was young. I think I was walking, but I can't remember. That police doctor said I hadn't got a . . . a template to work with, so I never learnt how to be a mam. Them kids get on me nerves, but if anyone hurt them, I'd swing for 'em.'

Kate reached across and took both Monica's hands. 'I do understand. I've been in a bad situation myself, and I sent Amelia to live with my parents for a while. How I might have managed to park four of them, I've no idea.' She looked into her new friend's eyes and saw pain. 'Monica?'

'What?'

'I trust you. Look at me, please.' She waited until they had achieved eye contact. 'I killed my first husband. He attacked our daughter, so I shot him.'

The woman across the table gasped. 'Bloody hell.'

'Oh yes. I thought I'd married a stockbroker and discovered that he was, in truth, the planning department of a London gang. He beat me several times, but when he turned on Amelia he signed his own death warrant.

'After I shot him I gave police the details of his three confederates — they'd done a big job, so what with what he'd done to Amelia and helping the police with their inquiries, I was found not guilty of murder and discharged. But I had to change my name, send my daughter away once she'd recovered, and escape to Liverpool. You're not the only one who chose the wrong life. But you'll be safe. You have the tradesmen, and a security guard stays every night. Alan does five nights, and his brother covers at weekends.'

Monica's skin paled, and she took a deep breath. 'So even posh people make mistakes, like?'

Kate shrugged. 'Look no further than royalty. I talk what you term 'posh' because my parents do, my school friends did — it was how we were raised. Had I been born elsewhere and into a different family, I'd have spoken differently. We all have to manage the hand we're dealt.'

'It's a bugger, isn't it?'

'It certainly is. Listen, Monica. I'm no expert, but I think you may have something other than OCD. Obsessive compulsive disorder can be part of a bigger picture. Tell me, can you remember whether you felt grim and depressed after giving birth?'

The little woman blinked a few times. 'I was always tired, fed up with life. Couldn't be bothered doing much.'

'And it got worse?'

'I think so. And I cured myself by finding a hobby. It kicked off with magazines that had photos of house interiors in them. I'd cut them out and save them. Once I started making our place nice, I felt cured.'

Kate nodded thoughtfully. 'It was a distraction, darling. Alex had stuff in his childhood that stopped him moving on, too. We know a man called Tim Dyson. He's abroad just now, but when he comes back Alex will talk to him about you — or I will. If post-natal depression isn't nipped in the bud, it can only get worse. My first few months with Amelia were difficult, so I got help. With four children and no treatment, you've never managed to recover. I could be wrong, but Tim will winkle it out one way or another. Agreed?'

Monica nodded furiously. 'You're right, I reckon.' She paused. 'Pete's got another woman, but he doesn't know I know.'

'We all need warm arms to hold us. You're not selfish; you're ill. This house will give you thinking time and a chance to be boss over men.'

'Ooh, I like the sound of that.'

'I thought you might.'

Before they both descended into a new bout of giggling, Kate led her new friend back into the big living/ sleeping/dining area and spread plans on the floor. 'This is flat one, and we're standing in it, so it will be the last to be worked on. There'll be a communal entrance hall with three private doors. Each upper flat, first and second floors, will have its own staircase behind its door.'

Monica was fascinated by detail. 'Them curtains is too long, Kate.'

'Muslin. A puddle of muslin on the right floor can be very effective. It's purely for decoration, because there'll be a blackout blind at the window. I've done some drawings of fireplaces for the upstairs living rooms. There are specialists in Liverpool — architectural antiques. We'll go together to choose.'

Monica bit her lip. 'Are you doing this because you feel sorry for me?'

'Good heavens, no. I went to your house with Pete and saw your work. You know what you're doing.'

'But yours is so much nicer, Kate. Real high class.'

'No, it's neutral. We make a blank canvas with a neat finish, which means very pale grey or the dreaded magnolia with white. If someone wants a purple wall, they can have one, but that's up to them. Skirting boards, ceiling roses and any architraves will stand out in bright white. Kitchens and bathrooms very modern, plain bedrooms and staircases — we're selling. The big selling point will be the fireplaces. Now, they must shine.'

'So you're being faithful — know what I mean? It's Victorian, this house, isn't it?'

'That's right. But if they want modern furniture it will still look good. They can choose a 1950s pink refrigerator, orange cups and those awful green plastic moulded chairs — retro is fine. Victorian buildings are very forgiving as long as you steer away from flock wallpaper and cheap doors.'

Monica was learning, and she was hungry for more. Pete would look after the kids, wouldn't he? For the first time in her life, she might feel useful, valued, appreciated. 'Should I feel guilty about leaving the kids?' she asked.

Kate smiled. 'I'd trust your Pete with a dozen of mine. I'll be buying more houses once I've sold the one in London, so there'll be work for you as long as you need it. But let's see how you get on here first, shall we? Now, on to the more serious stuff. I need a second sugar rush — are there any bourbons left?'

★   ★   ★

Max doubled back all the way to the city of Nevers, where he paid a further month's rental on his hired car. He bought a few essentials, including yesterday's *Daily Express*. He and Trev were in it; photographs, too.

At the tourism office, he was given directions to a campsite on the outskirts where he could pitch his tent. Bed and breakfast in Nevers cost an arm and both legs, so the decision to camp out was automatic. He walked to the quayside, sat down, and read the press article.

It stated that he and Trev were implicated in

208

the recent Hatton Garden heist. While the main players were in jail, these 'known associates' were believed to have been used as lookouts; they were also dealers in the handling and selling of class A drugs and were not to be approached by members of the public. That final statement shocked him. Drugs, yes. Too dangerous to be approached? That was just stupid. The law continued to live up to its reputation, then: it was an ass.

Walking back to the city, the *Express* in his pocket, Max was struck yet again by the cleverness of the French. A blue line painted on the road led visitors to places of interest. A simple yet inspired idea that ensured the area thrived, because sightseers needed to eat and felt compelled to buy souvenirs of the beautiful sites they visited.

Many of the old roads were cobbled; Max was glad he'd got rid of the bike. Bikes, plural, he reminded himself, though he scarcely needed the nudge, because Trev's dead face haunted him almost constantly. Trev would not have appreciated Nevers; no proper pubs, just bars and restaurants fit only for old fogeys and teatime with Mother. The lad had failed to recognize the sheer beauty of this part of the planet.

For Max, the Loire valley was perfect, though he was glad he had started to grow a beard. There were many English here, some as permanent residents, so he must disguise himself as best he could. And being alone might help, since police were looking for two men. Still, he wished he had some company, even if that company moaned and griped all the time.

Oh, yes, this was a clever place. A dense shopping area sat almost on top of the sites where historic buildings and monuments had been planted centuries ago; yet another point was gained by the French. They certainly knew how to do things, how to make them work. Paris was sensible, properly planned, everything radiating from a central point. In comparison, London was just a load of villages sewn together like some oversized quilt.

Wandering around, he found himself in a chapel in the church of St Gildard. The main attraction was the coffin of a nun, St Bernadette, who had died in the nineteenth century. A cordon prevented onlookers from actually touching the glass, but he could get close enough to see that she seemed to be merely asleep. 'Jesus,' he whispered.

The priest standing next to him smiled. 'Yes, she was a friend of Jesus and His mother.'

'Wasn't Bernadette from Lourdes?' Max asked.

'She is safer here. Lourdes pilgrims are sometimes hysterical.'

'Your English is good, Father.'

'Thank you. I worked in London for some years, but I wanted to come home.'

'Can't say I blame you. Now I'm here and just getting to know the place I don't want to leave, but I need work.'

The priest turned his gaze away from the coffin and looked his companion up and down. He took a breath and seemed to come to a swift decision. 'Good. I have work for you.' He blessed himself, and Max copied him, thanking the saint in her glass coffin for yet another miracle. He wondered what he was in for but figured he might as well see where this conversation took him. It wasn't as if he had many alternatives.

Outside, the priest introduced himself as Pierre Dubois. Max responded in kind, offering his new identity as Michael Shipton.

'Where do you stay, Michel?' the cleric wanted to know.

'In a tent, Father.'

'Are you Catholic?'

'No,' Max confessed. 'I just copied what you did in there to be polite.'

'Ah.' The man nodded. 'This is no problem to me. You may call me Pierre, and I give you room at *mon presbytère* — my house. If you prefer life in a tent, put it in my garden. But the work I have you must think of first. We need gardener for all churches. Also, gravedigger.'

Max swallowed audibly. He saw blue-white flesh, an open mouth, clenched fists and curled toes that had relaxed during the laying out. Trev had drowned. Perhaps the cold water had brought him round after the blow to his head, but he had definitely drowned. Water had dribbled from purple lips —

'I am sorry, Michel. You do not wish to dig graves?'

Max pulled himself together. 'I don't mind.' After all, he was experienced, wasn't he?

'*Alors*, you are big, strong man. At first, the French gardeners may not talk to you — it's just

211

the barrier of language. But you and I can talk sometimes in the evenings. I have good wine and beer — what more does a man want?'

At last Max smiled. 'My mates back in London would want pie and mash.'

The cleric laughed. 'I have missed Londoners, and now I have one living in my house, perhaps. Madame Hédouin is my housekeeper, and she is good French cook.'

'No snails,' Max chuckled.

'No frog legs,' Pierre added.

'No pie and mash, or jellied eels, or cockles.' Max counted on his fingers.

'Don't the English eat a lot of curry?' the priest asked.

'Some do, some don't. I'll go and get my tent.'

★   ★   ★

Kate insisted on accompanying me to work today. I told her I don't need supervision, but she wouldn't listen. I sometimes worry about not worrying about that; Pete got fed up with Monica, didn't he? But my girl's different. She torments me constantly, and that's part of the fun. So she's here in the boardroom, messing about with the coffee machine and asking did I buy it from Noah. Her language just now does not qualify as ladylike. Ah, here comes trouble.

In walks Amber Simpson. She's dressed in a suit fit for a garden party at Buckingham Palace. Her makeup is perfect, her hair is perfect, her body is honed to perfection, too. After two steps, she stands still and watches my girl having an unsuccessful battle with the coffee machine.

Amber sits to my left; I am in my CEO's chair at the top of the table.

Kate arrives bearing a tray that holds three suspiciously muddy cups of coffee. She announces that she can't work 'that stupid machine' and parks herself opposite Amber, telling the manager of Chillex that property is always a good investment and she's so pleased that Amber has found somewhere. So far, I am redundant. I decide to let it run. Do I have a choice?

Kate is in full stride. I watch her fine cheekbones, the shine on her dark, dark hair, her mobile hands as she explains how she might help Amber. 'Furniture's expensive,' she says. 'I have a houseful of it in London. My plan is to bring it up here for storage, keep a few things that might do for our house . . . ' she flashes me a bright, white smile, 'and you may pick and choose.' A sip of coffee makes my lover frown. 'Horrible,' she declares.

Amber blinks rapidly. She probably understands that this manipulative woman is attempting to manage her. 'I can pay you something,' she says.

'No.' The tone is firm. 'I'd rather give it to someone who'll treasure it.' Kate lowers her voice as if conveying a seldom spoken and special confidence. 'My first marriage was not good. Give my furniture a happier life, please.'

I feel a bit sorry for Amber.

Kate motors on like a well-tuned Rolls-Royce. 'You and I have similar tastes, I suspect. In your letter, you enthuse about original features, so I know that many of my items would fit your bill marvellously.'

The letter was addressed to me, so Kate has now implied that we keep no secrets.

'My husband will help you with the deposit, we decided.'

We? We decided? This is the first I've heard, I promise. Kate is trouble, but I already knew that.

Amber glances at me, and I simply nod. So far, I've delivered not one syllable. Kate's right. The coffee is bloody ghastly, but I'm enjoying the show.

'I'll take you to see the flats I'm designing if you so wish.'

Oh, yes, Kate; keep friends close, enemies closer. At last, I speak up. 'If you do take Amber to Merrilocks, use my car.' Then I address Amber for the first time. 'Her car's a large Ford boneshaker.'

A flustered Amber finally escapes the deluge of generosity. Meanwhile, Kate and I have something else on our minds.

★ ★ ★

When they reached home, Brian was in the huge garden with six dogs and a lawnmower. Castor and Pollux followed man and machine, while Alex's four ignored them. Brenda rushed to greet her boss and Kate, ticking off the things she needed to remember on her fingers. 'You've two bees out,' she said. 'And Kylie's keeping her baby. Tim phoned and said you've to turn your

214

bloody cell phone on. Does he mean your mobile?'

Alex nodded. 'A couple of weeks abroad, and he's talking American. Don't tell me anything else, Brenda — I've had one hell of a day.'

Kate tried to keep her face straight. Making love on a boardroom table was all well and good, but her back ached and she longed to lie in a hot bath. Even so, she followed her man outside and watched as he donned a glove and picked up bees clinging to the outer framework of their inside world. 'Will they sting?' she asked as the bees walked up his arm. With his sleeves rolled, he was exposing his forearms.

'They know me,' was his reply.

'How many are there?'

'It's hard to do a head count, Kate. They keep buzzing off.' He went through a complicated series of doors and returned his 'girls' to their beloved lavender. She watched in amazement as he changed colour while residents visited him; his white shirt was spotted, and his face was similar.

'He's marvellous, isn't he?'

Kate turned to see Brenda standing next to her. 'Yes. Alex is the most precious man I've ever met.'

'You love him.'

'I do. From the minute I looked into those dark chocolate eyes, I was lost.'

'And he held back?'

'Of course he did, Brenda. It was his coping mechanism.'

'Then I'm glad you understand him. He

doesn't allow many people in. His mother was away with the mixer.'

This was a new one for Kate, and she couldn't help envisioning an enormous Kenwood Chef with whirring blades to which a woman clung in the throes of desperation. 'Oh dear,' she managed.

'Oh dear is right, love. He brought their Susan here once with some of her teddies, but she screamed the place down. The nurse and doctor who came with her had to hold her down and give her an injection. She can't even visit her brother. Stephen very rarely comes back.'

'From Australia?'

Brenda nodded. 'The uncle's a millionaire with no kids, so Stephen will be set up for life. That's why the granddad and grandma left their pile to Alex. Families, eh?'

Kate watched while Alex, now bee-less, exited the honey farm. 'We're both sane,' she told Brenda, 'sane, but scarred. We can't choose our parents, and we can't be responsible for their mistakes. Mine are good people, but the man I married was a nightmare. I chose him. I'm the damned fool in my family.'

'Not this time, queen. You've won the lottery with Alex.'

'I know.'

He joined the two women, as did Castor and Pollux, who were now bored with lawn mowing. 'What are you talking about?' Alex asked.

'I was telling Brenda about our interesting day in the boardroom.'

'Were you, now?' The tone was dry.

216

'She never said nothing about no boardroom.' Brenda grinned.

He awarded his partner a grimace. 'Some situations are best kept secret,' he advised solemnly, 'and you interviewing a member of my staff is one of them.'

'And about what happened afterwards?'

He raised his eyebrows and then stalked into the house.

Kate leant towards Brenda. 'Did you say lottery? Well, perhaps three numbers for a few pounds. Or a lucky dip for next week?'

'Oh, give it up, love. The man's a prince, and well you know it.'

'I do.'

Alex dashed out again. 'Kate, come in. We have to be ready.'

'For what?' But he'd disappeared again. 'Oh, Brenda — what's he up to now?'

'No idea, queen. Just be glad he's not sulking with John Lennon in the inner sanctum. But when Alex says move, we move.' They moved.

'Inner sanctum?' Kate asked as they walked to the house.

'I'll tell you when we've time. Get upstairs and find out what he's up to. Sometimes, he gets excited like a little kid. So you see the lively child, then the dead serious boss of a sizeable empire.'

'I understand.' Kate bent to kiss the forehead of a startled Brenda before running upstairs. She found a dampish Alex running about in circles with a towel wrapped round his waist. 'What are you doing?' she asked.

'Getting dry. Finding socks. Tim's home. You're

going to meet Julia — Where's my new blue shirt?'

'I'll go and ask Brenda.'

'No time, no time. Get in the bath to stop your aches and pains.' He ran to the door. 'Brenda? Where's that brand new blue shirt?'

'In the walk-in wardrobe. I've took all the pins out,' Brenda yelled.

Kate closed the bathroom door and leant against it for a few seconds. The bath was already running; Alex had prepared it for her.

She didn't have time to linger in the sweet-smelling foam. The en suite door was opened by Alex, and his monologue, punctuated by curses, travelled through steam and the running of the telephone shower as she rinsed her hair. Tim and Julia were home. They'd arrived yesterday, but had been a bit jet-lagged. Julia's mother was dead. 'He sent me a lecture on keeping my phone turned on. We're expected at his house, so get a move on, please.'

★   ★   ★

Oh, I hope it didn't show in my face.

Tim is very handsome, though not as beautiful as my man, of course. Alex is, on the whole, a quiet person — almost unassuming, as if he would prefer invisibility. Not with me, though his manner at work or in social situations shows the old 'leave-me-alone' self. With Tim and Julia, Alex remains at ease. These three spent time together years ago when at the University of Liverpool.

The surprise is, Julia is plain. Aside from Elizabeth Taylor eyes, dark blue with a hint of violet, she is by no means pretty; the best adjective might be angular, as she is painfully thin, almost to the point of emaciation. Her cheekbones slice across her face like the blades on a pair of opened scissors, her hair is dull brown, and her mouth is unremarkable. She's flat-chested, though her legs, albeit rather thin, are shapely and long.

They came to the door together hand in hand, with Tim looking as proud as a peacock. This girl is the love of his life; his face glows with joy.

Alex hugs Julia. 'I wouldn't have recognized you,' he says. 'How much have you lost?'

Pain arrives in those lovely eyes. 'Around forty pounds at the last count, I'm afraid. But I'm not ill, I promise. It's just been . . . difficult.'

'She's lost too damned much,' Tim says. 'She kept forgetting to eat. I shall ply her with steak puddings, black puddings and treacle puddings.'

'Cholesterol,' Julia says. She shakes my hand. Her fingers are bony, and I handle them with care. The woman really does have the most amazing eyes. If she regains the weight, she might well be a stunner. I tell her I'm sorry about her mother, and she says it was a blessed release. 'Mom was ready. She wanted to be with Dad.' She has a soft, gentle voice.

In the living room hangs a massive painting of a beautiful town or city. Tim points to it. Julia did that before her father got too ill. She sent it to me years ago and made me promise not to hang it. I kept my word, though the painting was

219

propped against a wall in my bedroom for a very long time. I covered it with cellophane so that I could see it. Isn't she clever?'

My business head is doing sixty miles an hour in a restricted area. 'You must paint more,' I tell her. 'You are fabulous with architecture.'

'Thank you. But it's back to medical school for me.'

I bite back words about talent and how it should pay off, but it's her life, not mine. Inside, I'm screaming about Liverpool's remarkable buildings, but I know I must keep my thoughts to myself. I ask her about the place in the picture.

'Montpelier,' is her reply. 'Wonderful place to grow up in, not heavily populated, very pretty. We lived on the outskirts. Vermont's a lovely state.' She went on to sing the praises of her homeland before insisting that she adored Liverpool. 'And Tim's here.' The arrival of a rosy hue along those honed cheekbones proves that her circulation is in good order, but she's so frail.

'She's not going to college until I can get some meat on her bones,' Tim insists. 'One gust at the Pier Head, and she'll finish up in Speke.'

'Get to the point, honey,' Julia begs.

'OK. Alex, Kate — will you be our witnesses at the wedding?'

Alex delivers that beautiful smile, the one that threatens to alter the pace of my heart. 'You just try and stop us. We'll be there, won't we, princess?'

I nod, hoping and praying that poor Julia will

be closer to her normal self before the big day arrives. This is real, true love, the sort that survives a gap of several years and crosses oceans like seabirds riding thermals in the sky.

Julia invades my thoughts. 'I plan to gain twenty pounds first,' she says.

Tim laughs. 'I'll put suet on the shopping list.' He has relaxed visibly after Alex called me his princess. It hits me then; this man really does care about us. We're more than a pair of damaged people.

Julia smiles. She clearly knows about me. I see in her face every line, every bone made sharp by long-term suffering. I cannot imagine what she has been through, nursing both parents during their slow journeys to the grave. But I notice, too, how she leans on Tim, how her hand never leaves his, and I'm filled with hope for her.

She and I move to the kitchen, leaving the men to talk in private. We're having avocado with smoked salmon, beef with all the trimmings including Yorkshires and, for pudding, Tim's favourite since childhood, rhubarb and custard. I'm normally a chatty person, but this woman is quiet and sad because of her recent loss. 'Is your house sold?' I ask, mentally kicking myself for mentioning the family home.

'We think so. Three offers so far, so we're keeping our fingers crossed.' We sit at the kitchen table while the vegetables take care of themselves. 'Kate?'

'Yes?'

'I don't want to be a doctor.'

I nod. 'Have you told Tim that?'

'Not yet.'

Well, this is an unexpected honour; she confides in me first. 'Then don't be one, Julia. Do you need to work?'

She nods furiously. 'Lord, yes. Not for money, but for . . . '

'For you, for fulfilment, for the person you are.'

She beams at me, and those eyes light up like Christmas. 'Yes.'

We both ponder for a few seconds. 'Art college, then,' I advise her. 'Don't be afraid of disappointing Tim, because he's used to life changes. He often advises his patients to do a U-turn, I gather.'

She lowers chin and voice. 'I can't go through all that again, you see. You understand. As soon as I saw you, I thought you might. But watching people die, hearing them begging for euthanasia — I've been there. I wanted paediatrics, but children die, too. I have watched death for years.'

'Twice,' I say, though she needs no reminding. 'Tim knows you need time to rest and to regain your proper weight. Tell him tonight. He will be one hundred per cent behind you on this, I promise. Look. Take your time. You're about my height and build. I weigh . . . ' I try to calculate from stones to pounds and fail. 'I am five feet nine inches, and I weigh about nine stone or just over. Work it out and aim for that. Exercise helps build muscle, too. When did you last look after you, Julia?'

She tells me she can't remember.

'Be your own carer. Come to the beach with

us and the dogs. Try Chillex — one of Alex's clubs — because they'll help you build your core strength. Go to Formby and hire a horse, start riding again.' I grasp her hand. 'You need to learn how to be young.'

We jump up together to rescue vegetables and park them in the heated trolley. By the time we reach the table with our two plates each of avocado and salmon, I feel as if I've known the girl forever.

She winks at me. 'Tim?'

'What?'

'I'm not going back to medicine.'

'OK.' He doesn't hesitate. 'Put some weight on, and we'll start the baby factory.' He stares at her. 'What?' he repeats.

'Liverpool College of Art,' Julia pronounces.

'Fine,' he says. 'John Lennon went there.' He grins at Alex. 'After he got expelled from Quarry Bank.'

'Lennon was a genius,' my lover snaps back.

Tim will not be routed in his own house. I bite back a smile; this is like watching two hormonal teenagers fighting in a school yard. 'He had half a talent. Without McCartney, he would — '

'Would have been fine. Imagine.'

'Do you still play that dirge once a year?'

'Twice. Birthday and death day. Pass the bread and butter, Kate. I fancy a salmon butty.'

Julia is giggling, and I relax. She was right to return to Liverpool. For her, this city means happiness, God love her. So we are a contented party, the food is excellent, and Julia is going to art classes. This is a perfect evening.

223

Dr Giles Girling enjoyed his work at Alder Hey, yet he couldn't shift his mind off thoughts of Kate Latimer, Owen or Price. On his rare days off, he drove to a lane at the side of Price's house, hoping to catch just a glimpse of the woman who filled his dreams night and day. Twice, he'd seen her in the vast garden with half a dozen assorted dogs. Like an overgrown child, Kate played rough and tumble with the large animals, no fear showing as she fought for a ball or a Frisbee.

Once, he got to talk to her in Williamson Square where she waited for her husband to take her to lunch in the city centre, but he cut the session short in case Alex Price showed up early. Giles had no chance, and he should give up, but obsession had him by the throat, and there was no escape — he was stalking her.

But he found something at last, an interest apart from his research into childhood cancers. He discovered Chillex, one of the Price Partners clubs. It was great. The exercise side was superbly equipped, while the chill-out areas were brilliant. They had good, healthy food for normal people, for vegetarians, for vegans, and for the poor souls who needed gluten free. It was like a nightclub, though open all day and without booze.

There was Chatterbox Chill-out, Library Chill-out, TV Chill-out and Games Chill-out. He looked round, spotted the check-in desk and found a beautiful woman in charge of membership. Well, she wasn't as lovely as Kate, but she was more than simply pretty. 'I'm Giles Girling,' he said.

'Amber Simpson.' She tapped her name badge. 'We offer a free trial for your first session, just to give you the chance to get to know the place and the people who work here — also, feel free to talk to our members. Here's the form. Go to the library area — it's quiet in there. While you fill in your details, I'll find a trainer to do your assessment. Welcome to Chillex, Mr Girling.'

He wasn't a mister yet — he was still a mere doctor, but he didn't put her right. With the form, he found a brochure. They offered sauna, a massage service, hot stones, reflexology, physiotherapy, skin treatments, hair removal, facials, makeup lessons, manicure, pedicure — the list seemed endless. The basic price for a year's membership was low when compared to London facilities, although the list of extras meant more on top, but he could pick and choose whether or when he needed or wanted those treatments.

As he walked back to the reception counter, he watched the body language of Amber Simpson. She straightened her stance as he approached, and a hand raised itself to check on perfect hair. Her lips seemed to have received an extra application of gloss, so she was reacting to his presence. Promising, he thought. 'Here you are.' He placed the form on a counter, and she ran her eyes over it.

'Ah, you're a doctor,' she said, smiling at him.

'For my sins, yes. I'll be a general surgeon one day, though my interest lies in childhood cancers, particularly those originating in the bone marrow. Cancers of the blood.' Was he saying too much? He should keep his cards closer to his chest, perhaps.

Amber closed her eyes for a moment. 'My twin sister died of cancer when we were four,' she said, raising her eyelids. 'Are you at Alder Hey?'

'I am.'

'Then I wish you every success. Here's Drew.'

Drew was a mountain of a man with that very rare very black skin. He looked like a statue carved from an impossibly enormous piece of jet; muscular, flawless and as bald as a coot. Hair might well have spoilt his appearance, because the shine on his skin made him a black god. He led Giles past the small restaurant to the changing rooms. 'I'll wait for you near the treadmills,' he said.

Twenty minutes later, the doctor knew exactly how fit he wasn't. His heart was pumping like a pneumatic drill, and he felt exhausted. 'I'm a wreck,' he managed between gulps of air.

'You're a fit man,' was Drew's reply to that. 'I pushed you hard because I can see you're in good shape. Go back on the mill and walk, because we don't want lactic acid settling in your legs. I've stuck it on its lowest level.' He nodded. 'Get on with it. If you're a wreck, God help the thirty-stoners I have to deal with. Your massage will be free today. It's behind the blue door. If you think I'm pushy, wait till Big Babs starts knocking you about.'

'Big Babs?' Giles asked as he followed instructions.

'One of our masseuses. She's vicious.' Brilliant white teeth were allowed to show, courtesy of a huge smile.

Giles discovered that Drew had not exaggerated, but following the treatment from Big Babs he was walking on air. After a shower, he packed up his sweaty training clothes, dressed and approached the desk once more.

Amber looked up. The doctor was walking towards her. During her break, she had re-fixed her makeup and dealt with one or two wilful strands of hair. He was attractive and had a promising future. Closer to the point, he was single, and a surgeon was paid well. Yes, a doctor would be quite a catch. She flashed him a bright, expectant smile. 'You survived,' she commented.

'Drew accused me of being fit, Amber.' He noticed a slight dilation of pupils when he spoke her name.

'Will you join?' This was a question she had never before asked.

'I think so. The hours at the hospital are not regular, but I'll be here as often as I can manage.'

'I'm glad to hear that. You got Big Babs, then?'

'Yes. It hurt at the time, but she's a miracle-worker.'

'I'll tell her you said that.'

'Thank you.' He walked towards the door, stopped, and returned to the reception desk. 'Might you consider having dinner with me some time?'

'Yes, thank you.' Yes, indeed, she told herself. The ball was in the back of the net, and she could begin her plan to win the game. She would show Mrs Kate Price how well she could do by catching a doctor in her net.

This had been a good day. The flat was hers, and he was hers for the taking; any day with a plan in it was excellent.

10

It's been emotional. I have just stolen a line from Vinnie Jones — in Lock, Stock and Two Smoking Barrels, *I think.*

While we listened to the recording, I held Alex's hand, which went limp occasionally, as if he were responding again to the hypnotist's voice. All that blood, the lawn in his bad dreams turning from green to a muddy brownish red . . .

I stand and switch off the machine. Turning back, I kneel in front of him, and he places his hand on my head, threading his fingers through my cropped curls.

Finally he manages to speak. 'You've heard the nightmare; now, I must give you the real thing.' He pulls me up, and I return to my place next to him on the sofa. 'Aside from Tim Dyson, you'll be the first to know my terrible truth.'

I nod; this is a huge deal for him. Here it comes. I am ready for this. I have always been ready.

★　★　★

It was a bright, white day with a blazing sun so Alex closed the curtains, returned to the sofa, stretched out and placed his head on Kate's lap.

'It wasn't a great marriage,' he began carefully. 'Dad was silent, while Mum was quite the chatterbox when she took us out to parks or to the seaside — as long as he didn't come with us, Mum was great. She was extraordinarily beautiful, often compared to a star called Maureen O'Hara, a big name in old films, round about the middle of last century. Mum had long, wavy hair in a lovely shade of auburn; it hung down her back and shone like satin. I suppose her face was perfect when she was happy, but she was never happy at home.'

Kate stroked his head, gently scraping fingernails against his scalp.

'About once a month, Dad came home slaughtered, too drunk to get his key in the door. The shouting and subsequent arguing always woke me and Stephen. Strangely, I was devoted to Dad. He taught us to ride bikes, play cricket, swim, dive, catch fish, dribble a ball across a field.

'What neither of us knew was that he hit our mother.' Alex felt Kate's legs stiffening. 'Yes, darling, you're not the only one. My mother, anxious not to worry us, never screamed or cried. We found this out only after our father died. The doctor probably broke all the rules by telling my big brother the truth, but the person he was talking about was dead, so perhaps it was OK for him to speak.'

Kate stroked his forehead, found it damp, and patted it dry with a tissue.

'So our mother was quite the stalwart. Then Susan was born. At first, she did what all babies do — she suckled, cried, dirtied her nappy. She was late to walk. One of her legs seemed stiff, and she dragged it about from the hip for a while. Susan didn't speak. Mum's hair started to turn silver in streaks among the glorious auburn. She wore it shorter, and people asked where she got it coloured.'

'Oh, God,' Kate breathed.

'Or Satan,' Alex replied. 'Susan's tantrums began. They were so loud that the noise probably travelled from Darwen Road all the way to Manchester. By the time she was five, my sister was in a residential school for special children. My mother's hair was almost completely silver before she hit forty.'

Kate looked into his eyes. 'He did it?'

'Yes. The man I adored kicked my mother in the belly while she was carrying that baby girl. But Stephen and I didn't know that until later.' This was becoming difficult, yet he planned to motor on regardless. It had to be done. 'Just give me a minute, Kate.'

'Of course.' She kissed a finger and placed it on his mouth.

He managed to pick up where he had left off. 'We boys always had breakfast before our parents sat down for theirs. Dad was self-employed, and could work when he chose, as he had staff. We would go off to school and leave them to it, though we knew the score because of weekends and school holidays. She would sit, then he would place himself opposite her with the *Daily Express* hiding his face. He was a loud, sloppy eater, and the noise made her tense.

'We were not allowed to speak about Susan. He never accompanied Mum on her visits to the school, though we went with her several times.

231

There was very little improvement in our sister until we started with the teddy bears.' He gulped audibly. 'When she smiled, she looked very like our mother. I was afraid of beautiful women after what Mum did.'

'Do you want to stop?'

'No, no. There's just one big course to this meal, so digest it as best you can, sweetheart.'

'I love you.'

'Back at you, kiddo. I got a place at Bolton School, my father's alma mater. I was in my first year, eleven and a half years old, when the unthinkable happened. Another tissue, please, my love.' He sighed while she dried his fevered brow.

'Better?' she asked.

'Yes, thank you.' He visited once again that fateful day. 'I forgot my rugby kit, so was allowed to go home for it straight after assembly. As I got off the bus, I spotted Tim Dyson on the opposite side of the road. He was waiting for the bus back to school after visiting the dentist. Tim was thirteen, older and bigger than I was. He crossed the road and followed me into the house when I told him I would be just a second because all I needed was my sports bag.'

Alex groaned. 'My parents were still having breakfast. My mother didn't notice me. She was concentrating on the back page of Dad's newspaper, her mind clearly focused on what . . . what she knew she must do.' He swallowed again.

'I'm here,' Kate whispered. 'I'll always be here.'

'She took the Sunday carving knife, stood, pushed back her chair very quietly and thrust the weapon through the *Daily Express* and into my father's chest. I heard later that she used enough force to skewer him to his chair.

'The blood poured and spurted. She pulled in her own chair, sat back down, and continued to eat her toast. I couldn't move. Tim stood behind me, trying to shift me. I can hear him to this day; his speech was fuzzy because of the dentist's anaesthetic. He finally managed to drag me out to the hallway.

'We watched while Mum carried the cat upstairs. A bedroom door closed. It made no sense at the time — I can only suppose that she didn't want to leave her pet in the company of a corpse. She went into the bathroom and I heard a toothbrush scraping across her teeth, heard her spitting out the toothpaste. Water ran; she was washing her hands and face.

'Finally Tim got me out to our front garden, pushed me down on the grass and sat on me. I was trapped. The front door was wide open, and we watched her at the hall stand. She put on a bit of makeup, donned her best hat and coat, picked up her gloves and her handbag, and walked down to the gate. If you can believe it, she still hadn't seen us.'

'She was in shock, Alex.'

'As was I . . . as was Tim. I remember wondering why she'd chosen her best outdoor clothes on a weekday. They were usually reserved for church or for special outings, though there were very few of those. Tim allowed me to stand

233

and ordered me not to return to the house. We watched as she walked into the little police station on the corner across the road. It's no longer there.'

'I think she had tunnel vision that day, Alex.'

He sighed heavily. 'My father was dead, of course. The place swarmed with police and forensics people. Tim and I had to make statements.'

'Oh, Alex.'

'She killed him because of Susan. As far as he was concerned his daughter was already dead, because she wasn't fit for purpose.'

'And your mother had no gun, of course. Can't you see that I did the same but more suddenly? I killed Jim so that he could never, ever hurt my baby again. The anger in your mother grew until she could contain it no longer. He virtually killed your sister, just as my husband almost killed his own daughter. We both carry the same memory. That'll be why we're drawn to each other.'

'Damaged people,' he whispered.

'To hell with that. We're the two pieces that complete the jigsaw. What happened to you after that terrible day?'

He told her about his paternal grandparents and about his mother's slide towards insanity. 'I went home to Mum at weekends, but the place became uninhabitable. Stephen didn't seem to care about the conditions; he stayed with Mum, though he was out at work during the day. But an uncle arrived from Australia and managed to get permission to take Stephen over there. My brother was sixteen by then and could speak for himself. So our mother lost all three of her children.

'She never cleaned, seldom ate, and her personal hygiene was appalling. My grandparents got help, though that never worked out, since no cleaner would stay for more than a few days. After a while, I even gave up trying to start a conversation with her. Eventually, I was forbidden to sleep there any more, and one of my grandparents took me to visit her once a week. It was a nightmare. In the end, my mother committed suicide. She had no reason to continue living.'

Alex sat up and clung to Kate.

'Tim stuck by my side all the way through school until he left. Other boys started making comments about our relationship as the years passed, but that didn't bother either of us. He took good care of me, and I was grateful, and I remain grateful. Of course, the name-callers backed off when prefects told them to stop. It was and is a good school; bullying doesn't go ignored.'

She realized after a moment or two that her face was wet, and she wasn't crying. The hot baptism of tears poured down her face, and she simply let it happen, because he had to allow the pain to pour out; he shared it with her, and she felt privileged. When the door opened, she didn't even look to see who was there. 'Not now,' she ordered, her tone quite sharp.

The door closed softly. Holding him gently, she allowed the child to grieve, hoping that this catharsis would allow the man to let go of things he could not change. The only words she spoke were 'I love you'.

When the weeping stopped, she forced him to lie down and waited until he slept. Now, she could do her own crying.

In the kitchen, she clung to tiny Mrs Bee and allowed her heart to break. 'Bloody life,' she sobbed. 'Why do terrible things happen to good people?'

'Oh, love, has he told you all of it? Has he had the sense to let the truth out?'

Kate nodded. She was running out of words and crying too hard to say much anyway.

'Sorry I disturbed you before. See, I know just bits, and I don't want to learn any more bits. He loves the bones of you — you do know that, don't you?'

Again, the taller woman nodded.

Brenda swallowed hard. 'Go on holiday, queen. Take him to France and pick up your little girl. Alex likes fishing, and they live near a river, didn't you say? For God's sake, start looking after yourselves for a change.'

Another nod.

'See, I'll make you a cuppa. Get yourself sat down and try to take your mind off it. Where's Alex?'

'I'm here.' He was standing in the doorway. 'Hello, Other Mother. Kate, don't cry for me.'

'Argentina,' Kate managed.

He shook his head. 'Always the last word.'

'Too bloody right,' Brenda told him. 'Just look at the pair of you, both been bloody whingeing.

I've got madam upstairs knitting for her baby, keeps running down for me to sort her dropped stitches. My Brian's got bellyache, and he's blaming my potato hash. I ate the same and there's nothing wrong with me. Them flaming dogs have took his other work boot, but he reckons they might as well eat the pair, so thank God Bolognese sauce looks after itself, or I'd be up the pole with a nice fireman.'

She stared at Alex, then at Kate. 'That's all I need, isn't it? You two getting the historicals. There's not much to laugh about, anyway. Oh, Monica was on the phone saying there's a nice Victorian fireplace for sale up South-port and Kate might like to see it. Sit down, Alex. You cast a long shadow.'

'She's gone poetical,' Alex grumbled as he joined Kate at the little breakfast table. 'It doesn't happen often, but she always makes a meal of it. And you've been crying,' he accused his beloved.

Brenda continued. 'Pour your tears on a bright red rose, then see how your garden grows.'

He sighed. 'And the poet was?'

'Me,' the bustling keeper of the house answered. 'I made it up.'

'Write it down,' Kate cried.

'Don't encourage her,' was Alex's response. 'I don't fancy eating burnt Bolognese while my housekeeper goes all Walter de la Mere. Come on, let's take the dogs up the coast and let them pee on Gormley's men.'

When they had left, it was Brenda's turn to cry, but her tears didn't last long. Pete would be back soon with little Troy, and when it came to household staff, Brenda and Brian were the deliberate best. Alex's problems would be kept safe, as would the sauce. She extinguished the burner and washed teacups and saucers before peeling two enormous baking apples. Crosby beach would make them hungry, and she would do a crumble with fruit from his garden. That always cheered him up.

★ ★ ★

Max had gone strange. He knew he'd gone strange, though he seemed unable to rectify the situation. When he wasn't gardening or digging graves or filling them in, he spent some of his free time in the chapel with St Bernadette. A feeling of peace enveloped him as he prayed to her in his head. He asked for forgiveness, begging her to intercede on his behalf, because he wasn't the worst man in the world; nor was he the best.

After coming clean about drugs and keeping watch while the big four burgled houses and robbed shops, he informed the dead nun about Trev's accident and burial. He was terrified of being accused of murder, and he told her that, too. Trev hadn't wanted to stay in France. Trev had wanted to go home, and he wouldn't rest easy under foreign soil. It haunted him that Trev's wishes remained unfulfilled.

Father Pierre Dubois often stood at the back of the chapel, anxious not to be seen by his new English friend. Something was bothering Michel.

Some of the other gardeners had commented about his size and started to call him Max because of it, which had made the man very uneasy indeed. But it was more than being uncomfortable with a nickname. Something had to be done about this.

While Max blessed himself, the priest went outside and waited for him. It was time to talk.

The two men walked together in the direction of Pierre's house. 'You spend much time with our little nun.'

Max shrugged. 'It's peaceful in there. She's peaceful. I feel calmer when I've been inside and talked to her. I don't do it out loud — I just talk to her in my head. See, you Catholics believe that saints are close to God, so she can talk to God for me, can't she? I've never been a religious man, so it's just somewhere I go when I'm on a break.'

'You are troubled, my friend.'

Max produced a hollow laugh. 'Aren't we all? Wars all over the place, poverty, kids going blind or dying because they drink bad water. We've got climate change, melting ice-caps, polar bears eating their own young. And it's us what's done all that, Pierre. We got a beautiful planet and fucked it up. Oh, sorry. I should watch my language, yes?'

'Words are no problem for me. Let us sit.'

They claimed two chairs at a pavement table outside a cafe. Pierre ordered coffee and two pastries, while Max did his best not to feel embarrassed.

'Now,' Pierre began when the waiter had left,

'we begin to look at Bernadette, yes? I explain our little saint for you. There are miracles at Lourdes for people with physical illness. Is it possible that she reaches out now to you, on behalf of the Virgin Mary, to offer a cure for your worries?'

Max raised his shoulders. 'So she pulls me towards the chapel?'

'She may. You see, she was simple peasant girl with no education. She saw the vision, and people laugh at her. So one day, she told the Lady that no one took it serious. And the Virgin Mary said, 'I am the Immaculate Conception.' Bernadette did not know such language. Only then did people start believe her, and the miracles began after a while. Now, she calls to you in your heart.'

Max wasn't sure that he wanted anything or anyone calling to him in his heart. It was all crazy; even as a kid, when sent to Sunday school, he went instead to play football or marbles with other boys who truanted.

'Do not be afraid,' Pierre said. 'You will come to where you are going naturally, and I will help you along the way. I have some books in English that may guide you on the journey of the spirit. Do not fight this, *mon ami*. Some things happen outside us, but reach the inside. We lose the power to control our thoughts and behaviour, but this is will of God, of Jesus's Holy Mother, too. You have been invaded, Michel.'

'So I'm an occupied country? Like France in the war? Maybe I'm waiting for the Yanks to turn up.'

240

Pierre smiled. '*Oui.*'

'Why is that funny, Pierre?'

'My family. Resistance in Paris. They were very . . . what is word? Very casual when they put grenades in German vehicles. The tales that travelled through the house were funny and tragic. Is enough to say the family Dubois made some difference, helped English who came down in parachute, made life less easy for army of enemy.'

'He was a mad bastard, that Hitler. Why did a big country like Germany follow him? They can't all have believed in what he was preaching, could they? Some must have known he was mental.'

'Yes, he was ill inside the head, but Germany was desperate before he came to lead. Also, they did as told for fear of death. But this no longer a problem. We think now about your troubles. Eat your pastry, then we go home.'

Late that evening, Max received his first blessing from a priest of the Catholic faith. He was also given a special rosary that had been blessed by Pius XII, who had been Pope during the war. Pierre told him not to use it for prayer until he was ready, but to handle it as Arabs did their worry beads.

Max lay in the attic bed, counting his sins along the beads. He had many sins, too many for one decade. Then he found the single bead that separated each run of ten. On every one of these separate wooden globes, he prayed for Trev's soul. It seemed the right thing to do.

★   ★   ★

241

Monica was in a tizz. Kate was on her way with Kylie, Troy and some knitting patterns. 'I've never been no good at knitting,' she mumbled under her breath. 'Never been no good at nothing apart from tarting up houses.' Then she remembered that she knew how to crochet, because an old neighbour had taught her down the Dingle when she was nine. Crochet patterns would be the answer.

She took the ready cake mix, threw it in a bowl with egg and milk, then rattled it about a bit till it looked right. Then, the mixture got divided and shovelled into the bun tins, and she stuck the lot in the oven. Two of her kids were coming, and they would have fairy cakes. The icing was in the fridge, ready made by somebody else, but she squeezed it into one of Kate's proper icing bags. 'Why did I buy this stuff?' she asked the empty room. It was because she knew she was going to see the kids again, she supposed.

After dolling herself up a bit, she sat and waited. Who was looking after Britney and Chelsea? Ooh, she must hide the evidence. When the cake mix box was in the bin, she waited again. The muslin. Where had she put the muslin? Yes, yes, it was on the desk in the big everything room. She hoped that Kate would agree with her choice, because Monica had instincts about such matters. The cakes were done; she set them to cool on the windowsill. Only now, in the absence of her offspring, was she beginning to understand how hard a real mother and housewife worked. 'I avoided my duty,' she whispered. 'I must see that psy . . . psy . . . person Kate's been hammering on about.'

She heard a key in the door, and Troy shouted something unintelligible. Then he flew up the hall and through the door, a smile lighting up his face when he saw Monica. 'Mama,' he shrieked.

Tears threatened, but she held them back; she didn't know why she wanted to cry, anyway.

Kylie arrived. 'Hello, Mam. You all right?'

'Yes, I'm fine, princess. Come on, we'll ice our fairy cakes.'

Kylie did her best with the piping on warm cakes, but Troy, over-excited, threw hundreds and thousands everywhere, and Monica shrieked with laughter. Was this what she had missed while tiling walls and painting ceilings?

Kate entered the danger zone. 'This is a fine mess for somebody with OCD,' she said, giggles fracturing the words.

'Mam, he's got them silver ball things now,' Kylie cried.

Monica relieved her son of the silver balls and handed him some chocolate bits.

Kate approached the table. 'There's more topping than cake, Monica. They'll have their work cut out getting their teeth through that lot.'

The two women left Kylie in charge of the wrecked kitchen. Kate mentioned the fireplace in Southport, but Monica said it was sold. 'I want to show you this sample of muslin. It's plain white, but with a stripe in a slightly thicker texture. I thought it would suit Victoriana.'

Kate agreed. 'Well done, you. I see we're on the same page.'

Monica seemed to grow another inch on her abbreviated body. She was on the same page as somebody posh what talked proper. She was as good as any man when it came to sorting out these new flats.

'How are the trades coping?' Kate asked.

'Fine. With me having a foot up their arses, they shift like buggery. The man on the floor had to take wood back.'

'On the floor?'

'Replacing the floorboards upstairs. You said light oak, but he brought some stained rubbish, so I nearly sacked him on the spot. He's had one verbal warning, I think they call it, and he'll get another if he doesn't show some sense and shape up to the job. After two verbals, it's a written red card and cheerio, bog off and find a fool to work for.'

Kate laughed. 'I see you have everything in hand.'

'No, I told you. I keep a foot up their idle arses. We'd have been better off with Poles. Don't look like you don't understand me — I mean Polish people. They put twice the hours in for half the price, and they're usually good. I had Poles fitting my marble worktops in our back kitchen. Apart from ten minutes drinking black tea and eating some funny-looking sausages, they stuck to the job. It's true — you can't beat a Pole.'

'No, it would be silly to punch a pole.'

'Stop it, Kate. I'm going back to the kids.' But she halted and turned before reaching the door to the kitchen. 'Kate?'

'What?'

'She's keeping the baby, then? Our Kylie, I mean.'

'Yes. She believes abortion is murder.'

'Do you?'

Kate thought about that. 'I couldn't do it myself, but I've nothing against women who think it's right for them. And Kylie is a determined young woman.'

Monica nodded. 'Takes after me.' She left the room to clear up hundreds and thousands, silver balls and chocolate bits, but when she got to the kitchen she found that Kylie had cleaned up everything apart from Troy.

'I don't know where to start with him,' Kylie grumbled. 'It's in his hair, all over his legs and arms — he's a walking cup cake.'

Monica shook her head. 'No, he's a fairy cake.'

Kylie laughed. 'He's too young to be a fairy boy.'

'Kate says cup cakes are a Yankee thing, and there's enough Americanisms in the Oxford dictionary.' Oh yes, she was learning from Kate. 'I'll stick him in the bath. Have you any spare clothes for him?'

Kylie nodded. 'I always have spares. That's one of the things you do when you take a young child out everyday.'

The two females stared at each other.

'Was I that bad of a mother?' Monica asked.

'Yes, you were. You were bloody terrible. But the truth is, we still love you and you're wanted back home.'

Monica explained about the person she had to

see. 'It might have started off hormonal — you know, after having babies. I'll get sorted, but I want a job as well. Kate says you can all come here when you like. We can get a travel cot for Troy, and I have a massive bed big enough for you three girls. I don't mind sleeping on the couch. Weekends, I mean.'

Kylie wasn't too sure about that. 'We'll see about it. Dad wants Britney and Chelsea to stay in the house they're used to, and Troy lives with me.'

Monica picked up her son and took him to the bathroom. 'You've grown,' she grumbled playfully, 'and your hair's full of icing.'

He missed the meaning. 'Sing,' he ordered. 'Mama sing.'

She stripped off her clothes and got into the shower with him. She sang, 'If you're happy and you know it wash your hair,' thereby making a game of the cleansing of Troy. She changed 'hair' to legs, arms, belly, bum and willy until her only son shone with cleanliness. It was fun; she had missed all the fun by getting Pete or Kylie to bathe this sweet child.

'I'm sorry,' she told him.

'Sowwy,' was his reply.

With herself in a robe and Troy swathed in a towel, Monica returned to the kitchen. She handed the infant to Kylie, returned to the bathroom and picked up her own clothes and Troy's. 'These will be dry enough to take home with you. Kate has a washer-dryer — it does both jobs.'

As she pushed the laundry into the drum, Monica realized that she had enjoyed this time with two of her children. 'It won't be forever,' she told her eldest. 'Just till the man helps me get my head straight. I can still keep a job with Kate, and we can hang on to the childminder your dad got, so don't be thinking I'm not coming back.' As long as divorce didn't happen, of course.

Kylie pulled on the little boy's T-shirt. 'There you are, kid, all done.'

'Awdun,' Troy said.

Monica looked at them pensively. 'Sometimes, you have to stand away from something so you can see it proper. Like a diamond in a jeweller's window, I suppose. You need to put yourself in the perfect place to see all the colours bouncing off. I'm not well, our Kylie, and that's the bottom line, as Kate would say.' She paused. 'You're keeping the baby?'

'Yes, I am.'

'What about school?'

'It's OK, cos Alex has got me some tutors.'

Monica managed a smile. 'I'll be ready before the baby comes, I hope.'

Kylie gave Troy a few toys to play with. 'What about the neighbours, Mam?'

'It'll all be right, I promise. A house is a house, but a home is people.' She turned and saw Pete in the doorway. 'Hello, stranger,' she said shyly.

He smiled. It seemed that his nuisance of a wife might be trying to come to her senses, though it was odd to find her in a bathrobe during the day.

'I had to shower Troy,' she explained. 'We baked fairy cakes and he spread them about a bit. Make a cup of tea while I get dressed and his

247

clothes dry in the machine.' She fled, found something to wear, and returned to the bath-room. Was he still going for a divorce?

She arrived again in the kitchen. 'I'm seeing somebody about my nerves,' she told her husband. 'I want to get right and be a mam for these kids and a grandma for whatever our Kylie brings home.' She glanced at Troy. 'Another lad would be great, but we'll take what we get, eh, Kylie?'

Kylie burst into tears.

For the first time in years, Monica held her weeping daughter. 'Stop it, love. It's me what's been at fault, not you. Let me try — give me time. Tim, he's called. Rodney Street.' She looked at Pete. 'Where's Alex?' she asked.

'On the beach with six dogs, four bottles of water, three dishes and a pile of shit bags. He forgot the partridge in a pear tree.'

Kate entered the kitchen. 'Monica, about tiles for the bathrooms . . . ' She stopped when she saw what was happening. 'Kylie, calm down. It's too early to wet the baby's head.'

The girl stopped crying and started laughing.

'Don't be getting hysterical,' Monica said.

Pete gazed at her. If he could get her back the way she used to be, there'd be no need for divorce, no need for Lois. Lois was a great girl, but his family came first. There was a chance. He would cling to that chance and the hope that accompanied it.

★ ★ ★

Amber was living with Kate Price's furniture, and she couldn't quite manage to mind about that. The flat was beyond gorgeous; it looked like something out of a glossy magazine.

She lingered in her bedroom and looked at a four-poster draped in muslin tied at each corner, ancient wardrobes and chests of drawers, silk rugs, velvet curtains, a chaise longue, a group of twelve cameos on a wall. This was what she had always deserved, though she would swap everything without hesitation for a life with Alex Price as its pivotal point.

She didn't seem able to stop thinking about him. He was a mystery, a quiet man who had always been aloof. Until now, until the woman named Kate had stepped into his life. He was louder, happier, and Kate had changed him.

'It's not going to happen,' she reminded herself as she closed the bedroom door and entered the living space. It still took her breath away and, knowing that her sugar was low, Amber grabbed her weekend Milky Way from the fridge. Even the kitchen screamed Kate, as it was filled with expensive pots, pans and plates on a rack installed by a carpenter. They were all different and precious, and a very special one owned shallow cups in a circle; these circles were for oysters. Amber Simpson was now in the oyster class, though she had no intention of consuming seafood.

The living room had been two large bedrooms, which fact was announced by an RSJ across its centre. The area was massive, at least thirty-six feet long and sixteen wide. The end nearest the kitchen was for dining. A circular table stood on a massive central support with clawed feet, and there were six chairs, four of which sat at the table, while two carvers stood guard, one at each end of a Victorian dresser with drawers, cubbyholes, secret sections and a huge mirror.

The rest was a fabulous mixture of yesterday and today, but it worked. A display cabinet from the 1930s held china and crystal, all pieces donated by Madam Price, of course. Two bookcases, a piano, a bureau and Amber's own distressed coffee table completed the hard furnishings, and all the modern seating was in black and grey with red and silver cushions. Yes, even the cushions had been a gift from the woman she both envied and hated.

'The rugs and curtains are mine,' she reassured herself. 'But I have to say Mrs Price has good taste.'

She sat in an armchair. Rumour had it that Mr and Mrs Price had been carrying on in the boardroom as soon as Amber had left. Oonagh Murphy had been full of it. 'They were chasing each other round the room. Then it went quiet, so I think they were having sex.'

Amber had seen neither of them again until summoned to a storage unit in Liverpool about two weeks after the meeting. Mrs Price had affixed red spots to the items she wanted to keep — mostly small things like a Victorian writing slope, some prints, and a hexagonal sewing box on three legs. 'The rest is yours, so take what you like and I'll sell the rest.'

Thus Amber had acquired these riches. Dr Giles would love it, she supposed. Tonight was the night; he was coming for supper and would probably stay for breakfast. Did she want him? The truth was that she wasn't sure, but, having offloaded her virginity in her early teens, she was no shrinking violet. She couldn't have Alex Price, so she would take the next best thing. The next best thing seemed to be in love with Kate Price, so they had something in common, didn't they?

It was a daft situation. Giles had revealed he knew Kate when they'd met again at the club and was clearly crazy about her, while Amber's need for Alex lingered even now, long after he had pledged himself at the altar of some other female. Perhaps they could comfort one another, Amber and Giles. Oh well, this wasn't getting supper on, was it?

There would be no pudding; she had explained that to him. If he needed to end the meal on a sweet note, there was ice cream in the freezer. 'And I'm tasty enough to be afters,' she told herself aloud in the kitchen. Spanish omelette and a good green salad after a starter of homemade soup should be sufficient for a body-conscious doctor. After supper, it would be anybody's game.

As long as she was in charge, of course.

★   ★   ★

Père Pierre Dubois came home at three in the morning after ministering extreme unction to a

251

man who had reached his century two years earlier. People who lived alongside the glorious Loire had a tendency towards longevity, and even now, at so great an age, the frail soul had lingered at the gateway for hours.

The priest kissed the stole and put it away with the rest of his vestments. After swallowing a mouthful of single Scotch whisky, he went into the hallway, locked the door, and was preparing to go upstairs when a loud crash from two floors up startled him. 'Michel?' he called as he ascended the first flight. There was no reply. Was the man ill, or worse? Should he go back down for stole and oils?

The second flight was steeper, more difficult than the first for a priest in his fifties, one whose name had been put forward on a list for deputy bishop. He didn't want to be a bishop; he preferred to work at grass roots level where real people lived, and just at this moment he needed his English friend to be alive and unhurt.

Max was on the floor, eyes wide open, but unresponsive.

'Michel?'

There was no reaction.

Pierre knelt on the floor. 'Please wake, my friend.'

The man on the floor began to speak, but not to him. 'We never did the kidnap. Papers said they found the stuff. I didn't kill him. You know that, Bernadette.' After these few words, the rest was mumbled nonsense.

The man of God blessed himself and his guest, who was talking gibberish to the saint.

'She is trying to help you, *mon ami*. Unburden yourself and let her offer you comfort. When you are ready, you will come to me and I, too, will hear your worries.' Taking his rosary from a pocket, he began the first decade. He offered his prayers to Bernadette, who would put them in the hands of the Blessed Trinity and the mother of Jesus Christ.

'What happened?' asked the large man on the floor.

Startled again, the priest opened his eyes and looked at Max. 'You fell from the bed but did not wake. Is your head sore?'

'No. I had a dream.'

'Yes, you were talking.'

Max sat up, stood, and placed himself on a bedside chair. 'She woke.'

'Our little nun?'

'Yes. She floated towards me and talked in French. I've no idea what she was going on about, but she made me feel better. She was carrying a baby and pointing at me. About three times she said something like 'say twa''.

'*C'est toi* means this is you in your innocence. I think she tells you to be as innocent as you were as a baby. Bernadette has hope for you. See? She comes not to priest, cardinal, or Pope; she comes to you, a man who works the soil and digs graves. She is of the people and for the people.'

'You make her sound like a communist.'

Pierre laughed. 'Communism is . . . socialism *parfait* — perfect. But it doesn't work, because people in charge take money and hide it for the

253

day when they are no longer in power. Humanity is frail and quick to sin.'

'No need to tell me that. You could paper this room with a list of everything I've done wrong.'

'You have remorse. You will repent — this I am sure.'

'Glad you are. Have we any bread?'

Pierre nodded.

'Right, I'm going down to make some toast. Talking to a dead nun makes me hungry. It's hard work when they speak in French.' He stood and left the room.

Pierre scratched his head. Too tired for complicated thought, he remained sure of just one thing. Michel was going to be baptised a Catholic.

11

Tim Dyson fell in love with Monica as soon as she walked into his Rodney Street office. She greeted him with a lengthy monologue on the subject of chairs in the waiting room, which items she termed both ugly and uncomfortable. This complaint drifted into another, because his decor was all wrong. 'It's boring,' she advised him. 'You haven't got no vocal point in here or out there.' She jerked a thumb in the direction of his waiting room.

'What would you suggest as vocal points?' he asked, stressing 'vocal'.

She blinked several times, as she suspected that he was taking the piss. 'A bit of colour. Paintings over the fireplaces, a proper table in the waiting room with an unfinished jigsaw on it, something for people to do.'

'I could open a poker school, I suppose.'

'Don't talk soft. Them what's addicted to gambling would never go home. Don't be taking the wee-wee out of me, because I'm fit for you, lad. I might talk Scouse, but I'm an expert when it comes to things like decorating. I mean, look at these bloody curtains. As cheerful as a funeral in the rain.'

He laughed.

'What's funny?' Monica demanded to know. 'I work for Kate, so she trusts me. She knows I know what's what.'

'And what is what, Monica? Let's get down to business.'

She lowered her chin and pondered. 'There's something wrong with me. I'm a terrible mother. I'd rather paint or do a bit of tiling. I hate grouting, though.'

'Normal so far,' he told her. 'Most sensible people avoid grouting.'

'And most sensible women don't refuse to listen to a pregnant daughter, take another two girls to Spain and leave a two-year-old baby in his cot till his dad comes home.' She blinked again; her eyes were rather damp.

'I agree. Which is why I'd like to make an appointment for haematology at the Royal. Let's have a look at your blood and see what we can find. I don't believe you have anaemia, because you live up ladders, so you seem strong enough. This could be hormonal. HRT might be part of the answer.'

Monica folded her arms.

Recognizing this action as self-protection, he awaited onslaught.

'I'm not having a heart attack, not for nobody.'

'It would be a mini dose.'

'I don't care if it's a do-si-dose in country dancing, I don't want it.'

Tim managed not to grin. 'Do you still have sex with your husband?'

She gave him a stare that conveyed a very rude message.

'Well? Come on, Monica, tell me the truth. This can work as long as you stop hiding cracks behind wallpaper. Do you have sex with your husband?'

'No. He uses another woman for that. Lois,

she's called — I check his phone, you see. There was even a photo what he's deleted. All teeth and tits, she is, and her roots needed doing — about two inches were dark brown.'

'So which came first, then? Was it the chicken or the egg?'

She tilted her head to one side. 'For an educated bloke, you don't half talk some shit, shite and sugar.'

'I'm qualified in all three disciplines. Well? Sex?'

'Not since Troy.'

'The baby you left behind.'

'Yes.'

'So the egg came first — your baby boy. How were you after delivering him? Sad, tired, weak? Not interested in life?'

She nodded. 'Looking back, I was bad after Kylie, worse after Britney, screaming after Chelsea and . . . and angry after Troy. When I got brought back from Barcelona with my middle two, the police doctor said I had no pattern to follow because me mam died when I was little. Can it be that?'

He pondered. 'It might be. If you've had post-partum depression for fourteen years, that's nothing to joke about. Tell me, do you lose self-control?'

'Erm . . . not really. I just get on with what I'm doing.'

Tim walked round the desk and perched on the edge of it. He liked this woman. 'You cook for your family?'

'Yes.'

'Who puts the baby to bed?'

'My husband or our Kylie.'

'Never you?'

'Sometimes, like when everybody's out or doing homework.'

He looked at the floor and decided to go for broke. 'You've left Pete. You ran out on Troy and Kylie ran away from you. Your little boy is living with your pregnant fourteen-year-old and Pete's getting help at home. Am I right so far?'

'Stop it.'

'You're living in Kate's house and ordering men about.'

'All right, all bloody right.'

He gave her a broad smile. 'Monica, the soft-as-shit lefty psychologists would say you're finding yourself, and there may even be something in that. But all I know is this — you're a good and gifted woman whose communication skills could use work, but you'll get there. You married too young and had too many kids. So you looked past them and distracted yourself. Perhaps there's more to it, but we'll deal with that possibility another day. One last word — Pete.'

'What about him?'

'He doesn't want Lois, love. He wants you. Pete wants the ordinary life with his family around him.'

Monica burst out laughing. 'He wants the ordinary life when he wears a frock, a load of makeup and high heels?'

'That's his job, *his* talent. But the child-minder's a good idea.'

'Is she?'

'Yes, she is. You need to do some courses on design and all that stuff. Get qualifications on paper. Stick with Kate — she's the best. So. Blood tests, have dates with your husband, get used to the kids. See this job through for Kate, have a family dinner at weekends, take the young girls and Troy to the beach — it's not rocket science.'

'Are you qualified in that, too?'

'Of course. I'll see you in two weeks, then. You'll get a letter about the blood tests. We need to look at your endocrine system, too.'

'Eh?'

'Glands. Go on with you. Start enjoying life, Monica. But remember you have a family and you are missed. And loved.'

'Yes, sir.' She picked up her bag. 'How many Our Fathers and Hail Marys do I have to say?'

'Bugger off. I may allow you to improve my decor when you have time. Now, go home.'

She did as she was told.

Tim sat smiling to himself; he was looking forward to working with Monica.

★   ★   ★

I wake.

We're knotted together like a child's shoelace before said child has learnt to do the job properly. I always wake before he does, so I get the chance to look at him properly. Alex is the most beautiful creature on God's earth. That dark promise of beard has appeared, and his lips are slightly parted. Soon, his eyes will open; I

259

can tell that from the change in his breathing and some movement behind the eyelids. He's dreaming.

Since the hypnotist did his job, there have been no nightmares. My man used to shout and kick during the night. Occasionally, when waking him was difficult, it was like going eight rounds with a heavyweight wrestler, but Alex was asleep and didn't know what he was doing. Now he's more relaxed, since he told me his terrible truth.

We'll be going soon to visit my parents and to introduce Alex to Amelia. Luckily, she remembers nothing of the night when her father almost killed her, so she displays no fear of men. She knows her daddy's dead, and I've kept some photographs of him and one with the pair of them sitting on the front steps of my London house. I'll give her some of the truth when she's much, much older. For now, the story goes, 'You fell and banged your head, and the doctors had to look inside to make you better. Don't be sad. Your hair will come back.' And yes, it's growing well. The poor child's under guard because of Jim's missing minions, but she'll be home soon.

★   ★   ★

Amber Simpson was a strange girl. After several dates, Giles decided that while she was ace in bed, she spent the rest of the time talking about her job, her prospects, her ambitions, herself. Other than those subjects, conversation was centred on Alex Price and what a wonderful employer he was. She was selfish, determined and cold except when under the covers of her bed. Amber stressed the fact that this bed had not come from Mrs Price. He knew she was lying. The item was an antique four-poster, possibly French and definitely out of reach of Amber's limited means.

It took a while, but he found himself telling her more about Kate and the time she had spent with him after her daughter's 'accident'. While keeping quiet about small details like the fact that Kate Latimer had shot her husband, he admitted that he had grown fond of the woman, and that she'd suddenly moved away to Liverpool.

They were at Amber's table having breakfast in the flat, Amber's new home which was filled by furniture she said she had bought from Kate. So he was sitting at Kate's table, on Kate's chair, was looking at Kate's Victorian dresser.

'You loved her,' she accused.

'I'm not sure,' was his reply. 'She spent weeks in the ward while Amelia recovered, so yes, we became friends — '

'You followed her to Liverpool.'

'No, I came for Alder Hey and the opportunity to study childhood cancers.'

Amber stared at him, her face devoid of expression. He was OK, but he could never be what she wanted. What she wanted was life with another man, one who had been the prime object in a takeover bid by a rich and arty-farty woman from London. Kate Price was clever; she had created the interior of this flat without ever

261

stepping inside the place. 'I feel as if she owns me.' The words slipped from her mouth without permission.

'Kate?' Giles asked.

'Her furniture. I paid next to nothing for it.' She was incapable of admitting that everything had been free. It meant goodbye to a housewarming, as she didn't want everyone to know the provenance of all this splendour. 'She's very high-handed. She reads his mail, knows every step he takes, and she's a director of the company. So far, she's contributed nothing apart from a new coffee machine in the boardroom, plus a fridge to keep our bottled water in.'

'You don't like her.'

Amber glared past his shoulder and nodded. 'He loves her, you're fascinated by her, and I live surrounded by all this stuff.' She altered her expression and offered him a smile. 'I suppose I'd better tell you the truth — the bed was hers. So you've slept in her bed, and now I'm watching your expression. You look like a man suffering from home-sickness. I have another bed in my exercise room; we don't need to make love in her shadow.'

Giles flinched slightly. They didn't make love — they shared a sexual experience. Amber was bossy in bed, and he sometimes felt used, as if he were just a toy she played with for her own pleasure. There was a dark side to the woman, a place she fought hard to disguise, though he was wary of it. If he finished with her, there might well be repercussions, because she thought she owned him. 'In bed, do you ever pretend that

I'm him?' he asked.

'Do you pretend I'm her?'

'Don't answer a question with a question, Amber.'

'Fantasies are allowed,' she stated. 'I read about that.'

'Are your fantasies attached to him?'

'Sometimes,' she admitted. 'Are yours fastened to her?'

'Yes.'

'Then we're equal,' she said. 'Come on, now. Let's go and have our imaginings in my exercise room and on my own bed, the one I brought with me.'

Sensing that this relationship could end only in disaster, he followed her like a lapdog into the second bedroom. While undressing, he looked at a chart on the wall near the equipment she used to hone her body. The calorific value of every-thing she ate was in one column, while the next line carried the number of calories used during her sessions on the machines both here and at Chillex. It was rather frightening to see her obses-sive nature in figures that needed to balance.

Amber was mentally ill, and Giles had no idea of how to cope with her. He did as bidden, but had to be quick. She had a meeting, while he had work to do.

★ ★ ★

Amber Simpson was staring at Alex as if she'd crawled across the Sahara and he was provider of the bucket of water at the end of all the pain. He prayed that her expression would change before the arrival of the Queen of Sheba, who would be turning up shortly in her matron of honour garb, a ridiculously expensive dress that enhanced the colour of those incredible eyes. She should be here at the office at any moment.

Alex decided to address the issue. 'Do you have something to say?' he asked when Amber continued to stare after any other business was finished.

She didn't even blush. 'No. I'm just wondering whether your wife will be suggesting any changes at Chillex.'

He shrugged. 'No idea, Amber, because she hasn't yet discussed her plans with me. Don't forget that you all have the ability to negotiate; if you don't agree with her, she'll take that on board.'

The manager of Chillex cleared her throat. 'I hoped we would be finished by now. My deputy has an appointment this afternoon, so I may need to phone and ask him to postpone.'

Alex lowered his eyes, because he could no longer face the hunger this woman displayed. 'Do as you think best,' he advised the meeting. 'Kate won't be here for long, as we have a wedding this afternoon, which is why I'm dressed like a sommelier. I'm best man.'

Managers of the various clubs shared slight smiles. Fortunately, Martina Nelson of Checkmate had given up on him, so Alex suffered the unwanted admiration of just one woman at the table. Everyone here knew about Amber's desire for him, and she had become something of a joke, since the boss was clearly head over heels with his wife.

Kate stalked in, head held high, document case in one hand, small bouquet in the other.

'Good morning,' she said, smiling broadly, and turning to place the flowers in the sink with a little water. After taking her place at the table, she opened the case. 'Onward and upward, Mr Chairman. We haven't much time.'

Alex hid his grin behind a glass of water.

'Charm,' she announced. 'That's Lily and Ian, yes?'

The middle-aged married couple nodded in unison — they knew their dance moves.

'As far as I can see, it needs very little change. A new, thicker carpet and some better padded chairs in seating areas would be appreciated by older clientele. For salsa nights, coloured lighting would make a huge difference. I don't mean disco stuff, just colours that melt from one to another.'

Ian and Lily nodded their agreement.

'For Cheers and Checkmate, I suggest booths, half wooden, upper parts plastic that imitates stained glass set in frames. Bobby Ray, I know the club is half yours, so just think about my suggestion and talk to Alex. Cheers is brilliant as it is, but booths would afford a little bit of privacy to couples on dates.'

She motored on. 'Checkmate's booths would be a chance for people to get to know each other better, Martina. The panels would need to fold back against the walls for speed-dating nights. Yours is the smallest of the clubs, so just think about it. None of this is written in stone.

'Nick and Sandra, Champs aux Fraises needs colour. A freedom flag should beam on walls — a couple of cheap projectors would do just that. A balloon net, its contents echoing colours on the flag, could be used from time to time. The chairs are good, but perhaps they might be upholstered in the same shades. We'll talk about that.'

Alex waited for battle to commence; Kate had deliberately left Chillex to last on the list. He watched as she turned the page very, very slowly, until eventually she achieved eye contact with the enemy.

'Amber, Chillex should be left as it is unless you require equipment. The exercise areas are suitably clinical, and the lighting in the chill-out rooms is calming. Perhaps a little bit of red in the restaurant area might help, but I leave you to decide. Red improves the appetite and you'd sell more food.' She glanced at Alex, and he took over.

Standing, he dismissed the meeting. 'Questions and/or objections in writing to me, please. Kate and I have to be on our way.'

For the first time ever, Amber Simpson led the others out of the room. Kate gazed at Alex. 'Do you think I've upset her?' The words were coated with a thick layer of pseudo-innocence. 'She fled as if she had a firework up her bum.'

'Do you care?' he asked.

'No. I just need to blot the stems of my flowers, then we can be off.'

While she blotted, his arms encircled her

waist. 'You're magnificent,' he whispered. 'And you look almost edible.'

'As do you. Let's go and make sure they get married.'

On Bold Street, Amber Simpson hid in a recessed doorway and watched as the dynamic duo walked towards the company parking area. If Kate Price would just remove herself from the picture, he would need comforting, wouldn't he? Or if someone were to remove the damned woman deliberately . . . The wheels in her head began to move. Was she on the verge of creating a plan? She loved plans.

★ ★ ★

Monica was strangely restless in fits and starts. Her first meeting with Tim Dyson, psychologist and wonderfully sarcastic twit, had given her much food for thought. He was probably right about being qualified in talking shit, shite and sugar, because he dealt all the time with people who were more than merely troubled. According to Kate, Tim was a real psychiatrist who worked in real hospitals, so he must have come across all kinds during his career.

She was doing a bit of crocheting — not the lacy type that might trap little fingers, but closer work that imitated knitting. The true beauty of crochet lay in the fact that she couldn't drop a stitch, so she could throw it onto the coffee table whenever she got fed up. And she got fed up with monotonous frequency.

'Patience has never been my thing,' she told

the shawl she was working on. She had to make it her thing. She was thirty-four, she had four children and was about to become a grandmother. Things needed sorting out, and she wanted somebody to talk to now, this minute. The security guards seldom bothered her, and she didn't have much to say to them, so the house was echoey and empty once the trades had left for the day.

'Weekends are long, too,' she advised the fireplace. 'I'm sure I get two Saturdays and two Sundays rattling about in here by myself. I need a bloke — my bloke.' She wanted Pete, but she wasn't yet fit for Pete. How and when would she be in a condition to act like a wife? She was still fertile — did she want to risk a fifth pregnancy? The pill? She was terrified of the bloody pill.

She stood in the hallway and looked at the longest ladder she'd ever seen. Staircases hadn't gone in yet, so two wooden contraptions acted the part, and one of them had to go all the way up into the gods. 'Right. I'll have a look at that floor, see if he's shaped up to the job. If he hasn't, I'm getting a Pole. A Polish person, though a fireman's pole would make life easier on the way down.'

The second floor flat was looking good. The kitchen needed only kickboards and some tiling, while the bathroom was superb — a free-standing bath with clawed feet, a massive shower stall, twin washbasins that stood on top of a counter, all stark white and grey, with a touch of colour among the tiles. Lovely.

On hands and knees, Monica crawled about

the light oak floor in the living area, making as sure as possible that it was flat and laid properly. It was good, so he'd left her no excuse to sack him. 'Bugger,' she muttered. 'I was looking forward to that.'

After climbing down the oversized ladder, she attacked the shorter version which led to the first floor apartment. This one was still having its first fix completed — plumbing, electricity and gas. The layout was similar to the one she'd just visited; both were to have a little balcony to accommodate a small table and two chairs. The ground floor would be getting a wooden deck, while each flat would own a piece of the huge garden.

Monica loved this house, but she was becoming homesick. She missed the background music of kids arguing and laughing; she missed her husband and their own place. Neighbours? Surely she could make an effort, befriend somebody, admit that she'd been crazy?

In her temporary home on the ground floor, she made herself a pot of tea and re-addressed the shawl. If she didn't buck up, Kylie's baby might arrive before the article got finished. A grandmother at thirty-four? Suddenly, she found herself grinning. She wouldn't be the old granny sitting in a corner, the one who got invited at Christmas or New Year. 'I am going to get myself right,' she whispered. 'I'm going to be as good a mother and grandma as I possibly can be, because I'm having help.' Yes, Tim would show her the way. As for the being a wife bit — well, she might risk the pill after all.

She was just about to switch on the DVD player to continue watching *Gone with the Wind*. The title had always been a joke to her, and she had often aired the opinion that indigestion tablets hadn't been invented back in those days, so everybody was gone with the trapped wind. These days, she was trying to better herself, and there were several films Kate had suggested she watch. The next would be *Wuthering Heights*. What the hell was wuthering? Was it withering with a u instead of the i? Was it dithering, or wondering, or weathering? Maybe wuthering was a Yorkshire word; they talked funny, them Yorkshire folk.

With the remote poised ready to switch on the television, Monica heard something in the hallway. It sounded like a letter landing in the wire basket on the inside of the door. She also heard Alan, the security man, dashing out of an old wash house that now acted as a bedsitter. 'Funny bloody time for a postman,' he muttered as he ran towards the front door.

He returned and spoke to Monica. 'This is for a Mrs Latimer,' he said. 'There was nobody at the door when I opened it. What do we do about it? Do you want me to drive it round to Mrs Price tomorrow?'

'I'll phone her. Go in the kitchen and make yourself a brew while I talk to her.' But she didn't talk to her. It was after ten o'clock, and the newly married couple might have gone to bed, so she sent a text informing Kate that a letter had arrived hand delivered, stampless and addressed to somebody called Latimer. She

270

pressed Send and accepted a cup of tea from Alan. 'Sit here for a bit,' she said. 'I'm getting fed up with crochet and *Gone with the Wind*.'

'*Gone with the Wind?*' he asked incredulously. 'That film's older than Adam.'

'You don't need to tell me. See, it's North America against the Southern states, Bible belt, slave owners, half bad men and half daft buggers. But you can't tell who's what in the film, cos they're all covered in brown. There's blue and there's grey, but they're all messed up in brown muck and dust and they keep dying. It must have been one of the first films in colour.'

'There's the Southern drawl,' Alan reminded her.

'Nobody says much apart from the main ones like Rhett and Scarlett. The rest are all too busy dying. I worry about the horses.' Her phone rang, so Alan made himself scarce.

It was Kate. 'Monica.'

'That's me. There's a letter just come. Alan ran right through the house, but whoever pushed it through done a runner, too. It just says Mrs Latimer.'

Kate paused for a second or two. 'Open it, please.'

It was Monica's turn to hesitate. 'Are you sure? What if it's personal, like? I mean . . . I don't know what I mean. Anyway, who's Mrs Latimer?'

'I was. Open it and read it to me, please. You're one of the few I'd trust with my life. Just do it.'

Monica complied. '*Dear Mrs Latimer, This is*

271

being smuggled out by my mate Charlie, what's getting out of Walton today. I am going to send you a visiting order because I need to tell you some stuff. I know you was treated bad by Jim and I don't want you to suffer no more. With respect, I just want to say sorry about what happened to the kiddy, and this is my way of trying to set things easy in your mind. Eric Mansell.' Monica paused. 'You all right, queen?'

'I don't know. I'm going to talk to Alex. I've never visited a prison before.'

'Oh, you'll be OK. Take nothing in — they rummage through your things sometimes. I went once for Beryl next door down the Dingle. She was the nearest thing to a mam I ever had, taught me to crochet and make pies. Her Ned was in for stripping lead off church roofs. I went to Walton when she was in the ozzy with vericlose veins. Like blue ropes, they were.' Why was she nattering on? 'It was all right apart from being herded like sheep into a holding area. Find two forms of identification with Latimer on them.' She waited. 'Kate?'

'I'm still here. I have a credit card that's still just about in date, and recent utility bills from my London house. They should do, yes?'

'Yes. I'll . . . er . . . I'll let you go and talk to Alex, then.'

The call ended. Monica stared at the phone as if expecting it to tell her more. Posh people knew criminals, too.

Alan tapped on the open door. 'You all right, Monica?'

'I think so.'

'What about that letter?'

Monica shrugged. 'Kate was married to a Latimer, but he died. I read it out to her cos she asked me to.'

He opened his mouth as if intending to say more, but thought better of it. He was security, no more, no less, and letters were none of his business.

★ ★ ★

There's a long, long and very high wall. I suppose most prisons have the same arrangement. I'm sitting here holding fast to Alex's hand; there is nothing more to say, so we remain silent. Women and children alight from a bus; I could never drag Amelia to a place like this. Some people look rather drab and poor, possibly because there's no income, since Daddy is locked away. Others are well dressed and wearing makeup, but these women are young and filled with false hope for their contained men.

Alexander James Price is tense; I can tell by the set of his jaw. Of course, he wanted this to happen in a different way and, at first, demanded to telephone the prison and remind them of the nature of Mansell's offence, but I refused to allow that. Then he suggested obtaining a visiting order for himself, but that idea was stupid, since none of us was sure how to go about it.

Perhaps the wardens will recognize my old surname and disallow the visit anyway, but there's only one way to find out. I tell Alex I must go now, and he points to a side road whose very ordinary semi-detached council houses seem at odds with the huge building to our left. He tells me he will park round the corner.

After the promised herding of visitors and when I have proved my identity, a mountainous man informs me that I am Mansell's first visitor. 'So you live in London, then?'

'Yes.' I riffle through the imagination section of my brain, which seems rather arid at the present time. 'My parents know his,' I manage. 'They must have told the Mansells I was about to visit Liverpool, and given them the address —'

'I see. In you go then, Mrs Latimer.'

So in I go.

Twenty minutes later, I'm outside again and talking to my mother in France. I tell her what I've just discovered, my heart going at ninety miles an hour, sweat pouring down my face. When the call is ended, I walk to the edge of the pavement to cross the road. Alex is just round the corner. We must pack and get to France right away, because my father is ill and Mum and Amelia can't come home without him.

And that's when a car driving on the wrong side of the road hits me.

12

I hear it and race round the corner on foot; my darling girl lies in the road like a broken doll. Oh, God, no, not Kate. I run to her, my shoes crunching on the remains of her mobile phone, I think. I think? I can't think. Mental paralysis.

A woman — not young, steely gray hair — walks from the prison towards us. 'I followed her,' she says. 'She was in shock; I thought she might fall over in a faint . . . ' Words, words, more stupid words. Fear rips at my throat, my stomach, my head.

999. My fingers are rigid. 999. Why is this woman talking to me? I order police and ambulance, but we need a miracle, divine intervention. There's blood coming from her head. One of her legs is wrong. Bone protrudes from a calf. I don't know what to do. 999, yes, I've done that. Where are they? Where is God?

The woman bends and touches my Kate's wrist. 'Her heart's still working son. I can tell you this much — she got run over deliberate. Green car, wrong side of the road. No accident.'

Green car. I saw a green car passing the end of the avenue where I . . . 'Don't move her,' I manage to say. She's damaged, too damaged for the likes of me to understand what needs to be done. I want to pick her up, give her my life, change places with her.

The experts are coming, but they're taking

their bloody time. Bloody. The pool of red is growing. Another pool of red like the one I saw . . . Stop it, Price. Bugger the nightmares and bugger you, you selfish sod. But I know I can't live, won't live, without my girl. She found me and claimed me, and I reciprocated almost immediately in spite of my ridiculous rules. Don't leave me, Kate. Me, me, me.

The woman is talking again, something about being long-sighted and a four and a seven on the number plate. 'I'll stop with you, lad. Then the cops can give me a ride to the station, with me being a witness. They might even take me home after.' What's she expecting? A round of applause? Stop this. Be grateful, Price. I thank her just as two vehicles arrive and turn off their sirens. 'Have you come in a car?' she asks. I nod.

'Is it locked?' I shake my head. 'Round the corner. Black Mercedes.'

She takes the keys and goes to secure my Merc. 'Wait for me,' she orders the uniformed policemen. 'I seen it. I seen it all. Attempted murder.' She dashes off at a speed that defies her age. That's a good woman, bless her.

A policeman asks me if I am a witness, and I tell him I'm an ear rather than an eye witness.

I can't watch while they move Kate. When I get into the ambulance, I see she's wearing a neck brace, she's strapped to a hard stretcher to support her spine, and a drip is feeding something clear into an arm. A paramedic is mopping her head and talking to the hospital about O negative.

'She's strong,' I say, hope audible in my voice.

'Stronger than I am.'

'Are you her husband?'

The truth is required. 'I will be very soon.' I hope.

He awards me a hint of a smile. 'You'll have to wait till they get the pot off her leg unless you want her to hop up the aisle.'

I summon some courage. 'Is she bleeding internally?'

'Possibly.'

We scream through the streets, probably defying every rule of the road, but that's OK, because we are an ambulance and there's a police car behind us. Kate is now wearing an oxygen mask. She's so very pale, and her curls are matted with blood. The hand I am holding is cold. Don't die, sweetheart; dying isn't part of the picture, not yet, not for years. Stay with me. Was that Shakespeare's Sister?

'Stop,' the paramedic yells suddenly.

When the vehicle is stationary, he pushes something into my precious girl's chest. He looks at me. 'Punctured lung; just getting air out of her cavity. Try not to worry, because this is par for the course in road accidents.'

'Tell me she'll make it,' I beg. One lung. Firing on one cylinder only.

'We'll do our damnedest. There's a team preparing for her right this minute. Just try to keep calm — she might be able to hear us.'

If I'd had the chance to think and the ability to order my mind, I could have taken her to a better place, but do private centres take emergencies? All I can do is pray, and I'm not good at that, either. 'Let her live,' is all I manage.

Things get a bit blurred — well, more than a bit — when we reach the hospital. They rush Kate away and leave me with a couple of newly arrived policemen. I'm told the police at the scene have saved the SIM from her phone and are loading it into another. 'She talked to somebody just before she got hit,' the younger of the pair informs me. 'According to a witness, she'd been visiting a man in Walton, so we're going over there to question the prisoner and see what's what.'

I tell them it was Eric Mansell and that Kate would never talk on the phone while crossing a road. 'She's too careful, officer. And the witness says it was no accident.' Well, at least the thoughts are a bit clearer. 'The car was travelling on the wrong side of the road.'

'You didn't see that?'

'No. I was parked up the side road and heard the impact. The witness saw it.'

I'm in a waiting room now near ICU and ITU. I think the difference is that you get a nurse to yourself in Intensive Care, and one between two in the other place. Somebody told me that; can't remember who and don't know whether it's true. The boss, a young man in a blue cotton uniform, tells me Kate's still in theatre. He offers me a cup of tea, but I want only water. So I sit here gulping Adam's ale while my lovely girl is being drugged past the eyeballs so that the mending can begin.

Oh, here comes the witness woman, steely hair, a big smile and a shopping bag. 'I thought

278

I'd find you here, love. See, take no notice of me, but I've fetched you some bits. I won't stop. I told the cops what I seen.'

She places her bag on a chair next to mine.

And now I've got this big lump in my throat. She's poor and I'm not. Two nightdresses from when she was younger and slimmer, a little bag of toiletries, toothbrush still in its box, a couple of clean towels and some rubbishy magazines with the likes of Beyoncé and Lady Gaga on the covers. 'Thank you.'

'She'll not need nothing yet, not till she's sat up. I've put some butties in silver paper for you. Oh, me phone number's in the bottom of me bag on a Get Well card. Let me know how she's getting on.'

I study her, and she isn't as old as I thought. 'Sit down,' I say.

She chooses the chair at the other side of mine. When she takes my hand in hers, it's too much, and I start to cry. There's not much noise, just a load of water pouring down my face. 'So grateful,' I manage.

'Oh, son, we've all had our troubles. I've three lads in Walton, three buggers who sent me grey before I hit forty. Their dad died in there, and I was glad to see the back of him. I've a girl, a good girl, our Joanie. Now, you listen to me. That young woman of yours has every chance because she'll not leave you. You love the bones of each other, right?'

I dry my face with the tissues she offers. 'I will phone you. What about your shopping bag?'

'Keep it. See you, lad.' She stands and kisses

me on my forehead.

There's just me now in an empty room. That might be a good thing, because if Intensive Care isn't full, my Kate might get more attention. I suddenly feel exhausted, stretch out across three chairs and fall asleep immediately. Five minutes later, someone nudges me awake. Only it's not five minutes, because the clock on the wall says a few minutes past eight. It's evening, almost night.

It's the surgeon; he looks knackered too. 'She's in ICU,' he tells me.

'How long in theatre?' I ask.

He tells me it felt like a fortnight, but she came through with flying colours. 'Her head and neck bled outward for the most part — not much on the brain, no sign of bad swelling. The fibular fracture hasn't impacted on the ankle — that's a good thing. A rib pierced a lung and we've dealt with that, mended her diaphragm and saved her spleen.'

I thank him.

'She has other broken ribs, so she'll be black and blue for a while. We're keeping her asleep, because she's lively.'

'Yes,' I agree. 'Very lively.'

'Strong mind and good bones, Mr Price. In recovery, she opened one eye and accused me of not being Alex. So we've doped her again. She has her own nurse, and should she need help with breathing, the machinery is there. Have a quick look at her and go home. I don't want to keep her drugged, so we need her to be still. If she sees you, she might try to come home with you.'

I can't imagine Kate being still. Yes, I can; she

280

was motionless when lying in the gutter . . . 'So no harm to the brain? Concussion?'

'The brain got rattled, yes, but no serious bleeding. There's a coma chart just in case; that's normal procedure. Don't worry — she's in the best place.'

I stand by the bed. A little nurse with red hair is checking Kate's pulse. My girl looks as if she's gone a few rounds with some heavyweight boxer: black eye, scrapes on her lovely face, swollen lips. She's alive. If I'm right, she'll be alive and kicking with one leg at least by tomorrow. I whisper to the nurse, 'She won't do as she's told — never has, never will.'

The nurse looks me up and down. 'Don't worry — go home. We'll let you know if there's any change. We're going to put her on a heart monitor just in case.'

Life is returning to my own heart, to my whole body, and it hurts. I have never before hugged a nurse, but I can't hold my own adult baby just now. There are two other people in the unit, both on monitors, both with a million wires and tubes attached to their persons. I leave the little nurse to do her job. Kate must be in the ICU for a reason; perhaps they're waiting for something to . . . Give it up, Price. They're doing their job — isn't that enough for you, master of the bloody universe?

Oh, God, I haven't told anybody. Her mum and dad in France, my two Bees, Tim, Monica, who's become a friend to Kate, then Kylie, Pete . . . I stand in the foyer and think about my car. It's just a bloody car. There's a taxi rank, so I

281

grab the first in line and give him my address. I switch on my phone. There are ten missed calls . . .

'You all right, sir?'

'Yes, thank you.' Not for the first time, I also thank God for the existence of this city. The not-so-old grey-haired woman is Liverpool; this driver is Liverpool. Tears again. 'Apologies. My fiancée was hit by a car today. Take me home, please.'

'Sorry about that,' he says. 'I hope she's better soon.'

Oh yes. Like Kate, I am in the right place.

* * *

Alex's huge L-shaped sofa was fully occupied. Monica and Pete, both summoned by Kylie, sat with the sleeping Troy. Kylie occupied an armchair; she'd abandoned the knitting hours earlier. Brian, Brenda, Tim and Julia took up the other half of the sofa, and everyone had given up on conversation.

Thanks to the police, who had brought back Alex's car, they knew where Alex and Kate were. Tim, alerted by the Bees, had wanted to go to the hospital, but the rest of the company had held him back, with Brenda chiding him, 'You don't know him as well as you think you do. Let him be; he's a very . . . private man at times like this. The only person he needs is stuck in a bloody operating theatre.'

Untypically, Tim had been angry. 'I've been his friend since he was a child. He needs me.'

But Brenda had stuck to her sub-machine guns. 'If he'd wanted anybody, he would have phoned.' Thus all attempts at talking had been aborted unless it came to cups of tea or was anyone hungry.

A taxi arrived. 'Don't rush him,' Brenda ordered. 'Stay where you are and let him speak if he wants. I know this lad, Tim, and I know you've done him a lot of good. But Kate's his real cure. We both know that, don't we?'

Alex walked in, pausing as soon as he saw the congregation. All noticed that he sought eye contact with Brenda. 'Do her parents know?' he asked her.

She nodded. 'I told them you'd phone as soon as you got in.' The questions remained in her eyes.

'Hours in theatre, now in ICU but breathing on her own.'

Brenda blessed herself. 'Thanks be to God.'

'She's on a heart monitor, but she's tough. I have to talk to her parents.' Alex picked up the house phone and left the room. About to make the most difficult of calls, he needed solitude.

After twenty minutes he returned, shoulders sagging, suit looking as if he'd worn it for months. Standing with his back to the fireplace, he told them what he had only just discovered. 'There are kidnappers in France looking for Kate's daughter.'

Brenda staggered to his side. 'What? How do you know?'

'Kate phoned her mother just before . . . just after she left the prison. The man she visited was in her first husband's gang. Through the grapevine, he'd received news of two pond life named Trev and Max. They got forged papers and travelled to the Loire valley.' He ran a hand through dishevelled hair. 'The plan was to kidnap Amelia in order to force Kate to tell them about the missing loot.'

'But they found it all, didn't they?' Tim asked.

Alex nodded. 'But do the kidnappers know that? Kate's father is ill with a heavy cold that went bacterial and settled on his chest. He can't travel and can't be left alone in France. They're trapped.'

Julia didn't hesitate. 'We'll go, won't we, Tim?'

'Yes. Details on paper, Alex, or send me an email. I know you have to stay with Kate, so let us do what's necessary. Phone them again and tell them to expect the Dysons. We'll leave tomorrow and get Kate's daughter home.'

For the fourth or fifth time today, tears poured from Alex's eyes. He allowed Brenda to lead him into the kitchen, where she placed him at the table and stabbed at the cover on a ready meal. 'You'll eat, then get to sleep. Take plenty to drink. Before you drop off, write Tim's email sitting up in bed, and phone Kate's mum and dad from upstairs. If you want, I'll come with you to the hospital tomorrow. If Kate's awake, she'll be giving them hell.'

'Can you stop her?'

The little woman straightened. 'Just watch me, lad. Just you watch and learn. Do as you're told and get this sausage and mash down you, Sainsbury's best. If you don't eat, you'll be no good to Kate.'

'Yes, Other Mother.'

Brenda left him with his food and stood in the hallway with her back to the kitchen door. She looked heaven-ward. 'What else are you going to let him suffer, eh?' she whispered. Right. It was time to kick everybody out. It had been the longest day in history.

★ ★ ★

Kate had been taken off the monitor and moved out of Intensive Care because she was doing so well. She was in a surgical ward, but in the bed next to the ward manager's office so that keeping an eye on her would be easier. Her left eye was now closed and covered by flesh in several shades of red, brown and deep purple. Her face was marked, though the surgeon had said there would be no scars as long as she left the abrasions alone.

The good eye opened and fixed Alex where he stood. 'Where have you been?' she asked. 'My head is very sore, I'm black and blue all over, and — '

Brenda stepped forward. 'Where's he been? He's been here with you till gone eight o'clock last night. By the time he got home, he looked like the wreck of the Hesperus. He's been on the phone for hours and doing emails all night, because he was in a state worse than Ma Birtwistle's flophouse worrying about you yesterday.'

'Green car,' Kate said. 'It hit me deliberately. You must get Amelia. I can't remember why just yet, but she needs to come home. She's not safe.'

And now, she remembered why. 'Get her out of there.' She was becoming agitated.

'Julia and Tim are going for her today. Your dad's not well enough to travel, and I'm not the right person for the job. Anyway, I'm not leaving Liverpool while you're in here.'

Kate stared into the near distance. 'Are they still on their stay-at-home honeymoon?'

Where was she going with this? Alex scratched his head. 'Why, Kate?'

'Amelia mustn't see me looking so dreadful. Remember, she was in hospital for weeks, and all she kept asking once she started to speak was, 'Take me home, please. Why can't I go home, Mummy?' We mustn't put her through this, Alex. She's just a little girl, my little girl. Sorry I'm a bit forgetful — it's concussion.'

'It's all right, my love.'

Brenda had to stick an oar in the water, of course. 'Not much of a honeymoon with a kiddy to look after.'

Alex turned to face her. 'Then why don't you and Brian go with them? Amelia needs to get to know you, anyway. I'm offering a blank cheque here, Brenda. You might go over the Pyrenees into Spain, see a different way of life. Wherever you lodge, Tim and Julia can have their own room while you and Brian mind Amelia.' He left the ward to make some calls.

Brenda stared at Kate. 'I've never been abroad,' she said, her face paling towards the colour of new snow. 'I don't like aeroplanes. I don't like foreigners what don't talk no proper English, and I hate heat.'

Alex returned to find both women in silence. 'What's wrong now?' he asked.

'Aeroplanes, foreigners and heat,' Brenda replied. 'But it has to be done, or that baby will see her mam looking as if she's got bashed up and down Lime Street twice. Kate's right. Amelia has to be kept away till she's better.'

He pushed some money into her hand. 'Get a cab from the rank, go home and pack. You have an hour and a half before Tim picks you up. So you need to get your skates on, missus.'

She grabbed the money and glared at him. 'Listen, Alex. I'm doing this for her, not you. My blood pressure has just shot up right to the top of the thingumometer. I've never been to France before — never been to the Isle of Man. I get seasick on the Mersey ferry.'

'Just be grateful that I made sure you both have passports. Now, go and look at France, Spain or wherever. Bugger off and make a hole in my bank account. And look after that child as if she's part of the crown jewels. Amelia needs close vigilance, because there are people we don't trust looking for her.'

Brenda opened her mouth to speak, but her employer stopped her. With an index finger raised, he spoke in his meeting voice. 'Do as you're told for once. Who's the boss in this crazy arrangement?'

The housekeeper's eyes gleamed like cold steel. 'Kate is. And don't try denying it. She's got twice the sense you have.' She kissed the sensible one.

Kate held on to Brenda's hand. 'Keep her safe.'

'I will, love. You just concentrate on getting better.' She looked Alex up and down. 'And I want to come home to that house as I leave it — clean.'

'Yes, ma'am.' He watched as she disappeared down the corridor, then collapsed in a chair. He very much hoped he'd done the right thing in sending Brenda on this mission of mercy.

'Are you moving in?' Kate asked. 'I already have a police guard in the corridor.'

'Yes, I'm staying. I've made a contribution towards a new scanner. I shall make sure you get decent food, too, and not a lot of it. We don't want a full stomach pushing on your mended diaphragm, do we?'

'You'll get bored,' she predicted.

'I won't.' He lifted *War and Peace* from his briefcase. 'I brought a little reading matter. Go to sleep.'

★   ★   ★

I stand outside the hospital for a breath of air and inhale very tasty traffic fumes. Why do hospitals keep the heating on all year round? Surely MRSA and C-diff have a better chance of winning in that airless atmosphere? We must get out of here as soon as she can be moved. And the big question has to be answered. A green car. The vehicle failed to kill my girl, so the score is one nil, a win for the NHS. Who? Why? Will a second effort be made, and will it be successful?

I glance up and notice a figure coming towards me. It's Dr Giles Girling, and he's almost running. 'Alex?'

'Yes?'

'How is she? I saw it in the newspaper.'

I tell him she's on a ward and taunting me already.

He runs a hand through his hair. 'I know Kate had trouble in London because of that vile husband and his gang, but this could be much nearer to home.' He pauses, seems embarrassed. 'I've been seeing Amber Simpson. She has fixations, and you're one of them. Although I want rid of her, I daren't tell her I mean to end the relationship because she's toxic, and she hates Kate.'

I ponder for a moment. 'Does she have a car?'

'Not as far as I know, but the flats in her block have separate garages about fifty or so yards down the road. Hers is the second one — red doors. She has a licence — that's all I know.'

Licensed to kill? 'You think she's sick enough to try to kill Kate?'

'Yes. Her life runs as if she's keeping pace with a metronome. Every crumb she ingests is on a wall chart, as is every calorie she uses in exercise. No cushion must be disturbed, no cup hung out of line with the rest. A drop of gravy on a tablecloth, and she's furious. I hoped you'd be here, because I'd hate to tell Kate this; it could set her back. Amber's using some of her holiday quotient, so she's not at work.'

A cold finger makes its way down my spine. 'You don't know what's in that garage, then? It might well be empty.'

'It might be empty, and it might not. But she

289

probably believes that with Kate out of the way, you'll turn to her. Look, Alex, I'm as confused as you are. I know a bit about psychology and, at a guess, I'd say Amber had to keep herself under heavy control during formative years. That need to control has spread beyond herself, and she seeks now to be in charge of everything and everybody. That's an over-simplified diagnosis, but she scares me to death. The nearest she can get to you is me — if that makes sense. I love Kate, you love Kate, and Amber seeks control over me.'

'And me,' I add. 'If she kills Kate . . . if she kills Kate, I'll kill her.'

'No, you won't. You're not wired for killing.'

'Is she?'

'Possibly. Another thing — that bonus you gave her to help with the flat — I'm sure she'd get a buzz out of using it to dispose of Kate. She may well have paid somebody to do the deed.' Giles pulls an envelope from his pocket. 'I was going to leave this for you in case I missed you. What I've just told you is not for Kate's ears or eyes.'

'Thank you.'

'And please say goodbye to Kate from me. I'm leaving Liverpool tomorrow.'

'Does Amber know you're running away from her? Don't you need her permission? If she has abandonment issues — '

'She doesn't know, so she may go berserk. I'm going to Yale for research purposes, and I won't be coming back any time soon. I may be wrong to suspect Amber, but her behaviour suddenly

290

changed when I showed her the story in the paper and she realized that Kate is alive. She's become very pensive.' He thinks for several seconds. 'It has to be someone who followed you to the prison. Did anyone know where you were going?'

'No.'

'Then perhaps Amber followed you, or she set someone after you from the moment you left home. It's hard to understand a person who's so totally focused. Amber knows what she wants and she gets what she wants, fair means or foul.'

'I must find a way to get Kate out of here, Giles.'

He nods. 'She's had surgery?'

'Yes. Punctured lung, torn diaphragm, broken bone in her calf. She's tough. They saved her spleen, but she has some concussion and broken ribs.'

'And I'm damned sure Amber Simpson has borderline personality disorder. She reacts fiercely, does things without worrying about consequences, thinks about herself and no one else. I'm her spare. You know how royals are supposed to have an heir and at least one spare? Well, if she can't get you, she thinks she'll get me. A doctor's not a bad catch, but you're her real target.'

I smile ruefully. 'Good luck in the US, Giles. Will you see Amber before you go?'

'No bloody way. She thinks I'm busy writing a paper on childhood leukaemia.' He grips my arm. 'Don't let Kate out of your sight.'

'I won't. She has guards, too. My staff at work will keep the wheels turning. I won't speak to the police about your theory until you're out of the

291

country. Mind, if Ms Simpson gets arrested, you may be called upon as a witness.'

He shrugs. 'Que sera, sera. If she's under arrest, I'll be safe. Meanwhile, look after yourself as well as Kate. Amber isn't predictable — she may turn on you, because if she can't have you, no one else can. I thought she was going to kill me when I dropped gravy on her precious linen.'

We shake hands. 'I think the linen was probably Kate's,' I tell him.

'Everything in that flat is Kate's. Goodbye for now, Alex.'

I watch as he walks away from me, from Kate, from the hospital and Liverpool. When he disappears from view, I conjure up a picture of the elegant and perfect manager of Chillex, so laid back, unruffled no matter what might occur during any working day. Appearances can certainly be deceptive. And oh, my God, I've conjured her up in reality! That is uncanny. I hope she didn't catch sight of Giles, who's supposed to be doubled up over a laptop somewhere. I wipe all trace of surprise from my expression — she must learn nothing from me.

'Alex,' she says in a voice that's probably meant to be seductive. 'I came to visit Kate.' I notice the floral arrangement she's brought. 'A few pretty flowers might cheer her up a bit,' she adds.

My brain races when adrenalin comes to the fore. 'No visitors,' I tell her. 'Apart from family, that is. And because her condition is the result of attempted murder, she's under police guard.' I watch as she fixes her face in neutral mode.

292

'Also, she looks a bit of a mess, so she won't want people looking at her.'

She tries to hand me the flowers, but I don't take them. 'Use them at home, Amber. Kate can't see well at the moment, so she'll get little pleasure from them.' I look at her almost dead eyes, no feeling, no light, no life. 'If it takes me forever, I will rip Liverpool apart brick by brick until I find the freak who tried to kill her.' There's a flash of something in her eyes, a look that bears some relationship to hatred. I fold my arms. 'Can you imagine the mentality of a creature who sets out to murder a beautiful young woman?'

She shakes her head, reminding me of a toy animal that works on batteries, just movement, no emotion.

'To do this to Kate, he or she must place no value on life, on his or her immortal soul, on the laws of man and God.' She's looking now at some children coming out of the hospital. Ah, perhaps the woman can no longer meet my eyes? I continue. 'It was a green car speeding at well over the limit on the wrong side of the road. The numbers four and seven were on the plate.'

Her attention returns to me. 'I hope Kate's soon better.' She glances at her wristwatch. 'I must go. There are things I need to do in the flat while I have a few days off work.'

In her haste to escape my company, she staggers slightly. Amber Simpson never staggers. Every move, every calorie, every word is accounted for. Is it possible that someone so bright and confident might be mentally ill? I

293

can't talk to Tim, because he will be on his way to the airport soon.

The policeman called Terry emerges to have a cigarette. He and another constable named Chas are responsible for Kate's safety in the hospital. I ask him if Chas is in place, and he says he is. 'Any news on the car?' I enquire.

'Scrap,' is his reply. 'It's been written out of the system, so further investigations are ongoing.'

'Car graveyards, then?'

He nods.

Shall I tell him? No. I don't want a fleet of cop cars racing down to Sefton Park, do I? This is something I must do myself. 'Before you go off shift and when you've smoked your fag, will you go up and tell Kate something?'

'Yeah. As long as you don't blow me up for smoking in uniform.'

'Deal.'

'Well then, sir?'

'It's Alex. Tell her I'm going to work. There are a few things I need to sort out for myself.'

'No problem, Alex.'

'So that means there'll be free drinks for you and a friend at Cheers. One night only, not Friday or Saturday.'

'Thanks, Alex.'

'Welcome.' *I leave him to finish his fag.*

Must change cars. I'll go home and get the dog van minus dogs. Second garage, red doors. First, I phone the office to get Amber's full address so that I can update my system. Dark glasses — the sun is shining. Concentrate, man.

294

Kate is out of danger; Amelia will soon be safe.

Less than an hour later, I'm parked halfway between Amber's flat and the row of garages. Instead of my Kate, there are a number of items on the passenger seat — a cold bag containing soft drinks, chocolate and a pasta salad. Next to that, a bolt cutter and a pair of handcuffs reflect the sunlight.

★   ★   ★

She paced up and down the huge living area until she felt a drop in sugar level. As she preached often enough at Chillex, a person didn't need to be diabetic to suffer the shakes and sudden weakness that resulted from exercising on an empty stomach.

Opening a drawer in the dresser, she took glucose tablets from their packaging and placed them on her tongue; glucose would have to suffice, since she had no appetite. Protein? At this point in time, arsenic would be preferable. Where the hell was he? She'd paid him half to do the deed, while the other half was ready and waiting for him once his mission had been accomplished.

But he had failed; the bloody woman was still alive. Gus was a likeable villain who had been refused membership but still hung round endlessly behind the club. For Amber he would have done just about anything, because it was she who saved up leftover food or items whose dates had just run out, and she always gave him a drink of coffee, tea or pop to go with his meal.

Perhaps she'd suspected that she might need him one day?

How or where he had acquired the ten-year-old green Ford she had no idea. Very few people these days drove green cars. The colour was out of fashion, or was considered unlucky, but whatever the reason Gus's vehicle would have been noticeable. The sooner it was disposed of the better.

'Where the hell are you?'

The doorbell sounded at last. She pressed a button. 'Hello?'

'It's me — Gus.'

'Come up.' She activated the mechanism that opened the main front door.

When he tapped at her own door, she flung it open. As soon as he was inside, she turned on him. 'Where the hell were you? She's still alive.'

'I know. I'm sorry, but I did my best.' He looked round the room. 'Very nice,' he commented.

'Why a green car?'

He blinked. 'I didn't walk into a car showroom and ask for a test drive, love. There was no choice — I had to find a car what some daft sod had left for scrap with keys in the ignition. There's no time to be looking at colours or engine size; you just take what you can get.'

'Well, the police know part of the number plate. We have to get rid of it tonight. Did you put the can of petrol in the boot?'

'I did.' He paused. 'Do I get the rest of the money?'

'Yes,' she snapped. 'Once the car's been

cremated, I'll pay you.'

'You're a queen,' he said. 'Now, what do we do till it gets dark?'

She glared at him. 'The same as always — I give you food, and you eat it. I'll put the TV on for you. There's Sky, so you'll find something you want to watch.'

While cod and oven chips baked, Amber threw together a salad and cut some French bread. He ate on the sofa, but she decided to leave him to it; the sofa was a step up from paving stones outside the back door of Chillex. From time to time, she walked to the front window and stared out at the street. Nothing unusual was happening, and the van that had been parked down the road for several hours had moved away. Someone must have had a tradesman working on their house.

'All clear on the western front?' Gus asked.

'Yes. We'll be good to go once the light has gone properly. There's a spectacular sunset again.' Though she talked of matters mundane, her mind was fully employed in planning how to rid the world of Kate Price. Poison? A gun? Knives and other hand weapons were so messy . . .

'Why do you want her dead?'

This question from Gus cut through her thoughts with all the sharpness of a well-honed hand weapon. 'Personal,' was the only reply she offered.

'She's Price's missus, isn't she?'

'Yes.'

'And you want him.'

Amber rounded on him. 'It's not that at all.

She was given a directorship just because she married the boss. Some of us have given our all to the Price company, but she just drifts in from London, marries him, and gets the job. I'm not the only one who resents her.'

Gus blinked a couple of times. 'No, but you're the only one who wants her dead.'

'This conversation is closed,' she said quietly. 'You'll get your money, and that will be the end of it.' She walked out of the room and left him to his own devices. But he had better not get mayonnaise on that sofa . . .

13

'I don't think I like it.' Brenda was in the back seat of the hire car which Tim had picked up at the airport after they'd landed in France. She was white-faced and had been that way since arriving at the departure gate, when she'd caught sight of the aircraft they were to travel on. She'd spent the entire flight with her eyes tightly shut, shaking quietly. Nobody had ever seen her go so long without speaking before.

Now she was back on terra firma the shaking had stopped, but she was by no means back to her old self. Tim was driving on the wrong side of the road and so was everyone else. The machine that told them the way to go spoke in a foreign language, like everyone at the airport they'd landed at. It was all a far cry from Liverpool and she was deeply unhappy. But she didn't want to make a fuss as they were here with only one object in mind: to find Amelia, ensure she was safe, and bring her slowly back home. For that she was prepared to endure the torment of French motorways. But it didn't mean she had to like it.

'Après deux kilomètres, tournez á droit.' The satnav made no sense to her but Tim nodded as if he was expecting this instruction.

'Not far now,' he said, and she was comforted by the knowledge that he seemed to know what he was doing.

Julia, who was in the back seat beside her — having shorter legs than Brian, who'd bagged the front passenger position — put her hand reassuringly over Brenda's. 'We should be there in under half an hour,' she said. 'And remember, Tim's been driving on the right all the time he was with me in Vermont. He's had plenty of practice.'

Brenda nodded, still unable to speak, and slightly mortified that her terror was so obvious. But it was all right for people like Tim and Julia. They travelled all over the place all the time. Then she remembered that Tim himself was phobic about flying. She hadn't noticed if he'd taken anything, but she supposed with him being a doctor and everything he could prescribe himself whatever worked best. As long as it didn't affect his driving . . .

She'd been staring straight ahead through the windscreen ever since they'd set off, illogically afraid to look to either side in case that caused them to veer off the road and into a ditch. But now she cautiously let down her guard and began to take in the countryside they were passing through. Obviously it wasn't a patch on Merseyside, but all the same she was impressed with the lush trees and, as they turned off the main road and onto a more rural one, the buildings alongside. They looked nothing like houses back home. Everything was different, even the windows with their shutters, but she could see why people would come all this way on their holidays. Perhaps it wouldn't be so bad spending some time here. She tried not to think about the food — how it would taste foreign and unfamiliar. She must put the longing for a proper beef stew firmly out of her mind — it didn't do to dwell on what you couldn't have.

The satnav said some more strange things and Tim looked as if he understood what it meant. Finally Brenda plucked up the nerve to ask what was on her mind.

'Where are we going? I mean, are we going straight to find that poor child and her grandparents or what?'

Tim laughed from the front seat. 'We went through this at the airport, Mrs Bee, but you were probably too preoccupied to remember.' He swung the wheel around and she could see they were approaching the outskirts of a town. 'We're going to go to a hotel first, to settle in. We don't want to turn up at the Powers' all travel-weary and frighten Amelia, do we?'

Brenda approved of that. 'Very sensible,' she said. 'And where will that be?'

The satnav spoke again in its weird language.

'About five minutes away,' said Tim, manoeuvring through an increasingly narrow set of streets. Striped awnings hung over the buildings and the pavements were set with chairs and tables. Julia was smiling broadly.

'It's been many a long year since I was in France,' she said. 'I'd almost forgotten how they love dining al fresco.'

Brenda wanted to ask what this Alf had to do with anything, but just then Tim pulled up outside a stone building that was clearly very old.

301

'Here we are,' he said. 'That wasn't too bad, was it?'

Brian stepped out and stretched his legs, his joints creaking in protest as he did so. He looked around with a slight frown, but he couldn't help admiring the quality of the stonework. 'This place looks all right,' he stated.

Tim went to the boot and began lifting out their cases. Julia struggled with hers, and Brian came to her rescue. 'Here you go, love.' He felt very protective towards this still frail young woman who'd been through so much and was now giving up her honeymoon to rescue a child she didn't know from Adam. Or Eve, more like.

Brenda looked around the broad square, taking in the people dressed for sunshine, dark glasses propped elegantly on their heads, the relaxed atmosphere and the cool of the shade where they stood. It was a million miles from anything she'd known before and she'd never thought she'd ever end up anywhere remotely like this. But she was here to do a job, out of loyalty to Alex and that poor girl even now lying in hospital, fighting to get well enough to welcome back her daughter. She stood straighter, pulling back her shoulders. If she could be Other Mother to a big softy like Alex Price, well, maybe she could be Other Gran to the child who would one day be his daughter.

*   *   *

Alex paced around his kitchen, unable to relax, trying to gather his thoughts. He had to maintain his focus, keep everything clear, as he was in this

302

on his own. Kate was in no state to help him sort out his whirling ideas and there was no way he'd worry her with these details. Tim by now would be safely in France with his three musketeers — which meant there were no Bees to confide in either. He didn't think the ones out in the hives would be much use.

He'd found the garage with the red doors easily enough and the lock had been laughably simple to break. Nobody had taken a blind bit of notice as he swiftly went inside the gloomy structure, a small and grimy window at the back allowing in just enough light to mean that he didn't have to use his torch. The filtered daylight revealed what he'd hoped and feared to find: a rustbucket of a car in a bilious shade of green. No wonder that particular colour had never caught on. For his purposes it was usefully distinctive, though. A cursory check of the number plate confirmed his worst suspicions: it matched what they knew. This was the car that had aimed itself at his precious Kate.

He'd fought to contain himself, summoning all his self-control not to lash out at the wreck of a vehicle. Rage rose in him in powerful waves, but this was not the time or place to express it. Furthermore, he had to save his energy for later. He'd come for proof and he'd found it. Now he had to act.

Forcing himself to move calmly, he left the garage as quietly and unobtrusively as possible, pulling the doors closed so that they looked exactly as they had before he had broken in. He returned to his van and drove a short distance, parking round the corner. Then he called the police, stressing who he was and what he had found — that there was little room for doubt this was the car they were seeking in connection with the attempted murder outside Walton prison. And that the garage was rented by none other than his employee, Amber Simpson.

Then it was over to them. His best course of action was to return home and wait for news, which he had been assured would come. Thanks to his charitable donations the police were anxious to keep him on side, so they dispatched a team of officers to lie in wait for the owner of the green car to appear. Afternoon stretched into evening, day into night, before there was any sign of action.

It was after ten o'clock when Alex took the phone call. A man had been apprehended as he drove the car away from the garage, and a can of petrol had been found in the boot, leading the arresting officers to suspect his intention had been to find a quiet spot and torch the vehicle, destroying the evidence. The man was refusing to speak, but they were confident that a spell in the cells would loosen his tongue. Meanwhile their colleagues had gone in search of Amber Simpson.

There had been nobody at home. The pristine flat was empty, although signs of recent activity had been found in the bin: a thoroughly scrubbed container from a ready meal, wrapping from a packet of oven chips, the trimmings from salad vegetables. Of the occupant of the flat, however, there was no trace. The manager of

Chillex had vanished into thin air.

Alex had racked his brains as to where she might have gone. He gave the police the OK to go to the club and search within, although he doubted she would have chosen anywhere so obvious. The police guard at the hospital had been alerted, although again it was unlikely Amber would risk turning up there now she knew how closely Kate was being watched. Alex gave them the woman's former address over in Litherland, although that was even more of a long shot as Amber had made no secret of the fact that she hated the place, and had never mentioned any friends or even acquaintances in the time she'd lived there. In fact she'd never talked about friends at all. Giles had been the one person he knew of in her private life, and he hadn't been able to wait to get away from her. Now Alex came to think of it, Amber's life was desperately sad. She had no close relationships at work; her rivalry with Marty was widely known, and with everyone else she had been professional but decidedly cool. She had concentrated her energy on her obsession with Alex and, when a rival had stepped into her path, on destroying her. Destroying his wonderful Kate.

A day had passed since the operation at the garage and the Sefton Park flat but there had been no progress. CCTV of the area had been scrutinized but it was like looking for a needle in a haystack: a woman of average height, on her own, wearing who knew what, could blend into a crowd at will. The one thing Alex was convinced of was that she wouldn't be far away. She would not want to be out of reach of the object of her driving obsession: him. At some point in the not too distant future, he was sure she would emerge, and he would just have to be ready for that — unless the police could catch her first. But where was she?

★　★　★

Kylie glared at the vacuum cleaner and its odd attachments. She'd never bothered with the thing at home, and her mother hadn't seemed to have any trouble with it. But this was a whole new kettle of fish and looked completely different from their old one. Still, she was determined not to let Brenda down. She knew how house-proud the little woman was, and just because the housekeeper was away didn't mean everything had to fall apart on the domestic front. Kylie had decided to take her place as far as possible, but she might have bitten off more than she could chew — with this device at least.

She picked up the nozzle piece again and tried to work out where it went. The tube seemed to be a completely different size. Cautiously she poked around the body of the machine and pushed various buttons and panels. Finally one sprang back, revealing another place where the nozzle's tube might fit. With a cry of triumph, Kylie twisted it into place and pressed the on button. It worked.

Now she only had to drag the thing up the stairs, cleaning as she went. Bending over wasn't as easy as it used to be, now she was noticeably

306

thickening around the waist, but at least she wasn't being sick all the time like before. She wouldn't even think about it. She concentrated on not tripping over the lead as she progressed upwards to the top landing. Nobody was going to say the place had gone to rack and ruin in the Bees' absence, not if she had anything to do with it.

She didn't want to imagine what could have happened to Kate. Kate had been so kind to her, and she'd had absolutely no reason to be — she hadn't known her from Eve and might well have despised her for getting pregnant so young. Instead she'd taken her under her generous wing and helped her to see how she might have a future. It was almost as if someone had removed a blindfold. Kylie had been at the point of despair, unable to get past the enormity of having a baby and her mother's opposition, which led to a tidal wave of guilt when her parents separated. Now she was more certain of what she wanted to do, even if the way ahead would be fraught with difficulties. She felt that she was in a place where she could face them — and it was all down to Alex and Kate. Kate, who even now was lying in a hospital bed, her ribs broken and her eyesight damaged, all totally undeserved.

Well, there might not be much Kylie could do about that, but she could ensure that the house was as spick and span as possible for whenever Kate was deemed fit enough to return. She knew of the woman's OCD, how painful she would find it if the place was a tip. Everything had to be just right, and Kylie would do her utmost to live up to Mrs Bee's high standards. She might even venture into the inner sanctum, the shrine to John Lennon.

Kylie wasn't sure how she felt about that. Of course she knew who he was, who the Beatles were — you couldn't grow up in Bootle and miss that piece of information. Sometimes her dad would belt out one of the songs, to make a change from his usual favourites such as 'I Will Survive'. He'd taught her and her sisters the words to 'Yellow Submarine' and 'Octopus's Garden'. That wasn't quite the same as going into a small, windowless room dedicated to a dead man. There were valuable things in there, Mrs Bee had said, items that would fetch a lot of money if Alex ever wanted to put them up for auction. The whole idea made Kylie nervous — what if she broke something?

Perhaps everybody would be back before the little room was due its regular clean. That would be best. However, if it came to it, she'd gather her courage and go in there, give it a once-over, so as not to let Brenda down. Nobody knew how long they'd be away, or what they'd face when they got there. Kylie wasn't stupid. Although the grown-ups had tried to shield her from the details, she was fully aware that there were two thugs who'd once worked for Kate's husband now on the loose in France, on the hunt for little Amelia. They were dangerous men who would stop at nothing. Brenda, Brian, Tim and Julia were taking a big risk. There was no way of telling what they'd encounter once they got to the little village where Kate's parents had gone. Kylie briefly shut her eyes and tried to push away the thought that they might well be walking into an ambush.

No, that couldn't happen, wouldn't happen. Tim was a clever man, everyone said so. He'd think of something. He was smarter than any lowlife criminals, surely. Kylie gave her head a shake and her newly natural-coloured hair swung about her face. She finished the last tread of the stairs and switched off the vacuum. She'd play her part, however small, in keeping this show on the road and then, when they brought Amelia home, she could help look after her. If there was one thing she was good at, it was caring for young children.

14

Tim ran his eyes over the rack of newspapers in the shop opposite the hotel. Everyone else was taking the opportunity to rest after the journey, but he wanted to get going, test the lie of the land. For such a small place, the range of papers available was impressive. French ones, obviously, with today's date. Then there were German and Spanish ones — yesterday's. Finally he saw what he was looking for: British ones, two days old, most of them. He picked up *The Times* and for good measure the *Daily Mail*. Of course, he could have bought today's paper at the airport before setting off, but he wanted to see what news might have reached any British people around here. He glanced around, but the heat of the day meant that all sensible folk were inside in the shade. Well, he didn't need to be sensible, he just had to get the job done.

He took the papers to the counter and his loose change from his pocket. '*Parlez-vous anglais?*' he asked.

'But of course,' said the man behind the counter, emerging from the shadows. He was older than Tim, maybe in his forties, with jet black hair and a casual yet immaculate shirt, worn in the way that only the French could achieve. 'We 'ave a lot of English visitors 'ere.'

That was a relief. Tim had managed to understand the satnav but that was partly because he knew what sort of things it was likely to say. His schoolboy French was rusty and he didn't trust it to get him through anything but the simplest of conversations. He hoped it would improve once he got used to the sounds of the language again, but he didn't want to rely on it.

'Have there been many around recently?' he asked now, as lightly as he could, handing over his euros.

'Oh, quite a few,' the man said, handing some coins back across the counter. 'Some are just passing through; others stay for a few days, to see *la belle Loire*, you know.'

'Of course.' Tim nodded, aware that few other British visitors would have the same urgent mission as he did. 'We're here to see some family friends,' he went on, thinking he had better offer some information if he hoped to get anything useful in return. 'We think some other people who know them might be here too. I wonder if you have seen two men, one very big and older than me, and one about my age. They've got London accents.'

The shopkeeper shrugged. 'You English all sound the same to me.' He smiled. 'But mostly it is families or older couples. Sometimes students with their . . . how do you call them, bags on the back.'

'Rucksacks,' said Tim, with a sinking feeling. Max and Trev would not fall into any of those categories.

'Yes, rucksacks.' The man paused to think. 'But now you say it, I am remembering something. It was a little while ago . . . I recall

311

this man because he was very big. He was alone, though. He seemed . . . not afraid, but a little bit as if he has worries. Would that be your friend?'

Tim wanted to say Max was no friend of his, but stopped himself in time. 'Maybe,' he responded instead. 'I don't think he knows France very well, so he might be worried about that, you know, not being able to speak to people or find his way around.'

The man snapped his fingers. 'Yes. He ask me directions. He was a little bit lost. He had a map but it did not have the small streets on it. I say him where he find bicycles.'

Tim nodded. 'That might well be him. Thank you. That's very helpful.'

The man smiled back. 'I am 'ere to 'elp.'

Tim grinned and tucked his papers under his arm. He would find a pleasant little cafe to sip a coffee or maybe a cool drink and read the news. Then he would go in search of a bike hire shop, to see if anyone there remembered the man who he was increasingly convinced must be Max.

★   ★   ★

Max set down his shovel and wiped the perspiration from his brow with his forearm. The East End never got this hot. The trees in the middle distance seemed to swim before his eyes as waves of heat rose from the baked ground of the graveyard. Breaking the earth when it was this dry was exhausting. In his old life he'd have complained about it to Trev and Brains and Weasel — never upwards to any of the bosses, he wasn't stupid — but the four of them always shared their misery. Now, though, he couldn't do that as he still couldn't speak the lingo, though he was trying. Sometimes his colleagues spoke slowly enough for him to get the gist of what they meant, but a lot of the time it was impossible.

Somehow, though, he didn't feel like complaining now. He felt as if he'd been handed a second chance. Even if the work was hot and back-breaking, he didn't have the slightest urge to whinge. He loved this place. He felt as if he'd been reborn. The simple kindness he'd been shown, the food, the air, it was all unlike anything he'd ever experienced before. Sometimes he had to pinch himself to test if it was all a dream.

His hand brushed against his pocket and he remembered the rosary beads that he carried here. He'd taken Père Pierre's advice and started using them as worry beads, and was slowly getting accustomed to them. Back home he'd probably have been laughed at for getting them out in public, but here everyone seemed to think it was normal. He could walk along the street running them through his fingers and nobody batted an eyelid. Gradually it was becoming a habit. They were especially handy when his thoughts turned to Trev, as they frequently did. Poor Trev. If only he'd loved this country as much as Max himself did — but he hadn't and that was that. His death had freed his former partner in crime to move on to a new life — as long as he didn't get caught.

Max sent up a reminder to whoever was around to listen that he and Trev hadn't gone through with the kidnapping. When he looked back to how he'd been thinking on the way over here, seriously intending to snatch a little girl — one whose head had been bashed in, to boot — he could scarcely recognize himself. Would they really have threatened a kiddy with actual harm? What if she'd screamed, or been difficult in some other way? Was that who he was, a child abductor? Sure, he'd done some pretty bad things back in London, but he'd never knowingly hurt a child. Handed out the occasional slap, maybe, if one had been deserved. This was on an entirely different level.

At least now the child was safe — or safe from him. Now the loot had been found there was no point in stealing her in order to put pressure on the mother. But what if someone wanted to revenge themselves on Kate Latimer, who was still living the life of Riley if that big place they'd trashed was anything to go by? Once she sold Jim's London house she'd be sitting pretty once again. He didn't wish her harm any longer, but would all the people put out of work when the gang had folded feel the same? All the many associates of Gentleman Jim and his henchmen over the years? Maybe the heat was baking his brain and he wasn't thinking straight, but he was suddenly filled with anxiety for the child.

Should he try to warn the grandparents? Get a message to them somehow? Go and see them in person? But if he did that he'd not only risk blowing his cover, he'd have to take leave of absence from a job he'd only just started. He'd have to explain himself to Père Pierre. Max let out a big sigh. Realistically, one day he was going to have to do that anyway, to come clean to his benefactor. He had the strong impression that the priest wouldn't be judgemental, but all the same, who'd welcome a would-be child abductor into their home? Once the good father knew the truth he might feel differently about trusting Max. Who wouldn't? Max's face creased with anxiety. He wasn't used to having a conscience and he didn't really like it. It was inconvenient, to say the least. To live with himself, he was going to have to do something to protect the child and he would have to tell the priest what had brought him to this point in his life. He knew it was the only way to stand a chance of staying here. But if he did say something, it might all fall apart. He couldn't do it. Not yet. He didn't dare.

★ ★ ★

I sit and watch her eat, my Kate. I bring her small nutritious meals three times a day and make sure she's got healthy snacks in between or in case something happens to prevent my next visit. It's not that I don't trust the food at the hospital — they've been excellent about everything so far — it's just that I can't bear for her to have anything but the best. Especially now, when she's so pale and so injured. She's picking her way through a Marks & Spencer salad. I can tell she's trying to look as if there's nothing wrong, that she's enjoying it with a strong appetite, that she's not in pain, but the reverse is true. How can it not be when her face is so bruised? Just moving her jaw muscles must be agony. But she'll never admit it.

The doctors have impressed upon her that she must leave all the superficial facial injuries alone or she'll suffer permanent scarring, but it must be hell on wheels not to pick the scabs and scratches that pepper her once immaculate complexion. It makes my own face itch just to see them. I'd adore her even with scars but I know she will not want them as they will bring to mind the terrible image of the car bearing down on her, its murderous intent abundantly clear. She will want to return to how she was before that dreadful day, but will that ever be possible?

She looks up, in full knowledge that I have been watching her, and lays down her fork. The salad is only half-finished.

'Eat up,' I say, trying to sound upbeat and positive.

'I will. I'm just taking a break. It's allowed, you know.' She flashes a glance at me, and the undamaged eye still retains its bright fire. Its companion, however, remains resolutely shut, the bruising around it now turning livid purple and deep blue, from the former red and brown. The doctors have told me that's a good and necessary thing and when those colours begin to fade she may be able to open the eyelid again. There's no reason to believe the damage is permanent. Or at least that's what they say. I wish I fully believed them.

'Has there been any further development?' she asks now. 'Has that foul rogue broken his silence yet?'

I shake my head. I checked with the police before visiting her, of course, as I knew that would be one of the first things she would want to know. However, while we are desperate for a speedy resolution to the case, the pace of justice cannot be hurried.

'No,' I tell her. 'He's keeping to his vow of silence. The police have applied for and been granted an extension to how long they can keep him without charging him, though. So there is still room for hope.'

She harrumphs impatiently. She's all for flouting procedure, this goddess of mine. But even for her, they cannot bend the rules.

'Surely they have enough evidence to charge him.' She thinks they are dragging their feet.

'They don't want to risk him getting off if they aren't fully prepared,' I remind her. To us, from our point of view, the case seems obvious, but to a jury, all of whom must be unconnected to the characters involved, it might not appear so clear cut.

'Well, what about France? Any news from there?' She's desperate for some progress, somewhere. Lying confined to her hospital bed is torture for one normally so active and decisive.

'Tim's on the trail. Don't even begin to worry about that. They have all arrived safely and are just settling in before they go to meet your parents. And Amelia, of course.' In one way I am deeply jealous of the four of them, who are

317

going to make the acquaintance of this very special little girl before I do. And yet my love for her mother dictates that I must be here, guarding her, as no matter how much I wish it I cannot be in two places at once.

'No sign of the gruesome twosome, then?' She gives me a smile, which lifts my heart. If she can joke about this horrendous pair then her spirits must be bearing up. Their threat is anything but a laughing matter, as we are all only too well aware.

'He might have a lead — he texted a while ago. He'll let us know as soon as there is anything definite. You know Tim — he won't want to raise our expectations but he won't leave us languishing in ignorance either.'

'Ignorance is bliss.' She cocks her head to one side and attempts a pout.

'Knowing you is bliss,' I say, stepping forward and planting a gentle kiss on her forehead. God knows I want nothing more than to gather her into my arms but I know I cannot, or not for the moment at least. To think that I went to all those lengths to protect her, making it widely known that we were married, moving her into my house, and yet it still wasn't enough. Somebody wanted her dead and we were looking in the wrong direction, fearing recriminations from her late husband's associates, when all the time the real danger lay closer to home. And we still are none the wiser as to the whereabouts of Amber Simpson. The police are on full alert, as am I, waiting for her to make her move. Which they and I are fully convinced she will do, now her plot has been thwarted. The only question is when and where she will do it. For now, I have to remain on red alert at all times.

It will be agony for someone as obsessive as her to be uprooted from the order of her home and routine of her work. She must be growing increasingly anxious and liable to commit a desperate and random reprisal. I could do with Tim's take on her, how the balance of her mind will be affected by this major setback to her plans, but he's got a more vital role in this grim piece of theatre. He can fill me in later. Perhaps he can write a paper on it and make his name — there must be something good to come out of all this.

I mentally upbraid myself. I have to have faith that everything will work out, not allow myself to succumb to despair. That's not like me. Look what she's done, my Kate — she's got me feeling emotions after all these years and it's not at all comfortable. With love comes pain. For most of my life I dismissed that as a cliché, but now the truth of it has made itself all too agonizingly real.

Yet it is worth it. Life before Kate — I can hardly believe how rapidly that is receding into the far distance. Since I met her, colours have become sharper, sounds more vivid, tastes more pronounced; the very air smells different. I am more vitally, thrillingly alive than I've ever been, more indeed than I ever dreamed possible. She has done this, she alone. I am powerless to stop it, and I don't want to.

So, quite simply, I have to keep her alive.

Brenda twisted nervously in the back seat as Tim put the car into gear. It still didn't feel right, this driving on the wrong side. But she had to admit she felt better for a lie-down in the hotel. She had no complaints about the place, even if the pillows were a funny shape compared to the ones back home and there was a strange thing in the bathroom that looked as if it might be for washing your feet. All the plugs were wrong, too. Julia had come prepared and lent her a spare adaptor.

Tim had filled them in when he'd returned to the hotel. No lying down for him — he'd been out exploring the place and asking around to see if there was any news to help them. From the newsagent's he'd gone to the bike hire shop and what he'd heard there had sparked his interest. True, there had only been one English man, not two, but the assistant's description had matched one of the photos he'd seen in the papers. The assistant had been uncertain about the man's state of mind, as the language barrier had prevented his getting a clear picture, but the man's size was indisputable. It made him stand out and stick in the memory. The assistant had got the impression he was pretty jumpy, especially when he'd come back to return the bikes — he had brought them separately and the second time had been more nervous than ever. However, he had given no clue as to where he was going next, only that he had a car and so didn't need the bikes any more. There had been no sign of a travelling companion, but the fact that there had been two bikes suggested he wasn't on his own.

The assistant had checked the date when the bikes had been brought back and it was back in May, and there had been no sign of the man since. That didn't mean that Max was no longer in the area, of course, just that the assistant hadn't seen him, but in such a small village it would have been hard to hide if you were that conspicuous.

It was hard to know for sure based on such slender evidence, but it could be that Max and Trev had gone to ground for some reason. That didn't mean that they were no longer a threat, only that they hadn't yet carried out the act they had been dispatched to commit. In one way it was reassuring to know that the four of them hadn't set off on a wild goose chase: the criminals had almost definitely been seen in the area, or at least one of them had. It also meant that they were in time to save Amelia, if they acted fast. So they were now on their way to meet Kate's parents and the little girl. The beautiful green countryside flashed by the window, and Brenda took a deep breath and then sighed it out. They just had to hold their nerve and get this job done, for Kate's sake and for Alex's. Those two must be beside themselves with worry back in Liverpool, but she for one was determined not to let them down. She glanced over at Julia, whose thinness was more pronounced than ever in the bright sunshine and contrasting deep shadows.

Julia bit her lip. Then she realized that the older woman was looking at her and she smiled in what she hoped was a comforting way, knowing how anxious Brenda was about being away from home on foreign soil. She fought to hide her own anxiety, as it was something she could not share with anyone, not even Tim. It would have been selfish in view of what they had all set out to do.

She dreaded meeting Kate's father. Even when she said that to herself it sounded mean and ungrateful. But she'd spent so long nursing her mother, and her father had been ill before that — she could not stand the thought of encountering another sick old person. She knew this was a totally different scenario and she berated herself, trying to push away her fears, but logic had nothing to do with it. The sights and smells of the sickroom were too close still, her mother's death hanging over her, and she baulked at the thought of crossing the threshold into another place of illness. She shuddered involuntarily. She couldn't fall apart, not here, not when the Bees were relying on her and Tim. She had not hesitated to give up her at-home honeymoon to come on this rescue mission, but she hadn't quite thought it through — what it might entail. Too late now. Tim was barrelling along the country lanes, happy now that he was actively doing something, and she admired and loved him for it. She could not let him down.

'All right, love?' Brenda asked quietly. 'You're not getting car sick being in the back with me, are you? I know some people do and these roads are all windy, aren't they?'

'No, no, I'm fine.' Julia forced her face to relax and her voice to carry conviction.

'I'll wind down my window anyway,' offered Brenda, but she couldn't find the right button in the unfamiliar car.

Tim, overhearing the muttered conversation, obligingly slid down his own window, and a fresh breeze drifted back to the occupants of the rear seats. It carried the unfamiliar and tantalizing scents of the area and Julia breathed them in, knowing she should be glad of the chance to be here, despite the circumstances. She turned her face to the window so that the others wouldn't see her expression and read her thoughts. She had to steel herself for the coming encounter somehow.

'Not long now,' said Tim, thinking this would be exactly what his new wife wanted to hear.

'Lovely,' was Julia's reply. But she didn't mean it at all.

15

The old-fashioned brass bell clanged above the door as a very well-dressed woman entered the discreet antiques shop. She wore dark glasses and a neat dark red straw hat, which the shopkeeper thought could be because of the rare bright sunny day — you didn't see many of those in Manchester. Or, as was the case with so many of his customers, she might just wish to keep her identity hidden.

Since she removed neither hat nor glasses as she approached him, he assumed it was the latter.

Amber paused for a moment to reach into her capacious bag, which she'd just about managed to sling over her shoulder in an attempt to make it seem as if it was just another designer model, although it was straining at the seams. The antiques dealer smirked slightly; not only did his visitor wish to remain anonymous, she didn't want it to be known she was carrying heavy, and possibly valuable, items either.

Manchester was the ideal destination. It was easily reached from her current base, and she'd been able to prop her heavy bag on the train seat beside her without anyone's raising an eyebrow. The city had a large population, with plenty of big spenders — traditional fans of antiques, or newer media types keen to furnish their new homes; even developers seeking to make their refurbished properties look more authentic than they actually were. All of these groups added up to a decent market for her goods.

She'd assessed the contents of her new flat with a detached and practical eye. She didn't want to lose any of the gorgeous objects in it but if she was strictly honest she didn't need them; they were beautiful decorations but not essential. What was essential was that she got her hands on some cash. She knew she couldn't return to work after her few days off. That would be madness. Alex was on to her. It had to have been he who'd alerted the police so that they were waiting for Gus when he left the lock-up. She didn't know if he'd spill the beans or not, if she could rely on his silence, but he would probably crack sooner or later. She couldn't expect him to sacrifice himself for her, so she had to lie low until she could come up with a new plan.

The man at the counter was smiling encouragingly and she painted on her best, most confident smile as she brought the first item out of the bag: an elegant cut-glass vase. She gave him her carefully thought out story, telling him how she'd inherited a stunning collection of objects from a relative but simply didn't have the room to keep them herself. Even as she was saying the words she was reflecting on how it was almost true. Kate was Alex's first wife, sure, but if she played her cards right she herself could be his second. That made them all but related. It was fate.

The man nodded, reaching out to take the vase and then examining it with a practised eye.

He offered her a price and she pretended to think about it, having researched all the items first on eBay. She knew she dared not use the internet for the selling process itself, but that didn't mean she had to go into the negotiation totally unprepared. She countered his offer with a figure she knew he wouldn't accept. He raised his first bid, she lowered hers — and within a few minutes they had agreed on an amount that meant he could add his mark-up and make a profit, and she felt she'd done all right.

Secretly satisfied, she drew out the rest of the contents of the bag, and piece by piece she by turns haggled with and flattered the antiques dealer. He seemed more than happy to play along with the game, and was evidently in no hurry. Amber felt herself relaxing for the first time in days. Maybe this was something she could do in the future: source antiques and then sell them on. She thought she might have the eye for it.

Finally they concluded the deal. 'A pleasure to do business with you,' said the dealer, drawing his pad of receipts from behind the till and reaching for a stylish fountain pen. 'I'll just fill this in, so my records are straight.' He smiled broadly to indicate he wasn't one of these Johnny-come-latelies operating on the black market. 'Now, what name shall I put, Miss . . . '

Amber almost blurted out her real surname, so lulled was she by the success of her day. Then survival instinct kicked in. 'Sampson,' she lied easily. 'Amanda Sampson.' It was close enough to the real thing for her to remember if it ever came to that; she remembered reading that the best lies were those that contained more than a grain of truth. The man asked her to countersign the pad and she scrawled her initials. Job done.

Swinging the now unencumbered bag as she strode along the pavement in the direction of the train station, she congratulated herself on playing her hand as well as she had. There was a beautiful symmetry to the whole affair. Kate had pretty well forced her to accept her overwhelming generosity and showered her with all these hand-me-downs, and Amber was putting them to the best possible use: selling them off in the cause of destroying her benefactor. She wasn't yet sure of the details of Plan B, but she was as certain as she'd ever been of anything in her life that they would come to her. It was just a matter of time.

Amber wondered if it would be worth calling Giles once she was back in the city. She'd taken up residence in an Airbnb not too far from Sefton Park but on a very quiet street, where she could be anonymous. The owners hadn't asked her anything about herself. They were hardly ever there; they wouldn't care if she brought the handsome young doctor home for a little diversion. He must have finished his tedious research paper by now. Then again, Giles was getting a little insipid for her taste. When it came down to it, he was a very poor substitute for Alex Price. Perhaps she'd wait until she could savour the genuine article.

★ ★ ★

327

Even as Tim pulled the car into the wide gravel drive, Brenda caught a fleeting glimpse of pale yellow — a small child-size frock, no doubt attached to a small child who at this moment was running in and out of the trees which stood to one side of the picturesque building. It had those shutters at the windows, the same as the ones she'd noticed when they had first arrived in France — so different from anything she was used to back home. Then again, she thought they must come in handy on bright sunny days, as the light here was stronger than you ever encountered in Liverpool, even at the height of summer. She thought it must fade the upholstery in no time at all. If she lived here, she'd want shutters too.

As the four of them got out of the car, a woman appeared round the side of the house. Brenda nearly gasped. It was like seeing an older version of Kate: a little shorter, admittedly, but with those striking looks and a similar penetrating expression. The woman wore her hair in a sophisticated geometric bob which appeared to be subtly tinted, and her clothes were elegant but simple, in cream linen. If Brenda had stopped to think what Kate's mother might be like, this would have been the description she would have given.

The woman stepped towards them and held out her hand. Tim went to greet her and shook hands. 'Mrs Power? Very pleased to meet you.' He squinted a little in the sunshine.

'You must be Dr Dyson,' the woman said, and she even sounded like Kate, in those tones that only money could buy.

'Please, call me Tim. This is my wife, Julia. And here are Mr and Mrs . . . '

'Brenda and Brian,' said Brenda firmly, coming forward as well. 'Your Kate doesn't give us any of that Mr and Mrs nonsense and so neither will you. This is no time to stand on cemetery.'

Mrs Power barely batted an eyelid. 'Absolutely. I couldn't agree more. Now come around to the garden, where we can be more comfortable in the shade. There's someone who's very eager to see you.'

She led the way down a side path into a wide expanse of lawn, edged by a patio in pale stone, on which stood a weathered wooden table and a collection of chairs, some wood, some metal, with assorted cushions on their seats. 'Do settle yourselves. I won't be a minute.' She disappeared inside through a half-open door and re-emerged almost immediately bearing a large tray. Ice cubes clinked as she set a tall jug of still lemonade on the table, and half a dozen chunky glass tumblers. 'Now, you must be hot and thirsty. Do help yourselves while I go to find my granddaughter.'

Julia poured the lemonade as the others did as suggested and sat down round the table. A parasol stood to one side of it and Julia tilted it so they were all sheltered from the blazing sun. She realized how effective the air conditioning in the car had been. Taking her own glass, she pulled up one of the metal chairs next to Tim.

'All right?' he asked, angling a concerned

glance at her. 'Heat not too much for you?'

She shook her head, not wanting to come across as a delicate flower. 'I'm fine. This is a gorgeous spot, isn't it?'

'You're right there.' Tim gazed around in appreciation. Tall dark green trees surrounded the property, lush with summer, and there was a sound of birdsong coming from some of the topmost branches. Bees buzzed lazily in the long flower beds that stretched away to the furthermost boundary, and he wondered if anyone round here made honey. Alex would already be asking for details, checking which plants were most attractive to the insects, finding out which flavours of honey were most successful. Tim himself was content to listen to the creatures as they flew, while sipping the delicious lemonade.

'Cheers,' said Brenda, catching his eye and raising her tumbler. 'It's all right, this, isn't it? This beats the bottled stuff from the Co-op, I don't mind saying.'

'Totally different drink,' Julia agreed wryly.

Brenda looked at the cloudy lemon liquid. 'I'm going to try doing this when we get back. I bet it'll help Kate get better, perk her up no end. And that Kylie will like it too.'

'You may well be right, Mrs Bee,' said Tim, 'but remember, things that taste marvellous when you're abroad often fail to live up to expectations once you get them home.'

Brenda raised her eyebrows. 'Don't talk soft. This is grand stuff, and I can't see how it wouldn't be just as good back in Liverpool.'

Tim shrugged. 'It might well be. I'm just

saying, that's what often happens when you bring food and drink back from holiday.'

Brenda sensed a challenge and had no intention of backing down. 'That's as may be. I wouldn't know, being as I've never been anywhere foreign before. But I bet you right now I can make something like this and you'll love it just as much.'

Tim grinned. 'If you make it, Mrs Bee, I'm sure it will be delicious.' He turned as the noise of footsteps interrupted them.

On the patio, holding her grandmother's hand, stood a little girl in a pale yellow dress, her hair hidden under a soft cotton sun hat. If Mrs Power looked like Kate, this little girl's resemblance was even stronger. She had the indomitable air that was the essence of Kate — and it was even more impressive when displayed by one so young.

'Hello. *Bonjour*,' she said, and her bright eyes danced with mischief. 'Have you come to take me back to Mummy?'

For a moment Brenda's heart stood still. This poor child could have little idea of what was going on, the dangers which might be circling her here in the midst of what looked like Paradise. She had already suffered so much. She seemed none the worse for it, on the strength of this brief encounter so far, but Brenda had no doubt that the sun hat not only afforded protection from the hot rays but also hid the injuries inflicted by the late Gentleman Jim Latimer and the subsequent marks from the surgeon's scalpel. That the child was so cheerful and confident after such an ordeal was a testament to her mother, her grandparents and her own strong character.

Once again it was Tim who spoke first. 'If you'd like to come with us, then yes. We're all good friends of your mummy's.' He paused to look round at the others. 'We'd love you to come along. We might not go straight back, though — we're on holiday. Maybe you could show us around a bit? Your mummy told us you were learning French.'

'*Mais oui.*' The little girl giggled. 'I'm not very good yet. But I can ask for ice cream and chocolate and things like that, when Granny lets me.'

The older woman beamed down at her charge. 'And you're very good at doing that, but you know you mustn't have them every day or what will happen?'

'It'll ruin my teeth,' said the little girl, pulling a face. 'Then I won't be able to chew anything so it won't be worth it.' She paused as if to emphasize the unfairness of such an outcome. 'I can show you around here though. We go to the next town and I know the way, and where to have dinner. And where Granny buys me new dresses.' Her eyes lit up at the thought, and Tim smiled at the way the tendency to love shopping seemed to be inherited.

'Now, you know you've got plenty of new dresses,' her grandmother said gently. 'You probably don't need any more for the next week or two at least. Ah, listen, that sounds like Granddad. I expect he's woken up, but he'll want to meet you all right away. He's not been

332

well,' as a fit of coughing echoed across the patio, 'but he's slightly better now. He's so grateful you could come — he feels terrible about tying Amelia and me here.'

'We understand,' said Tim at once.

Julia stood up. 'You'll want to talk about arrangements, won't you?' She held out her hand to the little girl. 'Amelia, why don't you give me a tour of the garden? It's so lovely — much bigger than the one where I live. You can tell me everything about it.'

'All right,' said Amelia, with a look of undisguised pity that anyone could live some-where without a big garden. 'Come with me. This way.' She led Julia off around the side of the house with great authority, just as the coughing grew louder and the door through to the house opened.

★ ★ ★

Kate's father slowly and shakily took a seat next to his wife. Everyone instinctively allowed him a moment to regain his breath. Finally he looked up, and if they had expected a tired and defeated old man they were sorely mistaken. His breath might be ragged and his complexion too pallid for one who had spent several months in the Loire valley, but his eyes were as sharp as his daughter's.

'I must thank you for coming all this way, and two of you on your honeymoon, as I understand it,' he said.

'It's nothing . . . ' Tim started, but the old

man held up his hand.

'It is not nothing. It is a very big something, and my wife and I are immensely grateful.' He squeezed her hand and Mrs Power squeezed back. 'If circumstances were different, we would at this very moment be speeding back to England with Amelia. As things stand, though, as you can see, I am in no state to travel.'

Tim looked him straight in the eye. 'I agree, and as a medic I have to recommend you stay where you are until your lung function has improved.' He gave Mr Power what he hoped was a reassuring look, even though he had no real idea of how long that might take or even how likely it was to happen, in reality.

Mr Power nodded. 'So, I understand we are on the horns of a dilemma. Amelia cannot stay here if she's threatened with the possibility of being kidnapped. Yet she cannot return home either, since it would be too frightening for her to see my poor daughter in her current condition.'

'Exactly.' Tim took a sip of his lemonade, relishing the sharpness. 'It's our idea to ensure she reaches home safely, but indirectly. We are in regular contact with Alex and we will know as soon as Kate is ready to welcome Amelia home, which she is obviously longing to do. But meanwhile, it makes sense for us to take her on a tour. Brian and Brenda here' — he turned to indicate the Bees — 'haven't been to France before, and it would be a shame to come all this way and then not to explore the region. As long as Amelia feels comfortable with us, we'd like nothing better than to set out together.'

'And it will give you young people a chance to enjoy that honeymoon of yours.' Mrs Power's eyes crinkled with kindness. 'Even though it was many years ago, we haven't forgotten ours. Such precious memories. And actually we were in France ourselves — a little further south, near Avignon. What marvellous rosé wine.' She sighed. 'That was when we were young and able to get about a little more than we can now. I do hope you can make some time for yourselves, store some precious memories of your own.'

Brenda sat up straight. 'Don't you go worrying about that. Brian and me'll see to it. We're good with young children — we've just been looking after a little boy of two. Your Amelia will want for nothing. Then Tim and Julia can have all the time together that they want.'

Tim looked across at the often fiery little woman and realized she meant it. They sometimes fell out, usually over who was looking out for Alex's interest in the most useful way, and she was so fiercely protective of the man that she often didn't allow anyone else to get close. But now he could see that her phenomenal loyalty extended to Alex's close circle too — which now embraced Julia and himself. And, it would appear, Amelia too.

Mrs Power seemed relieved. 'Then our best course of action is to ensure Amelia gets to know you all as soon as possible. She's a friendly little soul, despite all she's been through. She's very bright, and has settled in to the ways of the region as if she was born to it. Never makes a fuss about unfamiliar tastes or things like that. I wouldn't go so far as to give her snails or frog legs, but I'd bet she'd try just about anything else.'

Brenda blanched at the mention of such items, but reminded herself that they'd passed several famous names in the world of global catering as they drove from the airport to their hotel, so the French must love pizzas and burgers just as much as the British did. You didn't hear as much about it, but the evidence was there none the less.

'In fact,' Mrs Power went on, 'why don't we celebrate your arrival this evening with a meal at a local restaurant? There are a couple in the village, even though it's so small. You'll find even the tiniest settlement over here has some sort of eatery, even if it's not much more than a handful of tables outside a bar. Fortunately we can run to something a little better here. You go and rest again properly, my love' — she turned to her husband and gave his arm a pat — 'and I shall telephone them to warn them of our arrival.' She turned back to her guests. 'It's not a smart place, you won't need to dress up, but the food is wonderful. Then Amelia can get used to you in a relaxed situation.' Her face became grave. 'Also, I feel it is much more unlikely that those criminals out there would make a move in a public place. So it will serve two purposes. Three, come to that, as it will give my husband and me a chance to get to know you too. Our rescue party.' She bestowed a dazzling smile on them, and each one of them realized afresh just how Kate had become the force of nature that she indisputably was.

★ ★ ★

Monica was nervous. She had never liked hospitals, whether it was visiting patients or being looked after herself, giving birth. She associated them with coming out more depressed than when she'd gone in. She hated the smell of disinfectant, the strip lighting, the shiny floors, everything. If she'd been in charge she'd have at least sorted out the decor. She hurried through the car park and in through the main doors, gritting her teeth, trying not to let her irritation show. She wasn't daft — she knew plenty of the people rushing around her would have serious matters of life and death on their minds. And she didn't want to get all het up when she was meant to be on a mission of mercy, but it was very hard. Look at that ugly colour they'd picked for the back wall. Did they seriously think that would help anyone feel better? 'Bleedin' ozzies,' she muttered.

She wasn't here to approve the interior decoration, though. Alex had called her, saying there was a meeting at his central office that he simply could not avoid, but it coincided with when he should be visiting Kate. He didn't want her to miss one of her regular meals; nor was he happy with the idea that she would be staring at the four walls, growing ever more frustrated. So would Monica step in and go in his stead?

Once Monica had ascertained that she wouldn't be expected to cook, merely to visit

Marks & Spencer and pick something up from a carefully chosen list, she had agreed with alacrity, because what sort of miserable bugger would refuse? She might not be over the moon about it but she absolutely had to go. So she'd visited the closest M & S and wandered up and down the aisles of the food hall, noting with approval how much ready-prepared stuff was available. No need for all that messy peeling and chopping. Then she'd applied herself to making a selection from Alex's list of specific foods that Kate would find acceptable. She found a balanced ready meal containing ingredients she'd never heard of, all foreign vegetables and strange grains, but it looked healthy enough, and colourful too — Monica nurtured a long-held suspicion of food that was too beige, thinking that particular colour belonged on soft leather furnishings but not on a plate. Unless it was that instant porridge . . . which obviously wasn't what was required here.

Now she clutched her carrier bag as she tried to follow Alex's directions to the ward. She didn't want to show herself up, trying to make out the complex signs with all the long words for the different departments. All very well if you'd been to university like Alex and Kate and Tim had, meaning they had no trouble with Haematology and Nephrology and Gastroenterology, but they floored her. She screwed her eyes shut for a second, trying to recall what he'd said, and when she was confident she'd got it right she set off. God, this place was enormous. She'd have worn lower heels if she'd thought, although she liked the added inches a good stiletto could provide. God knows she could do with them.

At last she reached the right door, and pushed her way through. Just as Alex had said, Kate was in the bed next to the ward manager's office. For a moment Monica thought the patient was asleep. Then she opened her eyes — both of them, though Alex had warned her that one eye had been very badly injured and was still part-shut. Monica gasped.

'He said you couldn't do that. He said you'd only look at me with one eye.'

Kate broke into a delighted smile. 'Not so. That man of mine doesn't know everything, as you can see.' She sat up properly. 'Come on in, Monica, make yourself at home. As you can tell, I've had to. I realize you won't approve of the curtains, and to tell you the truth I'd prefer something a little more neutral myself, but beggars can't be choosers.'

Monica pulled up the chair provided for visitors and perched on it, glancing uneasily around. There was that unmistakable smell of disinfectant, the special one that only hospitals seemed to have. God knows normally she was a big fan of any cleaning substance, but not this particular one. Still, she must put all that from her mind.

'Here, I got you this. Alex said you'd like it.' She took out the ready meal and little plastic fork.

Kate nodded in approval. 'Edamame. Just what the doctor ordered. Or he would if he had full control over the hospital kitchen.'

'Ed who?' Monica wasn't convinced, but then it wasn't her who had to eat it.

'I'll have it when you've gone. So rude to be the only one eating when others are present, I always think.' Kate tucked the meal and fork away into the utilitarian nightstand. 'So, tell me, Monica, how are you?'

'Me? I'm here to find out how you are,' Monica gasped. 'I'm the same as ever. You don't want to hear about me.'

'Oh, but I do.' Kate straightened herself on her pillows. 'I'm sick to death of being asked about me. It's so very boring. You must look upon it as your duty to entertain me, and what I wish to be entertained with is an account of how everything is in your life, as we haven't exactly been in contact since you took delivery of that letter.'

'No. Well.' Monica glanced down at her high-heeled shoes. 'All right. Things are going well at the house. I told them they had to get a move on to get the stairs in or I'll break my bleedin' neck one of these days going up those ladders. They tried to tell me I didn't have to go up to the upper floors but I told them straight I wasn't having none of that, or they'd get up to God knows what up there if I didn't check on them regular. So they've brought forward the delivery dates for the stairs, and they're sorting the last bits of tiling meanwhile. They're doing a good job with the grouting, I'll give them that.' She paused to draw breath. 'And I'm going to look for some proper bits and pieces to use as decorations when they've done. If I can't find anything I really like in Liverpool I might try a bit further away, somewhere like Manchester or Chester.'

'And you, Monica? How are you in yourself? Any news yet?'

Monica shook her head. 'I had them tests done but they're going to send the results to Tim's office. They won't be ready for a bit anyway. So I'm trying not to think about it. No point in worrying over something you can't change.'

'Very wise words,' Kate said with whole-hearted approval. 'Although I could probably have a word, see if they could redirect the results here and have a doctor talk them through with you, if you'd rather.'

Monica shook her head. 'No, cos then I'd just have to go through it all again with Tim explaining everything. Another doctor might not be so understanding — you know, what with Pete being the sort of singer what he is, and our Kylie being pregnant and all.' She sighed. 'I'll wait for them to come home.' Her hand flew to her mouth. 'Have I said something I shouldn't? You did know he's gone away, didn't you?'

Kate nodded. 'Don't worry, you haven't committed a faux pas.'

'A what?'

'An indiscretion. You haven't put your foot in it. Yes, I know that Tim and Julia have gone to France, along with the ever-faithful Bees. And very grateful I am to them, for rescuing my darling Amelia. They should be there by now, meeting my parents, and my precious little girl.'

Monica's shoulders sank a little with relief that

she hadn't gone and said something out of turn. Funny thing was, she was beginning to see why Kate missed her daughter so much. Just a short while ago she herself would have given an arm and a leg to be shot of hers, but now she was living apart from them she felt like she was missing those very limbs. Well, some of the time, anyway.

'So they can start bringing her back soon,' Monica offered brightly.

Kate sighed. 'Not while I look like this. My face is the size of a football. I can't frighten her like that, not after we've been apart for so long. It's a vile contradiction, actually. I'm bursting to see her, but I know I can't do so yet, for her own good.'

'But you are feeling better, aren't you?' Monica pressed. 'Your eye's open and that.'

'Yes, that's a huge relief. They tried to discuss it out of my hearing, but I know that they were worried I might lose my sight in the damaged eye. Fortunately, the vision's close to perfect already.' Kate pulled a face. 'However, it's only made me more aware what a total fright I look. My multi-coloured face would frighten the horses, let alone a little girl.'

Monica didn't know what to say. It was true, Kate did look as if she'd gone several rounds in the ring. 'But what about your other injuries? Surely they must be worse. A bit of bruising always heals in the end.'

Kate shrugged, and then winced a little. 'True, the ribs aren't great, but they'll mend in time. So will my spleen. My leg hurts, but at least it can't be seen. It's my face I'm concerned about. Would you do something for me?'

'Of course,' Monica said instantly, then wondered if she should have checked what it was first. You never knew how outrageous one of Kate's ideas might be.

'Be a darling and find me some arnica cream. It's excellent for bruises. I've mentioned it to Alex but he thinks I'm talking hokum and won't take me seriously.'

'Arnica?' Monica said doubtfully. 'Isn't that some mumbo-jumbo stuff? It's not proper medicine, is it?'

Kate glared at her severely. 'The likes of some doctors might not think it's proper medicine but I can tell you it works. Let's face it, I should know. Don't forget I've got plenty of previous form in covering up the after-effects of a good beating.'

Monica grimaced, knowing the effort it must take to be so casual when mentioning the savage attacks Kate had suffered at the hands of her late husband.

'I'm perfectly adept at masking the underlying injuries, the odd broken rib and suchlike,' Kate continued, 'but the state of my face is something else. I know that when the colour has faded and the swelling goes down I can do wonders with some carefully applied cosmetics, but before that can happen I need a little extra help. Arnica's the thing. So will you get some for me?'

Monica wavered.

'It will be no trouble. Boots will have some. Here, take some cash.' Kate pulled her purse

343

from the drawer of the nightstand. 'Can't have you spending your hard-earned wages on mumbo-jumbo potions.'

Monica hesitated. 'Well, if you're sure . . . '

Kate flashed her a smile and it was almost like the old Kate was back in the room. 'Of course I'm sure. I'm always sure of everything, you know that.'

Monica conceded defeat. 'All right, then. I'll pop down now so I can bring it back before visiting time's over.'

'That's the spirit. I'll be eternally grateful.' Kate's face set in an expression of determination. 'Because I need to get out of here as soon as possible and be in a fit state to welcome my little girl home. I'll do anything to speed up the process. Anything.'

★ ★ ★

Amber checked her phone, a snarl beginning to form as she did so. Getting back to her silent Airbnb room, she'd felt the need for company, to share her success at the antiques shop — not that she intended telling anyone about the details of that. But her mood was on the up, and she'd decided to call Giles after all. OK, he was no Alex Price, but he was sufficiently athletic and compliant. She wanted — no, needed — to work off her excess energy. A couple of hours on the treadmill wouldn't quite cut the mustard.

He wasn't answering, though. That annoyed her. Even if he was stuck in his research lab or the library he should surely have his mobile on vibrate, in case any urgent calls came in. As far as she was concerned, this was urgent. She'd left it for an hour and tried again but still answer came there none. What was he playing at?

She whirled around the room, noticing now how inferior it was to her flat only a few streets away. Compared to the old place in Litherland, it was luxurious and well presented, but now she knew what real quality was like she found it sub-standard. Her expression grew fiercer. She was ruined forever, and it was Kate's fault — giving her a taste of the good things in life, only to whisk them away again by failing to die when she should have done. The woman had no right to survive, no right to Alex Price and all the prestige and status that came with him. All of that should belong to her, Amber Simpson.

She forced herself to get a grip before her mood escalated into something uncontrollable. Losing it wouldn't help. She had to think straight. Giles might be working on a ward. He was attached to Alder Hey, wasn't he? That must be the solution. She'd ring him there, go through the switchboard, track him down that way. He'd probably be glad of the diversion — ministering to sick kids for hours on end must drive him mad. They'd be so demanding and yet so infuriatingly helpless. He'd welcome a call from her.

Before she could change her mind she found the number and dialled, focusing on sounding upbeat and polite. On no account must any trace of her real mood find its way into her voice. The eyes might be the windows to the soul but it was the voice that got you places — accepted as a professional, a rational human being worthy of attention and respect.

So when the receptionist refused her request to be put through she was startled. 'Why not?' she demanded, forgetting her resolution to hide her rising temper.

'Because he no longer works here,' said the receptionist.

'What? Since when?' Amber was flabbergasted. He'd said this was his ideal job, giving him the chance to conduct research into his favourite topic, and the prospect of making a real difference in his chosen field.

'I'm afraid I'm not at liberty to say, madam,' came the voice down the line. 'Now is there anything else I can help you with?'

Amber pressed the disconnect icon without deigning to reply. Madam yourself, she thought angrily. Could the woman have made a mistake? Confused him with someone else?

No, these people were trained to be accurate, otherwise they wouldn't have such a responsible position. It was highly unlikely there would be another Dr Girling on the staff. Something had happened and he had gone, left without telling her.

Amber's face twisted into a mask of pure fury. He had escaped her. He hadn't even had the decency to say goodbye or to tell her where he was going or what he was doing — he'd just vanished. She hadn't been enough for him. Just because he could see he wasn't going to get Kate, he'd done a runner. He hadn't spared a thought for Amber, despite all the kindness she'd shown him, all the times she'd welcomed him into her bed and the good times he'd had there. He'd counted all that as nothing. The despicable coward, the ungrateful monster.

Amber conveniently forgot that not long ago she'd been debating never ringing him again. Now she had been scorned her anger had grown to immense proportions in no time at all. She was beyond fury. No punishment was good enough for him. She had to deal him a killer blow, a lifetime of pain. There was only one thing she could think of which would achieve that — and by great good fortune it served her own purposes too. Kate Price could not be allowed to live.

16

Brenda stretched out and sighed with satisfaction. Even with the strangely shaped pillows, this was one of the most comfortable beds she'd ever slept in and she'd had the best night's rest she'd managed for ages. She wondered if that was because she'd been increasingly worried recently — all the trouble with Pete's family and Kylie in such a pickle, Kate's joyous appearance on the scene all too soon turning to near-tragedy, Alex coming out of his shell only to have his bubble of happiness burst in spectacular fashion. On top of all of that she'd had to come abroad. Brian turned over in his sleep and grunted, which at least was normal, and she felt grateful for his familiar presence.

Yet somehow yesterday evening had set her mind at ease. Kate's little girl was just adorable. Of course, all parents thought that about their own children, so Brenda hadn't put too much faith in what Kate had said about her daughter since she'd moved in, but she truly hadn't been exaggerating. Amelia was enchanting: extremely sociable and comfortable in the company of adults, even beyond what might be expected of an only child. She could hold a conversation, didn't make a fuss as it grew late, ate all her food with apparent enjoyment (and Brenda noted there was no kids' menu — she got what the grown-ups did) and left with her grandparents without complaint when they explained it was time to go.

This morning they were to pick her up from the Powers' home and begin stage one of their journey of adventure. Tim had arranged to swap the hire car for a bigger one, so they could fit in a child's seat and the extra luggage. They were to make their way slowly north, going where their fancy took them, until word reached them that Kate was in a fit state to welcome her daughter back. Alex had Skyped them yesterday and said she was getting more restless than ever at being restricted to her hospital bed, but the doctors wanted to keep her in to monitor her progress and there was no getting around that.

Brenda squinted at the lace curtains and the slatted shutters behind them, which let through the morning sunlight in bright white bars. Somewhere outside a bird was singing, and there were a few muffled shouts from what were probably tradesmen going about their early business. A few days ago she would have been terrified by this — they were shouting in their weird language and perhaps the birds sang in French too. Yet today Brenda had a sense that all was right with the world. She intended to hang on to that, and no London lowlifes were going to stop her enjoying this most unexpected of holidays.

★　★　★

'Happy, my darling? You've no regrets about doing this?' Tim propped himself up on one

349

elbow and regarded his new wife, the woman he loved more than anyone in the world. Her pixie-like face was relaxed in the soft light of the early morning but she was still far too thin.

'You needn't look at me like that, as if I'm going to break if you breathe on me too hard,' she said lazily.

Tim snorted. He'd been caught out and had his mind well and truly read. 'How do you do that? We've been apart for all these years and yet you still know what I'm thinking.'

Julia shrugged. 'Not difficult. Your face always shows exactly what's going on in your head.'

Tim recoiled in mock-horror, pulling his pillow to his chest. 'Oh no. You mean my patients haven't been taken in for all the time I've been in practice? It's a miracle I haven't been struck off.'

'Relax, honey. It's only me who can do it.' Julia laughed at him. 'Anyway, a few more meals like the one last night and you won't have to worry about me at all. I reckon I gained ten pounds just from the first course.'

Tim chucked the pillow to the bottom of the bed and drew her to him. 'It was fabulous, wasn't it? And those cheeses afterwards. Ones that you can't get back in England.'

'Let alone in Vermont. Guess I've made the right move. When I'm in need of cheese I can just hop on a short flight down to France in future.'

Tim smiled, and then laughed. 'I thought Brenda was going to keel over when she asked for the nearest thing to scouse and they brought her boeuf bourguignon.'

'She seemed to like it, though. Or if she didn't she hid it well, finishing it all off and wiping her plate clean with that crusty bread.'

'Stop it. You're making me hungry again. Wonder what's for breakfast? More bread? Croissants?'

'Ooh, yes please.' Julia rolled onto her back and stretched her arms above her head to the carved curved headboard. 'That would be most acceptable. Definitely makes me hungry all over again.'

Tim's eyes lit up. 'Is that all you're hungry for, Mrs Dyson?' As she smiled back up at him he drew her to him.

★ ★ ★

In the dim light of the presbytery scullery, Max was stacking plates, not at all resenting a task he would have considered beneath him only a short time ago. Kitchens were for women's work. But the housekeeper had a couple of days off and he found he was more than happy to lend a hand where he could. He hadn't volunteered to cook, as he realized that his skills were nowhere near up to the required standard, but everything else he could do. He carefully transferred the plates to the dresser. Back home he would have laughed at the delicate patterns on the crockery, but in this place it felt just right.

He sighed. He was living on borrowed time and he couldn't bear the thought of jeopardizing his new-found happiness here, but his recently awakened conscience was tormenting him more and more as the days rolled by. He didn't need St Bernadette to come to him in his dreams any more. Since she had spoken the mysterious words 'say twa' he had had no peace. Visions of Trev floated before his eyes at the most inconvenient moments. Images of a small girl separated from her family haunted him as he dug into the consecrated earth. Even thinking of Kate Latimer, or whatever name she was going by these days — Mrs Know-It-All, Have-It-All Kate — wrecked his composure as he considered all the ways he had helped to make her life hell. As if being married to Jim Latimer wouldn't have been bad enough.

Today was the day. He was going to speak to Père Pierre, although he knew full well it might cost him his position here. He'd put it off for ages but the truth was the savagery of his inner torment was outweighing the joy of living with the kindly priest. When he admitted to himself that this was the case he knew he had no option but to confess.

He stopped to run the rosary beads through his fingers once more. The steady rhythm of the movement calmed him. He would wait until the priest came in for breakfast after the first Mass of the day and then broach the subject. He considered whether he should have something to eat right now, in case the priest threw him out on his ear immediately, but somehow he had no appetite. His stomach churned in nervous dread. If he did this, it would be contrary to every self-serving act he had ever committed in his life. But if he didn't, he would be forever tortured by the pictures in his head — and they were what he deserved, he didn't kid himself otherwise.

As he pocketed the beads once more, he heard the outer door creak.

This was it.

'Father, I need to confess,' he blurted out as the priest entered the shadowy room.

Père Pierre regarded the man he had taken in, the man whose deep personal troubles followed him round like a black cloud. He had waited a long time to hear those words, unprompted and freely given. But now was not the time.

'*Mon fils*, I know you are in need of absolution,' he said, putting his hands on the big man's shoulders. 'However, I cannot hear what you have to say right at this moment. One of the young women in my congregation, she is, how do you say it, about to have a child. She is very sick and her mother fears the child will not live. I must be there when it is born in order that it does not die without blessing. We cannot leave the little one's soul in limbo, no? So I must go. Wait for me and I will hear your confession later. I cannot say how long I will be.'

With that he took an apple from the fruit bowl by the window and rushed out again. Leaving Max where he stood, stunned and defeated.

He'd geared himself up to admit to his many crimes, and now it seemed as if he'd have to hold on to them. He thought he was going to burst with the enormity of what he'd done and what he'd intended to do, and he didn't know if he could bear it.

The larger hire car was slightly more difficult to manoeuvre but Tim thought he was handling it well, considering he'd only been driving it since this morning. Amelia had been silent to begin with, slightly overawed at being in the presence of virtual strangers with no grandparents to turn to for reassurance, but it hadn't taken her long to perk up. She now sat in her booster seat wedged between Julia and Brenda, giving a running commentary on everything they passed.

Even inside the car she insisted on wearing her sun hat. It was as if taking it off was the one thing that made her afraid. Tim quietly wondered how deep the psychological wounds ran, for run they must. No human being, adult or child, could have gone through what this little girl had suffered and come out totally unmarked.

He could see in the rear-view mirror that Julia was beginning to doze off. They had stopped for lunch in a smallish town and wandered around aimlessly afterwards, not paying much attention to where they were, simply enjoying the new sights and sensations. Brenda had brought out the sun cream and insisted that Amelia wore it. Brian had refused, claiming it made him smell like a softy. Tim had accepted a dollop, as he'd forgotten to bring his own. It wouldn't do for him to get sunstroke — he was the only one insured to drive and if he let them down, where would they be?

He had checked for somewhere nice to stay the night on the internet but Brenda was unhappy about it, arguing that anyone could write anything and stick it up for all to see and you didn't know what you were getting. She relied on the now slightly dog-eared guidebook, which recommended another small town some way to the north. There was no reason to disagree; Julia surreptitiously checked it out online and gave Tim a quiet thumbs up. So they set off mid-afternoon, air con blasting away, and slowly everyone except Amelia and Tim fell asleep.

His eyes fixed on the road ahead, Tim counted the kilometres rolling by, and by the time they were approaching the town of Nevers he was distinctly pleased with their progress. Looking at a map it was easy to forget how great the distances between places were over here, as the country was so much larger than Britain, a fact he tended to overlook. He was trying to estimate how long it would take them to get to the town Brenda had chosen, and whether there would be time for them to all eat together before Amelia's bedtime, when the car gave a shudder.

Alarmed, Tim glanced down at the unfamiliar dashboard and let out a groan, which woke the rest of the party. Amelia pointed through the gap between the two front seats. 'Look! A big orange light! It's been on for ages.'

'That's pretty,' said Brenda. 'I wonder what it means? Tim, should it be doing that?'

Tim slapped his forehead in frustration as the car spluttered, gave a cough, spluttered again and, as he managed to pull into a convenient lay-by, conked out altogether. 'Well spotted,

Amelia. Yes, it's a nice colour, isn't it? A bit like peach juice. But no, it shouldn't really light up like that.'

Brian looked at him, knowing what it meant. 'We've run out of petrol, haven't we?'

Tim groaned. 'I've run out, more like. It's my fault, no one else's. I was concentrating on the road, and it slipped my mind that a bigger car would use more fuel.'

Julia immediately leant forward and hugged him. 'You shouldn't be so hard on yourself. Not one of us spotted it, and we even went to sleep and left you to do all the work. We'll sort it out. There must be a gas station nearby. What's this city called?'

Tim smiled gratefully. 'It's Nevers. It's a sizeable town and we should be all right. There's an empty petrol can in the back, I checked before we left the hire place. I'll walk into town along the main road, and there's bound to be something. You stay here with the bags and I'll be back in two shakes of a lamb's tail. I'll take my phone, so I can let you know when I've found somewhere.'

Amelia jumped up and down in her booster seat. 'Can I come? I'm good at buying petrol. Granddad lets me help. I know all the words.'

Tim shook his head. 'I'm not sure if that's a good idea. We'd have to walk along a main road and the cars are going very fast. Wouldn't you rather stay here with Julia and Brenda? Your Other Granny?'

Amelia shook her head very firmly. 'I can see a pavement. We can walk on that.'

Outmanoeuvred, Tim had to concede the little girl was right. He weighed up the risks — take her with him, knowing she could help with the language barrier but risking her getting tired, in which case he'd have to carry her plus the full petrol can? Or leave her here, possibly creating a scene? The town looked close. He'd give it a go.

'All right, you come with me,' he said, undoing his seat belt, checking that he had his wallet, and getting out of the car to collect the bright red petrol can. 'Stay close to me, mind. See you, folks. Wish us luck.' With that, the intrepid explorers set out.

★　★　★

Contrary to his expectations, there were no petrol stations along the main road, and no signs that Tim could recognize either. He soon realized that even if Amelia could say the words in French and understand them when she heard them, she couldn't yet read much. It was no surprise. She was still so young — easy to forget when listening to her conversation, but true nevertheless.

'I know,' he said, striving to sound positive and in charge of events. 'The next really nice-looking street we find, why don't we go down that and see if there's a shop or a bar, and then we can ask where the nearest petrol station is.'

Amelia nodded solemnly. 'I think that's a good idea.' She pulled her hat more firmly onto her head.

'You sure you're not tired yet?' Tim asked.

Amelia looked up at him with an expression exactly like her mother's. 'Of course not. I'm not a baby.'

'Of course you aren't,' said Tim. He knew when he was beaten.

Before long the older part of town came into view and a pleasant stone-walled street opened off to one side of the main road. 'Here,' said Amelia imperiously. 'We'll go down there.'

'As you wish,' said Tim, figuring it was as good as anywhere. A cluster of buildings a little way along looked promising, with colourful illuminated signs projecting from the walls indicating shops or bars or both. 'Come on, we'll try it.'

He gripped Amelia's little hand more firmly and they marched down the street, certain of finding what they needed. Before they could reach the first sign they noticed a dark alley to their right and heard footsteps coming from it. Out from its entrance stepped a black-clad man, clearly a priest, and behind him one of the tallest, broadest men Tim had ever seen.

'*Non, non,*' the priest was protesting. He switched to English. 'You must wait. I need to arrange for the doctor to visit *la pauvre fille*, then I may hear your confession. Wait. *Attendez,* I beg you.'

The big man's voice was full of despair. 'Père Pierre, I'm going mad. I have to tell you everything. Please, it won't take long, I've waited for ages and you don't know what it's doing to me.'

Tim came to a standstill. Desperate men of this one's size were probably best left uncrossed.

'Hang on a minute, Amelia,' he said. 'Let these two go by.'

But Amelia was staring at the big man, who now turned and noticed them. Tim drew himself up to his full height but he was still a good half-head shorter than the figure before them. He cleared his throat to say something, but Amelia beat him to it.

Pointing a finger at the giant, she raised her chin and said: 'I know you. You were putting that big dolly in a pit.'

★   ★   ★

I gaze at her as she sleeps and wonder if my fervent wishes are distorting reality. I have so longed for her to recover that I might be imagining it. And yet to me her bruising does seem less noticeable, her face closer to its usual exquisite shape. I know this cannot be so, that it's been a matter of mere hours since I last saw her, and still somehow my eyes seek to deceive me. Kate is looking better.

She stirs and turns on her pillows and I lean back a little, not wanting to wake her if her slumber is helping this miraculous restoration process. All disciplines of medicine from the ancients onward agree that sleep is the ultimate method of enabling the body to heal itself. Heaven forbid that I should deny my beloved her best remedy.

A moment passes and then she stirs again, sighing this time and rubbing her eyes. I want to tell her to stop, that she must not damage her injured eye any further, but when has she ever done what I've told her? She brings herself into a sitting position and opens her eyes. Both eyes.

I gasp in shock.

She grins in delight. 'Got you. You didn't think I could do that, did you?'

I admit she is right. I tell her how much better her face looks and she reaches over to her nightstand.

'You have this to thank — well, this and Monica.' She holds out a small white tube of ointment. I take it and examine it sceptically.

'Really? This is what you believe has helped you?' I'm all for complementary therapies, but arnica cream has always struck me as a waste of money, time and effort. However, the glowing face before me says otherwise.

'Of course. I've mentioned it before on several occasions. Monica was good enough to find me some, and you can see the result for yourself. A few more applications of this and I'll be as good as new.' She smiles brightly but I detect the wince she tries so hard to hide. Arnica cream might help the bruises but it won't have the slightest effect on the broken ribs and damaged spleen. I sit on the bed and kiss her brow.

'Almost, anyway.' I shake my head. 'You are impossible, you know that.'

She doesn't deny the accusation.

'Is there any news?' she asks, as she always does. I am sure she hates relying on me like this, but she has little choice.

'Amelia is safely on her way with the rescue party. I spoke to Tim at lunchtime. He seemed to be in a very picturesque part of the world, and said Mrs Bee had issued them all with regulation doses of sun cream.'

'Good,' Kate interrupts. 'I can't have my angel getting burnt. My parents would never have allowed it. I knew Mrs Bee would look after her as I'd wish.'

'He might ring again later with a progress report — apparently Brenda has selected their overnight accommodation with the help of her trusty guidebook and he dare not say no.'

Kate nods in approval. 'I'm sure she'll choose only the best. I can't see her putting up with anything remotely sub-standard. Besides, they all deserve the best.'

'They do.' I heartily agree. To bring back this most precious jewel, my darling's daughter, no expense need be spared. And yet they must continue to be vigilant and not appear too obviously extravagant, thereby drawing attention to themselves; it is a difficult balance to strike. Still, with the combination of personalities and skills involved, I am convinced they stand the very best chance of success.

'My love, I simply have to leave this place soon,' she tells me, fixing me with an intense gaze. 'Surely you can see that now I am so much better, I will recover more quickly at home?'

At once I am on my guard. I don't wish to distress her but I cannot condone jeopardizing her recovery by moving her too soon. 'Is that what the doctors say?' I ask.

She puffs out a sharp breath of frustration. 'You know it isn't. But those are the same doctors who hold an identical opinion to yours about this miracle cream of mine. And look how that's turning out.' She clenches her jaw. 'I cannot stay here. I can achieve exactly nothing, marooned here in this bed.'

Now I am worried. 'You must rest and heal, my love. I know it annoys you and it would do the same to me if we were to swap places — and how I wish we could. But for your own health, and crucially for your own safety, you must remain here.'

'Is there still no word of Amber Simpson's whereabouts, then?' Kate cannot hide her anxiety as she says this.

I shake my head. 'She's gone to ground. Giles texted me from America, where he's arrived in one piece, to say he's had a number of missed calls from her, so she's still up and operating somewhere, but she didn't leave any clues as to where she'd made the calls from.' At least he's got away unhindered and undamaged, or at least physically so; I suppose a part of me was expecting to hear that Amber had attacked him.

'What about Gus? Has he been charged?'

I smile. Here at least is some positive news. 'Yes, he finally cracked. He's admitted he was paid by Amber to launch that car at you. Moreover, he's confirmed that his instructions were to kill you. He's hoping for a reduced sentence now that he's collaborated with the investigation.'

I can see from Kate's expression she has little sympathy with the man, and I can hardly blame her.

'But he hasn't said where Amber is?'

'He claims he doesn't know. His only contact with her was via the health club or in her flat — he doesn't know where else she might be or anyone she might have turned to for help.' I can believe that, since as far as I know the woman has no friends. 'And therefore, my darling, it's much easier to guard you here, in a public place with plenty of people around, including the hospital security staff, than at the house.'

Kate looks mutinous. 'I simply don't accept that.'

I shrug. 'It's how things must remain for the time being.'

'For how long?' Kate asks the crucial question with her trademark directness.

'As long as the doctors decree.'

She shifts uncomfortably. 'I need to speak to Amelia. Not Skype, she can't see me like this, not yet. But with a day or two more on the magic potion, I might manage to appear respectable. I have to speak to her, you must understand that. I have to know she's really safe, and hear her voice for myself.'

I nod. I do understand. Kate fears for her daughter's safety just as I fear for Kate's, and every hour I am away from her is torment. 'I know, my love.' I sigh. 'I can't promise, but if we can sort something out in the next few days then I will move heaven and earth to do so. Just give it a little more time.'

Reluctantly, she gives in. 'But don't expect me to concede so easily in future,' she warns me, and that glint in her eyes reassures me that she genuinely is on the mend.

17

Although the light in the ancient walled street was far from bright, Tim could see that the big man's complexion had turned deathly white. This was nothing to do with his earlier agitation. It was a direct result of Amelia's peculiar comment.

'Dolly? I don't know what you mean.' But his voice was quavering, not at all the sort of tone one would expect from a person of his size.

'Yes, you do.' Amelia stood her ground. 'You pulled a big dolly from the river, and then you dressed it and put it in a pit. In the forest. Near Granny's house.'

The man stared at her in horror. 'No, no, you've made a mistake. I don't go round playing with dollies. That's for little girls.' He attempted a smile, but it came out as a cross between a snarl and a grimace of pain.

'I didn't say you played with it,' Amelia pointed out. 'You just took it out of the water and then put it in the big pit. That was all.'

The man sagged against the nearby wall of the alley's entrance, despair etched on his face. His companion — the priest — went to him. '*Mon ami*, what is this? What have you done?'

The big man groaned. 'That's what I've been trying to tell you all day. It wasn't a doll . . . '

The priest made a decision. 'I must find the doctor. He lives in the next street. Then you must tell me everything. Wait for me back at the presbytery. Does it concern these good people? Do you need to tell them something too?'

The man dipped his head. 'It's about this little girl.'

Tim spoke up. 'We can't come with you. We need to get back to our friends, but first I have to find some petrol. Our car broke down.' He held up the red can as if to emphasize his point. 'Although I would love to hear what you have to say.' He gave the big man a cool, searching look.

'Then it is decided.' The priest spoke again. '*Mon ami*, take these people to the petrol station near the *boulangerie*. It is not far,' he assured them. 'And then give them instructions how to reach the presbytery. You may park there. I sense this is important for all of you. But now I must fetch the doctor, who might yet save the young girl I have tended all day.' He nodded, and rushed off.

The big man put his hands to his face and groaned. It was as if he could not look at Amelia. Her very presence was causing him acute distress. Tim felt some sympathy, but if this man was who he thought he was, that sympathy was decidedly limited. However, the most vital thing right now was that this giant knew where petrol was to be obtained.

'Right,' he said with authority. 'Show us where this garage is or nobody will be going anywhere. Then you can come with us and show us where to park.'

The big man groaned again, but he was left with little choice in the matter. Reluctantly, he led Tim along the street, with Amelia clutching Tim's hand, her face full of curiosity at this turn of events.

★　★　★

Monica was on a mission and when that happened there was no stopping her. She'd set her heart on finding beautiful fittings for the almost-completed flats, and she could just imagine the exact lampshades that would work in the alcoves beside the fireplaces. She'd spent hours trawling every known antiques shop or vintage market stall in Merseyside, phoning those she couldn't physically get to, but none had the precise thing she had in mind. She was not prepared to give up, though. One dealer had mentioned a former colleague who often picked up lampshades for his clients, but he was based in Manchester. Monica had taken his number and rung him first thing in the morning.

They'd got on like a house on fire when the dealer realized this woman was as obsessed with lampshades as he was. He'd happily taken some pictures of his current crop and sent them over, staying on the line long enough to hear Monica's cry of triumph when she opened her email account.

'I'll be there on the next train,' she told him. 'Don't let anyone else see them till I get there.'

'Right you are,' the dealer said. 'We're near Piccadilly station so I'll expect you soon.'

Now Monica strode along the busy pavement, expertly avoiding other bodies as she looked at the screen of her phone, flipping between the street map and the pictures of the shades she hoped to buy. Part of her said it was silly; she should just get something plain from a department store, as whoever ended up living in the flats would want to choose something to their own taste. But another part of her brain argued that she had a duty to show what the place could really be like, make it seem as special as possible so that Kate would get a good price, and to have something small but distinctive such as period shades would add the finishing touch.

For someone in high stilettos she moved very fast, showing no trace of a wobble as she covered the short distance to the antiques shop. She was a hunter tracking down her quarry and God help anyone who got in her way.

The icon on the screen showed her that she'd reached her destination, and sure enough, here was the street. As she pushed open the door to the dealer's, the man behind the counter glanced up and his face broke into a wide smile. 'I don't have to ask who you are,' he said, and Monica beamed right back.

She took a moment to look around the place, and she knew at once she'd made the right decision in coming here. It was filled with gorgeous items, one-offs, treasures she couldn't wait to explore. There were exquisite ornaments, delicate pieces of furniture, and in the corner near the window, so that they could reflect the light, a collection of glass lampshades that took her breath away. It was like coming home; or, rather, to a home she'd always dreamed of.

She forced herself to be practical, and drew her notebook from her bag. She couldn't go buying any old thing; the dimensions had to be just so to look right in the alcoves. She studied the notes she'd studiously made, but knew that with such a choice she'd have no difficulty in finding what she was looking for.

'Let me lift down the ones at the top,' offered the shopkeeper tactfully, realizing Monica's lack of stature meant she couldn't really see the uppermost ones.

Monica pressed forward eagerly, putting her notes down on the counter so that the man could see them and help her find the most appropriate items. In what was possibly one of the happiest fifteen minutes of her entire life, Monica picked the ones she liked that were also the right size, and set about getting a good price for them. The man didn't put up much of a fight — he could probably tell that if the sale went well, he'd have a regular customer here in the shape of this exacting little woman with the immaculate taste.

Monica figured the delicate items were too fragile to cart down to the train station but that Kate wouldn't object if she took a taxi. It was while she was ordering one, as the man carefully swaddled the ruby glass in bubble wrap, that she spotted something which looked strangely familiar. She cut short her call.

'What's that vase doing there?' she asked abruptly.

The man looked up. 'Oh, that came in this week. Do you like it? It's in a very different style

368

to what you've just bought, I must say.'

Monica shook her head impatiently. 'No, I don't like it particularly. I thought I recognized it, though. My boss had the exact same one in the house she's doing up. Used to belong to some old aunt or other.' Monica's eyes narrowed in suspicion. 'Do you know who brought it in?'

The man looked taken aback. 'Is there something wrong? We're a respectable outfit here, you know. I hope you aren't implying anything's amiss.'

Monica tutted. 'I'm not saying that. But my boss has been in a whole lot of trouble recently and she didn't deserve none of it. Sorry, but I'm going to call the bizzies.' She hated to do that when she thought she'd just made a new friend who might well not welcome the attention, but a clue was staring her right in the face. There couldn't be many vases in the north-west with that intricately cut pattern. There had been one in Kate's kitchen in Blundellsands, left there because it was a good size for flowers — until, to the best of Monica's knowledge, Kate had given it to Amber for the Sefton Park flat. There was no getting away from it. If Amber had been in this shop less than a week ago, the bizzies would have to know.

* * *

The parlour in the presbytery was dark and cool. Tim had the distinct impression it was used only for best, and that it was an honour for them to be there. He wasn't sure what to expect. It was

369

close to Amelia's bedtime but she was wide awake, desperate to see what was about to happen, unable to sit still despite Brenda's best efforts to keep her on her lap. Brenda and Brian were now perched on the edge of the spindly sofa, their backs ramrod straight with tension.

Julia squeezed Tim's hand. Now that they were here, she was content to let events take their course. She sensed that this evening would bring everything to a climax, and there was little she could do to influence matters other than support Tim. Despite all that she knew of what had brought them here, her finely honed doctor's instincts led her to believe they were in no physical danger — she would never have allowed Amelia into such a situation otherwise. She wondered just what was going on in the kitchen, where Père Pierre had led the big man as soon as they'd all arrived. She strained her ears to hear, but either the soundproofing was excellent in this old house or they were talking very quietly indeed.

★ ★ ★

Max was slumped on an old wooden chair, sobbing into his hands. He'd let it all out — everything he'd done with the gang in London, selling drugs and trashing Kate's house in Liverpool, the plot to kidnap the little girl who was now sitting in the front parlour, and finally the business with poor old Trev. 'I never killed him, honest,' he'd pleaded, frantic for his friend the priest to believe him. 'I just covered him up, respectful like. I never knew the kiddy was watching. I wouldn't hurt a hair on her head now.' His shoulders heaved as all the long-bottled-up secrets spilled out, each one more horrific than the last.

'I know, *mon fils*, I know.' Père Pierre nodded his head sagely. He'd long since pieced together the gist of his English guest's past, from remarks he'd let slip, together with the obvious trauma the memories were causing him. It had to have been something bad. He gave silent thanks that Michel — or Max, as he now knew him to be called — had seen the error of his ways before carrying out his instructions to kidnap the child.

He truly believed Max to be remorseful, and that he no longer represented a danger to any of the people waiting in the parlour. When the man was ready he would welcome him into the Catholic church, baptize him, and then offer him absolution. Now, though, there was something Max had to do, for his own sanity.

'Come, *mon ami*,' the kindly priest said. 'You have confessed to me, but now you must seek forgiveness from those you intended to harm. You must tell them who you are and what you planned to do. They will have guessed much of it, but they need to hear it from you. You will feel the weight lift from those broad shoulders of yours if you do so, believe me.'

'I can't, Father.' Max shuddered with shame at the very idea. 'Don't make me. I can't face them. That beautiful little girl. What was I thinking of? I can't do it. I won't.'

'I can't make you. I do not have that power,

and nor do I have the right.' The priest regarded him gravely. 'You alone can do it. But it will be for the good of your eternal soul. What price a few minutes of pain now when your life everlasting is in question?'

Max shook his head in confusion. He didn't know what had come over him these past few weeks. He'd never cried back in London, let alone in front of anyone. If anyone had started to talk to him about his eternal soul he'd have run a mile. Somehow now it seemed perfectly normal. Was that what was at risk here — his soul? Père Pierre was watching, in anticipation. Max sighed heavily and lumbered to his enormous feet.

'All right. I'll do it. Come with me, Father, cos I don't think I can bear it on me own.'

'But of course,' said the priest, and held open the door, hoping Max would have the courage to carry out this act of penitence.

Max stumbled into the parlour, and stood before the ancient fireplace, his hands held in front of him, gripping each other tightly. He floundered for a moment, seeking the words to begin. Then, as when he'd confessed to Père Pierre, it all came flooding out. He tried to temper some of it so that the little girl wouldn't be shocked, and they didn't need know what the gang had done in London. Besides, he suspected that the adults already knew.

When he came to the plot to kidnap Amelia, he got down on his knees in front of her. 'I'm sorry,' he said, and for a moment he almost cried again. 'It was a terrible thing what we said we were gonna do. But as soon as I got to France I knew we couldn't do it. Please believe me. You're safe now. I won't cause you no harm. I'm so very, very sorry.' Max's face had gone bright red and he was sweating, although the room was getting chillier by the minute.

Amelia looked at him — their eyes were at about the same level. 'I know you won't hurt me,' she said in her small piping voice. 'You're a kind man. You showed us how to get petrol.'

Max gaped at her as if he couldn't believe it.

'But before . . . ' he said, wiping his forehead with the back of his hand. 'I wasn't a kind man before. I was the opposite of kind.'

The child nodded. 'Yes, you said. But you're kind now. So I forgive you.'

Père Pierre moved out of the shadows where he had been standing leaning against a wall. 'There, you see, *mon fils*. You did not even have to beg for forgiveness. It has been granted to you.'

'Out of the mouths of babes . . . ' murmured Tim, struck by the simple trust Amelia had showed this man who had intended to do her dreadful harm in order to hurt her mother, both of them completely undeserving of such brutal treatment. He could scarcely believe it: that this monster, who had had them rushing halfway across the continent, was now on his knees, full of remorse. He closed his eyes, and felt Julia squeeze his hand again.

Amelia was safe — they all were. They hadn't really discussed it, but it must have been in the back of all their minds, as it had been in his: something could go very wrong on this journey.

They'd kept it light, made it all about taking Amelia for an adventure, but he'd felt deep down that there was always the possibility they'd have to deal with two ruthless gang members experienced in violence.

Now they'd been told that one of those men was dead, a tragic accident by Max's account, and that Max himself had had a complete change of heart. Something about the French countryside had worked a spell on him and he was an utterly changed man. The professional part of Tim's brain was keen to work out exactly what had gone on, what had brought about this sudden conversion. Then he realized he didn't want to know. Questions like that were part of his day job and he'd left it back in Liverpool; his task here was to rescue Amelia and keep her entertained until her mother was well enough to see her. Certainly, if the threat of Max was removed, that had just become a whole lot easier.

The priest put his hand on the big man's shoulder. 'Come, *mon ami*. You have been given more than you had dared to hope for. Now it is best that you rest, and we will see what tomorrow brings, after you have had a good sleep. For I believe you will indeed have a good sleep.'

Max yawned at the words. 'Father, you might well be right.' He got to his feet once more and looked sheepishly at the assembled group. 'I'm sorry to have dragged you all the way out here. I only hope you get to see the place a bit and see how gorgeous it is.'

'Thank you,' said Tim. 'I'm sure we will.'

'And take care of that little one,' Max continued, a tear coming to his eye which he hurriedly dashed away.

Amelia glanced up at him and gave that dazzling smile she had inherited from her mother. 'Don't worry,' she said. 'I'll look after them.'

★ ★ ★

'So you're sure about this, are you, sir?' the policeman asked.

The antiques shop owner sighed in resignation. Even though all of his trade was above board, or at least as far as he knew, getting involved with the police was the last thing he wanted. It wouldn't do his reputation any good in the business. Some sources wouldn't touch him after this, if it got out. Still, when he realized what rested on finding the owner of the vase, he knew he had little choice but to cooperate.

'Yes, I'm as sure as I can be,' he sighed. 'Like I said, she wore dark glasses and had her hair tucked up in a sun hat, but that wasn't so unusual as it was a fine day when she came. I thought it was a bit odd she didn't take the glasses off once she was indoors, but we get all sorts in here. Besides, she might have had a headache or something.' He turned to his stack of paperwork. 'Here, I gave her a receipt and she signed it. I kept a carbon copy. A bit old-fashioned but that's what I like.'

'Very sensible of you if I may say so.' The policeman consulted his phone, clicked on an image and moved his fingers to enlarge it. He squinted at it and then at the piece of paper the man was showing him. 'Now I'm no expert, but they look pretty similar to me.'

'What's that you're looking at?' the shop owner asked, intrigued.

'It's a shot of Amber Simpson's signature, as signed at her place of work,' the policeman explained. 'As you can see, she prefers basically to scrawl her initials. Just as she has on your receipt.'

'Of course she gave a different name,' the dealer mused. 'Same initials, though. Must make it easier for her to remember.'

'Criminals often do that, sir,' the policeman said ponderously.

The dealer shrugged. The young woman hadn't seemed like a criminal to him, just a little over-cautious in some ways and edgy in others. He certainly wouldn't have put her down as the instigator of an attempted murder. That was a new one for him.

'Don't suppose you have any security cameras here, sir?'

The dealer shook his head. 'As I told you, I'm a bit old-fashioned. I don't hold with all that electronic stuff. I have a burglar alarm because I wouldn't get proper insurance without it, but that's it.'

The policeman nodded, as he hadn't expected anything else. 'That's a shame, sir. We really need to track her movements on that day. However, plenty of the streets around have CCTV and there is coverage at the station. So if you could just describe again what she was wearing . . . '

18

'I'd assumed you'd decided not to call,' said Alex when Tim rang him much later that evening. 'Has Mrs Bee's boutique hotel not got any signal then?' To be truthful he'd been alarmed by the lack of communication as the hours went on, fearing that something untoward had happened to the party since lunch, but he'd resisted ringing France as he didn't want to wake Amelia.

'I wouldn't know about that,' Tim said. 'We haven't got there yet. We're still in Nevers. Better late than never, though. Better still, we're at a guesthouse run by nuns.'

'Good lord, man! You haven't finally got religion, have you?' Alex had thought nothing Tim said would ever surprise him, but he hadn't expected this.

Tim laughed down the line. 'Not quite. Although the people who run this place are kindness itself and a damned fine advert for a life of service and contemplation. But you'll never guess who we ran into earlier, in the company of a priest.'

Alex acknowledged his friend was right. He didn't have a clue. 'So tell me.'

'You'd better make sure you're sitting down and maybe have a stiff drink to hand. It's not a short tale.'

Alex had in fact been standing at his kitchen window, but he took Tim's advice, pulled out a

377

chair and simultaneously treated himself to a generous glug of single malt. It was late, after all, and he deserved some indulgence after a day working in his head office combined with shopping for and visiting Kate, and managing to give the dogs two walks. At least Kylie had taken on Brenda's mantle and seen to the house, as well as producing a very passable casserole.

'You ready yet?' came Tim's voice.

'Fire away.'

And so Tim did, trying to convey the shocking coincidence of literally almost bumping into the very man they'd been trying to avoid at all costs, and then finding how very much he'd changed.

Alex listened in stunned silence, and spoke only when Tim eventually concluded with Père Pierre's insistence on their staying at the parish guesthouse. 'I was glad of the offer, to tell you the truth — finding somewhere else that Mrs Bee would deem acceptable would have been no mean feat at that late hour.'

'I'm sure.' Alex tapped his thumbnail against his teeth. He didn't want to spoil the moment but the account was, in fact, incredible. 'Look, I know you must be tired after all that driving, and I can tell this priest is a persuasive sort of fellow, but ... can you really trust him? Do you genuinely believe that this Max, who let's not forget sold drugs in my clubs and caused the death of a teenager, as well as ransacking Kate's house, has turned over a new leaf? Is it likely, after all those years leading a life of crime? Haven't you all been hoodwinked?'

Tim let out a deep breath. 'I can see why

you'd say that, but, hand on heart, I'm as certain as I can be that it's true. You know I'd never expose Amelia to danger, nor put Julia or the Bees at risk. If only you could have seen him, Alex. He's had a bona fide conversion. He sincerely regrets everything he has done in the past and wants to make amends. Père Pierre's going to keep him here, helping his good works, turning his remorse into something useful. It's like a miracle. Père Pierre puts it down to St Bernadette.'

Alex wanted to scoff. This was way beyond his comfort zone. Miracles rarely happened as far as he could see, and coincidences weren't to be trusted . . . and yet. He paused and took a sip of the Scotch. Wasn't a miracle exactly what had happened to him, that day outside Tim's consulting rooms? When Kate had lost her heel? Wasn't that the most bizarre, unlikely, impossible twist of fate? Perhaps he should be less cynical.

'Seriously, old man, you have to trust me on this,' Tim was saying now. 'I'm no pushover, you know that. And can you imagine Mrs Bee being taken in? That's simply never going to happen. Her bullshit detector's too well tuned. This is the real thing. Max is no danger to any of us any more. Amelia's free to enjoy her adventure. Although I have to say I think she would like to come back soon. I don't know how possible you think that is.'

Alex got up and began to stride around, unable to keep still in the wake of such news. It was hard to take it in: the fear they'd all had that this monster would take Amelia from them could now be consigned to the past. Kate would have to be told first thing tomorrow. Her joy would be beyond compare. He said as much to Tim. 'But,' he went on, 'we still have the problem of Amber to contend with. There's been some news on that, actually. The police rang me this evening — I thought it was you to begin with — to say they've had a lead. Amber has been traced to an antiques shop in Manchester and they're working on following her trail via CCTV and the like. It will take a while, but it's something.'

'That's good, as far as it goes,' Tim agreed. 'So, one cause for concern down, one to go.'

Alex exhaled heavily. 'I know. I want to shout and scream in delight that we don't have to worry about Amelia any more, but it's hard to rejoice when we have our very own psychopath on the loose somewhere nearby. I'm convinced, and so are the police, that she's only biding her time before she has another attempt on Kate's life. How can I ask you to bring Amelia back to a situation like that?'

'I know, old man. It's hard. But you do have excellent security to call upon,' Tim reminded him. 'Anyway, how is Kate in all of this? Today's news will pep her up, I'll be bound.'

'It will,' Alex acknowledged. 'She's healing remarkably quickly, Tim. Monica's found her some wonder potion that's putting paid to the bruises faster than anyone could have believed. She's desperate to speak to Amelia, but has avoided doing so up to now as the facial injuries slightly distorted her voice. Also, she was afraid Amelia would ask to Skype and she knew she

380

couldn't risk that. However, I think it's time to try it, just a call, no video. Should we see if we can arrange it for tomorrow?'

'Excellent suggestion,' said Tim at once. 'You know, I am beginning to wonder if we have underestimated this soon-to-be-daughter of yours. She's not asking to be flown home on the first available plane, she just wants to talk to her mother. She'll understand if Kate sounds a little different, and we can say that we can't get a signal for Skype where we are — which might well be true. But a short chat — what harm can that do?'

Alex nodded. 'You're right,' he said decisively.

★   ★   ★

My eyes mist with tears. It feels like a lifetime since I spoke to my daughter, the most precious child in the world. Just to hear her voice floods me with relief and joy in one heady cocktail. Relief that she has taken to this enforced road trip so easily, despite not having previously known any of her travel companions; joy that she is no longer under threat of kidnap. And I must confess to an element of pride too. That's one well-adjusted little girl, and she most assuredly didn't get that from her father.

I listen enthralled as she chatters on about what she's seen so far and how much she likes Mrs Bee and Julia. That bodes well for the future, as they are liable to play a major part in her life to come. Julia has helped her do some drawings and she can't wait to show them to me.

Well, perhaps she won't have to wait much longer.

Sure enough her next question is, 'When can I see you, Mummy?'

A lump forms in my throat but I can't let it show when I next speak. 'Soon, my darling. You know Mummy had a bit of a car accident? Well, I need just a little more time to get better. I'd hate for you to come back and then find I couldn't hug you as tightly as I would like to. I'm definitely improving every day, so you don't need to worry. It just takes a while and it never goes as fast as you'd want it to.'

'I understand,' says the light of my life. Well, the smaller one.

'Good girl. I knew you would.'

She laughs. 'Auntie Julia says that means we can all go to Paris. She promised to show me some famous paintings.'

'That would be perfect, darling,' I force myself to say. And after all, it's true. What an opportunity for my girl, and to think that she'll have someone with her who really appreciates art. It's the chance of a lifetime and I'm a fool to begrudge her these extra days away, apart from me. Heaven knows what Brenda will make of Paris, but I shall leave it up to Tim to diffuse her discontent. 'Say goodbye now and we'll talk again soon, and maybe by then I'll be feeling so much better we can decide when you can come home.'

'Yes please,' she says, polite as ever. She is a credit to my parents — they have schooled her well in my absence. 'Bye bye, Mummy. Au revoir.'

'Au revoir.' I cut the connection, knowing that it is indeed au revoir and not adieu, as I have feared ever since waving farewell to her.

Alex watches me as I set down the phone on top of my hospital bed. 'All right?' His marvellous eyes are full of love and concern.

'Absolutely fine.' I present my best optimistic face to him. 'Tim was totally correct to think that once she knew I'd had a car accident, she would understand. She wants to come home — but she also wants to go to Paris. So that gives us a window, in which I will endeavour to recover as much as possible, and Amber might be found.'

Alex nods in agreement and I see a trace of fury flash across his face, his rage at his former employee who could betray him in this way. 'The police are onto it. It might take time, but they will surely trace her now we have a confirmed sighting.'

'It's so infuriating.' I cannot contain my frustration. 'Surely they can speed up the process? What about facial recognition software?'

He raises his hands. I know, I know, don't shoot the messenger. But I'm stuck here, unable to help. 'We have to trust them to do this. They have to make sure the trail is watertight. If it ever comes to using it as evidence, you can understand why they are playing it by the book. Any shortcuts could make it inadmissible in court.'

He's right, of course, but it doesn't make it any easier. I just want them to find her and get her behind bars. I sigh and he reaches for my hand. 'But at least I can leave here soon,' I say, fixing him with my gaze. 'Do speak to the doctors again, my love. Get them to release me into your care. I'm so much better, I really am. My face is nearly back to its usual shape and I can disguise the bruises with makeup now. I really have no wish to become a bed-blocker.'

He snorts. 'Nobody can accuse you of malingering. Far from it — you know how anxious I am that you'll be moved too soon.' All the same, he's weakening, I can tell, and I press my advantage shamelessly.

'Think how much easier it will be for you if I'm home. You can work from there, we'll have the dogs to guard me and your own security. Kylie can tend to me. You won't have to come in here several times a day, keeping Marks and Sparks in business.'

Finally he nods. 'All right. I'll ask them, but don't be upset if they say no. We have to defer to their medical expertise.' He gives me one of his gorgeous grins, which melts my heart. 'My God, Kate, I can't wait to get you home.'

★ ★ ★

Detective Constable Watkins pulled her swivel chair closer to her desk and stared in concentration at the screen. 'Come and see this, sarge. I'm sure it's her.'

DS Marcom rubbed his eyes, itchy from a twelve-hour shift. There had been so many false dawns in the search for Amber Simpson that he didn't seriously believe this could be any different. Still, Watkins was young, and keen, and eager to make her mark in the department. She also had excellent eyesight, which is more than he himself could claim. 'All right, Watkins, what have you got?' He walked wearily over to her desk.

She pointed carefully to a figure on the grainy CCTV recording. 'Take a look at her. See, she's carrying that big bag we know she had at the antiques shop.'

Marcom bent down to see what his constable was referring to. She'd paused the shot, and the blurry figure could have been anybody to his mind. Then again, he couldn't have told the difference between two large handbags. Maybe his colleague was in a better position to judge.

Amber had been clearly identified on CCTV from a helpful bar owner on a street between the antiques shop and Piccadilly station, and then again on the busy concourse itself. Knowing what time she'd arrived there had helped. It should have been a relatively easy task to spot her getting off a train at Lime Street, but the sheer volume of people pouring across the platform there had made the task impossibly hard. Now they were combing the recordings from different cameras around the many exits from the station, for the time period in which they estimated she must have arrived. If she hadn't got off at an earlier stop or doubled back on herself, that was.

Watkins twirled the chair around and brought to life the computer screen on the adjacent desk. There was the shot from the bar owner in

Manchester. She froze it. 'See, her bag has distinctive long tassels hanging off metal hoops — one at each point where the strap attaches and one on the central zip.'

'If you say so,' said the sergeant, nonplussed. It was just a bag.

'It's from Accessorize, last year's winter collection,' Watkins explained.

'You're sure about that, are you?'

She rolled her eyes. 'When you recognize it, it's obvious. My sister had one. You can get them in several colours. Hers was brown — of course we can't see what colour this is, on this black and white film, but it's definitely the same model. Now look at the first screen again.' She zoomed in on the figure she'd pointed to before. 'See that? Three tassels, long ones.'

'Yes, but if it was available on the high street there must be hundreds — if not thousands — out there,' he pointed out.

'That's not all. Look, same shoes, same hat. It's her.'

Marcom tried his best to keep the rising excitement from his voice. It could still be a red herring. 'OK, so where's this?'

'On a side road just by Lime Street. Hang on, we should be able to go to the next available camera along.' Fingers flew across the keys and the sergeant looked on in envy, wishing he could control his computer like that.

'Here she is again. What's she doing?'

He screwed up his eyes but couldn't see clearly enough to tell.

Watkins drew back, pushing a strand of short

blonde hair behind her ear, and then leant forward again. 'She's heading for a bus stop. If I fast-forward a bit . . . there we are. Look, she's getting on a bus.'

'What number?' asked the sergeant, now deadly serious.

'Can't quite see. Oh, hang on. If I move it on a bit . . . it's a 75. Look, it's clear from this shot. Definitely a 75.'

'So it is.' Even Marcom could see that. 'Right, well, we track the route of that bus as thoroughly as we can and try to find out where she gets off.'

Watkins nodded. 'We can do that. But I was just thinking, it goes to Ullet Road, doesn't it? Back to near the flat she was last known to live at?'

'Surely she wouldn't try anything that risky. She's gone to all that effort to hide her identity — turning up on her old doorstep would be suicidal.'

Watkins shrugged. 'Maybe she's not thinking clearly. She must be feeling the pressure. We know she hasn't used her bank cards — what's she living on? How long will the money from that vase last?'

Marcom stroked his chin and thought for a moment. 'Right, we get CCTV footage from around that part of Sefton Park. We'll still track the bus — she could easily have got off before there. But, in some strange way, what you suggest could very well be right. Well done, Watkins.'

He turned away and left DC Watkins beaming with satisfaction at her desk.

19

'What did you like best?' asked Brenda as she nervously made her way along the Mètro platform. She held Amelia's hand tightly, as much for her own comfort as the child's safety. Normally the only public transport she took was the bus back home. The little girl didn't seem bothered at all by the heaving crowds, Parisians going about their daily lives and also plenty of tourists, wandering around more slowly, pointing at signs, looking at maps or dictionaries or their phones. Brenda supposed she must be used to all that from London.

'The big gallery with the triangle thing outside,' said Amelia promptly. They'd taken her to the Louvre earlier that day, and she'd been spellbound by everything there. 'I liked the lady with the dark hair.'

'What good taste you have,' said Julia, joining in. 'The Mona Lisa is reckoned to be one of the world's greatest paintings.'

Amelia nodded as if she agreed. 'And what did you like?' she asked Brenda politely.

'I liked the paintings in that other place,' Brenda said, trying not to panic as a group of unruly schoolchildren surged towards them, small brightly coloured rucksacks on their backs. 'The . . . splodgy ones.' She couldn't remember their name but she'd enjoyed the pictures, full of energy and life.

'The Impressionists,' Julia said quickly, to make sure Amelia remembered the correct name and didn't go home telling Kate that she'd seen splodgy paintings. Although this part of the trip was meant to be fun, she wanted it to be educational as well.

'Impressionists,' repeated Amelia dutifully. 'Look, this is our train.'

'How do you know?' asked Brenda uncertainly, quietly terrified of taking the wrong one and getting lost in this overwhelming city.

'Because they said so,' said Amelia. Brenda nodded — she herself had made no sense of the booming announcements, which sounded like gobbledegook spoken alarmingly quickly, but the child had clearly understood.

The three of them crowded onto the carriage. Tim had headed back earlier to make some calls from their hotel, and Brian had never left it in the first place. He'd claimed he had a stomach upset but Brenda suspected he was as nervous of Paris as she was, and had faked it to stay in the safety of their room. And a very nice room it was too, with a glorious view of Montmartre and all the tourists strolling through the streets. She couldn't begrudge him a day of people-watching from the sanctuary of their elegant ironwork balcony. He'd have hated the Impressionists anyway. He liked pictures which bore a close likeness to the real thing.

At least tomorrow they'd be starting their return journey. A few days in Paris were more than enough for her, if she was honest. It was all too hectic for her taste. It made Liverpool One on a Saturday afternoon look quiet and relaxing. Even better, Tim had sorted their tickets and they weren't going to have to fly. She had almost cried with relief when he'd told her. They'd be taking the train instead, all the way through to St Pancras in London, where she'd be able to get a proper cup of tea and ask for the food she wanted in her own language, without relying on a four-year-old. It couldn't happen soon enough.

They'd then spend the night in London so that Amelia didn't arrive in Liverpool late in the evening, but would be ready to see her mother after a good night's sleep. They'd all agreed this was the best course of action: after such a long separation, nothing must mar the reunion, and for all her precocious cosmopolitan ways the little girl still needed her rest. Brenda privately felt that they all did, and a brief stay in one of the capital's quieter hotels would do them the world of good, after their whirlwind trip around France, with all its rollercoaster of emotions.

She kept that thought firmly in her mind to shut out the horror of the crowded Métro train, with everyone pressing against her and no room to sit down. How did anyone do this day in, day out? She longed for the sharp tang of the Mersey and the open space around Alex's house, the dogs running wild and the bees diligently making their honey. She wondered how Alex was getting on, and if Kylie was keeping the house in good order. Well, she'd find out shortly. The sooner the better.

★　★　★

Amber could not sit still. She was heartily sick of staring at the walls in her Airbnb rental, the same old pictures, the boring little knick-knacks the owners had put there to make any guest feel more at home. Well, it wasn't working. Now that she'd had the best, Amber recognized these objects as the cheap tat they were. If she had the patience she'd have cleared them all away in a box for the duration of her stay, but she didn't. She was permanently on edge, furious with herself for hiring the wrong man to do the job, frustrated that she couldn't even see Alex, pining for his presence, angry that Kate was still able to see him and that they'd be enjoying cosy chats in the hospital while she was stuck in this tedious room.

She was unhappy with her current diet, too. She was forced to live on takeaways which she had delivered, minimizing the chance of being recognized outside. She was working her way through all the local ones, not using the same one twice just in case somebody knew her. She couldn't bear to eat Chinese, not after the old flat in Litherland, so that reduced her choices. It was impossible to eat healthily like this. She'd spent years avoiding the temptations of a good creamy korma or a pizza slathered with extra cheese, but now that was pretty well all she could get. She could feel the effect on her waistband. Another thing to blame on Kate: all that hard work put in at the gym or pounding the streets in running shoes overturned by a short spell of constant junk food. This was not part of her plan.

She could have screamed in irritation, but that might scare the neighbours, attracting undue attention. She mustn't do that. She had to keep her cool. She just had to bide her time and plan her next move carefully. The money from the vase and the other items she'd sold would last a little longer providing she didn't go mad, so she had a cushion, giving her time to think things through. What she really needed right now was a way of working off this destructive nervous energy. Damn Giles, the coward, for running away. She could have worked off some energy with him all right. Now that door was closed to her too.

Don't think about him, he's not worth it, she told herself. Good riddance to bad rubbish. All he ever did was pretend she was Kate. She didn't need someone like that in her life.

She balled her hands into fists and pressed them angrily against her thighs. She had to get out of here, if only for a short while. She'd go running in Sefton Park, that was it. If she put her hair up and tucked it into a baseball cap, wore sunglasses and hid her figure in a loose sweatshirt and tracksuit bottoms, she'd get away with it. Come to think of it, the loose clothes would be more comfortable now anyhow. Nobody would think this ballooning figure was her. It might be agonizing to her self-esteem to have visibly put on weight, but it was actually a decent disguise.

Acting swiftly so that she didn't change her mind, she flung off her too-tight blouse and jeans and got into the baggiest items in her limited wardrobe, grabbed her sunglasses, and twisted her hair tightly into an elastic band before jamming on a baseball cap. It was one she'd found in this room, left behind by a previous visitor, and it proclaimed ARSENAL across the front. That would throw anyone off the scent — she'd never dream of supporting a London team. Her family had been Everton for generations.

Finally ready, she tucked her key on a chain round her neck and headed outdoors, to burn off her grievances with a few circuits of the big park.

★ ★ ★

DC Watkins stretched her arms above her head, linked her fingers and pushed her palms away. Every muscle in her back protested in agony. She'd been sitting at the same desk for far too many hours, reviewing CCTV almost nonstop, certain the footage from around the Sefton Park area would show something significant. The trouble was finding it. The tune of the song 'Needle in a Haystack' was permanently stuck in her head. 'Give it a rest, change the record,' she muttered, lowering her arms once more and swivelling the chair round to check the second screen.

Yet again she stared at the section of road served by the 75 bus route. Watkins might not have been in the job as long as most of her colleagues, but every ounce of instinct she'd acquired thus far was screaming at her that she was on the right track. There was another bus, coming to a halt. Off got an elderly man, a young couple manoeuvring a buggy while trying to control a toddler, and a couple of schoolkids. Then, last of all, a woman on her own.

Watkins zoomed in, hardly daring to breathe. It was tricky to tell from this angle how old the woman was, or even exactly what she was wearing, but as she turned to walk down the pavement more details became apparent. She had on a pair of sunglasses, and her hair was obscured by a sun hat. She carried a big shoulder bag, and from her other arm there swung a carrier bag of some kind.

It had to be her. Watkins noted the time the footage had been taken, and quickly compared it to when they knew Amber had got on the bus. Unless the bus had got stuck in heavy traffic, the gap was much longer than they'd have expected. That was why they hadn't looked at this piece of film yet — they'd assumed she would have arrived ages ago. But that carrier bag . . . she could have got off the first bus, popped to a shop, got back on another bus on the same route. Now here she was, strolling along the side of Ullet Road.

Watkins tried to keep calm. It didn't mean Amber was still there, only that she'd been there on the day in question. She might be visiting a friend — just because they didn't know of any didn't mean she didn't have them. And yet . . . that carrier bag. Groceries? Something for wherever she was staying? Watkins knew it was speculation, and she couldn't zoom in close enough to see the logo on the plastic, but if she herself had been going to visit a friend, she wouldn't have taken a load of shopping along. A bottle or a small present, yes. Not a bagful of stuff.

Her senses humming, she reached for her phone and pressed the quick dial button for her boss.

⋆   ⋆   ⋆

I don't know whether to laugh or cry. Kate, my beautiful Kate, is coming home. The doctors have agreed she no longer needs constant supervision as her spleen, lungs and diaphragm are recovering and her ribs and leg will mend just as well in her own bed as in the one she's occupied so resentfully in the hospital ward. We have the option of hiring a private nurse for her but have decided to wait and see how she copes first of all.

I have agreed to the hiring of a private ambulance to bring her back, as the front seat of my car is no place for one with injuries such as hers. Besides, it will afford her better protection, should it be needed. Not that I believe even Amber Simpson in all her misguided aggression would attempt to attack Kate on the way back from hospital, but it makes sense to take all available precautions.

Kylie is in the midst of a flurry of activity, knowing how exacting Kate is when it comes to order and cleanliness. Despite her growing bump the girl is vacuuming the stairs, dusting the ceilings with Mrs Bee's special long-handled brush, and polishing surfaces until they gleam. For not only is Kate coming back tomorrow morning; tomorrow afternoon will see the long-awaited arrival of little Amelia, with her four rescuers. Kylie would die of shame if Mrs Bee found any cause for complaint, and so she's turning the house into something worthy of the Ideal Home exhibition. I've tried to tell her to slow down, that she's done enough, but she's having none of it. She has her mother's determination and eye for detail, I'll give her that much.

So I had better leave her to it. Time to gather the pack for their ritual outing — in all of the disruptions of the past few weeks, the one constant is the dogs' need of exercise, and plenty of it. They too will be beside themselves at Kate's return and it will be all I can do to keep them from jumping all over her, which would cause far more harm than they could ever imagine — if indeed dogs imagine. I feel they do.

Whistling to them I set off for the great outdoors, pausing to swipe six strong leads from their hooks. I cannot wait for the day when Kate is once again well enough to come with me, calling to her darlings and throwing their sticks as they hurtle around her. I swear they have found me second best in her absence. There's nothing like a dog's honest gaze to put you in your place.

Now, though, there's no stopping them as they bound around and about, full of the joys of spring, little realizing their mistress will be back

tomorrow even *if not exactly back on her feet,
and the element that has been lacking from their
lives will be restored to them. How we've all
missed having her here. If anyone had told me at
the start of the year that I would be feeling like
this before midsummer I would have laughed in
their face — but it is without a shadow of a
doubt true. One more day, one more night of
solitude and then the Bees, Tim, Julia, Amelia
and my most precious Kate will all be here,
where they belong.*

★ ★ ★

'Is that her, there?' Marcom had been known to
complain when rung up after already putting in a
long shift, but when it was for something like this
he didn't mind in the slightest. He had hurried
back to the station when Watkins had got hold of
him. They were closing in on the crazy woman
who'd paid to have Kate Price mown down, and
the sooner she was off the streets the better. She
was a walking liability, a danger to the public, as
she was so irrational. Now, watching footage
from just a few hours ago, it seemed as if she
could well be a running liability as well.

'It could be.' Watkins watched as a figure, definitely female, jogged past a camera mounted on
one of the entrances to Sefton Park. The quality
of the image was not of the best, and it was hard
to make a positive identification. The woman
wore sunglasses, but her hair was hidden by a
baseball cap rather than a sun hat. Her clothes
were baggy, and the impression she presented

397

was very different from that of the well-dressed young professional they were familiar with from work photos, colleagues' descriptions and the CCTV from the day of the visit to Manchester. The figure before them now seemed scruffy. But if she was avoiding detection, wouldn't she try to change her look? It made Watkins more convinced, not less.

'Can we get over there now?' she asked eagerly.

The sergeant sighed. 'Look, I appreciate you're keen, and you've done sterling work here, Watkins. But you've been here all day. You won't be in a fit state to tackle this homicidal bunny-boiler if that's what it comes to. You need to go home, get some rest, be ready for whatever tomorrow throws at us.'

Watkins's smile fell and her short blonde hair swung over her face. She was tired, yes, but adrenalin had got her through up to now. She desperately wanted to be part of whatever happened next. 'But, sir . . . '

'No use arguing,' the sergeant said, asserting his authority. 'We'll get the new shift on to it. Your work won't have gone to waste, Watkins, but you have to go home now. Whoever goes to Sefton Park has to be fully alert and at peak physical fitness, not half dead from being stuck at a desk all day. You'll be first to hear if anything happens, but I want you back in tomorrow good and ready, as although we're tightening the net we haven't got her yet. We'll be lucky if we snare her tonight; the odds are this will go into tomorrow if not beyond. Don't tell anyone I said that, but it's true.'

Reluctantly, Watkins reached for her light coat. 'Yes, sir.' There was nothing for it. She'd have to do as she was told, but as she walked towards the door she could hear her boss rounding up detectives and uniform constables to get themselves over to Sefton Park, and she wished with all her heart she was among their number.

★ ★ ★

Pete paused in the act of plucking his eyebrows, wondering if he'd done the right thing. He could have asked Molly Partington to babysit, but he had a strong feeling that he'd asked his neighbour for enough favours lately. He would be forever beholden to her for coming to the rescue the night Monica took off for Spain with the girls, leaving little Troy on his own. That didn't mean she would want to help out every time his life didn't go to schedule, as was the case only too often.

He'd deliberately not worked since taking sole charge of Britney and Chelsea, but tonight the club had been desperate. Their much-publicized guest act all the way down from Glasgow had called in sick at the last moment, and they had sold nearly all the tickets — a huge and angry crowd left with no entertainment other than to turn to drink was the last thing Sandra and Nick wanted. Could Pete come in, just this once?

Pete had ummed and aahed, and wondered if he could leave his daughters on their own for a few hours if it came to it — then realized that would be doing exactly what he'd blamed

Monica for. The girls might act as if they were nearly adults but he knew better. If either of them woke up from a bad dream they'd want to see a parent's face, not cope on their own in a cold and silent house.

In the end he'd bitten the bullet and rung Monica. Their conversation had been surprisingly civil. Ever since the dreadful day when they'd all heard the news about the threat hanging over Amelia, relations between the two of them had thawed somewhat. He understood her better now, and working for Kate had given her a focus for what he had to concede were impressive skills. She, in turn, realizing she had a condition which could in all likelihood be treated, had eased up. Admittedly she wasn't exactly what you could call laid back, but she wasn't simmering with anger all the time either.

He hadn't seen her this evening, as her taxi was just rounding the corner as he was on the way out, but he had no doubt that she'd look after the girls and he could rest easy on that score. Now he had to turn his attention to giving the punters what they'd paid for.

Grimly he assessed his appearance in the mirror. It didn't take long to undo the careful work of years of meticulous grooming. His eyebrows needed major attention. He sucked in his cheeks and pouted. Yes, he still had it — but he'd have to get plucking and fast. The stubborn little buggers had re-emerged the second he stopped his regular sessions with the tweezers. Maybe he should go all out, have them removed by electrolysis and then get gorgeously shaped ones tattooed back on, but was that really what he wanted? What if his grandchild thought he was weird? He didn't usually give a fig what anyone thought of him, but the prospect of a grandchild . . . somehow that was different.

After a few minutes of painful plucking, he sat back, satisfied. That was better. He'd have to hope the redness abated in time, or else slap on some extra-thick makeup to cover it. Now for the false eyelashes. 'Ma, he's making eyes at me,' he sang, as he delicately attached them. The beginner's mistake was to rush the process, but he knew that could be fatal. An eyelash at the wrong angle was worse than no eyelash at all. It would seem as if a spider had escaped over his face, and that wasn't the look he was after.

He could hear the crowd getting rowdy even though he'd firmly shut the dressing-room door. Time to put the big frock on and to wow his eager public. If he was honest with himself, he'd missed it — the way he'd go out on stage and get all the punters onside, even if they'd been hostile to begin with. Gingerly he slipped the shiny material over his newly adorned face and pulled the sequinned fabric over his specially shaped torso. He shimmied in front of the full-length mirror, then finally fixed on his most flamboyant wig. He flexed his toes inside his absurdly high stilettos and adjusted his balance — no point in getting all dolled up only to fall flat on his arse in front of everyone. Right, he was ready. He might not be a Glaswegian, but he was the best damned drag act in all of Merseyside and he knew it.

Two hours and two sets later, he was exhausted but ecstatic. The crowd had gone wild, not in the least disappointed that the promised act hadn't shown up when they realized they had their local favourite back again. It was like the return of the prodigal son. He'd been inundated with offers of drinks, food, after-show parties and the occasional suggestion of something so shocking that even he, who considered himself pretty broad-minded, had been momentarily lost for words. Clearly not everyone knew he was a family man at heart.

As he drove back to his house and his waiting children, he acknowledged that this was indeed the truth of it. He loved performing — it was in his blood. And he absolutely adored coming back to his family, who were the centre of his world. He'd never doubted it for a second, but recent events had brought home to him how easily it could all come crashing down. It was up to him to ensure that never happened.

Easing the key into the lock, he could hear gentle snoring from the living room, where the light of the TV screen flickered. He put his head around the door and saw Monica stretched out on the sofa, head propped on a cushion, mouth slightly open. He knew she'd be mortified if she woke up and found him looking at her and yet he made no move. Seeing her there like that felt completely right. Sleep robbed her of her sharp edges, her caustic tongue, and revealed her to be the same woman he'd fallen in love with all those years ago, before all the kids came along, before they'd got angry with each other and lost the ability to know instinctively what the other wanted. He knew he could never recapture the past; life had moved on. Monica still had to sort out her blood tests and see what could be done, for a start. Yet perhaps he wasn't being too naively hopeful to think that they might just make a go of building a new and better future.

20

DC Watkins was at once delighted and disappointed. Disappointed that the operation last night had come to nothing — or, rather, hadn't actually succeeded in pinning down Amber's exact location, though examination of still more CCTV footage revealed that if she wasn't living in the Sefton Park area then she was certainly spending an awful lot of time there. What a shame there had been a run of sunny days, Watkins thought churlishly, enabling the would-be murderer to wear dark glasses all the time without standing out as an idiot.

Delighted, though, because after a decent night's sleep here she was, all revved up and ready to go, waiting by one of the number 75 bus stops to see if there was any action. She did her best to blend in, glancing at the digital display, pretending that her desired bus hadn't shown up yet, tutting with the other people waiting when the display changed for no apparent reason. She hoped her demeanour didn't scream plain-clothes police. She'd put on her most informal clothes, dark jeans and an old blue shirt, and hoped people took her for a mature student.

She glanced at her phone, just as half of the other passengers were doing, but she was checking for any texts from the rest of the team, who were strategically deployed near the park gates where Amber had been picked up on film, or at other bus stops near the ones she was known to have used. Still others were interviewing owners of guesthouses or even landlords who'd recently let out properties — she was glad she hadn't had the tedious task of checking the details for that. But in a city with so many people passing through, whether they were tourists, business travellers or students, how could every newly available room be found? Even assuming Amber wasn't kipping on an unknown mate's sofa.

She couldn't think like that. She had to stay positive, trust the team. Amber was around here somewhere. It was only a matter of time before she had to venture out again, and when she did, they'd have her.

★ ★ ★

Amber was happy. She had a plan again, and that meant her world was coming back to normal. Without a plan, chaos threatened, but now she could ward it off, thanks to a new piece of information.

She had rung the hospital, pretending to be a concerned friend who wanted the visiting hours for Kate's ward. A helpful receptionist had checked and then dropped the bombshell — Kate would be leaving the establishment this very morning. Amber had narrowly avoided swearing, recovering just quickly enough to say, 'That's marvellous. Does that mean she's better?' But the receptionist didn't know.

Amber had initially been furious. How come

Kate had escaped with hardly a scratch? Then she reasoned that she was jumping to conclusions. They were probably keen to get rid of her — everyone knew all hospitals were forever short of beds. As long as Kate no longer required expert treatment twenty-four hours a day, they were most likely packing her off home. She'd still be in lots of pain — good.

In fact, Amber calculated, this could be to her advantage. The hospital had been like a fortress: cameras, police, zillions of staff members, all coming between her and her prey. Back at home, Kate couldn't be so closely guarded, could she? Alex had to go to work. He might manage some of it from home but his physical presence would still be required for some matters. It was simply a matter of finding out when. In fact . . . her brain raced along its obsession-driven tracks. She could engineer a crisis, get him out of the house. That would be perfect. Then Kate would be at her mercy and she'd make no mistakes this time. That was where she'd gone wrong before, trusting someone else to finish the job, when it was always more reliable to simply do it yourself.

She hugged herself in gleeful satisfaction. For the plan to work she would have to know the ins and outs of the household. No point rushing in like a bull in a china shop. Prior preparation was the key. She would get herself over there right away, and lie in wait for an opportunity to see who was around in the daytime, what the arrangements were likely to be, and what security measures were in place.

Looking around the hated rented room, she

glimpsed the sun hat she had worn to Manchester. That trip had been very successful — maybe this was her lucky headwear. Jamming her hair up under it and tucking her sunglasses into her jacket pocket, she hummed to herself as she slammed the door shut.

⋆ ⋆ ⋆

'That's it. Over that way a little — yes, careful now, and we're almost there.'

The paramedic guided his colleagues as they gently lifted Kate on her stretcher, carrying her out of the ambulance and into the house. She shut her eyes as finally, after what felt like a lifetime, she was back in the place she had so quickly adapted to thinking of as home.

Alex walked beside her, keen to ensure that the whole process went as smoothly as possible, anxious that the journey might have caused her additional pain and set back her recovery. Yet he was sure that the sheer relief of being back here would promote her healing. He would never have agreed to it otherwise.

The paramedics expertly handled the stretcher for the last steps of the way and then at last Kate was back in her own bed, her lustrous eyes now wide open and full of delight. She sighed with pleasure as Alex thanked the ambulance crew and escorted them out. At one point the landline rang but he dismissed it. 'Everyone at Price Partners knows what an important morning this is,' he told her, 'and so they're fully prepared to deal with anything themselves. If it's not work then Kylie can deal with it later.' A moment later Kylie herself appeared, smart in a crisp light blue shirt and dark trousers. 'I'm your new nurse,' she proclaimed, then ran forward to give her saviour a very tentative hug. 'Now you're to rest while I sort you out. How would you like a cup of coffee? I know how to make it just as you like it. Alex taught me.'

Kate nodded animatedly. 'Thank you, my darling girl. That's just what I have been longing for. The hospital was excellent but their coffee-making facilities weren't quite up to the standard I'm used to — their priorities quite rightly lay elsewhere.' She lay back gingerly against her own pillows, her own soft pillowcases with their impressively high thread count, and savoured the beloved and familiar view. She could hear the dogs running around downstairs. She would have to organize them to be brought up to her two at a time; even in her current optimistic mood she was aware she couldn't handle six in this confined space.

Kylie slipped out of the room, and Kate was alone — something that she hadn't experienced since her transfer to the hospital ward. It was a delicious sensation and she vowed to relish every moment of it. It wasn't that she was ungrateful, far from it, but her life since leaving London had often been solitary and she'd used those long hours to assess her situation with as much honesty as she could muster. Of course, her circumstances had changed for the better in just about every way and perhaps such self-scrutiny was no longer necessary — or not to the same degree — but she must make the most of any fleeting opportunity.

Casting her gaze around, she noted that everything was immaculate. Kylie had more than lived up to expectations. She had very nearly beaten Mrs Bee at her own game, Kate decided. She was going to have to rely on the girl quite considerably until her own movement was back to something approaching normality, and it was reassuring to know that Kylie knew what she was about. Mrs Bee would be delighted too — Kate was intensely aware of how much importance the housekeeper placed on everything running smoothly. Well, she'd be returning to a spotless house.

And she'd be bringing Amelia with her. If Kate could have hugged herself without sending jolts of pain across her ribcage, she would have done. Her own little daughter would be here soon, this very afternoon if all went to plan, after such an agonizingly long separation. Perhaps Kylie could help with the necessary camouflaging makeup, Kate thought. She had dared to Skype Amelia yesterday so that the child wouldn't be startled by her mother's appearance, having carefully applied plenty of foundation first, and the conversation had gone well. Amelia had wanted to know what hurt and where, but hadn't exclaimed in horror, and so Kate was confident that with appropriate precautions their physical reunion could be a success.

Kylie returned with the promised coffee, the very aroma of which made Kate gasp aloud. 'You're a genius,' she asserted after the first sip.

'Never mind the painkillers — this is the stuff to make me better.'

Kylie beamed in delight at the appreciation, and then set about making her patient as comfortable as possible.

★ ★ ★

Amber crouched low in the bushes, her eyes riveted on the house some distance away. She was not sure how close she could reasonably go without detection. She had seen the ambulance arrive, Alex — gorgeous as ever — and the paramedics get out, and the stretcher being lifted inside. From this distance it hadn't been easy to track where everyone had gone next, but she'd seen figures passing the windows and she could make a pretty good guess which room Kate had been taken to.

Annoyingly, Alex hadn't then left as he was meant to. She had put in a call to the main office of Price Partners, disguising her voice, claiming there'd been a break-in at Chillex and that there might be a connection to the drugs gang who'd wreaked such damage before. If anything was guaranteed to make Alex swing into action, that was it. Yet he'd failed to emerge. What was wrong with him? He'd got the damned woman home — now he ought to be refocusing on his business interests, as he infallibly did. Surely it would only be a matter of time.

Amber's legs were growing stiff and she flexed her muscles as unobtrusively as she could. It occurred to her that the red sun hat was too bright to blend with the greenery, and she slipped it off and shoved it in her back pocket. She mustn't let her impatience overtake her and do something foolish. All she had to do was wait, painful though that might be. She was confident she'd evaded any detection on her way here, changing transport often, keeping an eye out for any suspicious fellow passengers, while never taking off her glasses. She'd walked the last stretch, thinking that this would be the best way of approaching unnoticed. All would be well, if she could only hold her nerve for just a little longer.

★ ★ ★

The sun was already beginning to beat down hard on the good people of Merseyside, despite its being only mid-morning, and Watkins was regretting bringing her light jacket. The text had come about an hour ago: suspect seen leaving a house just off Ullet Road, and making for one of the bus stops close by. The nearest plain-clothes officer had hurried to the stop and got on the bus when it arrived, sitting behind the target, who was easy to spot thanks to the jaunty red hat. Watkins had got on the next bus heading the same way, and the chase was on.

Amber had clearly read all the right thrillers to pick up the techniques to avoid being followed. She'd changed buses, got on a train, even doubled back on herself, before walking the final part of the journey — when it had become obvious, if there had ever been any doubt, what she was doing. She was heading for Alex's house, the house to which Kate had just been discharged from hospital.

DS Marcom had endeavoured to warn Alex, but his mobile went straight to voicemail and the landline rang out unanswered. He had therefore advised his team that the suspect was approaching the house and nobody inside was aware of the danger. The team would have to proceed extremely carefully, and the instructions were to apprehend Amber Simpson before she could cause any further damage — ideally, before she made contact with any of the inhabitants of the house at all.

Watkins now found herself going along the very same road that Amber must have walked down not long before, wondering where the suspect had disappeared to. She glanced around for any sign of the red hat, but there was none. The best thing to do was to get as close to the house as possible and then tuck herself away as unobtrusively as she could. Her boss would decide if the occupants needed to be warned in person, but her job was to stop Amber getting in before such a warning was needed.

She was growing hotter by the minute. She stopped beside a wall of pale grey stone and rested her small backpack on it while she slipped off her jacket. So much for the mature-student look — she was roasting, and she'd be no use to anyone if she was on the verge of heatstroke. She reached into her backpack for her bottle of water, took a long swig, and felt better. If she rolled her jacket up very tightly it would just about fit in. She jammed her phone into her jeans pocket, minimizing her chances of its dropping out if she had to run. Then she selected a shady spot towards the end of the wall where she could remain hidden from anyone coming along the road but still retain a clear view of the house's front door.

Fifteen minutes of complete inactivity later, she was bored and beginning to wonder if this was all a waste of time — if Amber hadn't thought better of it and gone away again. Then a movement towards the back of the house caught her eye. A tall man strode out — that must be the famous Alex Price. He was being followed by no fewer than six dogs, all lively and competing for his attention. They all seemed to know where they were going, and for such big dogs they appeared very well behaved. Watkins sighed. She loved dogs and as soon as she got her promotion she had promised herself to get a ground-floor flat where she could have one herself — probably not an Alsatian or a husky, it would have to be something smaller, but a canine companion nonetheless.

She was jolted out of her dream of future pet ownership by another movement, from some bushes over to her left. A figure — small, blonde-haired, dark glasses — was dashing towards the door at the back, keeping low, most likely out of the view of anyone inside the house. Watkins didn't need to think twice. She set off in hot pursuit.

★ ★ ★

I still can't quite believe that I'm really home, after all that time in hospital. I realize some of the doctors were reluctant to discharge me, fearing it was too soon, but they were totally wrong. I am in the best possible place, with my darling Alex to guard me, and Kylie showing all the signs of being a more than competent nurse, as well as a stellar housekeeper. Everything is ready for Amelia's arrival this afternoon. Julia has texted to say their train is on time and that they'll take a taxi from Lime Street. All I have to do for now is lie here and rest.

Alex is wisely taking the dogs out while all is calm. His mission is to exhaust them completely. That way, they'll be less inclined to interfere when everyone gets here, and I can't have them jumping up and frightening Amelia. She's not used to big dogs, let alone six of them. I know they will all get along famously once they've had time to get acquainted, but until then caution must prevail. I'm hardly in a position to physically restrain them.

That pleasurable duty must fall to Alex, as I can't have Kylie attempting to do it. She's too small and now visibly pregnant. No harm must come to her on my watch. Anyway, it won't be long before the Bees are back in harness, which will make Castor and Pollux very happy indeed. I swear they love nothing more than to torment Brian, bless him.

That must be Kylie now, running up the stairs more quickly as she hasn't got a cup of delicious coffee in her hand. How clever of her to have perfected that most desirable ability before I got

414

home: the first taste of decent coffee perked me up no end. Truly she is to be commended, and I shall tell Monica of her eldest's new talent the moment I see her — which I trust will be soon. I wonder what progress she's overseen in the past couple of days, and if the final tiling has been completed to her satisfaction? Maybe she is already in a better frame of mind, more able to hear good of her firstborn daughter.

Except it isn't Kylie who bursts in. It's Amber.

★　★　★

For a moment I don't know what to say. The first thing that comes into my head is how different she looks from the self-possessed, extremely cool manager of Chillex whom I am accustomed to seeing at Price Partners meetings. The young woman before me might, to those unfamiliar with her, appear normal, but I know better. She's let herself go — the old Amber was immaculately turned out. This one is untidy round the edges, her top unironed, her shoes scuffed. More alarmingly, her eyes are wild. And, if I'm not mistaken, she's put on weight. That will make her furious — more furious than ever, I should say. This is a woman who has held a slow-burning, deep-felt grudge for as long as I've known her.

And as such I have to calm her down, talk her out of whatever she has planned. For whatever it is, I doubt it bodes well for me.

'Hello, Amber,' I say as evenly as I can manage. 'How have you been? Do sit down, make yourself comfortable now you're here.'

She does not seem to hear me. Instead she reaches forward and swipes away my packet of painkillers, which Kylie left within reach. Fortunately I have just taken two.

My gaze rests on my phone, also within reach on the small table next to the bed. Could I possibly use it somehow? But Amber sees where I am looking and grabs that too, dropping it to the floor behind her. I hope she hasn't damaged it. That would be exceedingly inconvenient.

'Would you care for a drink of some kind?' I ask politely. 'Something cool, maybe? It's a hot day.' Or at least it looks as if it is outside. It's perfectly regulated in here by the air conditioning.

She looks at me as if I am insane, which is a little rich. Finally she speaks. 'There's only one thing I'm interested in here and it isn't a drink.'

Very well, at least I tried to be hospitable. Nobody shall say otherwise. 'Are you referring to Alex?' I enquire.

At the mention of his name her face contorts. 'I know he isn't here at the moment. So don't bother shouting to him for help. By the time he gets back it will be too late.'

So she intends to do something swiftly, then. I must play for time.

'Why don't you tell me all about it,' I offer. All the same, I can't have her here when Amelia and the others arrive. I can't have her anywhere near my daughter. The very idea is insupportable. And I intend to stay alive to see my little girl — I haven't endured all these months of separation

416

to be denied by a crazy homicidal health centre manager. Ex-health centre manager. Who no longer looks very healthy.

She steps closer. 'What good would that do?' she hisses. 'I can see what you're playing at. It won't work. Talking won't get you anywhere.' She leans forward and shakes my shoulder a little, which of course sends a ripple of agony through me. Despite my best intentions, I cry out.

She steps back and nods. 'Thought so. They've let you out too early, haven't they? You're still in pain. Good.' Oh, my God, she really is mad. Perhaps talking to her isn't doing any good.

She wanders to the window and idly strokes the curtains. 'Nice,' she concedes. Yes, she's right about that at any rate. Alex chose well, back in those dark days before he knew me, and I have not seen fit to change them. I don't think telling her that would improve things right at this moment. She reaches in her bag and draws out a lighter, which glints gold in the sunshine.

'I didn't realize you smoked, Amber,' I say as casually as I can.

'I don't.' She glares straight at me, flicking the little gold lighter, causing a warm orange flame to burst from it. 'I'd never smoke. It's bad for you.' She glances back at the elegant cream curtain. 'Fire retardant, are they?'

'I wouldn't know,' I say truthfully.

She nods as if she expected no other reply. 'It won't matter,' she says. 'They'll go up eventually, like everything else in this room. A terrible accident, and you only just out of hospital. What a tragedy. Alex will be heart-broken.'

I gasp. 'You wouldn't want that,' I say quickly.

She laughs. 'But he won't be for long. How very lucky that I'll be free too. Your friend Giles has done a runner, did you know? But you didn't want him, did you. Turns out neither do I. I have someone better in my sights.' She waves the lighter ever closer to the fabric, enjoying this game of torment. 'I'll be right there ready and waiting when Alex needs consolation.'

I say nothing devastatingly aware that I cannot move. I'm trapped here with a madwoman.

Amber turns her gaze out of the window. 'Such a nice day,' she says conversationally. 'Ideal for walking the dogs. He'll be gone for a long time, I should think.'

Yes, he probably will. It's no mean feat to exhaust our pack. He'll imagine that I am asleep and, being exceptionally considerate, will stay away to give me some peace. Exactly what I don't need right now.

'Well, he's due back at any time,' I lie, but she isn't taken in.

'Then I'd better get on with it,' is her answer, and she holds the little lighter under the heavy jacquard tie-back. She flicks it and the dry material begins to darken. She holds the flame in position until it catches and then she withdraws her hand, slowly, as if she's impervious to the heat it must be throwing forth. She watches its progress, mesmerized, as the foul singeing smell permeates the room.

I cough, which is agony to my injured ribs.

There is a movement at the door which Amber has left ajar — a short figure, blonde-haired, blue top. Kylie, in her pretend nurse's outfit, which she thought was such fun. She mustn't come in here: the smoke will hurt her baby. I can't have that on my conscience, not when she's been so good to me. Despite myself I let out a sob.

The smoke is billowing more thickly now. 'Get out, Kylie!' I shout. 'Raise the alarm! Don't breathe in, whatever you do! Save yourself and save your baby!'

Amber laughs uncontrollably. She doesn't know about Kylie, evidently. 'Appealing for help to your imaginary friends?' she taunts, moving backwards towards the door. 'So sorry to have to say goodbye now, Kate. But it's time I was leaving.'

The figure outside, now made blurry by the wafts of smoke, doesn't obey me but steps into the room. When she speaks her voice is not at all like Kylie's heavily Scouse-inflected tone.

'Amber Simpson,' she says, and I realize this is a total stranger. 'You're under arrest.'

★ ★ ★

The next couple of hours were a blur. It was not until Kate was safely installed in a guest room at the opposite end of the house that the details came out: how DC Watkins had followed Amber into the house, alerting her colleagues, who were more than capable of restraining their quarry, now out of control with anger when she understood that her plan had come spectacularly unravelled.

One particularly quick-thinking detective had torn the blazing curtain from its pole and thrust it into the adjacent en suite, turning the shower head on it. By a miracle nothing else had caught alight, although there would be smoke damage to the whole room. But the main effects of the fire had been contained by the detective's swift action, and although the fire service had turned up they had found they had little to do.

'You're safe, my darling, and nothing else matters.' Alex smoothed Kate's hair as she leant against him, still shocked by the turn of events but determined not to let them spoil the arrival of her daughter. Thank God the party had decided to stay overnight in London and had not come back yesterday evening straight off the Eurostar — they too would have been in danger from Amber's murderous antics. 'I'm never leaving you unguarded again,' he continued.

'Don't be ridiculous,' she protested. 'There's no danger now. Threat number two has been terminated.'

'She nearly terminated you.' Alex's voice caught on his emotion. To think that he had nearly caused the very outcome that everything was planned to avoid, by taking the dogs out when there was nobody else watching the house.

'But she didn't,' Kate pointed out. She rubbed her eyes. 'No, don't worry, I'm not crying, it's just the effect of the smoke.' She pouted. 'I'll need my eye gel, and you won't know where to look for it. I'll ask Kylie later. At least it proved the doctors were wrong — I managed to hobble a little, and even to sit in the shower with a bit of help. So now I'm fresh as a daisy.'

'True.' Alex nodded.

'Anyway,' she went on, 'that bedroom was in need of an overhaul. Who uses fabric tie-backs any more? It can be Monica's next project, if she's amenable to the idea.'

'You can ask her yourself,' he said, shuffling a little on the edge of the king-size bed. 'Kylie rang her and she's coming over. So's Pete. They want to see for themselves that you really are all right, and that Kylie is as well. Oh, and to check the house is in one piece. So they might as well meet Amelia once they're here.'

'Oh, absolutely. Amelia might as well meet everyone at once,' said Kate, full of confidence that her little girl would be unbothered by a big crowd of people. Then a cough shook her and her composure cracked for a fraction of a second. Coughing was agony, though the doctors had warned her not to suppress it or she risked infection. They hadn't bargained on her inhaling smoke almost as soon as she got home, though. Then she rallied again. There was nothing to be done; what had happened had happened. She refused to let it spoil the forthcoming reunion.

'Can I get you anything?' Alex eyed her warily. He could tell she was putting a brave face on it. She must be in agony. 'More painkillers?'

'Kylie will bring them when the next dose is due,' Kate predicted. 'Then she can do my makeup. Can't have me looking red-eyed when they all get here.'

Alex laughed. 'My precious Kate. You'll look a million dollars, as ever. It would take more than a car accident and a house fire to change that.'

Kate smiled up at him. 'Isn't it strange, that policewoman being so similar to Kylie? I mean, I know they look very different when you see them together, but for a minute back there I was convinced Kylie was going to come in and perish in the flames. It gave me a bit of a shock, I can tell you.'

'Of course.' Alex stroked her hair again, unable to imagine the full horror of those moments in the burning bedroom. 'But, silver linings and all that, Monica was worried sick. Shows she loves Kylie after all, just in case we ever doubted it.'

'I didn't, not really.' Kate was adamant. 'She just has a terrible difficulty in showing it sometimes. Once Tim's back, he'll sort her out.'

Alex's phone beeped, and he glanced at the screen. 'Talking of the man himself . . . ' He opened the text. 'They'll be pulling into Lime Street in fifteen minutes. Bang on time.'

Kate straightened herself up in bed as well as she was able. 'Then I'd better summon Kylie. She has some repair work to do.'

'I'll find her,' Alex said, getting up from the bed and bending to kiss her very tenderly on the top of the head. As he strode from the room he reflected that a few months ago he would have been panicking at the threat to his house, the idea that his precious collection of Lennon memorabilia could have gone up in smoke. But

422

now nothing mattered except the miraculous escape of his beloved Kate.

★   ★   ★

Alex was checking that the dogs were quiet down in the mud room when he heard the sound of a car pulling up outside. He gave each furry head one more pat and then raced to the front door, flinging it wide. The taxi had just disgorged its passengers: the Bees, Tim and Julia and, standing in front of them, a little four-year-old girl in a pretty stripy dress. Amelia.

He knew how much rested on this moment. It was imperative that they got along, both loving Kate as they did. But he mustn't overplay his hand. So he crouched down to her level and said simply, 'Welcome. You must be Amelia. There's someone inside who can't wait to see you.'

She looked across at him, her eyes steady. 'Is it my mummy?' she asked.

'It is,' Alex told her, almost bowled over by the resemblance between this small child and her mother. Now was not the time to dwell on it, though. 'Come with me and I'll take you to her. I'm Alex, by the way.'

The girl went to him, holding up her hand so that he could take it, completely trusting. He would have thought she had been treated with nothing but love and affection in all her short life if he hadn't known otherwise. What strength of character she must have, to have overcome the injury inflicted upon her by her own father. 'Is she better now?' she asked.

423

Alex was aware of all the others waiting for his answer.

'Not quite, but she's much better than she was,' he told her. 'You can give her a hug if you're careful. This way.' He led her through the door, followed by Brenda and Julia, while the men turned to gather the luggage.

Amelia paused on the way up the stairs. 'Will this be my new house?' she asked quietly, as if she was still making up her mind about it.

Alex nodded. 'If you like it.'

'And will you be my new daddy?' was her next heart-stopping question.

Alex once more crouched down to her level. 'If you'd like that. I'd like to be.'

Amelia gave him a searching look and then nodded once, briefly. 'Yes please. I didn't like my other one very much.' Then she carried on up the stairs, leaving Alex to follow in her wake.

He had to run to catch her up. 'It's the door at the far end, the one that's open a bit.' He leant over her as she reached it and swung it fully open. The guest room was not quite as large as his smoke-damaged bedroom but it was still a generous size, and there in the white-covered bed at the end was Kate, now propped fully up on a mound of pillows, smiling in a way he had never seen before. She was also, for once, totally speechless, as she held out her arms wide.

'Mummy!' Amelia screamed, and flung herself across the room and onto the bed. Alex found his own eyes were smarting and his vision had blurred, the sight before him almost overwhelming as Kate hugged her daughter tightly, far too

424

tightly for her injuries but with no sign of pain, only the love that she'd had to keep locked away while separated from her child.

Alex turned away and took a sharp breath. This was it: his family unit of the future. Something he'd thought he would never have. Yet the nightmares of blood had not returned, and his once impermeable fortress against all emotion was well and truly breached. He felt his heart beating hard in his chest as mother and daughter murmured to one another.

Behind him in the doorway, Tim appeared. 'All right, old man?' Even now his habit of checking on his friend had not abated.

'Never better,' Alex assured him. 'Never better.' He turned back to the room and saw that Kate was reaching out an arm towards him.

'Come and join us,' she said. He needed no second bidding, taking his place beside her, one arm gently around her and the other, for the first time, around the little girl who would henceforth know him as Daddy.

It felt utterly right, as if he'd finally found his true place in the universe. Now nothing would ever be too much for his two girls. They deserved the best after everything they'd gone through, all that they'd survived, despite so many people's attempts to harm them. Well, now the world would have to deal with him first. He would go to the ends of the earth to defend these two precious beings.

'Who'd have thought it?' Kate laughed, speaking his own thoughts and not for the first time. Her face now appeared almost unmarked, thanks to Kylie's ingenious ministrations and of course Monica's magic potion. Their fears that she would be too damaged for Amelia to deal with were unfounded. Amelia's sheer delight at being back in her mother's arms was evident for everyone to see.

And there was everyone, crowding in at the doorway: not only Tim, but Julia too, hugging him closely — and did Alex's eyes deceive him or had she finally put on a little weight? Brenda was peering forward fiercely, eager to check how her newest little charge was faring, while still anxious for the man who was as close to a son as she would ever have; Brian was right behind her. No doubt they were both heartily relieved to be back where the food was familiar and the language intelligible. Peeping around the side was the diminutive form of Monica, with the towering figure of Pete behind her, and the body language between them was far from the recent antagonism. Perhaps they were on their way to recovering their marriage. And just visible behind them was the bright blonde head of Kylie, the girl who'd thought she was unwanted, but had come into her own just when they needed her. A swift movement at knee level revealed Troy pushing his way through the sea of legs, his eager face brightening as he saw someone close to his own size to play with at last.

Kate raised her eyebrows. 'Well, this is quite the audience,' she observed archly. 'Seriously, I cannot thank you enough for bringing Amelia safely home. What an adventure, wasn't it,

426

darling? I'm so happy to have you back, I truly can't tell you how much.'

Amelia nodded, calmer now after her initial excitement at seeing her mother again. 'It was. But now I want to stay with you.'

'And you shall,' Kate promised.

'Too right you will,' Alex echoed, his eyes sparkling. 'And when you are sufficiently recovered, Kate, I trust that you'll do me the honour of becoming Mrs Price in reality, legally, and forever.' He dropped to one knee, no elegant ring this time, but with all the certainty that this was absolutely the correct thing to do and what he wanted most in the world. 'Do you accept my proposal, Kate? Will you be my wife, not in a pretend marriage but one with all the love I can give you? And will you,' he turned to Amelia, 'be our bridesmaid? Do you want to do that?'

The little girl smiled even more, and both she and her mother answered immediately.

'We do.'

We do hope that you have enjoyed reading this large print book.

Did you know that all of our titles are available for purchase?

We publish a wide range of high quality large print books including:
Romances, Mysteries, Classics
General Fiction
Non Fiction and Westerns

Special interest titles available in large print are:
The Little Oxford Dictionary
Music Book
Song Book
Hymn Book
Service Book

Also available from us courtesy of Oxford University Press:
Young Readers' Dictionary
(large print edition)
Young Readers' Thesaurus
(large print edition)

For further information or a free brochure, please contact us at:
Ulverscroft Large Print Books Ltd.,
The Green, Bradgate Road, Anstey,
Leicester, LE7 7FU, England.
Tel: (00 44) 0116 236 4325
Fax: (00 44) 0116 234 0205

Other titles published by Ulverscroft:

DAUGHTERS OF PENNY LANE

Ruth Hamilton

In 1946, Alice Quigley returns to her childhood home on Penny Lane, having lost three sisters and her house in Bootle to the bombs that fell over Liverpool. Estranged from her husband Dan, who suffered from two strokes triggered during the Blitz, she moves in with her remaining sister, Nellie. But even though the bombs have stopped falling, tremors still rock the family when Alice's reviled mother is kicked out of Nellie's home and seeks vengeance.

When visions from the past resurface, she soon uncovers a dark secret that her mother has kept hidden . . .

MIDNIGHT ON LIME STREET

Ruth Hamilton

What possible connections might exist between an old shoe-seller, some ladies of the night, two nuns, a philanthropist, a serial killer, Liverpool Lime Street and a mansion in Southport? The answer lies in love, friendship and the determination to endure all the way to the winning post. Eve, owner and madam at Meadowbank Farm, is keen to secure a deal that keeps her in pocket and her clients happy. Meanwhile, a deranged killer walks the Dock Road. 'Inspired' by a vision, he seeks to clean up Liverpool. When he finds Eve's farm, he plans to cast his net on what promises to be a great catch.

MEET ME AT THE PIER HEAD

Ruth Hamilton

Comfortably settled into his expatriate life in post-war Britain, headmaster Theodore's secrets are set to remain deeply buried. Until she breezes in. Tia Bellamy cuts through his reserve and, for the first time in years, Theo finds himself able to confront his past and reveal the events carved onto his heart and seared into his soul. Together they form a strong bond, closely befriending Maggie Stone and her granddaughter, little Rosie. However, Theo and Tia soon realize that Rosie is the victim of an abusive mother. It isn't long before they decide to take drastic action, and all three lives are changed forever . . .

A MERSEY MILE

Ruth Hamilton

The residents of Scotland Road fear for their futures when government plans threaten to demolish their street and tear apart their community. Polly's Parlour café is the centre for resistance, where strategies are formed to fight back. But when local priest Father Brennan attacks little Billy Blunt, minds are instead turned to vengeance. Frank Charleson, the local hero after saving Billy's life, is increasingly fond of Polly Kennedy. But with his mother's harsh behaviour towards his previous wife, can he put Polly through the same? Can Frank provide the support she needs? And is Polly strong enough to keep their community together?